Acclaim for the novels of

TRANA MAE
SIMMONS

"Ms. Simmons has written a story full of wonderfully well-formed characters that seem to come to life as you read."
—*Old Book Barn Gazette*

"A delightful book . . . she has the ability to take her reader into the lives of her characters."
—*Compuserve Romance Reviews*

"In the hands of the extremely talented Trana Mae Simmons, readers get a refreshing, fun-to-read American historical romance."
—*Affaire de Coeur*

"Trana Mae Simmons's heartwarming, homey tale sparkles and shines. Another winner from this gifted writer!"
—Martha Hix

"This is an author who is going places fast."
—*GEnie Romance and Women's Fiction Exchange*

Southern Charms

Trana Mae Simmons

JOVE BOOKS, NEW YORK

MAGICAL LOVE is a trademark of Penguin Putnam Inc.

SOUTHERN CHARMS

A Jove Book / published by arrangement
with the author

PRINTING HISTORY
Jove edition / June 1999

The Penguin Putnam Inc. World Wide Web site address is
http://www.penguinputnam.com

ISBN: 0-515-12516-4

A JOVE BOOK®
Jove Books are published by The Berkley Publishing Group,
a division of Penguin Putnam Inc.,
375 Hudson Street, New York, New York 10014.
JOVE and the "J" design
are trademarks belonging to Penguin Putnam Inc.

PRINTED IN THE UNITED STATES OF AMERICA

10 9 8 7 6 5 4 3 2 1

To Louise Harper,
for her Louise'isms, but
mostly for her wonderful friendship;

and

To Lisa Simmons, my daughter-in-law,
in deep appreciation for her knack
for handling her Simmons man and
making him happy-ever-after;

and

To Ron and Wyletta Brown, in
appreciation for their daughter, Lisa.

May rainbows, romance, and the
happily-ever-after MAGIC always
be part of all your lives.

and

As always, to Barney,
my own Simmons man and
happily-ever-after MAGIC!

Prologue

~

Humans were such a pain at times—such fun at others.

Fatima woke leisurely in the bedroom of her opulent thirty-room castle hidden away on the edge of the universe. Lips curved dreamily in contentment, she contemplated her first waking thought. She so enjoyed interacting with humans—aiding their love lives with her keen matchmaking abilities and magic. But the best thing about her life was pampering herself in well-deserved luxury after an especially trying adventure.

Snuggling into the satin-covered, goose-down pillows, she wiggled into a decadently cozy position on the feather bed, then re-adjusted the silk sheets and downy comforter. A slight chill tinged the bedroom air, which was the climate she preferred when she slept. As intended, her snug cocoon was all the more toasty in contradiction.

No humans intruded here. No humans even knew this place existed. Their . . . well, *human* minds wouldn't understand the indolent leisure her magic afforded her. Might even be jealous of it.

She did share one trait with that race, however. After a while, an urge to find some industrious goal in her life had surfaced.

Pandora, her plump cat, also preferred the chilly air in the room and refused to sleep beneath the comforter.

She did, however, curl up in a not-so-dainty ball against the small of Fatima's back. Luckily Pandora slept in the same position the whole night through—most of the time. When the huge cat changed position, the feather bed and its occupant swayed with the movement.

Fatima's friend, Cupid, once horrified Fatima when he suggested she put the white cat on a diet.

"I would never think of doing such a terrible deed!" Fatima had told him. "Why, I know in my very bones Pandora prefers to look like a fluffy cloud gliding through life instead of a svelte but hungry shadow!"

Cupid didn't understand, of course. He'd muttered something about sleekness and attractiveness, like a typical dense male.

"*Some* people prefer to hold a proper armful of what they love," she'd told the silly man with the bundle of love arrows on his back.

When she had glanced at Pandora for confirmation, the cat's bright blue eyes blinked once in assent, her lips stretched into that smug cat's smile of haughtiness. The next time Cupid dropped by, he somehow missed seeing Pandora and tripped over her corpulent body, arrows flying in all directions. Fatima hadn't quite grabbed her magic wand in time to turn the marble-floored entryway into a bed of feathers, but Cupid bruised little but his dignity. Well, except for the small black-and-blue spot that showed up on his elbow after he cracked it against a stone table. Fatima hadn't heard Cupid disparage Pandora since.

The object of her thoughts stretched just then, a rumble purring in her throat. A few seconds later Pandora rose and stalked to the head of the bed, the mattress caving slightly in the wake of her progress. When she settled on the goose-down pillow next to Fatima's head and emitted a plaintive meow, Fatima sighed and turned over to face her.

Propping one palm under her cheek and reaching out to stroke the cat, Fatima asked, "Are you restless so soon, too? I have to admit, I'm about satiated with all this luxury myself. It's time to find another set of humans to work with, don't you think?''

Pandora yawned, blinked, and bobbed her head. The cat enjoyed their adventures as much as Fatima did. People who thought cats only wanted to laze their way through life, being spoiled and pampered unceasingly, didn't know the animals at all. Like Fatima, Pandora enjoyed their recuperation time, but after a while, the serene, carefree life paled. It was time to find another difficult set of humans completely unaware of their mutual suitability and show them they were meant for each other.

Cupid might fancy his arrows, but Fatima much preferred interacting with her chosen couple and sharing the period during which they fell in love. She and Pandora truly enjoyed watching their charges change as they helped them along that rocky trail to happiness. After all, what better deed could a fairy godmother do for her chosen young lady than show her the road to happily ever after?

Pandora meowed, and Fatima glanced into her pet's eyes. Was that a hint of hesitation in Pandora's blue depths?

''Now, Pandora,'' Fatima said. ''Granted, that last adventure was a little bit more difficult than I'd anticipated. But think of the fun we had. And think of the satisfaction when we finally did get those two to admit they loved each other!''

Pandora yawned and closed her eyes.

''Fine. So you don't want to think about it. But we allowed ourselves some extra time to recover from that adventure, so we should be in perfectly fine fettle to set out again. Besides, the easy ones aren't nearly as much fun, remember?''

Pandora sighed and opened her eyes. Fatima supposed the cat was agreeing with her.

Fatima frowned, pondering what challenge would strike her fancy this time while she continued to stroke Pandora's fluffy white coat. It was ten years yet until the turn of the century, and given the changes she'd seen the last few years, the speed of new wonders sure to develop in 1900 and beyond would no doubt dizzy a person's mind. Out of her nine hundred and fourteen years of being a fairy godmother, she hadn't enjoyed anything more than the period of the wild and woolly West. The excitement of frontier life was almost a thing of the past already, and she would miss it.

But, she mused, not in Texas. Texas was pretty much the last frontier. She doubted Texas would ever succumb to the civility and sophistication of the rest of the world. In Texas, cowboys, boots, and originality would never die.

"What do you think of going to Texas, Pandora?"

"Meow!"

That sounded like agreement to Fatima. Texas it was. But first her journey would lead her to New York City. She wouldn't stay there long, however. She much preferred wide open spaces, like the one where her hideaway was located in the beautiful solitude at the end of the universe.

One

Shane Morgan closed his mother's bedroom door.

Gently, he reminded himself. After all, his dear mother claimed a debilitating headache, despite the bright sunshine flooding her room. Everyone knew headaches responded better to shadow than light. He was willing to bet that if he were to pretend to walk away and then sneak back and peek into the room, his mother would be at her writing desk instead of lying on her bed, a weary hand thrown across her brow.

Shane shook his head, half in amusement and half in loving mockery at his mother's attempt to manipulate him. There was no ''attempting'' about it, he corrected himself with a chuckle. His mother left him no choice but to abide by her wishes—unless he wanted her sighs and mournful face to spoil every evening meal until he gave in. Mother yearned to experience the turn of the century into the nineteen hundreds. She'd just told him so. But she wanted no unresolved problems marring her life when she had that once-in-a-lifetime experience—even if it took ten years to clear them up.

Shane's expression sobered. God, what would he do when she actually did go? But the doctor assured him there was no reason to be alarmed about his mother's physical health. It was one thing, however, for his brain to understand that his mother could maneuver him so easily into fulfilling her desires, another to believe it in his heart.

Texas, he growled silently. His mood shifted from amused tolerance at his mother to sullen irritation at this irksome new demand on his time. Shoving his hands into his trouser pockets, he headed for the stairwell.

Who the hell in his right mind went to Texas in the summertime? Everyone with any sense left New York City during the fetid heat, but they were summering in the Catskills or at Martha's Vineyard. Not one of them went to a place where you had to weave your way through piles of cow dung to cross a street, and where the heat would make the town feel like autumn in comparison.

Texas. What the hell could make him go to that godforsaken state right now? It was not a *what*, but a *who* that possessed the ability to send him off to board a train and endure that long trip to Texas, a state with a climate approaching his minister's warnings about Hell's. He would rather walk naked down a busy New York City boulevard, but Mariana Catalina Morgan could send him to Texas with no more difficulty than she'd just affected.

Immersed in his thoughts, he rounded the newel post at the bottom of the stairs, plowing into the little housemaid-in-training his mother had hired last week, who was placing a vase of fresh flowers on a small table. Vase, water, flowers, and housemaid flew in all directions.

"Sir!" the maid gasped, after skidding across the polished oak floor on her rump and hitting the far wall.

"Good God!" Shane hurried over and helped her to her feet. "I'm so sorry. I didn't see you standing there. Are you all right?"

"Fine, sir," she said, although she was far from it, as her pained breathing indicated. "Please. I need to clean the mess before Madame comes down to see what the commotion is. I daren't let her see what I did."

"For pity's sake, it was my fault, not yours. Sit down a minute." Shane easily pushed her into a hall chair and then handed her his handkerchief to wipe the water from her face. But the longer he stood there, the more he could see that the maid was more worried about taking care of the broken vase and ruined flowers than herself. Sighing, he finally walked away and let her handle her duties. The maid would find out soon enough that his mother was a big push-over with her servants.

Mariana. His mother. The woman who, a few minutes ago, had begged him to follow up the latest report from the Pinkerton agent she had hired two years earlier. The mother who, when she turned sixty, had for no apparent reason begun believing that every day might be her last on this earth. Who wanted no loose ends left in her life—the most important of these being the reason she had hired the Pinkerton Agency.

And the agency had done its usual stellar job, no doubt with the assistance of the unlimited funds his mother made available to them. They had tracked down a woman they claimed was the missing heiress—the daughter of his mother's deceased childhood friend.

All that remained now was for Shane to confirm the information in the report—a job his mother would most certainly have undertaken herself if Shane had balked at abiding by her wishes.

Shane stomped into the library, which he also used for an office, and over to the well-stocked bar. Try as he might, he couldn't keep from glancing at the Queen Anne clock on the mantel as he picked up the brandy decanter.

Darling, drinking before the cocktail hour is just not done, unless it's in the privacy of that dreary old men's club you belong to. His mother's voice played in his head.

At that moment the clock chimed three. Four more hours until his mother felt it an appropriate time to partake of liquor. Shane picked up the decanter, jerked the top off and drank straight from the bottle.

The brandy went down the wrong way, and Shane choked, spitting brown liquor all over the carpet. After he quit coughing, he glared at the decanter as though it were at fault, then at the ceiling to see if his mother's disapproval from above had somehow caused the mishap. Sighing in acquiescence to at least one ingrained stricture of decorum, he poured a crystal goblet on the bar three-quarters full and carried the goblet with him to the chair behind the desk.

He sagged into the chair.

Don't mess with Shane Morgan.

Shane? He's honest as the day is long, but don't cross him or try to steal from him if you value your life and want to continue doing business in this town.

You try any shit on Shane Morgan, he'll shit back on you double.

Shane knew what they said about him; in fact, he fostered their attitude without qualm in the business world. But a tiny slip of a woman with a name way too large for her tiny body could let one tiny tear sneak from one mournful, beautiful blue eye and he'd cave in to her wishes!

He downed half the brandy. It made a safe, warm path to his belly this time.

He had reverted to his childhood custom of calling her Mama for months after the steamboat explosion a year and a half ago. But no one else except his aunt Blessing dared call Mariana anything short of Mrs. Morgan.

No one else could imagine the strength beneath Mariana's deceptively tiny frame the first time they met her. She looked like the perfect society matron, someone a man might want to take under his arm and shelter against the world. She often used this deceptive appearance when it behooved her, too.

Yet Shane knew how fast his mother could shed her feminine demeanor and bend everyone within striking distance to her will. How quickly she could erase any misconception that her tininess meant she was weak.

He finished the brandy and rose to refill his glass. Above the mantel hung a portrait his mother had commissioned a few years ago. He faced it.

"Mother," he said, saluting with his brandy. "To you."
As soon as he took a swallow to acknowledge the toast,
Shane sat down.

Mariana had proven her steely strength more than once.
After she received the telegram informing her that Shane
had been horribly injured, Mariana Morgan made it from
New York City to St. Louis in two days' time. She bullied
railroad executives into ordering her personal Pullman car
hitched to any train headed the direction she needed to go.
And she borrowed an engine and traveled alone on the connecting tracks that didn't have a scheduled train for her to
hook onto. Conflicting schedules were rearranged to suit
her need for swiftness and desperate desire to reach her
son's side.

Mariana's nursing no doubt saved Shane's life, but the
scars on his back and right arm and hand were permanent.
He wore long sleeves even in the summer, but refused to
wear a glove. Let his scarred and mottled hand remind people of what he had gone through.

It didn't do any good to hide it, since everyone knew
about it anyway. His fresh injuries had sure as hell made
Anastasia's eyes fill with revulsion, even when she couldn't
see the rest of his body.

He had heard the whispers. Anastasia broke their betrothal less than a week after he and his mother returned to
New York City. Anastasia told one friend, who told another, who spread the word around that Shane was now
loathsomely mutilated. Horrified, her friends whispered that
Anastasia couldn't bear the thought of living with a man
so disfigured.

Shane snorted and finished the rest of the brandy in one
swallow. Truth be known, Anastasia couldn't bear the
thought of making love to his less than perfect body. She
hadn't been after his money, since her own father was filthy
rich. But she enjoyed making love and intended it to be a
big part of any relationship with the man in her life. Too
bad Shane mistook making love for being in love.

She'd had no intentions of waiting until they were married before sleeping with him. Thought herself so modern and so up-to-date in knowing how to avoid pregnancy. In hindsight, Anastasia wouldn't have lasted through the engagement without lovemaking. She hadn't been a virgin. And she had torn at his back and meowed like a cat in heat, never sheathing her claws, the times he'd bedded her before the explosion. She couldn't have endured having to learn to avoid his scars.

"The Beast," Shane murmured, and tipped his brandy glass again.

That's what they called him. One of his friends got drunk one night and thought it hilarious to tell Shane about his nickname. The ex-friend hadn't thought it so funny the next morning when he couldn't see out of one eye and had trouble eating with his painful jaw.

"Sir?" Withers said from the doorway, wrenching Shane's thoughts from the past.

Grateful for his valet's appearance, Shane arched a brow in inquiry.

"Madame has instructed me to pack your things for a trip to Texas," Withers said. "I sent Cook's son to the station to retrieve a current train schedule and I will begin arranging your bags immediately. When will you depart and how long will you be gone, sir?"

Making a snap decision, Shane said, "I don't know how long I'll be gone, but *we'll* leave on the first available train in the morning, Withers. Pack a bag for yourself, too. You're going with me."

Withers's face paled. "To Texas? Oh, sir, please. I have no business in Texas."

"I haven't lost anything in Texas either," Shane spat, "but Mother appears to think she may have. And you're my goddamn valet, Withers, so you'll go where I go. Pack the sturdiest but coolest clothes I have. We'll stay in a hotel in Fort Worth, if they have one that's at all suitable in that

cow town. We can buy clothing more appropriate to the
territory there if we need it.''

Withers gulped. ''What do they wear down there, sir?''

Shane waved his brandy glass. ''Oh, you know. Those
Levi's and Stetson hats. We'll each need some. And we'll
want a pair or two of heavier boots than the English leather
ones we use for riding now. I hear there are poisonous
snakes by the thousands in that part of Texas, so we'll want
boots sturdy enough to deflect their fangs if we run across
one. Those should be available in that Western town.''

''S . . . snakes?'' Withers asked.

''Rattlesnakes. Huge ones, longer than a man and as big
around as a man's thigh.'' Shane caught sight of himself
in the mirror over the fireplace. An evil look filled his face,
and grim satisfaction seeped through him when he looked
over at Withers and saw the valet's hand tremble as he
smoothed his sparse hair.

For just a minute, guilt stabbed him at his rather heartless
treatment of his valet. But then he recalled all the times
Withers had helped his mother drill etiquette rules into his
head. These days, he totally enjoyed shaking up Withers's
prim and proper comportment.

''I understand they can make a complete pair of boots
out of one snake's skin,'' Shane mused loudly, ''and they
eat snakes down there, too. Grill them over a campfire, and
they'll feed a family for a week.''

Taking pity at last on the valet's stricken look, Shane
crossed to the bar and poured them each some brandy. He
handed Withers a glass and waited until the valet downed
it in one gulp.

''We'd really better start preparing for the trip, Withers.''

''Yes, sir,'' Withers squeaked.

Ellie dismounted with a groan of relief and knocked her
hat from her head, leaving it hanging down her back by
leather thongs. She whipped her bandanna off and wiped
her forehead, then draped the sweat-sogged bandanna

across the top fence rail. Both hands free, she resecured the pins holding her fine, platinum-blond hair off her neck. It took more than a hat to hold her hair against its flyaway nature; sometimes she wished for something more like an iron helmet to fasten down the dadblasted mess. Except a helmet would be even hotter than her hat.

The humid, pre-storm air hung as heavy as a blanket. Her split riding skirt and high-topped boots were as hot as the devil, too, and they wouldn't have let even a faint breath of air through to cool her skin, had there been one stirring. For propriety's sake, the best she could do to cool herself in addition to removing her hat was unbuttoning her top two blouse buttons.

Ellie and her three men, as hot and sweaty as she was, dismounted, pulling their hats off to fan their faces and reveal a variety of heads ranging from sweat-soaked locks to complete baldness. Dust from the churning hooves of horses eager to be turned loose didn't help matters. A haze of dust particles attached itself to the humidity in the air, then to the sweat beads on human bodies. Ellie grimaced at the dirt streaks on her bare arms.

She turned to her gelding, Cinder, and loosened the saddle cinch, while the horse stood patiently waiting for a rubdown. Unlike the other cow ponies, Cinder would be agreeable to Ellie's taking her sweet time caring for the horse. Cinder could unleash a nimbleness afoot far and above any other pony in the remuda when needed, but his patience was legend. That's one reason he meant so much to Ellie, in addition to the fact she absolutely adored the sleek gray gelding.

She didn't much adore the idea of what was waiting for her at the end of this day, though. Reluctance filled her at the thought of going in to supper.

No, dinner, she reminded herself. The ranch hands had supper; she and her adoptive mother and sister had *dinner*.

''Ellie!'' Darlene called from the back veranda. ''You're late!''

Ellie tensed and repressed a sigh of annoyance that her sister had already spotted her. Gosh darn it, what was Darlene's hurry? They had plenty of time, and Ellie wasn't late—not really, compared to the time she usually crawled in off the range. She had come in early this afternoon only because Darlene and their mother, Elvina, insisted.

"We plan on dinner in fifteen minutes, Ellie," Darlene called. "That barely leaves you time to bathe and change. Rockford has tickets for us to attend the evening performance of the circus. Remember? It starts at eight-thirty."

"I'll take care of Cinder," Shorty said from beside Ellie.

Ellie raised her head and gave the wiry man a grateful look. "Thank you. I knew we were going to be late getting in, but we couldn't leave that calf stuck in the ravine."

"Me and the men could've got it out by ourselves," Shorty reminded her, but the expression on his face divulged he knew why she'd stayed to help.

Shorty respected Ellie way too much to say anything to upset her. However, Ellie had overheard him telling one of the other hands a few evenings ago, with a shudder in his voice, that Ellie must be adopted, given the differences between her and that hoity-toity mother of hers.

Little did Shorty know, he was right. But the adoption, while not actually a deep, dark secret, wasn't an everyday topic of conversation, either.

"Ellie!" Darlene repeated. "Mother wants to see you for a moment before we eat, and I'm starving. Please come in."

"I'm coming, I'm coming!"

Ellie understood her sister's impatience. Rockford Van Zandt was the first man Darlene had truly fallen for. But for heaven's sake, if they arrived early they would have to wait on Rockford in the heat. It was bad enough that Rockford couldn't come out to the ranch and escort Darlene from here, since he'd received word that an important business acquaintance would be arriving that day. Giving in to her sister's pleading and knowing that Elvina was perfectly capable of forbidding Darlene to go into town to meet Rockford alone, Ellie had agreed to accompany her. It also meant her ranch hands could end their workday early and attend the circus, a goodwill gesture for which they would repay her in loyalty.

Her steps dragging, Ellie headed for the house. It was just as grand from the rear as the front, if you didn't examine it too closely. She had been trying to find enough money to have it painted for over a year now. Three stories, with a wraparound porch, it looked similar to pictures of Southern mansions Ellie had seen. When she let it, the towering structure also reminded Ellie of her yearning to see some of those actual mansions one day. A trip somewhere outside of Texas once a year would be nice, not that she ever wanted to be away from her beloved ranch overly long.

No, not her ranch, she reminded herself. The Leaning G was now legally Elvina's and Darlene's ranch. As the adopted family member, she didn't own an inch of the five thousand acres of pasture and sagebrush Darlene and Elvina had inherited when George Parker died unexpectedly five years ago.

Darlene went back inside before Ellie reached the rear veranda, and Ellie stole up the back stairwell to her bedroom without being caught. Birdie had filled the tub in her bathing room with tepid water, just the way Ellie liked it when she came in from a hot day on the range. But she couldn't enjoy her bath this afternoon. Elvina waited, along with *dinner*.

Barely an hour later, Ellie had explained once again to Elvina why they couldn't afford new carpet for the entire house right now and finished a meal made up of foods covered with such thick sauces she had to hunt in them to figure out what she was eating. Now she drove the buggy toward the outskirts of Fort Worth. Darlene sat beside her, restrained eagerness in every inch of her frame, which was more generous than Ellie's.

Ellie couldn't imagine having that sort of zeal to be in the company of a man, even Rockford. Her sister's suitor was nice enough, she guessed, but nothing special. For one thing, Rockford preferred his existence in town to living on a ranch, and Ellie didn't understand men like that at all. As long as he treated Darlene respectfully, though, she would tolerate him. She could even support her younger sister's wish for Rockford to propose, since all in all, she really did think he was the right man for Darlene.

Maybe Rockford wouldn't have the financial resources to help them get out of the ever-deepening financial hole the ranch was sinking into, given the stable but not very profitable state of his family business. But if he made Darlene happy, that would be what mattered. They would solve their financial problems somehow.

The circus had set up on the edge of town, and for once Ellie had to grudgingly agree with Elvina. It wouldn't do for Darlene to meet Rockford there alone. After all, Rockford hadn't actually proposed yet. Darlene continued to quake with anticipation, however, though she attempted to effect a studied calm. Ellie just wanted to get the evening over with and return to the ranch's accounting books. Somehow she had to squeeze enough money out of their tight budget to meet payroll in two weeks.

Rockford waited on the edge of the area roped off for buggies and wagons to park. Sunlight lingered in summertime, and even at six o'clock, there were a good three hours of daylight left. A good three hours of heat and humidity, also, although Ellie had read the signs enough times in her twenty years on this earth to know a storm would hit before morning. Summer storms in this part of Texas were rare, but normally a deluge while they lasted.

"Now remember, Ellie," Darlene reminded her, her hands flitting all over the place as she patted and probed her already perfectly attired figure, "give Rockford and me some privacy this evening. I just know he's going to ask me to marry him any minute. But he won't do it in front of you."

"I doubt he'd do it at a circus, either," Ellie said. "Nor would I think you'd want him to. It doesn't sound very romantic, a man asking you to marry him among all those smells of greasy food and animal dung."

"Ellie!" Darlene gasped. "You're my sister, and I love you. But oh, you are so blunt at times! Do please try to curb your tongue in front of Rockford. After all, his father is one of the scions of Fort Worth, and I'm sure he wouldn't want a daughter-in-law in the family with a sister who talks like an uneducated ranch hand."

Ellie shot Darlene a hurt look, and her sister clapped a hand over her mouth, then dropped it.

"Oh, Ellie, forgive me," Darlene said. "I wasn't thinking of what I was saying, because I'm so eager to see Rockford. But dear, it's not as if you don't know better. You've had the same training as I have in manners. And the same education, too."

"But you get to sit around and practice your needlepoint and pour tea for your friends all day, Dar," Ellie reminded her. "I have a ranch to run."

Darlene reached over and hugged Ellie briefly. "That doesn't mean you have to become one of those foul-mouthed ranch hands. I want to see you happy, too, Ellie, but I can't imagine having one of those ranch hands for a brother-in-law."

Ellie sighed and gave up. Darlene wasn't a bad person, but she was very full of herself. She couldn't much help it after being raised the favored daughter—the blood daughter. And she did desperately love Rockford Van Zandt, or at least, she had convinced herself she did. The love of Darlene's life just wouldn't take that final step into matrimony for some reluctant, hidden reason.

The object of their conversation walked toward the buggy as Ellie whoa'ed the horse and wrapped the reins around the brake handle. Glancing up, Ellie saw another man following Rockford. Clearly the two were together. The other man—a huge man—took the lead rein from Rockford when Darlene's love started to tie the horse and nodded for him to go on over to Darlene. Holding the lead rein, the man watched Rockford, but for some reason Ellie felt him looking at her from the corner of his eye.

She stared at the large man in fascination. Rockford wasn't small, but this other man dwarfed him. He had to be well over six and a half feet. Along with Rockford, he had removed his hat as the buggy with the women in it approached. Blond and thick, his hair was tawnier than her own nearly white, sun-bleached tresses, and she sensed without confirmation that his eyes would be as amber as hers were blue.

Amber, the color of a lion's eyes. His rugged face reminded her of a lion's face, also, stark and blunt with a don't-mess-with-me haughtiness. She thought Rockford had mentioned that his business acquaintance was from New York City, but he almost looked at home amid the horses, wagons, and buggies.

For some silly reason, Ellie looked down at her dress, wishing she hadn't chosen her second-best Sunday dress to wear to the circus. At once she shook off that feeling of inadequacy. Second best was her ultimate place in life anyway.

She was vaguely aware of Darlene and Rockford murmuring greetings as though they hadn't just seen each other for tea the previous afternoon. The buggy swayed, and Darlene giggled appreciatively as Rockford swung her to the ground with ease. The other man quickly tied the lead rope to a fence post and strode toward Ellie's side of the buggy.

"This is Shane Morgan," Ellie heard Rockford say as the man stopped in front of her.

Nodding a greeting, Ellie tore her eyes away from the man's craggy face. Propriety allowed men to remove their frock coats in a lady's presence during the hot summer months, and Mr. Morgan wore a long-sleeved, white shirt with a black bolo tie. The expensive material of the shirt was tailored to leave no doubt as to his physique. He also wore a pair of brand-spanking-new jeans and gray snake-skin boots, which must have cost him as much as her entire monthly payroll.

"Sister, dear," Darlene said, drawing Ellie's attention and making her realize she and Rockford had walked around to her side of the buggy. "Close your mouth. It's open large enough to catch a bat flying by in the evening air."

Ellie closed her mouth with a pop, and warmth totally disassociated from the hot weather flushed her cheeks. She realized the man—Shane—was holding out his hands, waiting to help her down from the buggy. Not knowing what else to do and not wanting to appear rude in front of Darlene's love, she gave herself over to the huge paws. She barely noticed that one of his hands was mottled with what appeared to be a scarred-over burn; she was lost too deeply in a mental contemplation of those amber eyes, while avoiding being caught in their gaze again.

Two

Damn, she was tiny. Soaking wet, she probably wouldn't tip the scales at ninety pounds. But Shane didn't for a minute forget that a tiny woman could rule a man every bit as effectively as a large one. Ellie Parker, née whatever else her name might be if the Pinkerton report proved true, was the exact same size as his mother.

His huge hands could crush her tiny ribs if he wasn't careful, so Shane forced himself to barely grasp Ellie's waist when she placed her hands on his shoulders. Swinging her out of the buggy, he barely noticed the feather weight of her. He set her down as easily as if he had picked a fluff of dandelion seed and blown it into the air.

Rockford babbled something beside him, and Shane caught the words "New York City."

New York City. Home. His mother. The Pinkerton report.

Shane quickly rerouted his thoughts about dandelions, summer days, and pretty women into the air and paid attention to Rockford's comments. He reminded himself that he was in this decadently hot and uncivilized state of Texas at his mother's behest. He needed to keep his head about him.

"Yes," he replied to Rockford's introduction. "Rockford and I are discussing expanding our mutual business entities. There appears to be quite a wide open market in—"

He thought he covered up his distaste at even speaking the state's name quite well as he continued, "—your delightful state of Texas."

Did he imagine it, or did Ellie's eyes fill with disappointment, then glaze over somewhat as he spoke? He should have remembered that women preferred not to have men discuss business in their presence. However, Ellie seemed extremely interested in Rockford's next comment, although the other man focused entirely on Darlene as he spoke.

"It'll be very beneficial to mine and my father's business interests here in Fort Worth if we can talk Shane into investing in our area," Rockford said. "I, for one, don't understand how he could overlook the charming company available to him, either."

Darlene preened and took the arm Rockford held out, but when Shane offered the same courtesy to Ellie, she didn't notice for a second. The look on her face wasn't so much disgust as puzzlement as the other pair strolled off.

Shane cleared his throat, and Ellie slowly turned her head. Evidently used to much shorter men, her gaze fell on his chest, although she tipped her head back—then tipped it back further in order to meet his eyes. He muffled the urge to tell her not to get a catch in her neck.

Funny, there were a lot of tentative things rolling around in his mind he wished he *could* say to this tiny mite of femininity. If only he could find someone like her in New York.

His jaw tightened. Damn, he'd forgotten for a minute. He would never subject a woman anywhere to his marred body—a New York woman or a Texas woman.

"It's really not necessary for you to escort me, Mr. Morgan," she said. "I'm sure I'll find plenty of friends to visit with."

Mariana Catalina Morgan's voice whispered a reprimand to him as Shane briefly thought of telling her fine and stalking away. To be honest, he thought in answer to the urge, she was proving a distraction to him he didn't need, and he would just as soon get out of her presence for a few minutes. But his mother would have his hide if he failed to fulfill her most recent request.

He unclenched his jaw. "It truly would be my pleasure to escort you, Miss Parker," he assured her, watching her eyes glaze over again. What was it about him? Every time he spoke, she looked as if it pained her to hear his voice. Surely she could appreciate his cultured tones compared to the hard-to-understand drawl infiltrating the speech of the rest of this state's population. Come to think of it, she had that drawl, too, but it sounded charming on her, not illiterate.

"Absolutely not." She reached out a tiny hand and patted his arm. "I know Rockford and Darlene want to be alone, and I've had practice busying myself before while they court. I'll see you when the circus starts."

Before he could move, she flitted into the profusion of buggies, wagons, and horses. As small as she was, he lost sight of her immediately.

Hell, how was he going to get to know this woman if she clearly didn't fancy being in his company? Forget the fact that for a moment he'd thought of deserting her disturbing presence on his own. He'd agreed—well, acceded to orders—to come here, and the faster he got his job done, the faster he could leave.

He sighed, with a mixture of resignation and—yes, he had to admit—a touch of eagerness. He would just have to find her again.

"Here she comes, Pandora."

The cat opened its eyes, but spoiled the pretense of alertness by yawning. Fatima scowled at her companion, then dropped the tent flap back into place. Hurriedly she swung her silver-tipped black wand, and a full-length mirror appeared amid a cloud of gold-dust sparkles. Waving the sparkles away so they didn't cloud the mirror surface, Fatima examined herself.

Her red hair was carefully coiffed, thick and luxuriant, not a tress out of place. The black-and-white ostrich feather curled above her left ear, then swept around and cupped the back of her head. The little black dot beside her mouth perfectly complemented her pretty features.

The red-and-gold full-skirted gown might be a trifle low-cut, baring her shoulders and a goodly portion of her breasts. But Fatima had always been of the school that if you've got it, flaunt it. Despite just coming off a few months of spoiling herself, she'd only gained a few pounds, and the gown tapered to a suitably small waist. The skirt flared out, filled by several layers of alternating gold, red, and black net skirts. It ended just below the knee, exposing a nice length of black net stocking on her shapely calves. She adored the high-heeled red slippers sparkling on her feet.

Propping her hands on her hips and tilting her head, she asked Pandora, "Do you see anything I need to give attention to?"

The cat yawned, no doubt bored with the perfection of her mistress's presence. Fatima sniffed at the cat, then quickly peeked out the tent flap again. Despite what Ellie had said about finding a group of friends to occupy her until circus time, she was strolling around alone.

That poor young woman spent entirely too much time alone. She was sometimes alone even when she rode with her ranch hands or spent evenings with her sister and mother.

Especially that mother! Fatima's irritation mounted at the thought of how Elvina ignored Ellie except for berating her about the ranch's finances whenever they were together. Her lips thinned even more when she thought of how Ellie catered to her stepmother as though it were Ellie's obligation and Elvina's due.

Time for a change in this young woman's life! A drastic change.

Fatima had chosen her spot well—back behind the animal cages. She assumed Ellie would stroll among the poor caged beasts, her heart aching at their restricted existence. At least this circus manager made sure his animals were well cared for.

Fatima waved her wand and made her tent visible to Ellie. As though she herself hovered overhead, she knew what Ellie saw—a bright red-and-white striped tent appearing out of nowhere amid a cloud of sparkling magic dust. Sure enough, Ellie halted as though she'd run into a brick wall, a stunned look on her face. She rubbed her fists in her eyes and dropped them, peering at the tent in disbelief—another typical reaction.

Fatima stepped out of the tent. "Hello, Ellie, my dear," she said. "I'm your fairy godmother. I'm here to grant your wishes."

Three

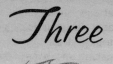

Good grief on a greased slide, she was going bonkers! Ellie had always feared there might be something strange about her. Hadn't her family sent her off to be adopted rather than keep her? Now visions threatened her sanity.

She turned to run. But the woman of the evening who had stepped out of the tent appeared in front of her, blocking her path. How had she moved so fast? The woman carried a polished black stick with a silver tip on it in one hand and wore a determined look on her face.

"Now, Ellie, dear," she said.

"How do you know my name? I don't know you! I've never seen you before in my life." Ellie tried to back away, but the woman pointed the stick at her feet, and they wouldn't move. "Let me go!"

She didn't know how the woman had frozen her feet— nor even how she knew that was what had happened. Oh, diddly! She'd be danged if she'd let herself believe for one second that the woman might possibly be carrying a magic wand.

"Let me go, gosh darn it," she repeated as the woman stepped closer. "I'll—I'll scream!"

"Ellie, please," the woman soothed. "I'm not going to hurt you. As I said, I'm your fairy godmother."

"There's no such thing as fairies! I demand you let me go!"

The woman sighed and shook her head. "Ellie, sweetheart, I'm not that sort of fairy, but you're wrong about them, too. I repeat, I am your fairy godmother. And I've come to bring you happiness."

"You're not making me happy right now," Ellie insisted. "And the only way you can do that—make me happy—is to release me and leave here yourself."

"Give me five minutes, Ellie. Then I'll—"

"You'll promise to leave?" Ellie asked when the woman fell silent.

"Well, no, but I'll try to convince you that I'm telling the truth. There. That's what I'll do. And you'll see that I only want you to be happy, my dear."

Ellie jerked frantically at one foot, but it was stuck to the ground as though glued. Hurriedly she bent down and tried to unlace her shoe. She would run away barefoot if she had to. But it would take her forever to undo her shoes, and indeed she only succeeded in making the laces tighter. A few seconds later, she wobbled and plopped onto her behind.

A tear of fright escaped, and she swiped it with the back of her hand.

"Oh, please, Ellie." The woman knelt beside her. "Don't cry. I truly don't intend to frighten you. Won't you give me those five minutes I asked for?"

"You and your tent appear out of nowhere in a cloud of sparkling dust, you glue my feet to the ground so I can't run away—" Ellie swiped another tear. "—but you don't mean to frighten me? What do you do when you *do* want to scare a person?"

"I—"

"Meowr!"

Ellie twisted her head sharply and saw a huge—decadently huge—fluffy white cat stalk through the tent flap. It was so large she could hear its footsteps on the hard-packed earth. It walked right up to her, gave the woman a look that Ellie could have sworn said you're-lucky-I'm-here, and climbed onto Ellie's lap. Rising onto its back legs, the cat licked Ellie's chin with a raspy tongue, then settled into Ellie's arms when she instinctively closed them. That cat's purr rumbled only slightly lower in volume than a train wheel's clickity-clack, but it soothed Ellie's fright.

"That's Pandora," the woman said, relief in her voice. "And I'm Fatima."

Ellie stroked the cat, her fingers losing themselves in the silky, feathery hair. She loved cats, although she didn't know where the love came from. Elvina had claimed to be allergic to them ever since Ellie brought a tiny kitten into the house to nurse it one winter. Elvina never came into the kitchen, anyway, but she heard about the kitten from Darlene and declared that it bothered her when she ate in the adjacent dining room. Only Darlene's pleas had persuaded her to allow Ellie to keep the kitten in the kitchen until it was ready to return to the barn.

"Hello, Pandora," she murmured. The cat rumbled on and lifted its head so she could scratch under its chin.

Before Ellie could protest, Fatima lifted her wand. The tent moved over and settled around them. Frightened at the enveloping enclosure, Ellie scrambled to her feet with Pandora still in her arms. The cat kneaded its claws on her arm, the action more comforting than hurtful, and Ellie was grateful to realize her feet were now free.

"I—" Ellie cleared her throat. "I don't believe in magic."

"Hardly anyone does," Fatima acknowledged with a sigh. "But magic is real. Here, watch this."

Ellie cringed as Fatima raised the wand again, but when the shower of gold sparkles from the silver tip subsided, the tent was filled with beautiful white roses. For the first time Ellie noticed the red silk walls. Outside it had variegating red and white stripes, but here inside, one color covered the walls. It draped and flowed all around them, caught here and there by diamond cluster pins, which shone in the light from candles burning inside crystal vases.

Somehow she knew those diamonds were real, also. The money to buy all that silk and those jewels would pay for every ranch and steer in her part of Texas!

The roses stood out starkly but beautifully against the silk. Their scent wafted pleasantly instead of over-poweringly around them, and Ellie breathed deeply. She loved roses. Elvina thought they made her sneeze, but since she never came into Ellie's room, Ellie kept a fruit jar there full of blooms from the plants Darlene tended when the blossoms were in season.

Lifting her head from Ellie's arm for a moment, the cat opened its eyes and meowed.

"Oh, Pandora, I know you like yellow roses better," Fatima said in a peeved voice. "But they don't go with the red silk walls."

"Meow!"

"Oh, all right."

Fatima waved the wand, and sparkles engulfed the tent. When they cleared, the walls had changed from red to white, the roses to yellow. If Ellie hadn't been able to make herself accept the first spectacle, this new change threatened her very composure.

She'd never fainted in her life, but blackness threatened on the edge of her vision.

"Ellie!" Fatima stepped close and placed an arm around Ellie's shoulders. "Here. Sit down."

Fatima pointed the wand at the floor—which Ellie now noticed was covered with a beautiful, thick carpet of gold—and a fainting couch in yellow-and-green patterned silk appeared. Ellie stiffened. No way was she going to actually lie down in front of this . . . this . . . whatever she was.

"Meow!"

The cat leaped out of Ellie's arms, and she realized she'd been squeezing the poor animal. It didn't go far, however.

It landed on the fainting couch and sat, then stretched out its left rear paw and started bathing it.

Ellie directed her gaze at the wand, then the woman's face.

"Uh—look, Miss . . . Mrs.—"

"Fatima," she repeated. "Just Fatima. We only need one name in my world."

"Fata—Fata—"

"No. No, no, no," the woman interrupted. "The way you're pronouncing it makes me sound obese, and I work extremely hard to keep my figure. It's not easy, you know. Why, I can conjure up chocolate or bonbons at my very whim. Lucky for me, I enjoy grapes and oranges nearly as well as all those oversugared sweets."

"Look, I don't care—uh—" Ellie placed a hand on her stomach. "Uh—chocolate and bonbons?"

"Oh, my, yes. And truffles. Why, Ellie, my truffles are to die for. Here, try one."

She waved her wand and a thin china plate appeared amid the gold dust, hovering in the air and holding a chocolate truffle. Before she could stop herself, Ellie reached for the truffle and brought it to her lips. She could smell the wondrous odor of chocolate and almost taste it even before she took a small nibble. Chocolate and nougat melted in her mouth, and she finished the truffle in two more ecstatically delightful bites.

"Would you like another one?" Fatima asked.

"No, Fatima. I wouldn't be able to fit in my clothes in the morning."

"Fatima," she gently corrected. "Fa-*tee*-ma. We're going to be friends, Ellie, and I do like my name pronounced correctly."

"Fatima," Ellie repeated. "And I do have to agree that your truffles are to die for."

Fatima's lips pursed in a self-satisfied preen. "It's not just sweets that I'm good at conjuring up. Why, I have the right touch with anything I make. Cupid is a steak-and-potatoes man, and he says I'm the only one who can grill his steak just the right amount—medium rare.''

''Cupid?'' Ellie blinked, then stared around her again. Fatima said something else, but Ellie let her babble on without comprehension as she adjusted her thoughts. For a moment there, she'd let that delicious truffle distract her and make her forget where she was.

She was standing in a silk-lined tent amid the animal cages at the circus, talking to a woman who appeared out of nowhere and who carried a magic wand. Who *used* a magic wand, quite capably, from what she'd already shown Ellie. A woman with a beautiful Persian cat called Pandora and who talked about her friend Cupid.

Ellie had always been a reader, curling up in her room alone evenings while Darlene and Elvina did needlepoint in front of a winter fire. Her reading often lasted late into the night as she made her way through the well-stocked library George Parker had collected. She read of Greek gods and goddesses and even found tales of fairies and elves. In novels about Ireland, she read about the little people, including brownies and the vicious leprechauns, who hoarded their gold at the end of the rainbow.

But she'd never believed. She knew the difference between fiction and reality—knew it well.

Fiction was the dreams she had of visiting all the far-flung places she read about. Reality was her situation at the Parker ranch. Her place was as the orphan who should appreciate having an actual home instead of living in a poorly funded orphanage, like those she'd read about in Charles Dickens's novels. Elvina alluded to her situation often enough.

Fiction was wishes and hopes and dreams. Reality was the ranch she loved beyond measure, but to which she held no claim other than her ability to make herself indispensable to Elvina as a manager since George died.

And now she was losing her mind—having visions of a prostitute who claimed to be her fairy godmother and a cat

who communicated with her. Could she possibly come
from a family who became deranged at an early age?

"Ellie?"

Fatima reached out and ran her hands up and down Ellie's arms. The so-called fairy godmother felt real, not magical.

"Ellie?"

Ellie jerked back, arms flying up and knocking Fatima's
hands away.

"No. You're not real. This isn't real. I'm *not* going
crazy!"

"You're not going crazy," Fatima assured her, then
glanced over her shoulder. "Oh, dear. Here he comes, and
I'm not ready yet for that part of this."

"Who?" Ellie demanded. "What part of what are you
talking about?"

But the tent disappeared around her, leaving Ellie standing in the middle of the area alone.

"I'll be back!" she heard Fatima say, although she didn't
see even a tiny spark of fairy dust in the air.

That settled it. Ellie had no further doubt she was on the
verge of lunacy.

There she was. Shane paused in his search, frowning for a
second. He could have sworn he'd already scanned this area
a few seconds ago and hadn't seen Ellie. He had searched
the entire circus, his height being both a help and hin-
drance. He could see over nearly everyone's head, but Ellie
was so tiny that he wove his way through thicker presses
of bodies to make sure she wasn't hidden there.

Now she stood there looking up into the air, hands on
hips and dainty foot patting impatiently under the hem of
her dress.

"I want you to explain yourself now!" he heard her say.

"Huh?"

Shane rescanned the area, trying to find whoever Ellie
was speaking to. But there was no one else around. At least,

not in the area Ellie appeared to be talking to.

To his right various animal cages held lions, tigers, and monkeys. The elephants and camels were chained and tied to their posts, nibbling at hay, or, in the case of one elephant, sucking from a tub of water with a long, snaky trunk.

To his left the big top sprawled, the lengthening ticket line finally moving forward. At Darlene's insistence, Shane had redoubled his efforts to find Ellie. Darlene assured him that she would save two seats, but from the looks of the crowd, that might not be possible.

The animal cage area had been the only place left to look, and he truly hadn't thought to find Ellie here. Now he couldn't figure out what on earth she was doing.

"Come back here!" she said.

Was she fey? His mother had never mentioned anything like that in the Spencer family. But he had better tread softly.

He softly treaded nearer.

"Miss Parker?"

The noise from a sudden disturbance over by the elephants covered up his words.

"Fatima! Pandora!"

Fatima? Pandora? Good lord, she's talking to imaginary people. At least, Pandora is a mythological character. I've never heard of Fatima.

Shane stepped closer. "Miss Parker? Darlene sent me to find you."

Ellie whirled, then distractedly glanced over her shoulder. He could swear she was still looking up into the sky. He caught himself before he shook his head in sorrow. From her actions, he almost thought her delusional. If that were the case, even if she were his mother's friend's long-lost daughter, she would never enjoy the riches waiting for her. She lived in a different world—or soon would.

"Miss Parker?" he said once again, his voice tempered with compassion. "Don't you want to go in and see the circus?"

"There's another circus out here," he thought he heard her say.

"What?" he asked.

"I'm sorry." Even her voice sounded distracted and distanced. "I said—uh—I lost track of it being time for the circus while I was out here. It's a beautiful evening, and I was enjoying the peace and quiet away from the crowds."

A lion roared mightily just then, and Shane chuckled.

"Peace and quiet? I believe it's ended now, since it looks like they're getting the animals ready to perform."

He nodded over toward the elephants, where a spangled and bejeweled woman patted the face of one huge beast. The lion roared again, sending a chill up Shane's back. He'd never been fond of cats, and the larger they were, the more he disliked them.

"Shall we go?" he asked.

She took a step, then started to lift her head and gaze overhead once again. Seeming to catch herself, she stopped in mid-motion and smiled at him.

"That's what we came for, isn't it? To see the circus?"

He bowed politely and held out his arm. She slipped her hand in the crook this time without protest, and Shane turned to lead her around the big top. Before they had taken three steps, the lion roared again.

It didn't only roar; it appeared in front of them. In fact, it bounded toward them.

Ellie screamed. Shane instinctively shoved her behind him, then threw his hands up and braced for the lion's charge. It roared again, and Shane realized he had closed his eyes in anticipation of the assault.

When he slit them open, the lion sat in front of him. This time when it roared, Shane saw straight down its throat, past the enormous white fangs and bloodred tongue to the waving tonsils deep inside. He imagined he could smell the fetid breath, and maybe he could.

The lion's roar ended in a creaking yawn, and it closed

its mouth, eyeing Shane as though *his* move followed next in this crazy, unpredictable dance.

"Ellie," Shane whispered.

"Yes?" she whispered in return. Her fingers were clenched in his shirt back, tiny and reminding him how extremely small she was. She would nearly fit inside that lion's mouth with room to spare.

"I'm going to move backward, step by step," Shane told her. "Move with me, but keep yourself completely hidden behind me."

"Don't worry," she breathed more than actually spoke. "I'm not about to show myself to that beast unless it's to run."

"For God's sake, don't do that! Just don't get under my feet and make me stumble, or you'll be wide open to him. I'm going to count to three over and over. We'll take a small step on each three."

"I understand."

"One. Two. Three." Shane cautiously moved one foot backward, and Ellie glided with him. They would have done well together in a ballroom.

The lion roared and moved a step closer.

"What did he do?" Ellie cried in a frantic croak.

"He—never mind. I won't let him past me. Let's go again. One. Two. Three."

He stepped back with the other foot, and Ellie went with him. The lion roared and moved a step closer.

"Goddamn it to hell," Shane said without thinking.

"What?" Ellie demanded. "What's he doing?"

Shane could tell by her movements that she was trying to see around him—to see whether the lion was preparing to spring. He wished like hell he knew that himself.

He shoved his arms stiffly behind him to hold Ellie in place. "One. Two."

"Darn it—" she said.

"Three."

Luckily for them both, she moved with him, but with a

sigh of impatience this time. Darn the woman anyway. Not only was she fey, she was evidently one of those women who didn't take kindly to letting a man handle things. She pushed at his arm, which barred her from peering around his wideness, but he stiffened it further.

"Quit trying to move around me, damn it," he snarled in a low voice. "That lion looks hungry."

She gasped and stopped fighting his hold.

"Hey!" someone to the left of them yelled. "Hey, don't move like that. It could be dangerous!"

"No shit," Shane muttered, though not loud enough for whoever spoke to hear him. Not loud enough to disturb the hungry beast in front of him. "But you think I'm going to stand here and be eaten?"

He took a breath, whispered a quick "One-two-three" and moved with Ellie. The lion advanced into his retreat, too, but only that one step.

"Hey!" the voice yelled again. "Stop moving. He thinks you're doing his trick with him!"

Shane risked a glance to the left. The sparkled-and-spangled woman walked toward him, the huge elephant trailing in her wake, its trunk dancing from side to side and its feet stirring up puffs of dust. Good God, if the lion didn't eat them, the elephant would probably trample them! Ellie wasn't big enough to leave even a faint grease spot in the dirt beneath that animal's huge foot.

He recalled an elephant-foot footstool in his mother's parlor and vowed to accidentally throw the damned thing into the fireplace when he got home.

"What trick?" he cautiously asked the woman.

"Just don't move again," she said instead of answering. Then she stepped aside and tapped the elephant on the trunk with the long, hooked pole she carried. "Now, Tiny."

Tiny? The elephant was named Tiny? The thought barely registered in Shane's mind before all three of them—Shane, Ellie, and the lion—were showered with an engulfing spray of water. The elephant. The damned elephant had sprayed them all with the contents of its trunk!

Shane took a step back and came up against a coughing, choking Ellie. His boot heel encountered her tiny foot, and somehow he managed to stop himself before crushing it with his weight. The jerky change of movement threw him off balance, and he started to fall, horrified when he realized his falling body would leave Ellie open to the lion's charge.

With one swipe, he caught Ellie to him as he went down. With a swift twist, he changed his direction of fall to land on his back, with Ellie cradled in his arms. The lion could still get her, and its roar sounded as though it were right in his ear. He flung Ellie to his side and scrambled into a protective crouch over the top of her.

The lion roared again. The elephant, trunk empty now, joined in the clamor with its own trumpeting bellow. Shane groaned and cuddled Ellie against his chest, waiting for the lion's fangs to pierce his back.

Something tapped him on the shoulder.

"You can get up now. I'm going to take Sinbad back to his cage. All he needed was for the water to shower him and let him know the trick was done."

Shane stayed frozen. Get up? He'd be damned if he would. He'd be eaten if he did.

Something tapped him again, this time on his upper arm. He glanced aside and saw the tip of the hooked stick the woman had carried. Hell, if the lion wasn't going to eat *her*, maybe he and Ellie were safe.

"I said, it's all right for you to get up now," she said. "I tried to tell you that Sinbad thought you were doing his trick with him—backing away like you were afraid of him. They do the same thing in the ring."

Very cautiously, Shane loosened his hold on Ellie and looked down into her face. Her little bonnet was missing and her white-blond hair was scattered all around her head. Her blue eyes gazed back at him, still filled with fear, and her terror jolted him—angered him. He got to his feet, pulling Ellie with him and shoving her behind him once again.

Furious, he glared at the woman and elephant. "What the hell do you mean, he thought he was doing a *trick?*"

"Just what I said," she replied with a shrug of a spangled shoulder. "Conroy, the animal trainer, does a trick like that in the ring. He pretends Sinbad is stalking him. Then Tiny squirts the two of them with water from his trunk, and Sinbad hightails it back to his cage." She flicked her head to the side. "See? Sinbad's over there by his cage now. I need to go let him in before he decides he's supposed to do the trick again."

She turned and started away, and Shane took a step after her. "Just wait a damned minute—"

The elephant trumpeted, sat down and lifted its front feet into the air. Shane froze, starting up, up at the potential footstools wavering over him. Damn, that elephant actually had teeth, too. Tusks, he thought they called them.

The woman turned back. "Oh, Tiny, quit it," she said. "You're scaring these people as bad as Sinbad did. Come on."

She tapped Tiny's front leg with her stick, and the elephant fell back to earth. Shane sneezed in the shower of dust Tiny's feet whipped up on the edge of the mud puddle where he and Ellie stood. By the time he cleared his nose and eyes, the woman and elephant were nearly to the lion's cage. Sighing in defeat and embarrassment, Shane turned to look at Ellie.

She stood there bedraggled and dirty, her hair trailing nearly to the ground. He'd never seen a woman with such long hair, even one undressed in her bedroom. But what caught his gaze even more was the front of her dress. The elephant's shower had soaked her as well, and the thin material outlined a pair of very adequate breasts for her tiny stature. The nipples on them perked toward him beckoningly.

He jerked his gaze free, but it didn't stop that randy part of him from stiffening in much the same manner as her nipples. She didn't seem to notice, thank goodness. Tears filled her blue eyes, and she sniffed, circling her arms around herself.

"This has been one horrible evening," she murmured. "I just want to go h—home!" Then the tears broke.

Shane pulled her into his arms. Surprisingly, she fit perfectly into the space he had initially thought too large for her. A strong urge to care for her—do anything within his power to stop her tears—filled him.

At the same moment he realized it was going to take an awful lot of power on his part to keep his mind on business and the reason he had come to Texas. He'd made the trip to verify this woman's identity, not fall for her.

Hell, if the Pinkertons were right, Ellie didn't even know for sure who she was herself. Given his already intense but confusing feelings for her, what on earth would happen when he tried to get close enough to her to confirm or deny her identity?

But he did have to try to get close to her, he reminded himself. Just not in *that* way. Besides, if he slipped and allowed something more than a strict friendship between them, she would hate him when she found out why he'd really come to Texas.

Four

She fit just exactly in his arms, Ellie mused through her dejection. Awareness of what she was doing and where she was suddenly sank in, and she struggled to free herself. Lucky for her, Shane released her accordingly. Had he been so inclined, he could have held her in place with one hand. Probably even one finger.

Rubbing under her eyes, she sniffled and then grabbed for a handkerchief in her skirt pocket. Shane handed her his instead, and she gratefully wiped her face. Beyond attempting to act like a lady, she blew her nose, too. So far this evening, she'd been faced with an incredibly attractive man, a woman who contended she could make magic, a lion that nearly scared her into wetting her drawers, and a monstrous elephant. She'd be diddly-darned if she'd feel embarrassed about blowing her nose in front of that same incredibly attractive man.

She folded the handkerchief and shoved it into her skirt pocket. "I'll wash it and return it to you."

"Good."

Ellie shot him a disgruntled look. "You sound as if you thought I'd give it back to you soiled. You shouldn't have offered it to me, if that was the case. I had my own."

"Hey," Shane said, "I didn't mean it that way." He tilted his head and studied her. "I only meant that your

returning the handkerchief would give me a chance to see
you again.''

''Oh, sure,'' Ellie said without thinking. ''I'm standing
here all dirty from rolling around in a mud bath an elephant
made for me, with my hair all straggly and a red nose and
eyes from crying because a lion scared me to death. And
you want to—''

She jerked and her eyes widened. Her mouth dropped
open so wide she almost had to push it closed to be able
to continue speaking. Her gaze flew up, up, to Shane's face.

''You want to *see* me again?''

He chuckled. He actually chuckled, and by all rights she
should have stalked away from him for daring to laugh at
her predicament. But his laughter soothed her, filled her
with a sense of self and wonder she'd never experienced
before in any man's presence. Anyone's presence, for that
matter.

She studied him. He wasn't in much better shape than
she was—muddy trouser knees and shirt, his tawny hair
waving loosely around his head, reminding her of the lion's
mane.

But dishevelment and dirt looked masculine on him,
while she must look a complete mess. She came in off a
hard day on the range a lot cleaner than this at times.

''I want to see you again,'' he said, heightening her sense
of wonder that he could say that in spite of her grubby
appearance. ''And it's not your fault at all that your attire
and composure have been ruined. I'm totally at fault, and
I do beg your pardon.''

''You? My attire and composure? My pardon?'' Shoot,
she sounded like a mockingbird.

But there he went again with those words no Texas man
even had in his vocabulary, spoken in that harsh, disagreeable northern accent. Yet somehow the accent wasn't quite
as disagreeable this time, the words more pleasing to her
mind. More often than not, she had to lower her own vocabulary level to far below the degree to which she'd ed-

ucated herself in order to carry on a conversation with a Texas male. Even Rockford occasionally used *ain't* and dropped his g's.

"I—" She drew in a breath and reached into her own store of education. "You are extremely kind, sir. But I do realize you are only trying to put me at my ease, so I will not hold you to your polite suggestion. I will see that your handkerchief is returned. Good evening."

Turning, Ellie headed for the rear of the big top tent instead of the now nonexistent ticket line in front. The buggies and wagons were corralled just past the entrance. She knew Rockford's conveyance, and she'd leave a note for him, telling him to please escort Darlene home himself, and that she had a headache and had gone ahead. Darlene wouldn't mind being lied to one bit, not when it meant she and Rockford could drive back to the ranch unchaperoned.

"Hey!"

Ellie ignored Shane and picked up her skirts, hastening her steps. She'd stood in front of him quite long enough in her muddy, disheveled state. He might change his mind about seeing her again—if indeed he wasn't just being polite—if she let him study her too long.

Elvina had told her once that her slight stature could possibly make a man think twice about taking her as his wife—especially a Texas man, who needed a strong wife by his side to bear his children. Of course, as an orphan Ellie never allowed herself to think she might attract a man of another class than the rowdy cowboys she worked with every day. After all, she had no way of knowing what sort of other secrets her background held.

Given his long, nicely muscled legs, she should have known she couldn't outrace Shane Morgan. He stepped in front of her, and short of bouncing off him like an ineffective piece of dandelion fluff, she had no choice but to halt her flight.

And flight it was, she admitted.

"Look," Shane said, jamming his hands into his trouser

pockets. "I realize I'm not exactly the escort you would have chosen this evening. You've made it quite clear my presence is distasteful to you."

"Distasteful?" Ellie gasped. "Why, hardly."

"I know you're just being polite, Miss Parker."

"Ellie."

He quirked a tawny eyebrow. "I might have your permission to call you Ellie?"

"Please." She shoved a tress of hair behind her shoulder. "It makes me uncomfortable to be called Miss Parker." She'd never tell him why the name bothered her, but then, she'd never have to.

"Ellie, then. What I'm trying to say is that I can't bring myself to abandon you until I see you safely home. Maybe in Texas it's all right for a man to allow a woman he's been escorting to drive home alone, but in my world it's just not done."

"You haven't really been my escort, Mr. Morgan—"

"Shane."

"Shane. I can't ask you to miss the circus, when I'm perfectly capable of getting myself home."

"Ellie." He actually seemed to savor saying her name, and something about the way it rolled off his tongue sent a not-unpleasant thrill up her spine. "Truthfully, I'm not a bit interested in that circus. My mother is a delirious fan of the circus, and I've been to both Ringling Brothers and Barnum and Bailey in New York City at least twice. Each time it was only because Mother insisted I tag along."

Ellie flicked at a piece of drying mud on her forearm, more to give herself something to focus on besides his earnest face and gold-dusted amber eyes than because it bothered her. Shane picked up on it at once, however.

"You can't be comfortable with that mud all over you. I know it's bothering me, and it'll just get worse as it dries during your drive home. Why don't you come back to my suite and clean up before I take you home, Ellie?"

His audacity earned him an astonished look. Maybe she

was a backwoods Texas girl, but she knew better than to visit a man's hotel suite.

"I will not, sir!"

He held out his hands, an injured look on his face.

"I didn't mean it that way, Ellie. My valet, Withers, is there. I can assure you, everything is proper, including my intentions. While you're there, I'll make myself scarce and arrange to rent a carriage to escort you home in."

"I have my own carriage, remember? I'll leave Rockford a note, and he can bring Darlene home. Darlene will be ever so grateful to me for the chance to be alone with Rockford, no matter what the circumstances."

"Then I'll need a mount to return to town. I'll arrange that while you clean up. So, will you allow me to try to make this evening end a little better than it began?"

He looked so earnest, so boyish, despite his hugeness. And Ellie had to admit, it sort of tickled her fancy to be in control of such a large man—to have him asking her permission rather than just barging ahead and expecting her to follow, as a Texas man would.

Before she could stop herself, she wondered what it would be like if that control carried over into a more serious situation with a man like him. Or maybe actually with Shane himself.

Could she make him groan in frustration because he yearned to kiss her so badly? Or even touch her in other ways?

Where on earth had those thoughts come from? Ellie shook her head in chastisement, her hair swinging freely with her movements and reminding her of her scandalous appearance.

"Elvina just might still be awake when I get home," she mused both to herself and Shane. "So I guess I would appreciate a chance to repair myself before I get there. All my friends are probably at the circus, even their parents, or I could ask one of them to let me clean up at her house.

As long as your valet is in attendance, I suppose it will be all right.''

"Excellent," Shane said, offering her his arm again. "Your idea was perfect, too. We'll take your buggy and leave a note on Rockford's, explaining that we've gone on ahead."

Ellie slipped her hand into his arm and accompanied him toward the buggy. By now the sun had set, darkness finally making its unrelenting presence known. Overhead pinpoint stars winked into sight, scattering and clustering in the inky sky just beyond grasp in the clear night.

Shane's next words indicated that the vista charmed him as much as it did her. "In New York City," he murmured, "we seldom see such beauty. There are still far too many factories on the shoreline."

"Do you live in the middle of the city, then?"

"Practically. But we have a couple of other houses, one in Cape Cod and one in the Hampshires, so we don't have to stay in town all year round. Mother would never miss the opera season and holidays, though."

Ellie sighed in yearning, and Shane once again seemed to know what she was thinking by reading that unspoken sound. They were in the corral now, and he stopped and looked down at her before helping her into the buggy.

"Do you ever wish you could attend the opera and season back East, Ellie?"

"Yes," she admitted. "Oh, I do love Texas and the ranch, and I would never, ever want to make my permanent home elsewhere. But it would be wonderful to see the sights of New York. Somehow, I've always been extremely interested in the East, and especially New York City. We have a cultural center over in Dallas where various artists perform, but Elvina has never seen fit to allow me to attend."

"Maybe we can do that while I'm here."

The stab of exhilaration surprised Ellie into speechlessness, during which Shane scooped her into the buggy seat.

He walked away for a minute, and Ellie peered through the darkness, her gaze following him, his white shirt a beacon. He paused at another buggy, which she recognized as Rockford's. Evidently he had found a piece of paper and pencil in the wallet he pulled from his pocket, because when he turned back to her, a note stuck on top of the buggy whip handle fluttered in the evening breeze.

He climbed into the ranch buggy, his weight creaking the springs, smiled at her and picked up the reins. As he guided the horse back toward town, a good half mile away, Ellie searched for something to break the silence. She couldn't think of a thing to say, though, and she'd been speaking so very easily with him up until now. She nearly always found men easy to talk to, having spent more time with them than women most of her life.

She had conversed easily with Shane until he mentioned taking her to the Dallas Cultural Center. She tried to tell herself she didn't want to bring that up again because he might change his mind. But the nagging thought that she really wanted to be with Shane Morgan again, wherever he wanted to take her, just wouldn't be ignored.

No, she adamantly told herself, she wanted so badly to attend that she would go to the Cultural Center with anyone who would take her there. She would consider it if even by any stretch of the imagination, Cecil Bedford took it into his head that the way to regain her favor would be to escort her to a cultural function instead of the barn dances that seemed to be his main repertoire of social activities.

Well, maybe not Cecil Bedford. She had avoided any further evenings with him after that first and only one ended with him heaving his dinner up on her dancing shoes in the middle of the square dance. No matter that he apologized profusely, claiming he had only drunk outside to be "one of the boys." Remembrance of the sour smell of vomit on her skirts all the way home kept her from ever giving that thwarted beau another chance.

They turned onto Main Street, and the hotel loomed partway down the block. All at once Ellie recalled her appearance.

"Stop," she implored Shane. "I can't go into the hotel looking like this."

Shane agreeably pulled the buggy over to the side of the street. Ellie frantically tried to arrange her hair, but most of the pins were gone. Unlike Darlene, who probably carried a full array of cosmetics, hairpins, and other feminine necessities in her reticule, Ellie knew all she had was a few coins and a handkerchief.

With her arms raised and hair held up into a knot, she realized she had even lost her bonnet and couldn't stuff her tresses into it.

"My bonnet," she murmured.

"It was in the mud hole," Shane informed her. "It looked irreparable, so I didn't retrieve it."

"It was new." Ellie couldn't keep the regret from her voice. She seldom got anything new, except at Christmas when Elvina grudgingly ordered her to buy herself a dress for church. She had saved the money for the bonnet out of the extremely scant wages she allowed herself, which had been nearly nonexistent lately. The men's payroll took everything she could dredge up.

"I'll get you another one, Ellie. We can go pick one out tomorrow."

Ellie gasped and stared up at him. "I can't let you do that! Women don't allow men to buy them personal attire."

"But it was partly my fault you lost it, so I'm not exactly *buying* you something. I'm only replacing something I was responsible for you losing."

Whether it was his gold-dust eyes or disconcertingly deep masculine voice, he made sense to Ellie. Or maybe it was the fact that he was once again making a plan to see her yet another time.

Good diddly, she hadn't even known Shane Morgan a few hours ago, and now she found herself pleased as punch at his open desire to see more of her while he was here.

"Look," he said, then clicked his tongue at the horse, guiding it into a turn when it began to move. "There's another way into the hotel we can use. As far as I'm concerned, it wouldn't embarrass me to be seen with you, because your appearance isn't your fault. It's mine. And it's none of the hotel help's business what happened. But I wouldn't want you to be embarrassed, so it's my duty to save you from that situation."

He guided the buggy horse into an alley behind the hotel, where the two-story buildings effectively shaded most of the moon- and starlight from them. Shadowy and dark, it would have been a perfect place for lovers to hide and seek their privacy for things better kept between the two of them.

In fact, it dawned on Ellie that that might be exactly what was happening when Shane stopped the buggy horse beside a rear entrance to the hotel. A set of stairs led up to the second-floor rooms, and she had a fairly good idea of what they were used for. Every once in a while, her men forgot she was around, although they were totally embarrassed when they did recall her presence. Still, she knew a few things her more innocent friends might not.

She held her tongue until Shane helped her from the buggy and placed a hand on the small of her back to guide her toward the stairwell. Then she balked.

"If anyone sees me, they'll think I'm one of the girls from Rosie's Place!" she said. "Isn't this how they come visit the rooms?"

"I wouldn't know," Shane said with a chuckle. "I'm new to town, so I'm not sure what Rosie's Place is."

"I'm sure you can guess by the name."

"Ellie," Shane said in a resigned voice, "no one's going to see you. You just said that everyone is at the circus."

"What if someone's not? I'll die if they see me going into the hotel this way. It would have been bad enough going in the front. If someone sees me—eeeek!"

Shane had plopped his hat on her head, although how he'd managed to keep the hat when she'd lost her bonnet she couldn't imagine. And he scooped her into his arms and bounded up the stairs before her shriek of surprise died. He reached the landing almost immediately, his easy breathing indicating he didn't even notice her weight in his arms.

Indeed, he shifted her into one arm and held her effortlessly while he opened the door and strode inside. In two more strides he reached a room door and retrieved a key from his pocket. Opening it, he carried her inside and kicked the door shut with his boot heel.

The man standing at the window turned, an astonished look on his face. Briefly, before Ellie buried her face in Shane's neck and the hat slid to the floor, she realized where they were. She'd only heard about the opulent Presidential Suite of the hotel, but had never expected to actually see it.

"Sir?" she heard the other man say.

"Is there warm water in the washroom, Withers?" Shane asked. "Ellie's in need of freshening up before I escort her home."

"Is the young lady all right?" Withers asked.

"As I said, only in need of freshening up. We had an encounter with a lion and an elephant, both of which we initially didn't realize were friendly."

"I see, sir," Withers said as though he actually did understand and wasn't a bit surprised. "Well, I wasn't sure when to expect you, so I ordered hot water just now. It should be—" .

A knock sounded on the door, and Ellie clenched her arms tighter around Shane's neck and buried her face deeper.

"Don't let them see me," she pleaded.

Shane chuckled and carried her onward. "We'll be in here while you replenish the washroom, Withers."

Another door closed behind them, and Ellie dared to lift her head. The room was dark, the curtain over the window keeping most of the streetlight from penetrating.

"Where—" Even in the darkness she made out the huge bed beside them. She started struggling. "I can't be in here with you!"

"Shhhhh," Shane whispered, placing a finger on her mouth. "The hotel bellboy is still out there. He's about your age, if I remember right. I imagine you know him, and he knows you."

"Hector," she admitted. No, she didn't want Hector to see her. The story would be all over town before morning.

"You could at least put me down," she said after a moment.

Shane shrugged, his movement rubbing her breast against his chest. Then he dropped her as though she had suddenly caught fire in his arms. The bedsprings creaked loudly even with her slight weight, and she knew without doubt they had been heard in the other room.

"Shane!" she gasped.

Eyes adjusting to the dimness, she saw him rub his chest, right where she had rubbed against him.

"Sorry," he muttered. "Just be quiet. Your friend Hector will be gone in a second."

"He's not my friend," Ellie whispered, but Shane didn't reply. He continued to stand there, and she sensed his gaze on her even though she couldn't see his gold-dust eyes. The gaze arced between them, the gold-dust path calling to mind Fatima's magic.

Ellie stifled a gasp when she realized she really did see the path of Shane's gaze. And could see Fatima hovering in the air behind Shane, the huge Persian in her arms. Fatima lifted a hand and wiggled her fingers.

Five

"What?" Shane glanced over his shoulder.

Ellie stilled, waiting for his reaction to the sight of Fatima floating in the air, dressed like one of Rosie's girls. Fatima only winked at Ellie, and the cat smiled serenely in her arms.

Instead of reacting, Shane reached beneath Fatima's folded legs and slid the curtain open a bit for more light, as nonchalantly as though the two of them were alone in the room. Then he pulled out a small drawer beneath the wall sconce and reached in for a match. While Ellie stared in amazement at his blatant disregard of the outlandish image in the air, he scratched the match head and lit the sconce. The smell of sulfur mixed with a slight hint of gas from the sconce before it flared brightly.

The sconce emitted a small stream of dark smoke, and Fatima floated a safer distance away while Shane adjusted the mantle in the center of it. Replacing the glass globe, Shane turned back to Ellie.

"There. Do you feel better now that there's a light in here?" he asked.

With an effort, she jerked her gaze away from Fatima, but Shane stared in the same direction and frowned. Clearly, though, he didn't see anything in the room to surprise him.

Shoot diddly! Could he be in cahoots with that woman and her cat?

Ellie glowered at Fatima, who mouthed the words, "He can't see me, Ellie," to her. Ellie heard in her mind every word the fairy woman spoke, but Shane obviously didn't.

"I was beginning to gather that much," Ellie said aloud without thinking.

"What?" Shane asked in a puzzled voice. "Are you talking to me?"

Ellie slid off the bed, straightened her skirts and tried to keep her eyes away from Fatima. "You and I are the only ones here, aren't we?"

"I thought we were. But for a second—never mind. I'll go check on the washroom. Please feel free to use my brush and comb there on the dresser, if you wish. I'll send Withers down to the hotel lobby, where I saw a small shop selling necessities when I checked in. Is there anything you need besides hairpins?"

"No, that's all." She opened the drawstring on her reticule, which luckily had remained on her arm throughout the evening's activities, and dug out a nickel. "This should buy a paper of pins."

He started to refuse it, then shrugged his large shoulders and accepted. With a nod of leave-taking, he went out the door, closing it softly behind him.

He moved awfully silently and smoothly for such a large man, Ellie mused. Even the deep carpet beneath her feet couldn't account for the grace and silence of his stride, which she'd noticed as they walked back to the buggy a while ago.

She glared around the room, surprised, then quickly irritated at not seeing Fatima and the cat. Gosh darn it! Now what were they up to?

Resignedly, Ellie crossed to the dresser and picked up Shane's brush. Guiltily, for she had another reason for doing so than to arrange her own scattered tresses, she glanced at the door. But the voices she heard indicated both Hector and Withers were leaving the suite.

Ellie plucked several tawny strands from the brush. She was right, she thought, running the strands through her fingers. His hair was as silky as it looked. Tawny blond in contrast to her white blond, but with lighter sun streaks indicating that even though he lived in the city, he spent time outdoors. His hair was full and thick, while hers was fine and flyaway, even with its considerable length.

She loved turning her hair loose when she had some privacy, galloping across the range and letting it stream behind her. Shane's hair would also blow nicely in the wind caused by a stallion at full gallop, since it curled down at least an inch below his collar.

"Is there anything you need that you can't find?"

Ellie started until she realized Shane's voice came through the closed door.

"I'm fine," she called, eyes searching the room and still not finding Fatima. "I'll be right out."

For some reason she stuck the hair strands in her skirt pocket, then snorted her distaste at her action, took them out and tossed them into a tin waste receptacle beside the bed. For heaven's sake, she had just met the man only a few hours ago. She hadn't paid that much attention to Darlene's rambling about the friend Rockford expected, so she had no idea how long Shane planned to stay. But he would leave when he felt like it—return to his world of culture and refinement, while she tried to find some way to hold onto the ranch and keep a home for Darlene and Elvina.

While she tried to carve out some niche of belonging in a world where orphans had to earn their love, not be born into it.

She hurriedly tried to brush the tangles from her hair.

Within a half hour, Ellie was ready for Shane to escort her back to the Leaning G, her hair safely secured on the back of her head. The dirt soiling her dress skirt had already set into stains, but she had brushed off the dried mud. The dress would have to be washed and the stains scrubbed before she wore it again.

The journey was for the most part silent, except when a jackrabbit exploded wildly out of the roadside brush and startled the horse pulling the buggy. Shane's sure hands on the reins steadied the horse before it could more than think of bolting.

He handled the horse as easily as the cowboys on the range handled theirs, Ellie mused, as though it were second nature. Most city men didn't manage a horse nearly as confidently.

The land lying in their path—west of Fort Worth—was cattle country, rolling and undulating, fertile and with plenty of water to grow nutritious grass for the herds. Most of the time, anyway. Last summer had been dry with drought, which had made the old-timers shake their heads and call it one of the naturally occurring seven-year dry spells. More than one ranch lost cattle, and the Leaning G had been hard hit. Given the sparsity of beef now, the market would be strong this year, if Ellie encountered no more disasters when culling her remaining herd for market.

Farther west the land was drier prairie, yielding to canyons and then a range of mountains. To the south mesquite and rock littered the hilly country. There were cattle ranches south and farther west of them, but it took far more land to fatten the herds than here.

The Leaning G had once been one of the most prosperous ranches in the area, but Ellie had discovered what she considered unwise use of the ranch's funds when she had examined the books after George Parker's death in the cattle stampede that spring five years earlier. Harsh spring storms and tornadoes spawned by the violent weather were prominent problems in their area of Texas, but George had been a cattleman to the bone. He rode the range with his men during the dangerous times of year for the herds, as well as the safe periods. And he died a cattleman's death, endeavoring to protect his herd.

From the state of the books, he had perhaps been more cattleman than businessman. Or perhaps been a little too much in love with Elvina to deny her anything, even at the detriment of the ranch's profits. No doubt George would have recovered from the most recent financial drainage, as he had from other profit valleys the books indicated, had he not died.

Ellie sighed, and Shane glanced down at her. "Something sad you're thinking of?" he asked.

"My stepfather," Ellie admitted. "I spent lots of nights out on the range with him and the ranch hands. Mostly during roundup. Nights like this remind me of those times—clear and pure and so very Texas-like."

"You worked along with the ranch hands?" he asked in astonishment.

"I not only did that then, I'm the one who runs the ranch now," Ellie told him in a firm, no-nonsense voice. "Someone has to, and you've already met Darlene. Can you see her out on the range, helping chase cattle out of the brush or branding them? Making bulls into steers?"

Shane shook his head. "Admittedly, I can't quite see you doing that either, but I'll take your word for it. What about your mother?"

"Stepmother," she corrected him. "Elvina is . . . well, she's Elvina. She's a typical Southern belle who always depended on her husband to take care of things and spoil her. Which George did. I can't blame her for the way she is, because it's the way she was raised."

"No brothers or uncles or any other males to help you?"

Ellie bristled. She worked hard, and she resented his attitude. "I'm doing fine. George had a brother, but he died in his teens. And Elvina was an only child."

The ranch loomed ahead, and as always, Ellie felt a warm feeling when she saw it. It was home; the only home she had. The only home she had ever had, as far as she knew.

It wasn't Elvina's fault that she couldn't bring herself to treat Ellie the same way she treated Darlene, her own blood daughter. Shoot, sometimes Elvina even got whiny with Darlene.

"What?" Ellie asked, realizing Shane had said something as the buggy went through the iron gate arching overhead.

"I said, I guess you were adopted then, since you call Elvina your stepmother."

"Yes." She hesitated, but then, it wasn't really a secret. And for some reason, it didn't bother her that much to talk about it with Shane. "I was on one of the orphan trains. George and Elvina had just found out they wouldn't ever have any other children. Darlene was three, and they wanted more, but Elvina contracted a fever the doctor told her would leave her unable to conceive again. They wanted a companion for Darlene, and there I was. On one of the trains that stopped in Fort Worth."

She sighed. "I don't remember it. Just what George told me once. He said I was the only girl left, and a girl is what they wanted. He thought maybe I'd been overlooked at all the other stops because I was so little. In fact, he thought I was only a year old at first, instead of two, like one of the chaperons told him."

Shane remained silent and pulled the horse up to a hitching post. Getting down, he tied the horse and then helped Ellie from the buggy.

"Don't worry about the horse," she told him. "I'll take it out to the barn and unhitch it."

He conceded with a shrug, and she noticed a look of deep concentration on his face. She started to thank him for the ride home, but he interrupted her.

"Where did the train you were on come from?"

Puzzled at his continuing interest in her story, Ellie nevertheless saw no reason not to answer him. "George said it had started out in New York City, but it made a couple other stops and picked up children. I'm not sure where I got on the train, because along the way robbers hit it. They stole a payroll from the mail car, and during the resulting fray, the car caught fire. Everything in it, including the papers on all the children, was destroyed."

Shane nodded as though deep in thought. When she started toward the door, he fell in beside her. From the way he took his courtesies so seriously, it would be useless to protest that she could very well walk up onto the porch and in the door by herself. Even at the door, he reached around her and opened it before he stepped back.

The wall sconce Elvina had left burning in the entrance foyer threw some light their way, but not enough for Ellie to see Shane's face clearly. Surely what she sensed was in error. He couldn't be studying her face as though he had a picture somewhere to compare it to.

Or—lordy, especially not that! As if he were debating whether or not he might chance a kiss.

She even thought for a moment that he bent his head, but undoubtedly it was a trick of the shadows. She took a careful step back anyway, although some strange pull followed her. With a jerk, Shane touched his fingertips to his hat brim, then strolled away without saying anything else.

He unhitched his horse from the back of the buggy and mounted before he seemed to realize he was being unmannerly—before he appeared to notice that Ellie hadn't gone on inside the house. Halting his horse, he removed his hat completely.

"Good evening, Ellie," he called. "Hopefully our next evening together will go more smoothly."

"Thank you for escorting me home," Ellie replied in a bewildered voice.

"It was my pleasure."

Turning his horse, he rode toward the ranch gate, keeping at a gentle walk instead of galloping off, as though perhaps continuing his serious thoughts. Ellie stared after him, trying to figure out his change of attitude. He couldn't be upset over her adoption, since he showed an obvious interest in that. And he mentioned yet again wanting to see her in the future.

So why was he so deep in concentration that he forgot those manners of his for even a few seconds?

At the gate, Shane halted his horse and turned in the saddle to look back. Finding her still standing there, he touched his hat brim once more before urging his horse into a lope and heading through the quiet Texas night back to town.

"Who was that?"

Ellie turned to see Elvina standing in the doorway. Small and diminutive, she was more like her stepdaughter in stature than Darlene, who had inherited George Parker's larger frame. Dressed for bed in her night rail and with her hair braided, she looked closer to the age of a young girl than a fifty-year-old woman. She took extreme care to keep her youthful looks, too. Being up this late was exceptionally unusual for her.

"It was Rockford's friend, the one from New York City," Ellie said. "I—uh—got a headache and didn't feel like attending the circus, so he brought me on home. Rockford will bring Darlene home later."

"You never get headaches, Ellie Parker."

"Well, I did tonight," Ellie lied. A lie was better than trying to explain everything that had happened. Especially going to a man's hotel suite to repair the damages to her attire. If Elvina found out about that, Ellie would hear about it for weeks.

"Are you up late for a certain reason, Elvina?" she asked to change the subject. Long ago, in her early formative years, Elvina had taught her to call her by name rather than "Mother." Or "Mama," as Ellie had slipped and tried to call her once or twice.

"I couldn't sleep. Ellie, I need to know if you're hiding something from me regarding the ranch's finances. I've been asking you for months now about the new carpet, and you keep putting me off."

Ellie frowned at her. Elvina had never shown an interest in the finances before, even when Ellie had to deny her a purchase. Something was going on.

"It's tight right now, Elvina," she said honestly. "Maybe after fall roundup we can—"

"Maybe?" Elvina cut in. "You're not sure that we'll even show a nice profit after roundup?"

"What's going on, Elvina?"

Her stepmother stared at her silently, as though considering what to say next. Then she turned and went back inside the house. "I think I can sleep now. I'm going on to bed."

"Elvina!" Ellie glanced at the buggy horse and decided it could wait a while to be put in the barn. Lifting her soiled skirts, she followed Elvina.

Inside she stared around in surprise. Surely Elvina hadn't been wandering around the ranch house in the dark, but there were no lights on anywhere other than the foyer sconce. She couldn't see which way Elvina had gone in the darkness, then caught sight of her stepmother on the stairwell, hurrying upward.

"Elvina!" she called again.

By the time Ellie was halfway up the stairwell, she heard Elvina's bedroom door close with a definitive thud. Sighing in resignation, she stopped and turned back, knowing better than to disturb Elvina in her rooms, as did Darlene. Even George Parker hadn't entered the mistress of the house's suite of rooms next to the master's without a proper invitation.

Deciding the buggy horse could wait another few minutes since Shane had driven the horse easily instead of asking it to exert itself on their drive home, Ellie headed for the study. She knew this house as well as Elvina did, and like her, had no need of lights.

The downstairs of the grand house George had built for his bride all those years ago contained six rooms, including the kitchen and two parlors, which could be opened into one huge room for entertaining. Upstairs each person had a private bedroom, although she and Darlene shared a washroom and dressing room. There was a guest room, and the master suite remained unused after George's death. Elvina was adamant about keeping the entire house clean, so all the rooms were dusted weekly, but the servants' rooms on the third floor were opened and cleaned only when needed.

After the kitchen, Ellie's favorite room was her stepfather's study, which she entered now, heading for one of the wall sconces. The Leaning G still employed kerosene lamps, although some of the houses in town had tied into the gas lines used for streetlights. Every once in a while, too, Ellie heard rumors that someone was looking into electricity for their area, but it remained a wishful thought for now.

Ellie reached for the lamp sitting on the huge walnut desk, jerking her hand back when she encountered the still-warm globe. The lamp had obviously been lit recently. Other than as a place her bills were paid out of, Ellie had never known Elvina to be interested in what went on in the study even when George was still alive. But since no one else was at home, Elvina had to have been in here.

Ellie carefully checked the globe again, finding it safe enough to handle. She removed it, lit the mantle and replaced the glass. Soothing light chased away the nearby shadows, leaving the corners of the room dim and serene. Ellie didn't bother with any other lights, since she preferred the more serene atmosphere the lone light provided.

She moved around the desk, studying the journals and papers on the surface as she went. By all means, Elvina had every right to examine the ranch's books and ask questions about the way things were running. After all, she owned the Leaning G now. What bothered Ellie was the secretiveness Elvina displayed. Ellie had worked on the journals the previous night and hadn't bothered to put them away. But she did remember closing them and shoving them back on the desk, in order to prop her elbows on the walnut surface and rub her eyes. The most recent journal was closed, but aligned with the edge of the desk, as though someone with short arms like Ellie's—or Elvina's—had been studying it.

Elvina wouldn't have seen anything she shouldn't have, and probably some stuff she should be interested in, Ellie mused. George Parker had taken out a hefty loan against the ranch a few months before he was killed, but even during the drought last summer, Ellie had managed to make the mortgage payment.

The payment had to be made, but what perturbed Ellie was what George might have used some of the money for. Not all of it had gone back into ranch expenses. There had been the breeding bull and several head of new cows. Ellie assumed, knowing what she did about the ranch, that the spring calf drop had been light on heifers and strong on bulls, which meant a dearth of breeding stock in the near future. And she verified that by checking the spring tally done that year when they rounded up the newborns, branded them and marked their ears.

Still, a thousand dollars had gone into bills Elvina ran up, and Ellie was fairly certain what George had done with another missing thousand dollars. She had prodded Shorty for information once after she took over the books, reminding her foreman of the high-stakes poker game everyone in Fort Worth talked about a month or so before George's death. Her stepfather's one indulgence had been his gambling, but she never would have thought him into the bigger games. At least, not with money he needed to keep the ranch solvent.

Shrugging, Ellie extinguished the lamp. She couldn't do anything about the misused money at this late date, but she decided to at least try to find a time the next day to discuss whatever concerns Elvina had with her. Ellie didn't believe in secretiveness or underhandedness. Nothing made her dislike a person more than finding out the person had blatantly lied to her or deceived her. She dismissed the thought of her recent lie to Elvina about her headache as a necessary courtesy for her stepmother's state of mind.

She went back down the hallway and out onto the front porch just in time to see Shorty unhitching the buggy horse.

"I was going to take care of him," she told him.

"I know you would've," Shorty said. "But I was up anyways. Thought I heard that coyote out by the corral, but if he was around, he took off a'fore I got there."

"Well, thanks. Everything else all right?"

"Right as rain. You have yourself a good time at that there circus? I stayed home so the rest of 'em could go, and we was glad to see you goin' off to enjoy yourself, Miss Ellie. You work too hard."

Ellie smiled at him through the darkness. What would he do if she told him? She decided she *would* tell him, just to see his stricken face.

"I guess if you call being attacked by a lion and nearly drowned by an elephant fun, I had a good time," she said.

Moonlight glowed bright enough for Ellie to see Shorty's jaw drop, and she hid her smile of delight at having jolted him to the point of shock behind her hand. With one deft twist of his wrist, Shorty retied the buggy horse and approached the porch.

"You don't say?" Shorty said. "Reckon I'd like to hear about that."

Ellie laughed and sat down on the steps while Shorty leaned against the hitching rail. Maybe the poor buggy horse would get into its stall sometime tonight.

A couple of times while she related the evening's activities to Shorty, Ellie found herself looking around her, wondering just where on earth that fairy woman had gone. But she pushed the thought firmly aside. Circuses were famous for illusions, and probably the woman was a gypsy who knew how to work the circusgoers' minds and trick them into believing they saw things impossible to be real.

She left out that part of her story to Shorty.

She tried, too, not to ponder how Fatima had worked the illusion in Shane's hotel suite.

Six

Ellie never heard Darlene come in, but when she glanced into her sister's room the next morning before dawn, Darlene lay sprawled on her back, a pillow clutched tightly in her grasp. Imagining Darlene thought the pillow Rockford, Ellie didn't disturb her. Darlene might be rather spoiled, but she did her share as long as it was things she considered suited to her femininity. She always rose later than Ellie, however, although never as late as Elvina, who considered anything before ten A.M. an ungodly hour.

Dressed in range attire—a split riding skirt and loose cotton blouse—Ellie joined the ranch hands for breakfast. She never saw any reason to make herself a solitary breakfast in the ranch house kitchen when the bunkhouse cook fixed heaps of food for the men. Cookie was a great cook, too, and for the most part, Ellie preferred his plain cooking to the fancier dishes Elvina planned for their meals with Birdie, the lone servant they could afford. Their housekeeper/cook took advantage of the late-rising mistress, arriving sometime before ten and leaving for her own home right after the evening meal.

After ham, eggs, potatoes, and hotcakes, which Ellie would work off long before noon—and after retelling her tale of the lion and elephant—she joined her men in tacking up their chosen mounts for the day. As always, she lassoed

Cinder herself and tied the gelding to the corral post next to where her saddle hung.

After they were all mounted, the men waited for Ellie's orders.

"I noticed last week that the pasture where we have the remuda horses is nearly overgrazed," she told Shorty. "We need to move them."

"You and me can handle that," Shorty agreed. "Dan and Cal can check the north fence. We ain't rode up that way all month."

Ellie nodded and they rode out of the ranch yard, splitting once. outside the gate. This time of year she only needed a crew of four: Shorty, Cookie, Cal, and his brother Danny. During spring and fall roundups, she hired extra hands.

Her small crew got along well, and she considered herself lucky. She hated firing men, but any troublemaker had to be sent packing, as she had done twice since George died.

Years before, the free range had become only a memory as every rancher fenced and cross-fenced his land with barbed wire. But new chores sprang up due to that, which entailed riding fence, checking pastures to make sure they weren't overgrazed, and moving cattle or horses if they were.

By late afternoon, the horses grazed in their new pasture, and Ellie was hot, covered with dust and dirt, and ready to call it a day. She and Shorty headed home, and when they rode over a small rise that hid the ranch and barn from sight, Ellie groaned under her breath.

Rockford's palomino stood in the shade of a cottonwood tree beside the house, a strange horse beside it. Darlene held court in the swing on the porch, while two men served attendance on her, their rears perched on the porch railing. It took Ellie only one glance to ascertain who the man with Rockford was.

Shane probably heard the horses' hooves, but Darlene

jumped from the swing and waved at Ellie, making sure the men would notice her.

"Yoo hoo!" Darlene called.

Ellie wished like diddly her sister would find some other form of getting her attention. Or better yet, ignore her until she could change clothes.

"Ellie, hurry on to the house! Rockford and Mr. Morgan have come to call, and they'll stay for dinner."

Ellie waved an acknowledgment, but continued on to the barn. But while Rockford stayed on the porch with Darlene, Shane stood and headed down the steps. Surely he wouldn't come out into the heat when he could wait on the much cooler porch.

But he did. He strode toward her, and she avoided Shorty's questioning gaze and kicked Cinder into a lope on around the house and toward the barn. The gelding whinnied in surprise, since he had already put in a hard day's work and expected to be allowed his rest; but once inside, Cinder headed for his own stall, where Ellie kept her curry-comb and hoof picks.

Even though she had Cinder unsaddled and a gunny sack in hand to rub him down, Ellie knew the minute Shane entered the barn. His presence infiltrated the shadowy gloom and familiar smells like a breeze on a hot summer day. Gritting her teeth, she refused to reach up and tidy her hair. If the man had the audacity to visit a working ranch at the end of a workday, he would just have to put up with her appearance the way it was.

And her smell, too, she realized with a tentative sniff. She was still sticky and hot from the day's work. Even the ride back in hadn't stirred up enough breeze to dry her completely.

"Need any help?" Shane asked, coming up beside her.

"Cinder prefers I take care of him," she said honestly, taking her gunny sack to the other side of the horse without looking at him. "Why don't you wait up at the house? There's no sense in you having to suffer in this heat."

"It isn't even the end of June yet. How bad is the heat in August here?"

"Bad. But you know what they say."

"No. What?"

"It's not the heat, it's the humidity. They say that down around Houston, closer to the Gulf, you could almost wash your clothes outside without a tub of water in the summer."

Shane chuckled, and she realized she was coming to know that chuckle. Expect it, even. Like it, even.

"*They* are obviously right," he said.

Smiling, she finished wiping the sweat off Cinder and picked up her currycomb. Tried to, anyway. She heard the rasp of it on the other side and realized Shane had found it on the shelf and was already currying the gelding.

So much for what she had said about Cinder preferring her to care for him. Had the horse been a cat, it would have been purring in contentment at the sure strokes to its hide. Shoot, the gelding's eyes drooped to half mast in enjoyment, his skin rippling in pleasure at Shane's strong strokes.

Grabbing her hoof pick instead, Ellie bent to examine Cinder's hooves. She hadn't noticed any problems with his gait on the way in, but experience had taught her that a stone hidden in a loose shoe could cause later problems.

The rear hoof was fine. She backed up and picked up Cinder's front hoof. Hearing a grunt, she glanced over her shoulder.

Shane stood there, staring at her, the currycomb ready to fall out of his grasp. A violent blush heated Ellie's cheeks at the picture she made—rear sticking inelegantly in the air while she held Cinder's hoof in her hand.

She dropped the hoof with a thud, and Cinder let her know he didn't care for the rough treatment. He turned and butted her on the rear. She stumbled and caught herself against Cinder's rump.

"Hey, horse, quit that," Shane ordered. An instant later, he peeled Ellie away from the horse and turned her in his grasp. "You all right?"

"I've been butted by horses before," she insisted, struggling against his hold.

Ellie's blush heightened as she attempted to move away from him. Her embarrassment put a sharp bite in her tone. "Not only does Cinder prefer me taking care of him, I prefer it myself. Do you mind waiting up at the house?"

"Hey." Shane spread his arms in an innocent gesture. "I was only trying to help."

Grabbing the currycomb from his hand, Ellie put her back to him. She curried the other side of Cinder with vigorous strokes, and when she didn't hear Shane move off immediately, she sent a quick glare over her shoulder. He guiltily jerked his gaze upward from studying her bottom again.

"I'll see you up at the house," she growled.

Shrugging, he turned and stuck his hands in his trouser pockets, then sauntered away. He didn't once look back, which she knew because she watched him all the way out of the barn. Disgusted when disappointment stabbed her after his broad back disappeared, she bent back to her task.

A moment later, as she was getting ready to turn Cinder into the corral and give him a measure of oats, Ellie heard a thunder of hooves race into the ranch yard. No one galloped a horse after a hard day's work in this heat without a good reason—and usually the reason meant trouble. Leaving Cinder tied to his stall door, Ellie ran from the barn.

Cal drew his cow pony up in front of the barn in a shower of dust and leaped from the saddle. Having heard the commotion from inside the bunkhouse, Shorty was right behind him.

"Danny's out at the north water hole," Cal said without preamble. "Either the stream broke through one of the underground alkaline shelves or someone poisoned the water."

"How many?" Ellie asked.

"Two dead," he replied succinctly, catching her meaning without further explanation. "Danny's keepin' the rest of them away, but we'll need to fence off that hole or more will die."

"Saddle a couple fresh horses while I hitch the wagon up," she ordered. "There's posts and wire in the supply shed. Shorty, get it open and be ready to load soon as I pull the wagon over there."

"Can I help?" Shane stood at Ellie's side, having turned back to the barn to see what the trouble was.

"We'll probably be out there until after midnight," she warned. "It's a fairly large water hole. And you're not really dressed for range work."

"I don't have anything better to do. And I don't mind if these clothes get dirty. They'll wash."

"Then we would definitely appreciate your help," Ellie said honestly. She wasn't foolish enough to turn down an extra pair of hands in an emergency—strong hands, at that.

She headed for the other pasture on the far side of the barn, where her two draft horses lazed away days when she didn't need them to pull the wagon for ranch chores. She whistled, and the well-trained animals responded with plodding but certain steps. Quickly she caught them and led them into the barn, where she harnessed them and hitched them to the wagon. By the time she drove the wagon over to the storage shed, Shane had piled a good stack of fence posts outside.

Shorty watched Shane in awe as he picked up six fence posts and heaved them into the wagon bed, while Shorty had trouble managing his three. Shane started to grab a roll of wire, but Ellie stopped him with a cry.

"Here." She dug into the wooden box on the wagon where she kept tools and gloves. Pulling out the largest pair of gloves she could find, she tossed them to him. "That wire is sharp. That's why they call it barbed wire."

"Thanks."

As soon as the wagon was loaded, Shane climbed onto the seat beside her. Ellie clucked to the horses, heading them out in a trot. It was quite a drive to the water hole, but they would make the trip easier if they drove slowly than if they hurried in this heat. On fresh mounts, Cal and Shorty galloped ahead, leaving her and Shane to follow.

As they passed the bunkhouse, Cookie came out and Ellie pulled the wagon up. He loaded several canteens into the wagon, then went back in and brought out a wooden box covered by a white cloth.

"I'll have a regular meal ready when y'all get back in," he said.

Ellie nodded and sent the horses on their way again.

"You seem to have a well-trained crew," Shane mused after a moment.

"You mean, for being bossed by a woman?"

"No, I didn't mean that at all," Shane said in an exasperated voice. "It's just that Rockford said you had several thousand acres here, yet you run the place very efficiently with a small crew. I have to admire that in a male *or* female foreman."

"You don't have any experience at knowing how a ranch is run."

"No, but I do know about running a business efficiently. And at the bottom line, that's all a ranch is—a business where you need to make a profit over and above your expenses."

Grudgingly Ellie admitted he was right. Still, she had a long-standing prickliness and ready defensiveness whenever anyone discussed the subject of her being a female in charge of a cattle ranch. Not that other women hadn't successfully run ranches in the West. Shoot fire, she knew of at least two other ranches in their part of the state with women who were widows running them.

For some reason, though, she wanted Shane Morgan's respect a tad more than she'd ever wanted any other man's. Why, she had no idea. He was only an eastern tenderfoot, who was more at home with smokestacks than buffalo grass.

Wasn't he?

• • •

It was well after midnight by the time the weary group re-entered the ranch yard. Cookie kept his word, and a hot meal waited for them, although Ellie was far too tired to eat much after they cared for the horses and went to the bunkhouse. Talk swirled desultorily, mostly consisting of their certainty that the poisoned water hole was a natural disaster rather than a manmade one.

Ellie had made sure she sat close by the doorway, and after a few bites, she stood.

"Why doesn't everyone take an extra hour in the morning? I, for one, am going to. But right now, I really need to clean up and get to bed."

Shane stirred beside her, and Cookie said, "I fergot to give you the message from your sister, Miz Ellie. She said that there other'n, that Rockford, went on back inta town. But he put that 'un's—" He nodded at Shane. "—horse in a stall first."

Understanding Cookie's cryptic words—that Rockford had put up Shane's horse before he went back into town—she realized it would be an insult to Shane to force him to make that long ride back tonight. He had worked as hard as the rest of them—perhaps even harder.

"There's a guest room always prepared at the house," she told him, knowing her men would expect Shane to stay up there and not with them. "And a bathing room off the kitchen you can use before you retire."

When she moved out the door, he stood and came after her.

"You can finish eating," she told him when he caught up to her slow, tired stride. "I'll light a lantern in the room you can use and leave the door open."

"I ate ten times as much as you did while you toyed with your food," he said with that nice chuckle that took the sting out of his words. "I'm more than ready to clean up and catch a few hours' sleep, and I definitely appreciate the offer of a bed for the night."

"By the way, Shane," Shorty called after them. "Thanks for all your help."

"No problem," he called back.

"I'm the one who should be thanking you," Ellie said as they walked. "We'd still be out there if you hadn't helped."

He only nodded and strode on beside her, matching his stride to hers. The night had cooled the air to a tolerable degree, although later in the summer the nights would swelter in tune with the days. For now, the sky overhead—clear, pure, and cloud-free—reached endlessly into the far corners of the universe, yet the stars and planets filled the vastness. A bright moon sent Shane's shadow skittering ahead of them as though they chased it to the porch. It climbed the steps silently before they did.

Shane held the door for her, but remained on the porch after she entered the house.

"I think I'll stay out here and have a smoke before I go in."

"You smoke?" she asked. "I hadn't noticed."

"Not often, but once in a while I enjoy one. Please don't feel you have to keep me company. I was in the kitchen earlier and know where the bathing room is. And I can find the guest room and put myself to bed."

"All right." Ellie stifled a yawn. "I'll see you in the morning."

She hurried out of sight, and Shane closed the door. He stared into the dimness on the other side of the screen until he realized what he was doing and that his thoughts were too unclear to make any sense. Strolling over to the porch railing, he propped a hip on it and leaned back against a post, taking his makings from a shirt pocket.

He didn't smoke that often and, in fact, had thought about quitting. Supposedly tobacco was only an enjoyable vice that men kept away from the ladies due to their disgust at the vile smell. But Shane had noticed some of the heavier

smokers at the club hacking and coughing unpleasantly as
they aged.

He deftly rolled the fine-cut tobacco into a paper and
licked it closed. Few people he knew rolled their own
smokes, most of them having succumbed to the ease of pre-
rolled cigarettes. They just didn't taste the same, though.

He struck a match on the porch railing, touched it to the
cigarette, and inhaled. The smoke found its place in his
lungs, and he enjoyed the easing of tension and sense of
looseness it fostered. Dropping the match into a nearby
flowerpot, he studied the ranch and the people he hadn't
even known would enter his world a few days ago.

Despite the energy-draining heat, he had enjoyed the
work of fencing off the water hole this evening. The men
treated him as one of them instead of a city-slicker outsider.
Had Rockford joined them, it might have been different,
but Shane didn't suppose the other man even gave a
thought to helping out. Probably had been surprised when
Shane rode out with the crew.

Granted, the man was besotted with Darlene Parker, but
you would think Rockford would grab a chance like helping in an emergency to win some points with her. After all,
the ranch belonged to Darlene and her mother, from what
Shane had found out in the Pinkerton report.

Is that what he had done with Ellie? Tried to win points
with her? Tried to impress her, win her admiration by helping her with her all-important ranch? Clearly, the Leaning
G meant a lot to her, given how hard she worked.

Shane dragged on his cigarette, denying the contemplation as soon as it crossed his mind. He hadn't even known
Ellie two days ago, and he had absolutely no reason to try
to impress her. He only needed to gain her confidence long
enough to see if she remembered any further clues to either
prove or disprove her identity.

Given what he had already found out—that the records
on the train had been destroyed—he doubted he would be
able to find firm evidence one way or the other. With Ellie

admitting she was only two when she arrived, he doubted very much she would recall anything of her former life. He assumed, though Ellie hadn't said so, that the chaperons on the train had told George what Ellie's name was along with her age. But George had given his adoptive daughter his own last name. Maybe changed her first name, also. Indeed he had, if her identity panned out.

But the Pinkerton report indicated that the two elderly women accompanying the orphans were both dead now, after eighteen years. So there was no way to question anyone directly associated with the orphan transport.

There was that one strong coincidence, though. Rose Spencer's daughter had been two years old when she disappeared.

Shane had no idea what he would do if he couldn't prove Ellie's identity one way or the other. He wouldn't even think of allowing his mother to become involved with Ellie without proof she was truly Rose's daughter. It would break Mariana Morgan's heart if she fell in love with Ellie and then found out later that Ellie had accepted the place in life as an heiress under false pretenses.

He finished his smoke and ground the butt out in the flowerpot. Ellie Parker sure didn't fit the picture of a missing heiress. Physically, maybe. She had that delicate, fine-boned stature that came from a background of blue blood, and she would blend right in with the crowd of the season's debutantes.

No, she would probably outshine the lot of them, he admitted. Not strictly due to her physical beauty, either. She had an assurance and capability most women lacked—a maturity he admired. It took a special person to be able to supervise a crew of men and have them not only accept her rules but work without resentment under them.

He actually enjoyed her company, too, he admitted.

"Keep your mind on why you're here, Morgan," he reminded himself.

He needed to finish his business and get out of here. He

couldn't imagine how these people tolerated this hot, barren state. This western culture. This *Texas*. Even in town, he felt like he was in a foreign country where he had trouble understanding the language. The sooner he got back to New York, the better.

He had accompanied Rockford out here today not only to get to know Ellie better, but in the hopes of meeting the elusive stepmother.

He actually admitted that lie aloud. ''Sure you did, Morgan. You came out here because you wanted to see pretty little Ellie again.''

He did need to feel out the stepmother, though, but the woman hadn't made an appearance. When he managed to bring her name up casually in the conversation, Darlene said her mother didn't receive visitors in the heat of the afternoon, but she would join them for dinner—the same dinner he had missed because he went out on the range to help out that pretty little blonde.

At this point, the stepmother would be the most likely one to know any further background on Ellie. Even with the records destroyed, she might have talked to some of the chaperons of the orphans. Or found out what her husband had been told. Might be able to at least confirm the point of Ellie's entry onto the train.

But how could he question the stepmother without raising suspicion? The only idea he had come up with so far had been discarded as soon as he met Ellie Parker and found himself admiring her drive and independence.

He couldn't bring himself to evidence a false interest in Ellie—to play on the fact that he wanted to know more about her before he took the final step of asking her to be his wife, which was the only reason Elvina Parker probably would answer his inquiries.

He snorted repugnance at himself when the thought crossed his mind that courting Ellie wouldn't be an unpleasant chore. He would have to walk a fine line in order to pursue his investigation without giving Ellie the wrong idea—that he was indeed trying to build a relationship with her.

He turned and went on into the house. For an instant, he thought he saw someone over beside the window curtains, but on closer examination, it was just the breeze blowing one of the curtain sheers. He walked on to the kitchen, wishing he were back at the hotel and could take a full, soaking bath, given his tired muscles.

In the bathing room, he found his wish fulfilled. A marble tub stood there, with spigots for both hot and cold bathing water. Someone had laid out a man's nightshirt, which he supposed had belonged to George Parker. It was probably too small, but he wasn't picky right then.

Seven

As soon as Shane disappeared into the kitchen, Elvina emerged from behind the curtain at the window and climbed the stairwell. From her invisible stance in a corner of the room, Fatima watched her. She had no idea why Ellie's stepmother skulked around in the dark, but then, it didn't matter much. At least, not to Fatima and her goals. As long as Elvina didn't interfere with the blossoming romance between Ellie and Shane, Fatima wouldn't let Elvina's prowling bother her.

''I think things are going swimmingly, don't you, Pandora?'' she asked her cat. Not hearing an answering meow, she glanced around until she saw Pandora asleep on the love seat over by the fireplace. Sprawled lazily across the cushions, the cat lay on her back, paws spread to the four corners, her body covering fully half the seat.

Fatima smiled at her pet, then walked over to the love seat and squeezed herself into the remaining space. Stroking Pandora's fluffy belly fur, she willed the cat to wake and offer up her end of the conversation.

Some people thought it impossible to communicate with animals, but while Pandora never answered her in words, her actions and various tones of meow gave Fatima feedback. When Pandora wanted to, that is, which the cat didn't seem to feel like doing right now. One paw batted away

Fatima's stroking hand, and Pandora shifted into an even lazier sprawl and settled back into sleep.

"I like that," Fatima told the cat. "Didn't I conjure up fresh salmon and caviar for your supper? Now all you want to do is sleep."

Pandora slit open one eye, sighed a cat sigh, and slowly shifted to her feet. Ponderously she glided over into Fatima's lap and resettled herself. She purred for a few seconds while Fatima stroked her, then laid her chin on Fatima's knee and went back to sleep.

Fatima shook her head. Given Pandora's weight, she almost wished the cat had stayed on her end of the love seat. But as always the close companionship of her precious Pandora afforded her a measure of serenity. Fatima laid her head back and imagined the beautiful wedding Shane and Ellie would have.

Oh, yes, this would be a wonderfully easy assignment. After the last one, she deserved an easier time of achieving happily ever after for the two people she chose. She shuddered delicately, not even liking to remember the problems associated with that last assignment. The woman she had chosen—as wild and woolly as Annie Oakley—had had no intentions of settling down with a gentleman painter from France. But the last time Fatima checked, she saw the woman happily bossing around the crew setting up her husband's latest show of Western art in Denver, her belly heavy with child.

The only fly in the ointment currently was the lack of clues to Ellie's true identity. It was already clear that for the love relationship to fall into place, the mystery of Ellie's background needed to be unraveled. That had a direct bearing on whether the love between her and Shane would flourish.

Should Ellie fall in love with Shane as Ellie Parker, then find out she truly was the missing heiress Mariana Morgan searched for, her entire world would be tumbled upside down.

Should Ellie *not* be that heiress, nothing would change.

Unless Ellie found out Shane's true purpose here in Texas.

For once in her various adventurous episodes, Fatima wished she had a companion with whom to discuss how they might help uncover Ellie's true background. Her magic couldn't take her back in time, and she'd spent her centuries on earth dealing with human love lives, not mysteries involving detective work. Pandora was a wonderful companion, but the cat would need more than a series of various meows to carry on a discussion with her mistress about the possible repercussions solving this mystery in either vein would have on Ellie's mental attitude.

"Ellie!"

Ellie covered her head with the pillow, but Darlene grabbed it and tossed it to the floor.

"Ellie, wake up!"

How her sister could whisper so piercingly, when she normally had such a nice, smooth voice, was beyond Ellie. She pulled the comforter over her face, realizing her mistake when the heat stifled her. Goose down apparently didn't breathe at all.

Darlene swiped the comforter off, dancing away when Ellie surged upright and grabbed for it.

"What on earth do you want so early, Darlene?" Ellie halfway snarled. "I gave the men an extra hour to sleep in this morning, since we didn't get in until well after midnight. It would've been nice for me to get some extra sleep, too!"

"Oh, I'm sorry." Darlene's pretty face fell in true humility. But not for long. "I didn't know you got in so late. I tried to wait up for you last night, but I fell asleep."

Ellie scooted up against the headboard. "Well, I'm awake now. What on earth's on your mind?"

Smiling ecstatically, Darlene hugged the comforter in her arms, rocking it back and forth in excitement. "Rockford, of course. I think he's going to ask me to marry him!"

"You've been saying that for a couple of months now,"

Ellie grumped, not really wanting to deflate her sister's happiness but still groggy from lack of sleep. "But I've yet to see a ring on your finger, so I don't see why you had to wake me up."

As soon as the words left her mouth, Ellie wished she could take them back. Darlene's smile crumbled, and her lower lip pouched out resentfully. Dropping the comforter to the floor, she determinedly strode over and bounced down on the edge of the mattress.

"He *is* going to ask me to marry him, Ellie!"

Ellie hugged her sister. "I know he is, Dar. I can tell he's desperately in love with you. And I'm sorry. I'm still tired and I took my grumpy mood out on you. Forgive me?"

Darlene hugged her in return before settling herself more comfortably, her actions indicating she wanted to talk further. Repressing her sigh, since she knew any more sleep that morning was now out, Ellie leaned back to listen.

"Rockford and I talked yesterday afternoon, after Shane left with you," Darlene said. "He was so earnest, Ellie. And very, very honest with me. And sooooo romantic."

She closed her eyes in bliss, silently contemplating her adored future mate. Ellie stood it as long as she could, biting back her amusement, but she just couldn't imagine feelings for a man that would make her act that foolish. The words *simpering silliness* flashed in her head, and it was all she could do not to laugh out loud.

"You haven't explained what he actually said," she prodded finally.

"Oh!" Darlene opened her eyes wide in wonder. "He said that there was someone he wanted very much to ask something very important. But that when he asked this someone that something, he wanted to be able to offer that someone the world."

Ellie laughed delightedly. "I'm assuming this someone is you, and the something is a proposal," she said.

"I'm positive it is."

"Then why didn't he ask you?"

Darlene blinked wisely. "Because he isn't able to offer me the world right now. There are just a couple of teensie problems with his and his father's business, but it looks like those are going to work out. That's why Shane's here, remember? To look into expanding his business down here. And to consider expanding Rockford and his father's business, perhaps offering them the opportunity to expand into New York City."

Darlene bounced up and down on the mattress in unrestrained glee, unaware of her childish silliness. "Rockford said that Shane's help would expand their business enough for the profits to support *two* families! And since he's the only child, I do believe the family he and I would have would be that second one. Don't you?"

"I can't deny it must be," Ellie mused. "I gather Shane Morgan must be fairly well off himself, then."

"Rockford says Shane has enough money to buy half of Texas if he wants, and still have enough left over to consider buying Louisiana. They met when Rockford went to school back East, and Shane's family is one of the richest and most prominent ones on the entire eastern seaboard."

"We've never heard of them in Texas."

"Oh, maybe *you* haven't, Ellie. You're always buried in the ranch or your books. But those newspapers Mother gets have society pages, you know. I always read them after she's done, and I'll bet I know as much about New York City society as the New Yorkers themselves."

Ellie stretched her arms above her head, easing her sore muscles, then leaned forward and pushed a stray lock of dark hair behind Darlene's ear.

"I'm not interested in the people in New York society, although I admit I'd enjoy attending some of the entertainment they frequent. But I am very happy for you, if Shane Morgan's being here helps you and Rockford with your betrothal plans. I love you, Dar, and I want you to be happy. Rockford is a good man."

"I agree with that," Darlene said dreamily.

Drawing her legs up, Ellie scooted past her sister and started out of the bedroom to the water closet.

"El?"

Ellie turned at the door. Hardly ever did Darlene call her that childhood nickname, although she still periodically shortened her sister's name.

"Uh—Rockford said that expanding the business might mean they will have to open an office in New York City."

Darlene could have punched her in her stomach and not made a bigger effect on Ellie. Her voice froze in her throat as she waited for Darlene to continue—feared beyond doubt that she knew what her sister was going to say next.

Darlene's words confirmed Ellie's foreboding. "He said that his father would probably want him to be the one to move up there and handle that office."

"Oh, Dar," Ellie whispered.

"That . . . that's not all, Ellie."

With a frown, Ellie slowly walked back over to the bed and sat down by Darlene. What could be worse than her beloved sister—the person in the world who meant more to Ellie than anyone else—moving halfway across the country?

Darlene's hands twisted in her lap. "I'm so very afraid Mother might want to come with us. You know how she dislikes living on the ranch. And I really don't want to start my married life with my mother living with me."

"What—" Ellie cleared her throat. "What would she do with the ranch?"

"Probably sell it, Ellie. While you've been out on the range lately, she's been going over the books. She never ordered me not to tell you about it, so you have a right to know."

Sell the ranch? Her beloved Leaning G? Cold dread crawled into Ellie's stomach. What would happen to her if they sold the ranch out from under her?

Reaching out, Darlene took Ellie's hand, her words coming as though from a distance.

"You'll always have a home with me, El. It would be different having you rather than Mother live with me. And . . ." Her sister gulped. "And if it meant you having a place to stay, also, I'd put up with Mother."

Rigidly Ellie took a grip on her emotions. Despite Darlene's being a year older, Ellie had always assumed the position reserved for the older sister in their relationship. She had matured much faster than Darlene, given that Darlene was pampered more as the blood daughter.

"Please don't worry, Dar," Ellie assured her as she rose to her feet again. "You know I can always find employment in Fort Worth. Why, Mr. Jenkins at the dry goods store has offered me work as his bookkeeper for years now."

"Ellie, you'd shrivel up and die in an old office all day long. I won't see that happen to you."

"I'll be fine, Dar. You just concentrate on your plans with Rockford."

Ellie managed to dress and slip out of the house without encountering anyone. Dawn was just breaking as she crossed the ranch yard to the barn. Normally this hour would be filled with noise—men at the corral choosing their mounts for the day; whistles piercing the air, along with jokes and teasing as lassoes swirled and horses milled, trying to avoid the day's work; Cookie, finished serving the men and busy feeding the flock of chickens or slopping the hogs he raised each year. This morning the sunrise filled the sky unnoticed by anyone except Ellie as the men took advantage of the extra respite of a late morning start.

Despite the turmoil in her mind, Ellie paused a moment to look at the gorgeous sunrise spectacle. Normally she barely had time to notice the glory, and today she caught herself thinking maybe it had put on this awesome display to soothe her troubled spirit. Or perhaps to remind her what she stood to lose.

Gold and violet colored the sky, streaks of vermilion highlighting the less than intense yellow and pink. The lack of clouds indicated another hot, pure day. Ellie couldn't bring herself to resent the fact that another sweltering day was on the horizon. Not when each day on her beloved ranch might now be her last.

Never had she resented being the adopted daughter more than today.

Dragging her eyes away, now misted with tears that blurred the beautiful sunrise, she strode on into the barn. Before she reached Cinder's stall, she halted as abruptly as though she had run into the stall door.

That fairy woman stood in front of Cinder's stall, dressed today in colors that rivaled even the sunrise. Shiny silver threads sparkled in the red laces running up the front of the black, sequined bodice of the dress. Once again, the bodice bared her shoulders and barely covered her nipples. Gold and purple stripes wove through the skirt, and it ended today at least two inches above her knees. This time her net stockings were red to match the laces, her high-heeled slippers a gold glowing even in the dim barn.

That silky, extremely red hair was piled on her head and caught with jeweled hairpins matching the various colors in her attire. The white cat in her arms stared at Ellie with piercingly blue eyes.

Ellie glanced over her shoulder, prepared to run, but the barn door swung shut behind her, eerily silent when normally it squeaked on its hinges.

"We need to talk, Ellie," the fairy woman said.

Oh, sure! The fairy woman had already told her no one could see her and her cat except Ellie. That's exactly what Ellie needed right now—someone coming into the barn and catching her talking to thin air.

She could try to tell whoever saw her the truth.

Sure she could!

She could tell them that a redheaded lady of the evening had begun appearing to her. A woman who carried a white Persian cat nearly as large as a newborn calf in her arms. A woman who claimed to have magical powers. And gosh-diddly-darn, the woman actually *did* appear to create magic!

Ellie wouldn't need to worry about what would happen to her if Elvina sold the ranch. She would be locked away in an asylum, with no one believing she was truly sane.

Whirling, she raced to the barn door and tugged frantically. It refused to budge, and she yanked harder.

"Open this!" she screamed over her shoulder. "Let me out of here!"

The door swung open, and she fell into Shane Morgan's arms. Shaking and trembling, she wrapped her arms around his solid, comforting presence and buried her head on his chest. He hesitated slightly, then gathered her close to him, rocking her and murmuring soothingly.

Several long seconds later Ellie fathomed what she was doing. Hot humiliation surging through her, she struggled to escape Shane's embrace. He loosened his arms enough for her to pull back, but refused to drop them completely, his more than adequate grasp effectively unbreakable.

"What's wrong, Ellie?" he asked. "What happened?"

Ellie threw a glance over her shoulder. The fairy woman—Fatima, she remembered her name was—still stood outside Cinder's stall, holding that beautiful, blue-eyed cat in her arms. She quirked one eyebrow, and wiggled two fingers of one hand at Ellie. The rest of both hands—and her arms—were busy holding the cat.

Ellie bit her tongue to keep from asking Shane if he saw the woman. When she glanced at his face, she could tell by his puzzled expression that he didn't. She looked back into the barn. Fatima waved again.

"Ellie?" Shane asked again. "Did something in there frighten you?"

"Frighten me?" She couldn't halt the harsh laugh that

emerged. "Now, what on earth could frighten me in a barn? I've been in there a million times."

"With the door propped shut from outside?" Shane questioned.

"Oh. Is that what was wrong? Gee, the wind must have blown the prop against the door."

Shane turned slightly to look at the heavy wooden prop they used to hold the barn door shut when necessary. It weighed at least fifty pounds, as Ellie knew from having to struggle it into place herself when a ranch hand wasn't around. She bit her bottom lip and kept her mouth shut as Shane casually perused the quiet, early morning air. Not one sign of a breeze stirred the humid heat.

While his attention was distracted, Ellie slipped out of his arms. Funny how reluctant she had been to make that move for such a long moment.

"I think I'll—uh—go check and see if Cookie has any coffee ready. I know I gave them all an extra hour off this morning, but Cookie is so used to getting up before dawn, I'll bet he at least made coffee."

"I could use a cup myself."

"Oh." She bit her lip. He was coming with her. "Oh, of course."

They walked out of the barn and headed toward the bunkhouse, and Ellie unyieldingly kept herself from looking back over her shoulder. It didn't help much. As they approached the bunkhouse, Fatima and the cat appeared on the roof, the fairy woman once again waving at Ellie.

Fatima sighed when Ellie refused to acknowledge her greeting and hurried into the cook shack. The cook shack and bunkhouse were really two parts of the same L-shaped building, connected by a short breezeway. Cookie reigned as king of his end of the building. Fatima had wandered around the bunkhouse when she first arrived at the Leaning G, but the men's messiness in the bunkhouse sent shudders up her spine. At least Cookie kept the kitchen sparkling clean.

"I've never had this happen before, Pandora," she told the cat as they settled on the roof. "Ellie's desperately afraid of us. Of course, just about everyone is a little scared when I first contact them, but they usually see the good I can do for them and become friends with us. Selfishly, at times, but even that gives us a chance to build a good relationship with them. I don't understand Ellie's fear at all."

"Meow."

"I *have* been thinking about it, and I can't—oh! Oh, Pandora, you don't think— But if that's it, and what it looks like might happen after what's going on with Darlene and Rockford— And with what Elvina's been up to— If all that happens, it's going to devastate Ellie."

Fatima hugged Pandora tighter, worry filling her. "And we'll have about as much chance of Ellie and Shane falling in love as . . . as a monkey ever flying to the moon! I've never failed at an assignment I set myself before, Pandora. And I've already come to admire and care so much for Ellie. I surely would hate for this to be the first time I failed."

Eight

Ellie at last had to admit defeat in her fight with a blinding headache when she and her men finally rode out of the ranch yard. The sun now hovered an hour above the horizon, and even with her hat brim pulled down almost to her nose, the bright light slivered stabs of pain through her brain. Pulling Cinder up, she motioned to Shorty.

"I never get headaches, Shorty, but I've got a horrible one this morning. I'm going back and take some powders, then lie down for a while, until it goes away. You and the men go ahead, and I'll catch up with you later."

"You take the whole day off iffen you need it, Miz Ellie," her wizened second-in-command told her. "We can handle things."

"I know you can," Ellie assured him, turning Cinder toward the barn.

And honestly, Shorty and her men didn't need her supervision. They would do their work well because they took pride in being top hands. She wouldn't have any other kind on her ranch—no, Elvina's ranch, she reminded herself with a sigh.

Shane had left before she and her men mounted up after breakfast, as soon as she thanked him for his help and turned down his request for her to join him for dinner in Fort Worth that evening. The headache was already stirring then, but she'd thought it only a result of her early-morning talk with Darlene and the appearance of the fairy woman and her cat. A warning that the tension of not knowing her future and worrying about her sanity was causing the pain.

Now, as she unsaddled Cinder and turned him back into the corral, she wondered if there was a physical cause for her illness. Perhaps some summer malady was making the rounds. Her stomach started hurting and nausea threatened. Losing the fight for control of the roiling, turbulent nausea, she dropped Cinder's saddle outside the barn door and raced a few feet away to vomit up her breakfast.

"Ellie, let me help."

Straightening, Ellie saw the fairy lady by her side, holding out a wet cloth. Her nauseating illness at the moment left no room for fright. Accepting the cloth gratefully, Ellie wiped her face and mouth, the coolness of the cloth a welcome surprise. Then Fatima placed an arm around her.

"Let me help you to the house," Fatima said.

"The saddle . . ."

Fatima lifted her black stick, and the saddle floated through the air and disappeared.

"I put it in the tack room," the fairy lady said. "That's where it goes, right?"

Ellie nodded, leaning heavily on Fatima as the woman steered her toward the house. The huge white cat padded ahead of them, leading the way.

Birdie hadn't arrived yet. Her hours matched Elvina's waking time, not anyone else's, and she would get there in time to prepare a tray of coffee and rolls to carry up to Elvina's room around ten o'clock—not before. Clutching her stomach and praying she would make it to her room before she needed to vomit again, Ellie let Fatima help her up the stairwell. At the top of the stairs, she saw Darlene's door closed, her sister having returned to bed after her early-morning rising. She was probably smiling in her sleep, dreaming of her life with Rockford.

Ellie barely noticed when Fatima conjured up a thin silk

nightgown rather than the cotton one she always wore, insisting Ellie undress and don it before she slipped into bed. However, the new gown did feel wonderful against her flushed skin.

"What's wrong with me?" Ellie asked around a moan. Before Fatima could answer, Ellie gagged and surged over the side of the bed. Miraculously, the chamber pot slid out from beneath the mattress, lid off, in time to catch the contents of her stomach.

When she lay back, Fatima wiped her face again, then held a glass of something bubbly to her mouth. A straw stuck up from it, and Ellie eyed it warily.

"Take a little sip, please," Fatima insisted. "It's only soda water to settle your stomach."

Ellie grimaced, but right now she would probably drink anything the devil himself brewed up if he said it would help her feel better. She sipped, and the lemony-tasting liquid slipped down her throat. Immediately her stomach settled.

"Thank you," she told Fatima with honest gratitude. "It worked instantly."

"It won't get rid of your illness any faster, I'm afraid," Fatima said. "You're going to have to stay in bed and let that run its course. But the drink should make it more bearable, and I'll be here to watch over you."

"I feel like I've been run over by a herd of cattle," Ellie said with a moan. She closed her eyes, hands clutching her forehead in pain.

"Here."

Lifting Ellie's hands, Fatima laid a cold pouch on her forehead. Astonished, Ellie opened her eyes and felt of it.

"It feels like it has ice inside," she said in wonder.

"It does."

"But . . . but there's no ice here—"

"I did it with magic, Ellie. Don't worry about how it came about. Just enjoy it."

"Oh, I will." Closing her eyes again, she luxuriated in

the icy coolness, drifting toward sleep within moments. Just before she dozed off, the mattress sank, and the huge cat nudged against her side. Its purr soothed Ellie, and she laid one hand on the cat and surrendered to slumber.

Twice she woke, tossing restlessly. Each time Fatima gave her a cool drink and replaced the ice pack on her head, and she drifted back into healing sleep. The third time she woke, although she felt a lingering weakness, her headache was gone and her stomach growled with hunger. Fatima sat in the rocking chair beside her bed, and the cat still curled by her side.

"You're looking much better," Fatima said when Ellie glanced at her.

"I'm feeling much better. What time is it?"

"Nearly dinnertime. It's a good thing I'm here, too," Fatima huffed. "No one's bothered to check on you all day!"

"I don't imagine they even knew I was home," Ellie said in defense of her stepmother and Darlene, although dejection stabbed her at their unintentional neglect. "I'm usually out on the range all day."

Fatima rose to her feet and indignantly plopped her hands on her hips. "That doesn't excuse them. Your horse is in the corral. Even that housekeeper didn't come in here to clean your room after she arrived!"

"She doesn't clean my room, only the rest of the house. I prefer it that way."

"Ellie Parker, you could die and no one would miss you!" Fatima strode around the room, a red curl falling from her piled-high hairdo as a result of her angry movements. "Your men would think you were taking some time off and your stepmother wouldn't think to look for you until she needed some money to buy something! You need someone to take care of you."

"That's the way it is, Fatima." Ellie closed her eyes again. "Please. I'm really not in shape right now to argue with you about this."

Fatima hurried over to the bed. "Of course you're not. Oh, I'm so sorry. I—"

The sound of angry voices from downstairs penetrated the air, and Fatima paused, cocking her head. "Who's that?"

"It sounds like Elvina and Birdie," Ellie told her. "I suppose they're having another fight."

"Another one?"

"They've never gotten along. But Birdie needs the money we pay her, and she's a wonderful cook—at least with the things Elvina likes to eat. But Birdie has her ways about her."

A door slammed, and Fatima hurried over to the window. "She's out in the yard, untying that horse she rode up on earlier."

"I done told you," Ellie heard Birdie say, her grating voice floating through the window. "I done already fixed supper—"

The door slammed again, and Elvina's voice cut in. "And I told you it's called dinner, not supper!"

"Dinner, schminner, supper, dupper!" Birdie shouted. "You shoulda told me earlier I was wastin' my time fixin' you something to eat. That you was goin' inta town! I wouldn't've bothered, and I coulda gone home two hours ago!"

"You're paid for your time whether you spend eight hours or six here, Birdie!"

"Iffen I can get my work done in six, ain't no skin offen your nose!"

"Oh, dear," Fatima said. "She's on her horse."

"I quit!" Birdie yelled. "Miz Monroe, she came over yestiday and said she'd pay me a dollar more a week iffen I'd come to work for her. I told her one of the reasons I stayed on and put up with your fussiness was 'cause I got off early now 'n' then. Since you're gonna get huffy 'bout that, you can find yourself someone else to take your guff!"

"Don't you dare ride away from me, Birdie. I'm not done—"

"And Miz Monroe likes eatin' regular meat and 'taters! I don't haveta make all them stupid, fancy sauces!"

Horse hooves sounded, and Ellie saw by Fatima's grinning face that she was enjoying the scene below. In fact, she almost sensed that Fatima felt Elvina deserved having her cook and housekeeper walk out on her in such an uproar—or was there some other explanation for the contemplation mixed in with the glee on the fairy woman's face?

Fatima wasn't the one who would have to find a new servant for her fussy stepmother, though. Ellie's stomach clenched in renewed nausea. And Birdie wasn't one to be muzzled when she got a burr up her butt. By the time she got done spreading her discontent and reasons for leaving the Leaning G all over the entire county, Ellie would be lucky to find someone she could afford.

She groaned and fell back against her pillow. "Fatima? Do you have another one of those ice packs?"

Fatima hurried over to the bed, picking up her black, silver-tipped stick from the nightstand.

"What *is* that thing?" Ellie asked.

"Why, that's my magic wand," Fatima said. "Watch."

Holding out her free hand, she waved the wand back and forth over her palm. Gold dust sparkles showered from the silver tip and filled the air. When they cleared, a new blue pouch like the previous ones lay on Fatima's hand. She gently placed it on Ellie's head, and the ice inside settled in a curve around Ellie's forehead.

"I don't care if it is or isn't magic," Ellie mused, closing her eyes and sighing in absolute pleasure. "It feels completely wonderful."

"It's magic, Ellie. Have no doubt about that."

Fatima's voice faded, and Ellie looked up to see her back over by the window. She heard a murmur of voices, but this time she couldn't make out the words. Even though Ellie didn't ask, Fatima explained what she was seeing.

"Your sister Darlene must have gone out to the bunk-house to get your ranch cook to hitch up the buggy, Ellie. The cook's heading back to the cook shack, and Darlene's driving the buggy over to the porch where Elvina's waiting for her."

"Elvina hardly ever goes into town," Ellie mused. "And when she does, it's never this late in the day. Unless there's some performance going on in town, but there's never anything other than the traveling circus this time of year. The heat keeps people away from our area until later in the fall."

"Well, she and your sister are all dressed up. There they go."

Once again horses' hooves sounded leaving the ranch yard. Still weak from her bout with stomach sickness, Ellie drifted back to sleep.

She woke once during the night, and Fatima fed her some of the most delicious soup she had ever eaten. Tender beef chunks that melted on her tongue floated in a rich broth along with carrots and corn. She had always heard that a person with a sour stomach should avoid everything except liquids while ill, but the soup was exactly what she needed. Stomach at peace, she drifted back to sleep.

When she opened her eyes the next morning at her usual time—just prior to dawn—Ellie felt so well it was almost as though her illness had never been. But when she looked around for Fatima and Pandora, they weren't in sight. For a hopeful moment she tried to tell herself she'd been so sick she imagined the fairy woman and her cat—hallucinated them. Nearly before the thought could form, she admitted lying to herself. Ellie Parker had herself a fairy godmother, and the fairy godmother wasn't about to go away until she was diddly-darned good and ready.

But why was Fatima here? Surely she wasn't going to stay with Ellie the rest of her life. She must have some mission.

Ellie sighed and scooted out of bed. She would have to

wait until Fatima appeared again to ask the fairy woman that overdue question.

She washed, the beautiful silk nightgown giving further evidence that Fatima and Pandora weren't hallucinations. Dressing in her range clothing—a split skirt and clean, white blouse—she hurried down the rear stairwell leading to the kitchen.

Suddenly the enticing smell of coffee and bacon was real, not imaginary or an odor carried on a breeze through the open windows from the bunkhouse. Had Elvina found a new housekeeper that quickly? One who didn't mind preparing something for Ellie, so she didn't have to eat with the men?

She wandered on into the room. Fatima stood at the stove, chatting gaily with Shane, who was eating from a piled-high plate at the table. The shock of seeing Shane calmly sitting there as though it were the most ordinary thing in the world to have a lady of the evening serve him breakfast glued Ellie's boots to the floor.

Nine

Ellie blinked, then glanced at Fatima again. Shane hadn't seen Ellie yet, but Fatima winked, though she continued talking to Shane.

This morning Fatima wore gold. A gold dress shone and sparkled in the lanterns hanging from various pegs placed around the kitchen. As with her other dresses, the gold one plunged to a daring neckline. Today several gold chains with charms dangled around her neck; gold-tipped hairpins held her coiffure in place; gold stockings covered her legs and gold slippers barely covered her feet. Her cheeks flushed charmingly in the heat from the stove, her green eyes sparkling.

For some reason, a stab of what Ellie thought could possibly be jealousy cut through her. Surely not. What could it matter to her that a devastatingly beautiful woman in a devastatingly daring gown stood talking to Shane Morgan? Shane didn't mean a thing to Ellie except for his promised assistance with Darlene's future plans.

While Shane laughed at something Fatima said, the devastating woman greeted Ellie. "Good morning, Ellie. My, you're looking much better this morning."

"I—" She glanced at Shane, who rose to his feet in her presence. His appearance stunned the words in her throat. He wore a blue work shirt, like the ranch hands wore, but the light material would be cool even with the long sleeves buttoned around his large wrists. The sleeves barely fit around nicely muscled arms, and the shirt tapered from broad shoulders to a trim waist. A red neckerchief was knotted around his brawny throat. Instead of trousers, he wore the jeans her hands preferred, and they wandered endlessly, and tightly, down long, well-toned legs.

Ellie cleared her throat. "I feel fine today. Good morning, Mr. Morgan."

"Shane," he reminded her. "Good morning."

Fatima hurried over to Ellie. "I've got breakfast ready here, Ellie, so you don't have to eat with those burping, cursing men."

"They don't curse when I'm . . ." Ellie defended them.

But her words died in her throat when Fatima's clothing changed in front of her eyes. And not only her clothing, but her appearance. Her red hair faded to gray, although it was still coiled nicely around her head, now in braids. Her dress changed to a long, neatly pressed gray-and-white calico, with a full pink apron covering the front. No chains, and no jeweled hairpins.

Ellie glanced at Fatima's feet, and as though sensing her curiosity, Fatima picked up her skirt hem a tiny bit so Ellie could see the sensible black shoes on her feet.

"This is how others will see me," she said sotto voce and with another wink. Then more loudly, "Come on over to the table, Ellie, love. I fixed your favorites this morning. Ham and eggs and home fries. Oh, and my biscuits. If I do say so myself, my biscuits are so light, I have to cover them to keep them from floating out of the pan!"

Dazed, her words still dammed in her throat, Ellie followed Fatima over to the table. She sat down across from Shane, and Fatima placed a cup of steaming coffee, already liberally laced with cream as Ellie preferred it, in front of her. Ellie heard a thump, and looked down to find Pandora settling in the chair beside her. The cat nearly covered the seat, especially when it plopped its bottom down and raised one paw, licking it and then smoothing its fur.

Shane eyed the cat warily, but Ellie easily read the flickering emotions crossing his face. First he grimaced a little at the cat's proximity to the breakfast table, then glanced at his plate, then at Fatima, the cat's owner. A decisive resignation settled last on his face, as he evidently thought better of antagonizing the owner of the cat, the person responsible for the delicious meal he enjoyed.

Already in love with the cat, Ellie petted Pandora as Fatima set a plate filled to nearly overflowing in front of her. Pandora's ears perked.

"Meow."

With a laugh, Ellie tore off a piece of ham and held it out. Pandora accepted it daintily and arranged herself more comfortably on the chair to eat.

"You'll spoil her," Fatima said with a tolerant smile. "I was so lucky that Mrs. Parker agreed that I could bring Pandora with me, too, when I accepted the position of housekeeper and cook she needed to fill. But then, I wouldn't have taken it without Pandora."

"That's some name for a cat," Shane put in.

"Isn't it?" Fatima said without further explanation. "Now, the two of you eat up. There's more if you want it."

"I don't understand—" Ellie began, but the smell of ham tickled her nostrils until she cut off a large bite. The questions in her mind could wait. Neither Birdie nor Cookie had ever served a meal as delicious as this one, and Ellie chewed dreamily. The ham edges curled crispy brown, as nicely turned out as the home fries mixed with onions. The egg centers were nice and mushy in firm salt-and-peppered whites. When Ellie tore open a biscuit, steam feathered from the hot center, and the fresh-churned butter she slathered on melted at a touch. She added pear preserves and ate half of the biscuit half in one bite.

She noticed that Shane also centered his attention on his

own plate, finishing his food without the normal courtesy of chatter.

Huh. He had been carrying on a nice enough conversation with Fatima, she grumped to herself. He wiped his plate with a biscuit and handed Fatima the plate.

"More?" Fatima asked.

"Please," Shane said with a nod, before he plopped the biscuit in his mouth.

Her hunger assuaged somewhat, Ellie took the opportunity to ask at least one of the questions crowding for notice in her mind.

"Why are you here so early, Shane? It's almost as though you spent the night," she said before forking a fried potato slice into her mouth.

"We did," a voice said from the kitchen doorway.

The bite of potato clogged Ellie's throat when Shane's valet, Withers, spoke from the doorway. "And might I say, Miss Ellie, you have a most charming abode here."

Ellie choked and coughed, and Fatima hurried over to pound on her back. The potato dislodged, landing on her plate.

Able to breathe again, Ellie stared at Shane, moved her eyes to Withers, and then glanced at Fatima, the questions crowding her thoughts making her frown in warning. Fatima ignored her. Her eyes were on Withers, an apprising looked mixed with what looked like admiration on her face.

The heck with good manners! She had been faced with a fairy woman claiming to be her fairy godmother, who kept appearing and scaring her half out of her wits. Now the man who had haunted her dreams ever since the night of the circus sat across from her in these early-morning hours, much as though he had moved into the same house. And his valet appeared to confirm that it had indeed happened.

Ellie exploded and surged to her feet. "Just what on earth is going on around here?" she demanded.

The kitchen filled with gold dust, and when it cleared,

Shane sat across from her with his fork halfway to his mouth, frozen in time. Ellie's mouth dropped, and she fearfully stared at Withers. He stood with one leg raised in the middle of a step, unmoving also. Cutting her eyes very slowly to Fatima, she saw her—now dressed in her gold clothing—holding her magic wand and tapping it against one palm.

"Ellie, I would have told you what was going on if you'd waited a minute until we were alone. Now I—"

"What have you done?" Ellie whispered. "Turn—turn them loose."

"In a minute," Fatima said calmly. "You need to know something, Ellie. Your stepmother hired me when she came into town last night. I left you sleeping, and I just conveniently happened to be at the hotel when she arrived to see Shane. Of course, I had impeccable references and I wore appropriate attire when I applied for this position."

Ellie gulped, cutting her eyes back around to Shane, then Withers. "Will—will they know what you've done to them?"

"Fiddle dee dee, of course not. So don't worry, we can have as long as we need to talk."

Reaching a shaky hand out for her chair, Ellie felt her way back into the seat. Pandora blinked blue eyes at her. At least the cat was still alive. But then, surely Shane and Withers were alive; they were just . . . just frozen.

"Yes, they're alive," Fatima said, making Ellie realize she had voiced her fear aloud. "And I'll release them in a moment. But you need to know—"

Ellie whirled toward Fatima. "What was my stepmother doing at the hotel, wanting to talk to Shane? And why is he staying here now?"

Fatima sighed and tapped her wand harder on her palm. A few sparkles of gold dust shook from the end of it, and Ellie stared at them in trepidation.

"Elvina has decided to look into selling the ranch," Fatima said. "And since she knew Shane was in the area look-

ing for investments, she decided to ask him if he was
interested. Or if he knew someone who might be.''

Although she had suspected as much, Ellie's heart
twisted in agony. ''The Leaning G is the only home I have!
But then, Darlene insinuated the same thing yesterday
morning, so I don't guess I should be so surprised.''

''One day you'll marry, Ellie . . .'' Fatima began.

''Never. No man I could fall in love with would ever
want an orphan who doesn't even know her own background for a wife.''

For a moment, Fatima looked as though she might say
something more but shook her head. Ellie rose.

''I'm going out on the range with the men. I assume
you'll turn Shane and Withers loose.''

She raced out of the kitchen before Fatima could reply,
not wanting anyone to witness the tears threatening to
course down her face. They burst free as she stumbled
across the rear veranda and down the steps, and she wiped
the heels of her hands across her face defiantly.

''I will *not* cry,'' she said, even though the tears gave
lie to her words. Sniffling, she went on to the barn. When
Shorty mentioned her stuffiness, she explained it as a lingering trait from her illness the day before, but assured him
she felt fine.

Before she could mount and head out with her men,
Shane appeared in the barn, looking none the worse for
having been in the frozen state Ellie didn't dare mention to
him. Given that Fatima promised only Ellie saw her true
appearance, the fairy woman was well aware asylum doors
could close on anyone professing to see her as she was.
But Fatima could use her magic wand and disappear. Ellie
would spend her life inside those dark, dreary walls if she
voiced what she saw. She had been imprisoned for her own
good, everyone would tell her, since she was obviously
having delusions.

''Can we talk for a minute, Ellie?'' Shane asked, bringing her thoughts back from that scary road.

"I need to get out on the range. I missed yesterday."

"Fatima told me you'd been ill yesterday. Are you sure you feel like riding out today?"

"It's my job," she told him firmly. "Now please excuse me."

He caught her arm before she could get in the saddle. She kept forgetting he could move so fast for such a huge man. His hand was warm and . . . and big on her arm, though its hugeness was in no way threatening. Instead, it gave her comfort in her distress. Those darned tears jumped back into her eyes, but she backhanded them away.

"We can talk later," she managed in a rather calm voice.

"I thought you would be interested in why I'm here."

"I know why." She kept her gaze on Cinder, stroking the gelding's dappled neck for something to do. "Darlene said yesterday morning that Elvina was thinking of selling the ranch. With the drought we had last year, few of the other ranchers around here have a lot of ready cash—or would want to expand right now, even if they did."

"You know quite a bit about ranching."

"I told you. That's my job—to run this ranch."

"Can you show me how it's done? Running this ranch?"

Ellie chuckled wryly. "In what? A week? It took me years and years of following George around and being quite the little tomboy to know what I do. And even then, like the drought showed, there are unavoidable pitfalls."

"Seems to me there should always be a financial cushion put aside in case of things like drought."

"Should be," Ellie agreed abruptly. "Tell that to Elvina when she gets hold of a mail order catalog."

He reached one of those large hands around and cupped her chin, turning her head to face him. Resistance was futile, even though her mind clamored with danger warnings. Her heart won, wanting for just a few seconds to savor the comfort flowing from his strong fingers. To enjoy the thrill of his index finger, gently, so gently, stroking her cheek, almost as though he wasn't aware he was doing it.

A little curl of sensation twisted her belly and meandered downward.

"Have you been crying, Ellie?" he asked softly. So softly for such a huge man.

"No!" she insisted, jerking free with an effort she had to dredge from the bottom of her toes. "Now, excuse me. My men will be wondering where I am."

She fairly leaped onto Cinder's back, and the gelding shied in alarm and surprise. Shane quickly stepped back, slipping his thumbs into the rear pockets of his jeans and drawing her attention once more to how nicely they fit his backside—almost as though he'd had them tailored. She snorted and pulled her hat down firmly on her head, urging Cinder forward with only a slight touch of her heels. Given Shane Morgan's pile of money, he probably had bought Dan the Tailor's entire shop, just to make sure he had proper clothing to wear!

Given Shane Morgan's pile of money, he would never be interested in a poor little orphan girl from Fort Worth, Texas. He was only being nice.

But lordy, lordy, nice felt awfully . . . nice from him.

Frowning, Shane wandered over to the barn door and watched Ellie ride out of the yard. Her dappled gelding's well-curried hide shone silvery in the morning light, and not for the first time he considered that the horse might have some Arabian blood. Ellie's white-blond hair, a marked contrast to the darker shade of her horse, was covered with her hat this morning, the lovely locks tamed in a braid down her back—a back that sat as straight and as tall in the saddle as her short stature allowed.

He didn't understand her distress over the possibility of Elvina selling the ranch. What on earth could there be for a woman with her potential here in this dreary, dry, desolate country? In *Texas*?

He could offer her so much more—

"Whoa!" he cautioned himself, blurting the word out so

loud he startled a pigeon from the barn rafters. The bird swooped toward the door, and Shane ducked instinctively.

I'm only here to figure out whether she's really Cynthia Spencer instead of Ellie Parker, he reminded himself silently. *If she does turn out to be Cynthia, she can buy this ranch herself twenty times over if that's what she wants to do. And my time here won't be wasted. Mother will want me to advise Ellie, or Cynthia, on any investments she decides to make, so I might as well see whether or not this ranch has any potential.*

And I might possibly see more potential for a good investment with Rockford's company than I do now. So even if Ellie's not Cynthia, this trip could be worth some money to me. And if not, examining Rockford's business to see if it's worthy of expansion has served its purpose—to give me an in to get to know Ellie.

"And I'm not looking for a wife, Ellie," he mused quietly. "Even if I do admire the hell out of how much strength and ability you've built in yourself inside that tiny body. Even if that tiny body does have every curve in every right place and make you about the loveliest thing I've seen since I visited the Louvre in Paris and saw an exhibit of Delacroix's paintings. Even if I can't stop thinking about how well you fit up against my back that night the lion stalked us and wishing I could find out if you'd fit in my arms that well, too."

Shane pulled his arms to the front and stared at his right hand. Reaching over with his left, he unbuttoned his shirt cuff and rolled it upward. The skin was even more mottled and distasteful on his arm than on his hand, and although he refused to look in the mirror when he was naked any longer, he knew what his right side and back looked like. It was a nightmare—a nightmare that had turned Anastasia's stomach the first time she saw him back in New York City following the steamboat accident. And one that had her delivering his ring to him by messenger within an hour after she left.

Oh, her note had been polite. Overly polite.

I'm sorry, Shane, but it just wouldn't be fair to you. You deserve someone who can share your life completely. He snorted to himself. What she meant was share both the days *and nights* completely. *I am going to give you your freedom so you can find someone. You are far too wonderful a man to have to marry someone as shallow as me.*

Within a month, Anastasia was betrothed to one of the Vandergoods, the oldest son even. The heir apparent, though she would have to wait for the old man to die, which hadn't been the case with Shane, whose father had passed on years earlier.

Ellie could find someone like that, also, if that's what she wanted. Or stay here in Texas. Lord, he still found that word distasteful. She could stay here in *Texas* and find herself a rough-and-tough cowboy if that tickled her fancy after the life she had been raised in. Someone who could ride the range with her and take her to circuses and barn dances, instead of operas and museums.

Damn, it had twisted his gut when he saw the tear tracks down her cheeks.

Damn, the idea of her marrying a cowboy—any other man, for that matter—twisted the knot in his belly tighter. But it was best for all concerned.

He went back into the barn. Ellie apparently hadn't seen the stallion Shane had put in the far stall last night. He needed a large horse to carry himself around if he planned on spending entire days on the range. Blackjack fit the bill. Shane had found him at a Fort Worth stable yesterday afternoon and decided immediately after riding the horse to take him back to New York with him when he went.

For such a huge, wild-looking beast, the stallion was incredibly tame. Shane offered him a couple of sugar cubes, and the horse slurped them from his palm and nickered his thanks. Shane curried him briefly, then tacked him up and headed out.

"Yoo hoo!" Fatima called from the porch as soon as Shane got out of the barn.

He reined Blackjack over to the porch and leaned down toward the woman. "What can I do for you, you wonderful cook?" he asked.

"Here." She handed him a cloth sack, bulging with whatever she had inside it. "I want you to make sure that Ellie stops and eats at noon today. No matter what she says this morning, she was extremely ill yesterday. There's also a canteen of lemonade in there, and I've wrapped it well so perhaps it will stay cool until noon."

"I doubt that." Shane glanced up at the sky, already turning white-hot this early in the morning.

"We'll see about that." Fatima waved a nonchalant hand. "Just make sure she eats, will you, please?"

"I will." He reined the stallion away, his pleasure at his assignment filling his thoughts a hell of a lot more than it should have. It wasn't until he was a mile from the house, pulling Blackjack up and scanning the horizon for signs of dust to see which way the men had gone, that he took time to wonder once again about the coincidence nagging him: the housekeeper and her cat having the same names Ellie had called into the air the night of the lion attack.

He thought that Fatima had met Elvina only yesterday, when she applied for the job. It had seemed that way on their trip back to the ranch, when Fatima and her cat rode in the buggy alongside Elvina and Darlene, with Shane and Withers escorting them.

Maybe he hadn't heard right. Or maybe Elvina had told Fatima about Ellie's illness. He doubted Elvina Parker would have hired a woman she had just met without checking out her references first. A woman who was going to be living in her house, unlike the housekeeper who quit on Elvina.

Huh. Fatima had also known exactly Ellie's favorite foods for breakfast. Seemed strange, since logically, they had only met this morning. Now that he thought of it, they hadn't even introduced themselves.

But it wasn't his business. His business was finding out if Ellie Parker was indeed Cynthia Spencer.

Ten

Gosh darn almighty! Shane and that overgrown elephant of a horse silhouetted the skyline every which way Ellie turned all morning. There was as much chance of ignoring the man as tuning out the Fort Worth community marching band during the Fourth of July parade every year. And he was every bit as brassy as the horn section—in his quiet way.

He asked questions, and if she didn't answer, he rode over and asked one of the men. Shorty especially preened like a proud bandy rooster who had just made sure every one of his hens would lay a nice spotted egg that day when Shane deferred to his knowledge of the range and ranching.

Yeah, Shane, she mentally mocked the comment Shorty had just made. *A dogie's a maverick calf. Usually his mama's been et by somethin'. Maybe a coyote, but they kin only ketch the old cows. We git pumas around here, tho', and iffen they start makin' too many kills, we gits a bunch of hands together and go lookin' for the cat.*

"So what do you do with an orphaned calf? A dogie?" Shane asked now.

"We hope another cow'll take it on," Shorty said. "But iffen it won't, we take it back and let Cookie raise it. Only problem with that is, Cookie, he don't like us to eat none of the ones he raises. Or sell them for meat, neither. So he uses his wages to buy them offen the ranch, and he's got a smart little herd goin' down in the south pasture."

"You suppose he plans on starting his own ranch someday?"

"Of course he does," Ellie put in. "Lots of the big ranches now were once small, one-drover spreads. With careful management, a ranch can grow."

"Without someone draining profits that should go back into the herd, I assume," Shane said, keeping his gaze fixed on her as though glad he finally had her attention.

Shorty took the opportunity to ride over and check a nearby cow and calf. With a measure of privacy now, Ellie told Shane what he wanted to know, but grudgingly.

"George could handle Elvina. But the ranch belongs to her now, and her word outweighs mine. Sometimes it's just too much effort to try to argue with her. I'm just the orphan who was given a home with the Parkers. A dogie calf taken in by them. Part of the time, Elvina will listen and put off what she wants. Other times, come heck or high water, she wants what she wants."

"Heck or high water?" Shane said with a chuckle. "Ellie, for a woman who spends her days with a bunch of cowboys, you do avoid picking up their language, don't you?"

Ellie glanced down at her dusty split riding skirt. Thought about the other five skirts exactly like it hanging in her closet, among her two lonely church dresses.

She faced Shane, warmed by his tawny eyes and the glint of humor in them. Somehow she knew he wasn't laughing at her; his amusement resulted from admiration.

"I don't get many chances to remember I'm a woman," she admitted in a quiet voice. "Not succumbing to foul language is one of the things that reminds me I'm different than my hands, even though their language doesn't bother me all that much. I'm used to it, I guess."

"Oh, you're definitely a woman, Ellie Parker." His appreciative voice sent shivers up her back, cooling her in the humid day. "Don't ever for one minute doubt that."

He looked up at the sky, and Ellie suffered an almost physical wrench when their eyes lost contact. Good thing, though. She had been staring at him like one of those dogies mooning over a prospective new mama.

"Looks to me like it's about noon," he said. "I saw a nice little stream back there with some cottonwood trees for shade. How about we go eat our lunch there?"

It took a minute for Ellie's befuddled mind to process what he said, then she straightened in the saddle and briefly glanced at the sun. "Uh . . . uh, yeah, it's time to eat. But I forgot to bring anything with me today. I'll just finish checking this line of fence—"

"Fatima packed us a lunch, and she'll have my hide if I let you go without eating, Ellie. She told me so in no uncertain terms. So come on."

He turned his stallion, and called, "Hey, Shorty! Ellie and I are going back to that stream and have lunch. What about you men?"

"We're gonna ride up to the line shack and fix some stew on the stove," Shorty called back. "Y'all are welcome to come with us."

Shane waved them onward. "We'll catch you later."

Shorty and the other two men rode off. The orders Ellie had issued earlier meant this would be the last she saw of them until supper time. From the line shack, they would travel on to check the newly fenced-off water hole, then try to find the old pregnant brindle range cow, who somehow avoided roundup each spring. And somehow always avoided getting bred until it meant she would drop her calf far later than the rest of the herd.

They had spotted the brindle a couple of days ago, and she looked like she was ready to calve any minute. She always had wonderful calves, but if they didn't keep an eye on her, they would never find her and the calf and get the calf branded in case it wandered onto some neighbor's range.

The orders she had given them also meant Ellie would be alone with Shane the rest of the day.

So what? He was only putting up with the heat and dust and long hours in the saddle because he wanted to see if the ranch was worth investing in. If it would make him a few more dollars to add to the mountain of money he already had.

"I really need to go ahead and finish checking this fence. Cows could wander out if there's a break somewhere."

Shane shrugged and picked up his reins. "Let me know when you're ready to eat. But I hope we don't have to ride too far back to the stream by then. Unless you know a nice shady spot further on down the line?"

Ellie stared longingly over her shoulder. Sweat dribbled down her back and between her breasts in front, and the tiny stream beckoned. She had eaten numerous lunches along it; she knew well how nice and cool it was beneath the cottonwood shade—how the break made the hot, humid afternoon easier to take.

Right then the cottonwood trees shivered as though a breeze blew through them, and her yearning to feel it persuaded her.

"All right," she said. "I guess it does make sense to eat at the stream, since we're already so close."

Shane smiled, a purely masculine, satisfied smile at getting his way that made her heart beat triple time. Had he been that lion they saw the other night, he might have licked his lips at the idea and anticipation of getting her alone on the stream bank.

Well, where the diddly-darn had that silly, self-satisfied thought come from? He was only smirking because he would get his own way—get to eat his lunch when he wanted.

Surely that was it.

Nudging Cinder with her heels, Ellie headed for the stream at a lope. Following, the stallion's larger hooves drowned out Cinder's hoofbeats—or was that her heart thudding louder than Cinder's hooves?

Beneath the cottonwoods, Ellie dismounted and removed Cinder's saddle and bridle. The gelding wouldn't wander off; he had spent thousands of working days on the range and knew the day wasn't over yet. Ellie removed her hat and lifted her braid off the back of her neck. The breeze feathered against her skin, making her feel so good she unbuttoned the top two buttons on her blouse. Then she sat down on a fallen limb and reached for her boots.

"I'm going to wade in the water for a few minutes before we eat," she answered Shane's inquiring look as he laid his own saddle aside and carried the sack that had been tied over the back of his horse to a sandy spot on the shore. "If you feel like taking your shirt off and cooling off yourself, please don't mind me. The hands work shirtless on hot days, and I don't pay them any never mind."

"That won't be necessary," Shane said, dropping the bag so hard that anything in it would have been broken if it hadn't landed on sandy soil. His tone of voice told her that she had trod on some feeling he didn't want her near, but she shrugged it off.

"In case you haven't noticed yet," Ellie said with a chuckle, "this isn't New York City. We're not nearly as formal here in Texas. But suit yourself."

Leaving him to make his own decision, she tossed her boots aside, stood and stuck a toe in the water. The stream began somewhere underground not far north of here, and the water stayed cool even in the blasting heat of August. Today, in June, it was even cooler, and she relished the chill.

Ellie's left foot overturned a sharp rock when she balanced her weight on it, and she flinched at the small stab of pain. Her right foot submerged in the water, sliding on a moss-covered stone.

"Whoa!" she said, then, "Brrrr!" But she danced on into the water, out past the rocks lining the shore to the more sandy bottom. Just before the water would have reached the hem of her riding skirt, which fell halfway between her knees and ankles, she stopped and bent down. Cupping both hands into the cool water, she sipped some, then poured the rest over her face, allowing it to run down her neck.

The water cooled more than her physical body. She felt her pique with both her life and Shane sliding off her shoulders with the icy droplets. Rarely did she get such a refreshing break in the middle of a backbreaking day, and she wanted to savor every blessed minute of it without the restraint of all her disturbing problems.

She would enjoy having some company in her relaxation, too, if only Shane would drop some of his proper formalities. She drenched herself with another brimming handful of water.

"Ummmmm," she said. "I'm glad you talked me into stopping here. You definitely should come on in and cool off, Shane."

When he didn't answer, she glanced at him. He stood as though glued in some of the dangerous red-clay mud downstream, holding his hat in one hand, his other palm dangling by his side. Gosh darn it, it looked like he was glaring at her. But maybe the shadows from the trees gave his face that glower.

She cocked her head to find a different point of view of his face, and Shane abruptly turned his back and reached for the sack containing their lunch.

Well, she liked that. Such a stuffy old Yankee man.

"Hey, stuffy old Yankee," she called.

When Shane turned back toward her, she threw two handfuls of water straight at him. She had good, strong arms from all the physical labor she did, and the silvery trail of water raced true, with plenty of impetus to splatter his face—a face that took on a stunned disbelief as the water dripped from his chin.

Uh-oh. The disbelief turned to a reckoning glower, and

Ellie suddenly remembered how huge he was compared to her tininess. But for some reason, she wasn't one bit afraid. She clapped her wet hands over her mouth loosely, deliberately letting her giggles escape.

He sat down, and she dropped her hands and propped them on her hips.

He took off his boots, and the taunt she had been going to throw at him died in her throat.

She kept forgetting that he could move so fast! She barely had time to splash out the other side of the creek before he caught her. He lifted her as easily as he did the large saddle on his stallion and carried her back to the stream. She giggled wildly, flailing in his arms, but knowing she had no chance of escaping a dunking.

"Don't," she pleaded anyway. "Don't drop me in!"

He paused, but not before he waded to where the water was a little deeper beneath a huge cottonwood a few yards downstream. He stared down into her face. "Take it back."

"What?" she managed around her laughter.

"About me being a stuffy Yankee."

"But sometimes you are—"

She hit the water without warning, submerging completely, then kicking against the bottom and streaking back up like one of the seals she had read about out on the West Coast. Her braid came half undone, and her hair hung sodden and heavy across her eyes. Giggling some more, she pushed it back.

And stuck out one trim foot between Shane's spread legs, catching him by surprise when she coiled her toes and jerked back on his knee. He tumbled into the water also.

She half-swam, half-lunged to shore again, standing beside the lunch sack and watching as Shane wiped his eyes and pushed his dark-blond hair back out of his face. He looked at her, his tawny eyes warm with laughter, shaking his head.

"I can't believe a little bit of a thing like you got the

better of me," he said, then threw back his head, his laughter roaring through the treetops.

Smiling, Ellie sat down on the dead limb and started untangling her hair with her fingers. At last Shane stumbled out of the water, standing on the shore and letting the worst of it drain off him before he approached.

"I thought you were mad at me because I was interested in buying the ranch," he said.

Ellie sighed and continued working her hair. "I've been thinking, and I guess it's not your fault. I mean, Elvina approached you, not the other way around. I should have expected it after George died." The sunny day dimmed for her, and Ellie continued, "It's like almost everything else in my life. I really don't have a claim to anything. It all belongs to someone else."

Shane ambled over and sat down near her on the ground, his face a mixture of seriousness and sadness. "And then some stuffy Yankee comes along and starts thinking of buying something you've worked so hard on and that means so much to you."

Ellie shrugged, cutting her eyes at him. "You *are* stuffy sometimes. And I don't need your pity."

"You're good at making me unstuffy. And it wasn't pity—it was concern."

"Is there such a word as that?" she asked with a chuckle, trying to lighten the mood again. He was getting too close to her hidden feelings now. "I never learned the word 'unstuffy' in school."

Shane slowly and solemnly shook his head. A wet curl fell over his forehead, drawing her gaze and pointing out the teasing glint in his eyes, which belied the solemnity. He pushed the curl back, and Ellie fought noticing how his wet shirt clung to his wide chest, leaving not one bulge or muscle to her imagination.

"Why, ma'am," he said in a laughingly poor imitation of a Texas drawl, "I guess y'all's backwoods schools down hyar just don't keep up on the latest in the English language. Unstuffy, it's been in use for yars and yars back where I come from.''

Ellie laughed again, reaching for the lunch sack. Shaking her head and pulling it over between them, she tore open the top. With the tension broken between them, ravenous hunger suddenly filled her.

She started removing things from the sack, then looked around for somewhere to set them down.

''Here,'' Shane said, holding out his hands.

She gave him a loaf of bread and the ham, then excitedly opened the sack wider and reached in again. Out came a quarter wheel of a cheese, the smell telling her it was cheddar, her favorite. Next a bag of half-a-dozen apples, and then a bar of butter wrapped in cheesecloth. She handed all these to Shane, then bent back to the sack.

There was a small jar of sweet pickles; lucky it hadn't broken when Shane dropped the sack. Another wedge of cheese—Swiss, this time. How had Fatima known she loved this cheese, which she had had only once at a nice hotel George had taken her and Darlene to in Dallas?

Emptying her hands, she reached for a paper bag. When she opened the top, her eyes widened. Chocolate chip and raisin cookies. Oh, lordy, she would never get any work done this afternoon.

''Uh . . . Ellie.''

''Shhhh. There's something else . . .''

She found some tin plates and cups, then a tablecloth and napkins. Something was wrapped in the tablecloth, and she shoved the plates, cups, and napkins at Shane to unwrap it.

''Uh . . . Ellie.''

The shape inside the tablecloth was round, like a canteen. It *was* a canteen, and it felt cool beneath the cloth covering. She unscrewed the top and smelled lemonade. Cold, tart lemonade. Perfect on a hot day. Fatima must have used her magic to keep it cold somehow.

''Oh, it's—''

She turned a delighted face on Shane just as the mound in his arms started trembling, ready to fall. Hastily propping the open canteen against a rock so it wouldn't tip over, she grabbed the sack of cookies and the ham, giggling as she tucked them in one arm and spread the tablecloth in a lumpy mess with the other hand.

"There," she told Shane. "Set everything else down now."

"Ellie, if I try to set everything else down, everything's still going to land in a heap."

Smiling at him, she rose to her knees and started taking things from his arms, placing them on the tablecloth. The last thing she tried to take was the cotton napkins, but he held them tightly in his fingers. She tugged, then looked up at him in question.

His intent gaze was on her face; his head bent and his lips only about the width of an easy movement away. His gaze entrapped her like a jackrabbit she had seen one night when she caught it in the beam of her lantern light. Her nipples puckered against her wet shirt in reaction.

She studied that purely masculine, so close, so very attractive face, as she had wanted to do in real life but had only done in her dreams at night.

His hair was slicked back, outlining a broad forehead, with a crease of concentration in it at the moment. Her fingers itched to smooth it away, but she resisted. His eyebrows matched his hair, resting above those captivating gold-dust-sprinkled eyes. His eyes were the most expressive she had ever seen—ever reacted to. She truly loved his eyes. The light-colored lashes didn't look that long until you got this close to them. They were dark at the roots and golden at the curled tips.

A straight nose bisected his face between nice cheekbones, and his mouth—oh, that mouth. Full and firm and perfectly masculine. She sighed, the movement rasping her breast tips against her shirt and pebbling them into further hardness. The woman who married Shane Morgan and got the right to kiss him would truly enjoy his mouth.

She had been kissed a couple of times, once rather pleasantly, but once in a wet, sucking motion that made her think her beau was trying to swallow her. That was the same beau who tossed his stomach on her skirts.

"If you don't quit looking at me like that—" Shane said in a gravelly voice.

"Like what?" she mused.

"Like a cat getting ready to lap up a bowl of fresh cream," he growled.

Her eyes flew back to his. "Oh! Oh, I'm sorry. I—"

He kissed her. Without any warning, she found his lips on hers, and it was every bit as wonderful as she had imagined. Their mouths fit together perfectly, and his lips were warm and gentle, firm yet caressing. The only other place he touched her was on her fingers, still clutching the napkins along with him. He feathered a light touch back and forth across the tops of them.

Sensation raced up her arm, joining the thrills cascading over her from his lips.

He drew back a bare inch and said, "I've been wanting to do that for a very, very long time."

She sighed. He caught the sigh in his mouth when he bent to kiss her again. This time he gently ran the very tip of his tongue across her upper lip, and she somehow instinctively knew what to do. She opened her mouth. With a groan, he deepened the kiss, took it to another degree and slipped his arms around her.

Slipped backward, pulling her with him. When she stiffened—in surprise, not resistance—he cupped her head and slid his lips down her neck, then traced his tongue back up the side of it to her ear. She heard a muffled whimper of longing, and realized it was hers.

"Ellie. Oh, God, Ellie," he said with a groan she felt in her breast tips pressed against his chest.

He pulled her lips back to his, and the world receded. Hungry, hot, and claiming, he kissed her as though brand-

ing her. After only a second's shock—not at the kiss but
at the pleasure racing through her—Ellie greedily joined
the dance of his tongue in her mouth.

At her first touch, Shane growled his declaration of satisfaction and deep enjoyment. Not needing to hold her,
since there was no way their mouths would give up their
greedy joining, he ran his hands down her back and to her
hips.

Something long and hard—and pleasurable—sprang up
between them. Ellie's foggy mind told her it had been there
for several seconds, but when Shane snugged her hips
against it, the pleasure raced up her stomach and joined the
swelling longing in her breasts with a force that almost rang
in the air.

She didn't think she voiced the longing for him to see
what his touch felt like against her breasts, but maybe he
read her mind. The next thing she knew, all her sensations
pooled in her left breast, which had somehow escaped her
blouse and found its way inside a warm, tugging mouth.
But the clamor of a new, untried sensation beginning to
swell farther down, right below her belly, overpowered the
scandalously decadent uproar in her breast.

And scared the diddly-darn out of her. Scared her back
into her senses.

He didn't try to stop her when she scrambled off his
belly. Clasping her hands over her mouth, she backed away
from him, and abruptly came up against the dead limb.
Legs weak, she welcomed the seat.

The scalding sensation below her stomach lingered, and
she tightened her thigh muscles one time before realizing
what she was doing. The pleasure sharpened again, and she
released her muscles. Horrified at herself, she stared at
Shane.

He lay flat on his back, eyes closed and his right hand
flung out as though reaching for her—fingers curled as
though in longing. She firmly ordered her wayward eyes
not to look below his chest—and they disobeyed her just

as firmly. That part of him that had scared her was visibly outlined in his tight jeans. It throbbed one time against the material, as though sensing the touch of her eyes.

Ellie gasped and jumped to her feet. Wildly, she scanned the area for Cinder, finding the gelding grazing more than a hundred yards away. She tried to call him to her, but the whistle he always responded to clogged in her throat. Frantically, she kept trying, but all that came out was a faint, tiny sound.

"Ellie?"

She froze. Her wayward eyes disobeyed her once again. He was sitting up now, a look of deep concern on his face. Thank you Lord, his bent leg hid—the rest of him.

"Ellie, I'm very sorry that happened. It got out of hand way too quickly."

She cleared her throat—strenuously. "I understand."

And she did. Mr. Big Shot Moneybags was afraid she might think there was more to what they were doing than just a dalliance on his part with the poor little orphan girl. Well, she could put his mind at ease in that regard real fast. Succeeding in her attempt to whistle for Cinder this time, she rose to her feet.

"I'm really not hungry any longer, so I'm going to get back to work. I—"

Gosh darn his fast movements! He was on his feet and standing in front of her before Cinder got to the top of the creek bank.

"I'm the one who's to blame for spoiling our lunch, Ellie. I'll leave, and you enjoy yourself."

His stallion hadn't wandered nearly as far as Cinder, and it stood at the top of the bank. He reached down and grabbed his saddle and strode to it. Less than thirty seconds later, while Ellie chewed her lip and tried to keep from begging him to stay, he was on Blackjack's back. Tipping his hat at her—she hadn't even seen him put it on—he nudged the stallion and galloped away.

Ellie sank back onto the limb. She looked at the tablecloth, where the formerly delectable lunch still lay spread out. Now the cheeses looked unpalatable, the ham unappealing. She bent down and retrieved one of the apples, tossing it up the bank to Cinder. The gelding chomped it greedily.

Shane's lips had been greedy, too . . .

Snorting her disgust, Ellie grabbed the sack of cookies and the canteen. Maybe the staple foods didn't appeal to her, but sweets always succored distressed feelings. She ate one cookie in two bites, washing it down with tangy, sweet lemonade, and then reached for another one. She didn't stop until every cookie crumb was gone.

Eleven

Fatima gazed deep into the bowl of water, disgust at both humans in her care clenching her lips. Sweet Venus, what on earth was it going to take to show those two how perfect they were for each other? There sat Ellie, munching on those delicious cookies Fatima had made for her, tears running down her face. And there was Shane, on down the creek bank, wading in the cold water to cool his ardor. He could have cooled his ardor with Ellie, and they both would have enjoyed the interlude completely!

Fatima wasn't of the school that said a man and woman had to wait for a piece of paper before they shared the pleasures of their bodies with each other. At least, not if the two people truly loved each other. Despite Ellie's stupid preoccupation with being an orphan, and despite Shane's dumb priority setting that said he had to find out Ellie's true identity before he fell in love with her, they had both already fallen.

"But humans are so obtuse at times," she muttered. "They've got all these silly emotional stumbling blocks in the way of facing their real feelings."

Someone gasped, and Fatima stiffened. Uh-oh. She glared at Pandora for a second, stretched out there in front of the stove on a fluffy rug—a fluffy rug Fatima had conjured for her so her poor little padded body wouldn't suffer on the hard pine floor. The cat always warned her if a human was slipping up unnoticed and Fatima needed to shield her appearance. This time Pandora had shirked her duty.

Fatima erected the shield into place anyway. A second later, she turned and found Shane's valet in the kitchen doorway. Withers's face indicated in no uncertain terms that he had seen her in her true dress—at least from behind. And silly her, she hadn't realized until this minute that the mirror beside the dry sink reflected the front of her.

Nonetheless, Fatima attempted nonchalance. "Uh—hello. Can I do something for you, Withers?"

"Who are you, madam?" he said in that oh-so-proper English accent.

"You know who I am," she evaded. "I'm Fatima, the cook and housekeeper."

"No." Withers barely breathed the word, then continued, "You are the most ravishing beauty I have ever seen in my entire life."

"Oh!" Fatima simpered, batted her eyelashes and preened. "Oh, that's so nice of you to say that."

"It's bloody true," Withers insisted. He slowly walked toward her. "You're even beautiful the way you look now. Have you not noticed how drawn I am to you?"

"Drawn to me? Why . . . why, I can't say that I have. I've been so busy trying to get Shane and Ellie together, I haven't thought about myself."

"We may just have to do something about that then, my beautiful Fatima. I would truly like you to pay some very serious attention to yourself, my darling. And to me."

"Oh, Withers," she said with a heartfelt sigh. "You are so forceful and masculine."

He kissed her, and Fatima's shielded appearance and her defenses all crumbled to the floor.

Pandora smiled that cat's smile of satisfaction and licked a pink tongue across her upper lip. Then she yawned and settled down for a nap. Fatima wasn't the only matchmaker in this partnership.

Shane's boot sank in something gluey, and for the first time he noticed that the creek bed here was lined in red clay mud, not nice sand as in the spot where he and Ellie had planned to eat lunch—where he had planned on fostering his friendship with Ellie and finding out more about her possible identity.

Hell, friendship had been the furthest thing from his mind the moment he touched his lips to hers. And he hadn't lied to Ellie. That same moment he realized he had wanted to taste her since the first moment he saw her in that rather worn dress in the buggy at the circus.

Maybe it was the contradiction of her shabby mode of dress and his knowing there could be a fortune waiting for Ellie that interested him.

Sure! And he kissed her just because she was a handy female and he hadn't kissed one in a while.

Damn it to hell, he hadn't felt such passion even those nights with Anastasia, the willingest woman for sex he ever ran across. But, he honestly told himself as he tried to pull his boot free from the mud, a few minutes ago he learned the difference between sex and lovemaking.

Look at how his relationship with Anastasia fell apart after his body was scarred. How quickly Anastasia realized she didn't want to be between the sheets with a marred body. Sex was empty passion, something two people mistook for what it took to make a lifetime commitment when they didn't know any better. That's what he had with Anastasia. Sex—something that satisfied their bodies, but not the more important needs they didn't even realize they were entitled to—like companionship, admiration, respect.

Damn it! Like love!

Hell, that's why they called it lovemaking. He jerked on his boot, lost his balance and landed on his ass in the cold water. Instead of getting up, he bent his head and buried his face on his knees.

Lovemaking. That's what he would have had with Ellie if she hadn't came to her senses before he did. That's where they had been heading. The differences between how he had felt when he held Anastasia and how he felt with Ellie were nothing short of profound.

Ellie.

He could have companionship with Ellie. When they weren't sparring, they enjoyed each other's company. Hell, even when they sparred, *he* enjoyed it. In just this short time, she had made a huge impact on his life.

Admiration? Oh, yeah. He admired that little bit of a woman so much it was like a disease sometimes. He had never seen a female who could run a ranch and take care of so many people the way Ellie could. She didn't even realize how much her men, her sister, and her stepmother depended on her. She just went about taking care of them, expecting nothing in return.

Respect? It was tied in there with admiration. He respected her independence, her confidence in herself—which she didn't flaunt, at least as far as running the ranch went. Which maybe she didn't even realize she had. Maybe those other insecurities outweighed everything else. Wasn't that what happened to people at times? No matter how well they did in most facets of their life, the things they obsessed on were the negatives in their lives.

What had she said earlier that day on the range?

I'm just the orphan who was given a home with the Parkers.

Some faint sound made Shane lift his head, but his thoughts remained occupied with Ellie. Could it be? For the first time he found himself wanting desperately to prove that Ellie was indeed Cynthia. He had lost his objectivity about the matter, if he had ever had any.

Probably not, he admitted. He came to Texas . . . *Texas* . . . with his mind made up that he would find a woman with a similar background, but not Cynthia Spencer. That's why he had hidden his true reason for being here.

But most definitely, when Ellie found out he was here under false pretenses—not to look for investments but to prove or disprove her identity—she would hate his guts for deceiving her.

What the hell had he done?

The sound drew his attention again—a faint bawling he recognized as that of a young calf. Then a louder sound joined it, the moo of a much larger animal. He recognized the distress in the moo, a result of hearing both types of sounds this morning—contented moos from cows with calves by their side; frantic moos of separation when the cows searched for calves lost in a herd that milled and raced away at the approach of the ranch hands.

Shane rose to his feet and, with an effort, jerked his boot out of the sticky red mud. Waiting until he'd climbed out of the stream before replacing his boot, he grimaced at the sodden leather. Hell, he shouldn't have waded into the water with his boots on, but he hadn't even thought about that when he stopped here. All he wanted to do was soothe the ache in his groin before he ended up with a case of long-lasting, excruciating blue balls.

Stomping his feet, he jammed the right one down into place, then looked for Blackjack. The stallion stood near, ears perked as it listened to the sound of the cow, now bawling repeatedly and agitatedly downstream.

Gazing at the red clay soil, Shane figured out immediately what might have happened. Shorty had said earlier that his men checked this creek periodically when the calves were young, due to the chance the tiny calves might wander into the gluelike mud. The calf he heard was no doubt stuck, needing just such a rescue.

He didn't have a rope with him, but he remembered one hanging from Cinder's saddle. Besides, he could never keep that cow away from her calf while he rescued the baby without some help. Some of these beasts had awfully long, sharp horns.

Reluctantly, he climbed into his saddle, then urged Blackjack toward the distressed cow. He'd better find out how bad the situation was before he went for help.

Hooves thundered, and Shane glanced over his shoulder. Ellie rode toward him, and he pulled Blackjack to a stop.

She paused beside him. "I heard that cow bawling." She avoided his face, a hint of blush lingering on her cheeks. "Have you checked to see what's wrong?"

"I was on my way. But just in case it's a stuck calf, I'm glad you came along. I don't have a rope."

She nodded and settled her hat on her head, then kicked Cinder into a gallop. He followed, but not far. When they rounded a bend in the creek, Shane's theory proved true. The little calf was stuck in the mud, its head barely above the waterline. Its mother stood on the creek bank, bawling her distress.

"That's sure a small calf for this time of year," Shane observed.

"It's the old brindle," Ellie told him. "She always calves late. And she's vicious, so we need to be careful."

"We better figure out what we can do both carefully and quick. That calf's going to drown in about ten seconds."

They started forward, and the brindle swiveled toward them with a roaring bawl of confrontation. Lowering her head, she shook a pair of six-foot-long, sharp-tipped horns at them.

"Jesus," Shane muttered.

"While you're at it," Ellie said quietly, "ask Him and everyone else you can think of to help us out here."

She snapped her rope loose from the saddle horn and shook out a loop. Twirling it by her side, she walked Cinder toward the cow, murmuring soothing words.

"Come on, Brindle. Come on, you pretty thing. We're here to help your baby, not hurt it. Come on, girl."

Heart in his throat, Shane watched, afraid any move he

might make would be the wrong one—would result in the cow charging. At one point, the brindle did actually lower her head further, pawing one front foot on the ground. Cinder stopped, although Shane hadn't noticed Ellie pull on the reins. Probably the cow pony knew as much about what needed to be done as Ellie—and a lot more than Shane, who didn't usually find himself on the waiting-for-orders end of a situation.

Cinder moved a couple of cautious steps forward. The cow charged. Cinder nimbly swerved and pounded away, the cow after him.

"Get the calf!" Ellie shouted over her shoulder.

Shane urged Blackjack forward and slid from the saddle on the edge of the creek. Stumbling in, he grabbed the calf and pulled it free of the sucking mud a second after the first wave of water lapped over its head. Securing it in his arms, he turned toward shore.

And saw the brindle cow racing back toward him, snorting like a house on fire, horns swerving wickedly from side to side as she ran.

With a neigh of terror, Blackjack deserted him. Well, hell, the stablemaster had told him the stallion was a breeder, not a stock horse.

The cow thundered on, and Shane tried to decide whether to throw the calf at the bank and head for a tree or just close his eyes and wait. He prepared to toss the calf.

A lasso loop circled almost lazily, then dropped over the cow's horns. She slid to a stop on her ass, right on the edge of the creek. Glancing past the huge, sprawled, spotted body, Shane saw Cinder on his haunches, the rope stretched between him and the saddle horn, Ellie wildly waving her hat at him.

"A cow won't attack a man on horseback as quickly!" she yelled. "Put the calf down on the bank and get on your horse!"

Shane did. He scrambled out of the water, dropped the calf beside its mother—not too near—and raced after

Blackjack. Luckily the stallion hadn't gone far, and when he saw Shane, he ambled forward. Shane met him halfway, caught him and lunged into the saddle.

He looked back at the cow just as Ellie somehow flicked the rope off the animal's horns and she scrambled to her feet. Kicking Blackjack into a gallop, Shane raced away and gave the brindle privacy to clean her calf.

After a few seconds, Ellie joined his mad gallop, racing Cinder alongside. When Shane looked at her, he saw her swaying dangerously in her saddle. God, had she somehow gotten hurt?

He slowed Blackjack, but before the horse stopped completely, Shane realized why Ellie was swaying. Her laughter shook her so hard, she nearly tumbled out of the saddle!

Shane gritted his teeth. It wasn't one damned bit funny! That crazy cow could impale them both on her horns and go looking for other prey with barely a pause to clean the horns off!

"Stop that damned cackling!" he shouted at Ellie.

She straightened in the saddle, blue eyes dancing and sparkling with tears of laughter. She bit her lips for a second, then collapsed again. Nudging Cinder into a gallop, she left Shane and Blackjack behind in her dust, Cinder's hard pounding hooves failing to cover up the sound of the chortles carried back to Shane on the wind.

Twelve

When Cinder showed signs of tiring in the heat, Ellie slowed the gelding. For an entire five seconds, she firmly refused to look over her shoulder and see if Shane had kept up with her. In the sixth second, she saw him far back on the flat horizon, Blackjack ambling slowly along.

Nudging Cinder to a fast walk, which would cool the horse after its run, she headed on to the ranch. The rest of the fence check could wait until tomorrow, even if it was hours earlier than she normally went in. If anyone asked, she could blame her illness from the previous day. Not that Darlene or Elvina would ask, she reminded herself. They weren't even aware she had been ill.

In the barn she quickly unsaddled Cinder and gave him a cursory grooming, promising him a better one later that evening. It was too hot right now, she told herself, and he would be fine with a roll in the dirt in the corral.

Sure, and pigs fly. She wanted out of the barn in case the big black horse decided on a faster gait and carried its rider here before Ellie made her escape.

After turning Cinder into the corral—and not seeing Shane riding up yet—Ellie hurried to the house and through the empty kitchen. Crossing to the stairwell in the main part of the house, she noticed how clean and fresh everything smelled, much nicer than Birdie had kept it. To be honest, though, Birdie had never really given them any cause to complain about her abilities. It must be the comparison, Ellie guessed.

Shrugging, she went on up to her room, where she retrieved a clean set of clothing, her second-best dress again. With her clothing in her arms, she tried to get into the upstairs bathing room.

"Who is it?" Elvina's voice called.

"Oh," Ellie answered. "It's only me. I'll use the room downstairs."

"You may have to wait for more hot water, Ellie," Elvina called back. "I just finished filling the tub."

"All right."

Musing that Elvina hadn't even thought to ask why she was in off the range so early, Ellie turned and headed for the back stairwell, which led down into the kitchen. Her stepmother didn't give a diddly-darn how Ellie spent her days.

All the way down the rear stairwell, Ellie smelled something cooking. Surprised, since the room had been empty a few minutes ago, she emerged into the kitchen to find Withers and Fatima sitting at the table over cool glasses of lemonade. Fatima giggled girlishly at something Withers said, then looked up at her.

"Ellie! Ellie, dear, are you feeling all right? You're home early."

The concern in Fatima's voice filled Ellie's eyes with tears. Once in a while Darlene worried about her, but she was the only other person on earth who did that.

Even her parents hadn't wanted her.

Ellie sniffed back that thought before it took hold and dissolved her into a sobbing heap. Lordy, she was emotional today.

"We had a hard morning, and this afternoon one of the cows gave us quite a problem," she explained. "I decided to come in early."

Fatima stood. "Well, you go on into the bathing room

and have a nice, hot soak in the tub. While you're relaxing in there, I'll bring you a cold glass of lemonade and a couple of the fudge brownies I made.''

''Elvina just used all the hot water,'' Ellie said longingly. ''I'll have to relight the boiler and wait for more to heat.''

''Oh, the fuddle you will. Here.'' Fatima picked up her magic wand, which Ellie hadn't noticed lying on the table, and pointed it at the bathing room door. Gold sparkles flew from the end, and Ellie stared at Withers in horror.

''Fatima!'' she said. ''Withers—''

''Pooh. Withers knows who I am,'' Fatima told her, with a nonchalant wave at the valet. ''We've been having the most marvelous time getting to know one another better. I used magic to clean the house and do all the chores, then we had a nice walk. We were just talking about maybe going into town tonight after dinner to see what we can find to do. I read in the local paper that there's a little stage show going on.''

Closing her mouth, which was open so far in stunned amazement her jaws ached, Ellie looked from Fatima to Withers. Indeed, the valet merely sipped his lemonade and winked at Ellie when he caught her eye.

''In case you're wondering,'' Fatima said with a fond glance at him, ''he does see my true appearance. And it seems to please him.''

''Very much so, my dear,'' Withers said.

Fatima sighed with pleasure, then picked up her wand again and pointed it at the door. The door opened, a floral scent wafting into the kitchen from the bathing room.

''Go, Ellie,'' Fatima ordered. ''I've put some nice shampoos for your hair and lotions for your skin on the counter in there. Take your time and pamper yourself.''

Drawn by the wonderful scent, Ellie wandered into the bathing room. The scent was stronger here, of course, a wonderful mix that somehow reminded her of every Texas wildflower she had ever smelled. Bluebonnets and Indian paintbrushes. Black-eyed Susans and wild roses. Others she recognized, but her eyes found the array of bottles on the vanity top and rounded in wonder.

She examined them; took off their tops one by one and smelled them. Heavenly. There were creams for her face, and creams for her feet. Elbow cream and knee cream. Body cream. Oh! Breast cream. Oh, my!

Two more bottles sat by the tub. She bent down to check them. One was shampoo for her hair. One was actually a rinse for after the shampoo! Good lordy, did women elsewhere really use all this? No wonder some of the women she read about in the books she loved took hours and a maid's assistance to dress each day. Let alone how long it took them to prepare for an evening ball!

Fatima had conjured all this up with one wave of that magic wand out there. And here Ellie was, eyeing the decadent tub of floral-scented water and the various lotions as greedily as the chickens Cookie kept behind the bunkhouse eyed him when he came out with the meal scraps. Eyeing them as though they hadn't come from magic—or, worse, as though she believed that the woman out there could truly perform magic.

That Ellie herself wasn't slowly becoming totally unbalanced.

Not only was she falling straight into love with a man who was the absolute opposite of a man she could ever hope might love her with a forever kind of love in return, she was adding more assurances that the gap between them could never be bridged. If by some wild stretch of the imagination, Shane might overlook her being an orphan with no idea of her background, he could never accept a woman he might have to put in an asylum some day.

But right now, a tub of very real-looking, steaming water beckoned. Magic or not, she couldn't find the willpower to deny herself this pleasant interlude. She took off her clothing.

By the time she settled into the steaming water, not the least bit unpleasant on such a hot day, Fatima was tapping on the door. At Ellie's agreement for her to enter, Fatima carried in a tray holding a pitcher of lemonade, ice cubes clinking, and a plate of chocolate brownies, looking absolutely sinful with a full half-inch of chocolate frosting slathered on their tops. Moisture gathered in her mouth, and Ellie sighed in anticipation.

Fatima conjured up a little table beside the bathing tub and Ellie didn't even blink at that bit of magic. The fairy lady set the tray down, then turned and glared at Ellie's worn dress. Before Ellie could protest, Fatima tapped the dress with her wand, and a different dress appeared. Then new under things and a nice pair of soft leather walking shoes.

"Oh, you can't!" Ellie said. "Elvina will wonder where I got them."

"I thought of that, and it's not a fancy dress, Ellie. Look, it's just a blue-and-white checked gingham, which will look nice with your hair and eyes. Knowing how much attention Elvina pays to you, she won't even notice what you're wearing. If she does ask, just change the subject."

Ellie stared longingly at the gingham dress. Maybe it wasn't fancy, but it was every bit as nice as her one good dress for church. Nicer, even. It had been a long, long time since she'd had a new dress. Not since the old ones had grown too tight around her blossoming bosoms.

And Shane would be joining them for supper—

"Thank you, Fatima. By the way, what was that delicious smell on the stove?"

"My special beef stew. And I'll make some biscuits, and we'll have some nice fresh-sliced tomatoes. I made a chocolate cake, too, with chocolate frosting."

Ellie laid her head back on the tub. "How did you figure out that chocolate is my favorite? I hardly ever get any."

"I know lots about you, Ellie," Fatima said softly.

When Ellie turned her head toward the fairy woman, she saw only a closed door. Then she heard a well-recognized voice rumble in the kitchen. Shane had made it in off the range. She closed her eyes, recalling the moments by the creek when he had held and kissed her senseless. Remembering how she had kissed him back.

Remembering her fear when the brindle quit chasing her and whirled to race back to her calf. How her laughter after they were both safe was as much hysterical relief as the recollection of Shane's uncertain, panicky face as he watched the cow charge, holding the calf in his arms.

Smiling, she let the sound of his voice wash over her, fluttering her hands in the water to make some waves, which lapped over her breasts in accompaniment. The combination of the warm, scented water on her skin and his deep, sensual tones stirred the most luxurious feeling she had ever experienced.

"Ellie, I'd like to speak to you after dinner."

Elvina issued the order as a command, not a request. Ellie pushed another beef chunk to the far side of her plate, hoping Fatima would think she had eaten a little something. Somehow she choked down half a biscuit, washing it down her throat with swallows of cold milk.

"Ellie?"

Her head jerked up. "Yes, Elvina, I heard you. I'll wait for you in the study after dinner."

Satisfied, Elvina returned to her meal. She babbled now and then for the rest of the time about how wonderful the food was; how much better than Birdie's. Hadn't it been fortuitous rather than disastrous having Birdie quit right when Fatima was available and seeking employment?

Ellie murmured brief acknowledgments or denials at the appropriate points while her thoughts wandered down other paths. She and Elvina were alone at the huge, formal dining-room table, where Elvina always insisted on having the evening meal. Shane had gone into Fort Worth, escorting Darlene to see Rockford, since he claimed to have a meeting with Darlene's beau.

All the care Ellie had taken with her appearance was for

naught. Elvina, as Fatima had thought, didn't notice whether Ellie came to dinner properly dressed or with mud from the hog pen on her shoes.

A crash sounded in the kitchen, but Elvina didn't seem to notice. Picking up the tiny silver bell by her plate, she rang it, signalling for Fatima to bring in dessert.

Ellie pushed her chair back. "Excuse me. I don't feel like dessert this evening. I'll see you after a while."

Elvina nodded regally, dismissing her, just as Fatima came through the door from the kitchen. Ellie took one look at Fatima's angry face and frowned, but Elvina didn't pay any attention to the fairy woman's glower. Leaning back in her chair, Elvina merely waited for Fatima to remove the dinner plates and pour her cup full of coffee again, then set a piece of chocolate cake in front of her.

Not having a taste for finding out what Fatima's problem was, Ellie escaped to the study. She had at least a half hour before Elvina would appear; her stepmother lingered forever over dessert, whether or not she had company.

Elvina had been at the books again, although Ellie had no idea whether she understood anything. She hoped for once that Elvina did. Knowing of her stepmother's continuing examination, Ellie left a list of upcoming expenses and the funds available to pay them prior to the fall roundup inside the most current ledger. It showed barely enough money remaining from the working loan they took out at the beginning of every year to meet payroll and other expenses, such as the loan payments. In the second column on the page, Ellie listed the expenses that would go unpaid until after the roundup, such as the general-store bill. George had always made sure everyone got paid after roundup, and the various suppliers extended the same credit to Ellie.

She hoped she could continue to maintain their outstanding credit reputation. Another drought like last year would strap them, especially if the cattle prices fell again due to the poor quality of the beef raised on a water-starved range.

Elvina swept in, and Ellie reflexively got up and gave her the large chair behind the desk, standing beside her. Elvina sat and pulled the ledger closer.

"I know Mr. Morgan has told you that I asked him if he would be interested in buying the ranch, Ellie."

"Darlene," she murmured.

"Darlene?"

"Darlene told me," Ellie said. "So yes, I'm aware of why Shane is here."

"Well, I want you to know that whatever happens, I'll always make sure you are taken care of, Ellie. I took on a responsibility the day George brought you home, and I won't ever shirk it."

A responsibility, Ellie mused. Not another daughter to love. Nothing new there in Elvina's words.

"Now," Elvina continued, "I'd like you to show me what . . . what are they called? Oh, yes. What assets we have. You'll have to be the one to set the price for the ranch, since you're the only one I would trust to do something that important. You're so smart in that area."

Elvina sighed a sigh that Ellie had come to know well. "I surely wish you had grown into a great beauty like Darlene, but we'll have to accept that your brain is your better attribute. Maybe some day there will be a man who can appreciate that in you, dear. But if not, as I said, I'll ensure you are provided for."

Thirteen

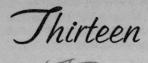

Ellie tossed and turned until well after midnight. Near that witching hour, Shane and Darlene rode into the ranch yard. Her sister surreptitiously slipped into Ellie's room on her way to bed, whispering heartfelt entreaties for Ellie to wake, but Ellie feigned sleep. Shoot, no, she wasn't going to listen to Darlene's excitement, while her own life crept toward the hole beneath one of the outdoor privies they had used before George put in indoor facilities.

She woke the next morning determined to pull herself out of the self-pity pit. And the only way to maintain her resolution to not let her unhappiness overshadow her life was to stay busy. She slid out of bed, dressed, and went through the main house instead of the kitchen, ignoring the tantalizing smells coming from Fatima's cooking. After taking the long way around to the barn, she saddled Cinder. She stopped by the bunkhouse, but only long enough to drink a cup of coffee and grab two of Cookie's biscuits to take with her. She ate on Cinder's back, riding out to check on the brindle's calf.

She escaped until noon, just after the men left to go to the line shack for lunch. Not hungry, she decided to check the fence around the poisoned water hole, although Shorty said he'd checked it the day before and found it fine.

Shane was waiting there.

"Hi!" he greeted, as friendly as before. As though he hadn't spent the evening with Darlene yesterday. "I was wondering when you'd get here."

Ellie leaned on her saddle horn instead of dismounting. "How did you know I'd be here?"

"Fatima told me," he said with a shrug. "I assumed you let her know what your plans were for the day. She sent out food, like she did yesterday."

Ellie clenched her jaws at the thought of Fatima using her magic to keep track of her, but then her mutinous stomach growled.

Shane heard the sound. No use to lie and say she had already eaten now.

The tablecloth already waited in the meager shade cast by a couple of tall mesquite bushes, food spread out temptingly. Ellie refused to look directly at it for nearly ten seconds by pretending to study the fence around the water hole. She finally realized there could be a ten-foot gap in the fence and she wouldn't see it.

Sighing in defeat, she dismounted and started to remove Cinder's saddle.

"Here, I'll get that," said Shane from right beside her.

"I can take care of my own danged horse," she growled through still clenched jaws.

A quick glance at Shane confirmed that a puzzled look crossed his face, but at least he stepped back and gave her some room. Tucking his fingers in his back pockets in that incredibly appealing stance, he waited for her to care for Cinder to her satisfaction.

She finally moved over to the tablecloth, but instead of sitting, she took bread and cheese and ate them on her feet. Shane realized her standoffishness, remaining where he was instead of joining her, steadily watching her. She poured lemonade from the canteen into a tin cup, drank, then picked up two apples and a fried pie. Sticking the pie in her shirt pocket, she bit into one of the apples and turned to see where Cinder had gotten to.

The gelding cropped grass almost exactly where she left him. She strolled over and fed him the other apple, then gave him the rest of hers. A few seconds later, she had her saddle cinched back in place and was mounted again.

Shane still stood in the same spot, the same position. Ellie swallowed bitter disappointment that he hadn't tried harder to talk to her.

Lordy, lordy, what was wrong with her? She made no bones about wanting him to keep his distance, and then grew irritated because he did!

Pulling her hat brim down over her forehead, she neck-reined Cinder in the opposite direction from where Shane stood. With an indifferent wave over her shoulder, the casualness of it taking every bit of effort she could dredge up, she nudged Cinder with her heels.

"Thanks for bringing out my lunch," she called as the gelding loped away. She smiled grimly, satisfied her tone of voice was the same as she would use to speak to one of her ranch hands—maybe even more dismissive.

Fatima met a similar cold shoulder from Ellie when the fairy woman confronted Ellie in the bathing room that evening. Ellie tuned her out, although she did take advantage of the lotions still sitting on the vanity. Wrapped in her dressing gown after her bath, she went through the kitchen and fixed herself a plate of food. Carrying it with her, she climbed the rear stairwell to her room.

She locked her door, something she never did, and when Darlene knocked later, Ellie claimed a headache. As soon as Darlene gave up, Ellie picked up the book on her stomach and tried to read again.

A second later, she caught her breath and pulled her bottom lip in to chew on it when she heard Darlene speaking, still in the hallway.

"She says she has a headache, Mother."

"She's had a lot of those lately, but then, let her sleep it off," Elvina's voice replied. "That's about all you can do for a headache. Have you seen my riding gloves? I can't find them in my drawer.''

"I think I noticed them down on the little table inside the front door.''

"Wonder why Fatima didn't pick them up and put them back where they belong?'' Elvina mused. "But let's don't say anything to her. For the most part, that woman is worth her weight in gold, especially her delicious meals. Just because she has one little lapse doesn't mean she needs chastisement.''

"Why do you need your gloves anyway, Mother? It's too late to go riding this evening.''

"Of course it is. But I'm going out in the morning with Mr. Morgan to look over the ranch.''

Ellie's heart dropped, and she nearly drew blood on her lip before the pain forced her to turn it loose.

"And,'' Elvina continued, "he feels we need to leave at the ungodly hour of eight A.M., so I have to have my things ready. I guess, given Ellie's headache, I'll tack a note on her door, informing her to be ready to accompany us tomorrow morning. If I let her get out of here earlier, we'll never find her all day.''

"Rockford's coming for lunch, remember.''

"I wouldn't forget that, my dear. We'll be back in plenty of time. How long can it take to show Mr. Morgan some grass and a bunch of cows?''

Turning over with a jerk, the book falling to the floor, Ellie grabbed a pillow and covered her head. She wasn't going to do it, that was all there was to it. She wasn't going to ride over the ranch with Elvina and Shane to point out all the attributes of the Leaning G, which would make it a profitable investment for Shane. Let Elvina get Shorty to accompany them!

At eight A.M., Ellie sat on Cinder in the ranch yard, waiting for Elvina and Shane. She had tried to avoid the breakfast Fatima prepared, grumping around in the barn and attempting to work up the courage to let Elvina think she hadn't seen the note fluttering on her door before sunrise that morning. But Elvina herself came out to the barn and called Ellie to breakfast at seven-thirty. She must want to sell the ranch desperately, Ellie had thought as she obeyed and trudged behind Elvina back to the house.

Ellie ignored Fatima's concerned look. And one from Withers, too, who helped Fatima serve a sumptuous breakfast of hotcakes, eggs, bacon, sausage, biscuits and gravy.

Just then, Shane led Blackjack and one of the gentler mares out of the barn and joined Ellie in front of the porch. As though on signal, Elvina came out of the house, thankfully making it unnecessary for Ellie to carry on any polite conversation with Shane while they waited. Shane bounded up the steps—darn, those jeans were scandalous—and extended Elvina his arm. Ellie could tangibly imagine what Elvina felt when she slipped her hand into the crook of Shane's elbow. Those muscles in his arm invaded her dreams over and over again every night—and in reality during the day.

She stared pointedly off into the distance while the two of them mounted.

"Ellie, dear," Elvina said from beside her. "Please get over this pouting attitude you have."

"I'm not pouting!" Ellie told her, a sulk in her voice.

"Of course you are," Elvina refuted. "You haven't been yourself for several days now. I do hope your headache isn't lingering on. If so, I guess we could ask Shorty—"

"No!" Shane interrupted.

Elvina's inquiring gaze settled on Shane's face. "I mean, Shorty's only the foreman," he said. "I really want Ellie with us this morning. She'll have a much more overall, broader view of things."

"As you wish, Mr. Morgan," Elvina agreed. "I promised you every cooperation while you consider your purchase of our ranch." She picked up the reins and nudged her horse, leading the way out of the ranch yard.

Elvina rode well, Ellie mused to have something besides the big horse and rider extremely close beside her to concentrate on. She always had ridden easily, the few times Ellie saw her on horseback instead of in a buggy. Ellie vaguely recalled the scant number of times she, Darlene, George, and Elvina had ridden out as a family, usually during bluebonnet season in the spring, before it became too hot to enjoy the days. Even then, as today, Elvina wore full, ankle-length skirts and a fitted-bodice riding outfit, with a bonnet perched on her head instead of the wide hats the cowboys preferred. To counteract the sun, she always carried a parasol.

Shane must not have been paying attention to his stallion, because suddenly his leg nudged Ellie's, their stirrups catching.

"Whoops," Shane said, pulling Blackjack immediately to a halt, as she did Cinder. He bent down to untangle the stirrups, taking an inordinately long time, at least in Ellie's opinion. Then the back of his hand brushed up her boot, not withdrawing until it encountered her bare skin beneath the hem of her riding skirt.

Ellie's eyes flew to his face.

"Whatever I've done to make you angry with me," he said in a low voice, "I humbly apologize. Please tell me what I can do to make you smile again."

Kiss me again, Ellie's heart cried. She had sense enough not to trust that her tongue wouldn't say the words, and she tore her gaze from his lips and kicked Cinder up beside Elvina's mare.

"What did you have in mind seeing first, Elvina?" she asked.

"Oh, whatever. My, it is a nice morning, isn't it? Remember when we used to take Sundays off and ride out with George? Pick bluebonnets and Indian paintbrushes?"

"I remember."

On those outings Ellie had almost felt like a true member of the family. George treated her that way, anyway, as did

Darlene as they got older. But in more than one of their sibling rivalries in their early, just-out-of-toddler stages, Darlene had yelled that Ellie was ''only 'dopted, not borned like I was!''

Only once had George overheard a squabble and followed Ellie into the barn, where she sobbed into a tiny colt's mane. He took her small shoulders and turned her to him, saying in a soft voice that the next time Darlene made that remark, Ellie should remind her that she had been chosen, not adopted.

Funny, though, her sister had been right behind George, sobbing out her sorrow at hurting Ellie's feelings.

''. . . at least, in my opinion,'' she became aware of Elvina saying. ''Don't you think that would be best, Ellie?''

''Ummmm . . . sorry, Elvina. My thoughts were wandering. What did you say?''

Elvina frowned at Ellie, then reached over and patted her arm. ''I know you are very unhappy at my considering selling the ranch, Ellie. But I'm afraid you're going to have to get used to the idea. Wouldn't you much rather spend your days not working so hard?''

Ellie knew better than to argue with her stepmother. Had Shane not been a witness to the confrontation, she might have tried, but she stilled her tongue. Shrugging, she stared around her to get her bearings.

''I guess we should start at the lower end of the ranch and head north,'' she said.

''That's what I just said,'' Elvina said in exasperation. ''So, shall we continue?''

Ellie led off, but given the dry soil, within moments Shane and Elvina both rode up beside her to keep from eating her dust. Assuming Shane was more interested in the property today than the workings of the ranch, as he had been when he rode out the other times with her and her men, she showed him the pastures and cross fences at the southern end, which they used for grazing in either summer or winter. Spring and fall, she explained as they headed northward, the cattle were slowly moved pasture by pasture closer to ungrazed areas of the main ranch. It made roundup easier for the men if they could ride back to their bunkhouse each night to eat and bathe, instead of camping on the range.

"When you read about roundups," Shane mused at one point, "you always think of chuck wagons and days on end camping on isolated ranges."

"Even Texas, as big as it is, is becoming civilized today," Ellie told him. "Back in the times you're thinking of, there weren't any fences to keep the cattle separated. Why, that's how Texas began to grow and recover after the Civil War. Most of our men went off to fight. And the men who did return found thousands and thousands of cattle roaming wild and unclaimed, since there weren't that many men left to take care of them. More than one well-off rancher today got his start by rounding up a herd of longhorns and driving it up to Kansas to sell. The market was strong, and one herd could bring enough money to start a ranch."

"Interesting," Shane said. "Still, it's a hard life."

"It's a good life," Ellie told him staunchly. "A satisfying one."

"Some people have different ideas of what makes a satisfying life," Elvina interrupted. "Look. Isn't that a creek up there? The one where we used to eat our lunch on Sundays?"

Ellie heaved a sigh of resignation. "Yes. We can cool off there. But be careful. The brindle's hanging around here still."

"One of the cows?" Elvina asked.

"One of the meanest cows I've ever seen in my life," Shane told Elvina with a mock shiver. "Did Ellie tell you what happened that day?"

When Elvina denied knowing, Shane launched into the story with plenty of flourishes and expansions of the tale, even stretching the height of his fright. By the time they got to the creek bed, the sandy part where they had nearly made love, Elvina was laughing in delight. He continued the tale as he helped Elvina dismount and turned to Ellie, but she was already on the ground.

Ellie turned her back to keep from Shane the wide smile threatening to split her face. That man could truly tell a tale, but she would be diddly-darned if she would let him see he had finally made her smile.

After Shane finished his story, Elvina bent down and delicately wet her handkerchief in the creek. She patted her neck and face just as delicately, staring around at the trees and rippling water.

"George and I used to come out here alone sometimes," she mused. "You children never knew that, did you?"

"No," Ellie said in astonishment.

"A long time ago. I hated those trips, but I never let him know that." Elvina shook her head slightly, then pulled her lady's watch from her skirt pocket. "Oh, my. I promised Darlene I'd be back in time for lunch with her and Rockford. I've barely got time to make it back to the house and bathe first."

Shane got to his feet from the limb he was sitting on, but Elvina waved a hand at him.

"No, no. I want you and Ellie to go ahead and finish touring the ranch. I—"

"We've already seen most of the north part," Ellie put in hastily. "When Shane was out with the men and me before."

"But not all of it." Elvina's look appraised Ellie in an enigmatic manner. "So please proceed, Ellie."

With a dismissive nod, Elvina moved to her mare. Shane went with her and helped her into the saddle, and she thanked him politely. For a long few seconds, she stared at Ellie with that contemplative look, then murmured a good-bye to both of them and turned her mare.

The silence, broken only by the mare's retreating hoof-beats, actually seemed heavy to Ellie. It weighed on her shoulders, pressing down so intensely she found it hard to breathe. She took an inordinate interest in a school of tiny minnows flashing around in the creek, waiting for Shane to make a move. But after the mare's hoofbeats faded, she heard only some grass tearing as Cinder and Blackjack grazed, and now and then the jingle of a bridle part.

From experience, she knew he moved very silently for such a huge man. More like a panther than the lion he reminded her of. But surely she would sense him if he came up behind her? Smell that masculine Shane smell of sandalwood soap and aftershave, mixed with the odors of a day on the ranch, such as a tang of sweat and saddle leather.

Perhaps he had gone up the bank to check on the horses.

Perhaps he had sat back down on the dead limb.

But she hadn't heard the distinctive creak the limb made when weight descended on it.

Shootfire darn! This was silly!

She turned—

Fourteen

—right into his chest, nose jammed into its broadness. She jerked back, and her boot slipped in the sand.

Shane grabbed her before she fell, murmuring an apology for startling her. To steady herself, Ellie had no choice but to accept his muscular arms, one of which Elvina had touched.

But she held on only long enough to steady herself. Sneaking out of his grasp—she noticed he didn't try to stop her—she scrambled up the creek bank.

"We better get going if we want to see the rest of the ranch," she said, heading for Cinder.

"Ellie."

If he had shouted angrily, she could have ignored him. But his soft, entreating voice stopped her dead in her tracks. Very slowly, she turned to face him.

His hat hung in his fingertips, hiding one blue-clad thigh, his tawny hair creased and damp with sweat. The cotton-wood leaves danced overhead in a sudden breeze, mottling his face with light and shadow, but his gold-dust eyes stared unflinchingly at her. The deep hurt in them cut her to the quick.

"I very humbly apologize to you for pawing you the other day," he said in a husky voice. "That's the only thing I can think of that I've done to turn you so staunchly against me. I'm sure it wasn't pleasant for you to be mauled by a disfigured man."

She gasped in shock, then her eyes narrowed. "What the diddly-darn . . . what the *hell* are you talking about?"

He shrugged and stuck his thumbs into his front pockets this time, the stance rounding his shoulders forward, as though he were ashamed. She hurried to him with no hesitation, not stopping until she was nearly jammed into his chest again.

"I asked you a question, Shane Morgan. Answer me!"

He shrugged again. "You know what I mean. Don't make me spell it out, because it's not easy for me to talk about."

"Why—why—you—you—!"

She took a breath and snorted it out at him as the old brindle cow had done two days before. Sticking her finger out like a schoolteacher's pointer, she poked him in the chest, once with each word she said.

"You . . . did . . . not . . . *maul* . . . me! I . . . cooperated . . . fully . . . with . . . that . . . mauling! If . . . anyone's . . . embarrassed . . . *I* . . . should . . . be!"

He plopped down onto the dead limb, his eyes now on a level with her face. "You? Why?"

"Why?" She waved her arms in the air in exasperation. "I crawled all over you like a mare in heat! I've never acted like that in my entire life. If what I was feeling hadn't scared the bejesus out of me, you might have found yourself saddled with a wife, Shane Morgan."

Shane flinched as though someone had shot him, and Ellie's eyes constricted to mere slits as something niggled at her mind. "Or was that the idea? Did you think you could only dally with me, and maybe keep me around to entertain you after you bought the ranch? Not as a legal wife, but as your mistress?"

"Never," he denied vehemently. "How can you even think such a—ah, hell."

He kissed her. With a quick movement, as before, he

bent his head and captured her lips. And as before, that was all it took to capture Ellie's entire body, her entire soul. She could no more have denied herself the pleasure of his kiss than run naked down the main street of Fort Worth.

She closed her eyes and leaned into the kiss, such relief and joy at finally having his lips on her again filling her that she couldn't decide which would win the dominance battle— relief or joy. Didn't care. The important thing was Shane's lips on hers in reality instead of in her dreams.

He lingered over her mouth, continuing to kiss her as he slowly reached out and cupped her hips, drawing her into that spot between his knees with absolutely no resistance or hesitation on her part. Her arms settled around his neck, fingers tangling in his hair.

Sensations cascaded over her, but Shane maintained uncompromising control this time. He slowly traced her lips with his tongue tip, but didn't push inside as before—as she longed for him to do—as her body clamored for him to do. He held her as though she were something very precious, something revered beyond worth.

Leaving her lips, he kissed a path to her ear, his breath spilling goose bumps in its path, and his whisper bringing tears to her eyes.

"I'm so very damned scared you're going to pull away from me again."

Somehow she controlled her desire for him to continue his caresses. Somehow she knew the next few moments held something a lot more important than physical pleasure. She pulled back far enough to see his face, and cupped one hand on his cheek.

"Why?" she asked quietly. "Can't you tell I want you holding me? Kissing me? Caressing me?"

He evaded her gaze, staring toward the creek.

"Who hurt you, Shane Morgan?" she asked with a wisdom far beyond her experience with men.

His gaze flew back to her. "Tell me who she was," she insisted. "And tell me why."

"It's not important any longer," he lied. "I've accepted it."

"Oh?" She raised a brow in inquiry. "So you *are* just dallying with me?" But her tone came out far from teasing. A serious tinge of hurt settled in it.

"No!" He tightened his arms around her, pulling her against his flat stomach, and against something that stirred at the contact. Shane groaned under his breath, but held her in place with an almost fragile grasp.

"Ellie, that's part of the problem. You're definitely not the sort of woman a man dallies with. You're a forever kind of woman, Ellie, and the man who winds up with you is going to find a treasure worth more than he can put a measure on."

"But not you?"

He shifted uncomfortably, shuttering his eyes for a moment. She took advantage of his inattention and balanced on her tiptoes to kiss him. Another groan rumbled in his chest, and he surrendered, pulling her tight. He greedily deepened the kiss and stroked her back. Her hips, her sides. Her breasts.

Ah, her breasts.

His thumbs stroked her nipples to rigid longing, and finally his mouth conceded to their need. Not taking time to disrobe her, he suckled through the blouse, and she cupped his head, whimpering an entreaty for him not to stop.

Her other hand found his belt, his shirttail. She pulled one side free and slipped her hand inside, running it up his side and finding a male counterpart to her own pleasure. Unable to contort herself enough to taste it, as she longed to do, she flicked her thumb across the much smaller nubbin. Startling her, it crinkled into a hard kernel.

Abandoning her breast, Shane's mouth renewed its quest of the soft skin on her neck, while his large hand settled over her small one on his breast.

"Ellie," he said around his groans of pleasure, "don't. You can't . . . Ellie, I—"

She twisted her head and found his lips again, stilling whatever protest he was trying to voice. For one scant second, she thought he would resist her, but her thigh encountered the near-to-bursting buttons on the front of his jeans. Instinctively, she nudged against it, and he filled her mouth with his gasp of pleasure and his thrusting tongue.

Her hand wandered around to his back and encountered ridges of hard, gnarled flesh instead of the smooth masculine flesh covering banded muscles on his chest. The moment Shane became aware of her fingers there, he froze.

His tongue withdrew, as did his lips. He straightened, reaching for both her hands and pulling them in front of his chest. She tilted her head to study his face, focusing on a tiny tic beside his mouth, jumping and twitching. With a grin, she caught him by surprise and licked the tic with her tongue tip.

Something told her being serious about what she had felt on his back would send him running for Blackjack. Leave her alone here with no more idea than she had before about the depths to this man—the feelings he buried deep inside that huge body, which contained plenty of space for buried feelings.

As inexperienced as she was, all at once she knew how to hold him here, almost as though something whispered it to her. When he frowned at her, she giggled and slid onto his thigh, settling herself and cocking her head at him until her braid slid over her shoulder. Eyes locked with his, she tossed her hat to the ground and reached for the yarn holding the braid at the end, untying it and tossing it fluttering into the creek.

Shane rewarded her unspoken speculation as to whether what she had in mind would succeed in keeping him with her. He licked his lips and unblinkingly watched her fingers unplait the braid. She took as long as she wanted, then ran fingers through her hair, which the shampoo Fatima supplied had made even silkier and heavier than normal. Tossing her head, she scattered the platinum locks around her shoulders.

''Well?'' she asked at last.

''Well, what?'' he growled in a dry voice.

''What happened to your back, of course.'' It wasn't a

question; it was a demand for information, and she tossed her head once more. This was rather nice, knowing she had such power over such a huge man. "If it bothers you for me to touch it while we're touching each other, I can avoid it. There's plenty of the rest of you to touch."

He closed his eyes to elude her perceptive gaze. She moved her leg. Still rigid and hard, as she knew he would be since her own pleasure lingered close to the surface, he appeared ready to explode with one new touch.

And that touch got his attention.

"Ellie—" But he bit off anything else.

So she stroked her leg against him like a cat seeking to be petted.

He groaned, and the object of her attention jumped against her leg.

"Ellie, you've got no idea what you're doing to me."

"I don't," she agreed. "But you yourself called me a woman a while ago. I guess I have the right to explore what that means."

Releasing her hands, he grabbed her leg when it made another tentative foray. When he glared at her, she reflected that perhaps she might be confronting an unmistakably wild lion this time, instead of the aged escapee from its cage the night they met. Sensing danger, she nonetheless welcomed it, because beneath everything lay the sure serenity that this man would never physically hurt her.

Maybe he might hurt her emotionally, she conceded. Worlds separated them, just like the tame lion and its free-roaming counterpart. But she was drawn to him with a fierce need, leaving no room for denial. It went well beyond the loneliness of her growing-up years. It went into her burgeoning desires to become her own woman, make her own life instead of existing on the fringes of someone else's family.

"You haven't even begun to explore, Ellie," Shane breathed at last. "There's a new world here that you have only touched the surface of."

His hand on her thigh moved, his fingers stroking and inching upward. Her mouth dropped in astonishment and her eyes rounded in wonder. But only for a moment. The lassitude accompanying the return of pleasure spread over her body and her eyes drooped lazily.

"No, you don't," Shane murmured. "Open up and look at me."

When she did, the sensation stunned her into near immobility. Between the fingers inching their way to the deep yearning between her legs and the depths of the longing and need in Shane's gold-dust eyes, she nearly exploded with pleasure. At least, that's what she thought was going to happen, and the fact that she didn't set her wiggling on his thigh.

Then his fingers reached their mark, and she found what she hadn't even known was missing. Found it with a vengeance, and never wanted to leave it. When she regained her senses, she lay over Shane's arm as weak and helpless as a newborn kitten.

"Like that?" he whispered.

"Lordy, is that what it's all about?" she forced out.

"Not completely," he told her, an evil grin that didn't scare her one iota on his face. "There's more."

"More?" Darn, she even sounded like a tiny kitten now, her voice meek and squeaky.

"Want me to show you?"

"Please."

He picked her up as though she were a leaf floating down the creek and carried her over to a shady, grass-covered spot on the bank. Laying her down as though she were a precious bundle, he settled beside her and kissed her. Immediately she fell into a world containing only the pleasure of their two bodies. Shane kept her upper body occupied with his caresses and tongue, while he somehow removed her clothing at the same time. When she was naked and writhing against him, she demanded he take off his clothing in turn. Demanded it in a hoarse whisper she didn't recognize at first as her own voice.

She never saw a man able to remove his boots so fast,

but he only unbuttoned his shirt and let it hang. Through passion-lazy eyes, she saw him reach for his jean buttons, and nimbly beat him to the mark.

"Ellie!" he growled in clear warning not to toy with him.

Which she ignored completely. Smirking, she slowly took her leisure with each individual button. By the time the last one was free—along with what they had hidden from her—her trepidation had her wondering if she had made a mistake. Surely the two of them would never fit together. It would be like trying to mate a pony and a draft horse.

Shane scooted his jeans down, then lay back beside her.

"You're so tiny," he said, voicing her fears. "But it will work. I promise you."

"Oh, I surely hope so," she breathed.

"God, it has to," he said in return.

He bent his head and settled warm lips on her breast, and once again crawled his fingers to that spot between her thighs. The twin sensations sent her into a whirlwind of writhing once again, and when she next was aware of anything except her own body, Shane poised over her. Nudged her where his fingers had been a second ago.

"Let me know if I hurt you, Ellie, my love."

An instinct as old as time wrapped Ellie's legs around his hips. Shane nudged harder, his constraint and control so well in place, a drop of sweat fell from his forehead and hit Ellie on her cheek. His effort heightened her need for him to possess her completely rather than slacking it with fear.

She wrapped her legs tight, and Shane groaned with a sound so filled with craving it sated her sense of femininity and dominion over this huge man. She barely noticed the pain of his final thrust. But she felt his possession inside of her, felt it and gloried in it and willingly participated in his complete ownership of her entire being.

"Are you all right?" he asked through gritted teeth.

She answered him with her body, and he showed his gratitude by sending her pleasure swirling with his retreat and advance back inside her. She peaked once, then clenched her legs so tight around him that he couldn't escape when he started thrusting faster. He rode with her this time, the sounds of their pleasure mixing and filling the world their bodies created for the two of them.

Fifteen

Shane rolled to his back and gripped Ellie's hand in his. His stentorian breathing calmed about the time Ellie comprehended how closely her own exhalations matched his.

Were his eyes closed, too?

She opened hers, but without moving—an effort she couldn't dredge up just then—she could only see high-up treetops and leaves against a brilliant blue, cotton-cloud-dotted sky. It would take far too much additional effort to turn and study Shane.

He turned, but not a bit of guilt at his generating that action when she couldn't invaded her. After all, he was much larger.

"Are you all right?" he asked.

Physically? She thought about it for a few seconds, mentally scanning her body. It lay collapsed with satiation around her mind, a testament to her femininity and Shane's masculinity.

Emotionally? Ah, emotionally. To be honest, she didn't want to deal with that right now. So many repercussions could result from the last hour or so.

"Physically or emotionally?" she responded.

"Both."

She focused on a trembling cottonwood leaf, spotted, dry and dusty in the heat. "Physically, I never knew or even imagined it could be so beautiful. Emotionally? Scared to death. I never knew it could be so beautiful. You?''

''The same, although I'd add that I've never felt better in my life.'' Shane traced her cheek with a tentative caress from his index finger. ''Are you sorry?''

Finding her energy slowly seeping back, she turned toward him, cupping her cheek on a palm.

''Physically or emotionally?'' she asked.

''Both,'' he repeated.

''Physically, no. I'm very, very glad I became a woman at your hands. Emotionally? That remains to be seen, I guess. I just crossed a lot of lines, which I've been told would make a girl into a fallen woman if she crossed over them without the benefit of marriage.''

''We could—''

She slammed her hand over his mouth. ''Don't you dare offer to marry me.'' Sitting up, she looked around for her blouse. She found it within retrieving distance, grabbed it and slipped it around her. Feeling a whole lot less exposed—physically and emotionally—she gazed at Shane again.

''I'm not blaming you for what happened, so don't start carrying that load of guilt on top of whatever else you have on your mind.''

''That's where you're wrong, Ellie.''

''No—''

He placed a finger on her lips. ''Yes, you are. You were a virgin, and you had no idea that what we were doing could send us over the edge that quickly.''

Wiping his finger away, she frowned at him. ''How many times have you practiced?''

''All of them were before you, so they don't matter,'' he replied, then chuckled wryly. ''For that matter, it's never happened that quickly with me, either. But . . . I knew what could happen. My only excuse is that I've never in my life wanted to make love to a woman as much as I wanted to make love to you just now. And I wanted it *because* it was you, Ellie. Not just because it was any woman, but because it was Ellie Parker I was holding. Ellie Parker I wanted to make love to so badly.''

She gazed at him solemnly, his words whirling in her mind. ''Still, we've . . . well, put the cart before the horse, I guess,'' she said with a sad smile. ''We've made love before we courted and got to know each other. I supposed I could use the excuse that you weren't going to be here that long. From what I do know about you, you'll be going back to New York as soon as you can complete your business here.''

Without answering, he brushed a long white curl of hair behind her shoulder with a tender caress, then lay back down beside her. He reached into his shirt pocket and pulled out cigarette makings, which he held negligently on his flat belly.

Wrapping her arms around her legs, Ellie propped her chin on her knees. His nonresponse—no, she admitted, his nondenial—cut her to the quick. Though what did she expect? She'd told him not to ask her to marry him, and that's about the only way she would have a future with Shane Morgan.

Shane Morgan, though, had no use for a poor orphan girl from Texas for a wife. Especially one who might be suffering preliminary derangement.

She had successfully avoided Fatima the last couple of days, but probably only because the fairy woman appeared to have her sights set on Withers and was busy with her own relationship. Ellie had a faint hope that, given the fact Withers also saw Fatima in her true state—evidently also watched her perform her magic and accepted it—perhaps maybe she wasn't really going crazy.

She didn't need that complication in her life.

She frowned. Of course, she only had Fatima's word that Withers could see her true state.

She fervently wished Fatima would leave.

Suddenly a grating noise drew her gaze. The noise was

a snore! Shane Morgan lay with his cheek pillowed on his arm, sound asleep. The cigarette makings scattered on his belly, and a gust of wind lifted the papers into the air like rectangular snowflakes.

Madder than a wet hen, Ellie scrambled to her feet. She slammed her hands on her hips and glared at him, realized her hips were naked, and glared some more. Whirling, she splashed into the creek water and flung handfuls of water over herself, including the soreness between her legs. Despite her noisy bath, Shane never moved.

If this was how men acted after making love, she would be diddly-darned if she ever gave him the chance again!

Splashing out of the water, she dressed and went after Cinder. Even the gelding's plodding hoofs when Ellie led him back to the creek bank to saddle him didn't wake Shane.

Before she mounted, Ellie walked over and stared down at him, her teeth gritted in frustration. A sunbeam filtered through the cottonwoods, and she glanced at the sky. The sun was moving on its downward path, and shortly the cottonwood shadows would crawl past the creek bed, leaving the bank on this side unprotected from the heat. Shane's body would burn in minutes.

Good, she told herself in satisfaction, noticing exactly where the sun would hit him first. Just then, he rolled over onto his stomach. Ellie gasped, and dropped Cinder's reins to move even closer when she saw that his shirt hem had caught on the far side of him, riding up to expose his back.

The livid scars and gnarled flesh looked too fresh to be very old. A sickly pink pucker against his untanned skin, they covered the right side of his back and shoulder, that hip, and the underside of his arm. Whatever had happened also scarred his right hand, because she had already seen those marks. But these were much worse. Variegated ridges with smooth, nearly shiny areas interspersing them covered him, all the more repulsive because of the healthy skin on the other side of his body.

Once she had gone into the blacksmith's shop on the outskirts of Fort Worth to ask him to fix a loose shoe on the horse she had ridden into town. The smithy, a freed black slave, normally wore his shirt, but this day he had it draped around his waist and didn't hear her approach. He had evidently been beaten as a young man, but twenty-five years after the war, he carried those whip marks, pale and gnarled against his ebony skin.

Shane's scars looked similar, though different enough to make Ellie wonder how they had come about. Some of the areas almost looked like the spot on Cookie's arm where he had inattentively spilled a pot of boiling water on himself one day.

Shane shifted in his sleep, and Ellie waited another few seconds to see if he would wake. When he didn't, she bent forward and tugged his shirt loose to cover him. Then she mounted and rode toward the Leaning G.

Lately she shirked her duties an awfully lot. Seemed like every day she found some excuse to ride in off the range well before the day's work should be over with.

Shane stabled Blackjack in near-darkness. He couldn't believe he had slept so long. Why the hell hadn't Ellie awakened him?

Or had it all been a dream? A wonderful, beautiful dream.

No, it had been real—absolutely as real as possible. As real as the vibrant, wonderful sprite in his arms. The vibrant, wonderful *woman* in his arms.

But had she fled in embarrassment over her first time at lovemaking and the loss of her virginity? He heard that women were like that the first time.

Or had she glimpsed his horror-filled body while he slept? He tossed and turned restlessly even in deep sleep since the accident, and he nearly always fell asleep after satiation. Especially a deep and satisfying satiation like the one he had experienced with Ellie.

Crossing the yard, he walked around the side of the house to enter through the kitchen, assuming he would find Fatima there. He had noticed the buggy missing in the barn, so Elvina and Darlene must be gone into Fort Worth for the evening again. He didn't know enough about their daily lives to figure out if this was normal for them or not, but it seemed like they did a lot of gadding about while Ellie ran things and kept a roof over their heads.

He was going to have a talk with Ellie about that—among other things.

Entering the kitchen, he found it dark and empty, also. Hell, where was everyone? Where was Withers, whom he usually found fawning over Fatima?

The valet and the elderly housekeeper seemed an unlikely match, but who could understand Englishmen like Withers? Still, that fact actually made the match more surprising—snooty, prim and proper Withers with a lowly housekeeper much older than himself.

"Withers!" His shout echoed emptily in the vastness. "Damn it, Withers—"

What was that? It sounded like a water splash. In the bathing room, off the kitchen. Moving toward the door, he caught a delicate scent on the air—a scent he had come to associate with Ellie.

Dear God, was she in there taking a bath? In a house empty except for the two of them? Naked—in the bathing tub? Water cascading over that delicate, rosy-pink, satin-soft skin? Droplets forming, which his tongue could lap off around her peaked breasts?

His erection made itself noticed, and he reached for the doorknob and turned it.

"Don't!" she shouted from within. "I forgot to lock the door!"

Oh, Jesus.

He didn't release the doorknob, but he leaned his head against the wall and quit twisting a hair before the final click disengaged the tumblers. He probably should pound his head against the wall and shake his brains up. Release the doorknob and get the hell out of there. But the effort was beyond him at the moment.

"Shane?" she called again. "Is that you?"

"Yes," he responded hoarsely, then realized she probably couldn't hear him. "Yes," he said more loudly. "We need to talk, Ellie."

"Not in here!" she shouted back. "Please. Go to the study and wait for me there."

He jiggled the doorknob. "Maybe I don't want to."

"Don't you dare come in here!"

Water splashed noisily, sounding as though it cascaded over the tub rim and soaked the floor.

Had Ellie climbed out of the tub? Leaped out of it, scared he might actually enter? Hell, he had more sense than that. Didn't he? She was probably still sore from this afternoon.

But was she standing there delectably naked, a waterfall sheeting down her breasts and legs? Hair swinging wildly as she searched for her towel to cover herself?

He jiggled the doorknob again. Something thumped against the door, and the lock inside clicked into place. He could almost hear her sigh of relief through the wooden door.

"I told you I'd talk to you in the study, Shane," she said more calmly. "I'll be there as soon as I dress."

Lifting his head, he smiled evilly at the door. "Do you think that flimsy lock could keep a man my size out of there if I really wanted in?"

For a long, bated moment, she didn't answer him. When she did, her voice squeaked. "Probably not," she admitted. "But please don't break the door down. I could never explain that to Elvina."

"You could unlock it and let me in yourself," he replied logically.

"No," she said around a breathless gasp. "No, I don't think I could do that. Not until we talk, anyway."

That much of a concession on her part satisfied him at

last. Nodding, though she couldn't see him, he turned away. "I'll be in the study," he called through the door.

He walked out of the kitchen and down the hallway, into the study, where he had already spent time talking to Elvina. Debating for a moment, he finally decided to leave the chair behind the desk for Ellie and took a seat in the larger rawhide-slung chair in front. Positioning it so he could see the door, he waited.

Need to see Ellie vied with his fear that she was now repulsed by him, as Anastasia had been. He had told himself all the way back to the ranch that Ellie wasn't Anastasia, that she had already felt his scars and still made love with him. That even if she had seen the full horror of his scars while he lay exposed in sleep, she would feel sympathy rather than revulsion—the Ellie he was getting to know, anyway, or thought he was.

The growing strength of his feelings for her nearly made him believe he could accept her sympathy, if that was all she had to give. But not quite.

Still, nothing refuted the fact that she had left him instead of waking him. Was it because he had been insufferably rude enough to fall asleep on her, right in the middle of their discussion? Because she wanted to be alone for a while to sort out what had happened in her own mind? Or because he had inadvertently exposed his horrible disfigurement to her?

Nothing she had felt in the scant time he had allowed her fingers on his back could possibly prepare her for the actual sight of his body. Nothing had prepared him the first time he escaped his mother's eagle eye and angled two mirrors to examine it.

And not even his debilitating weeks of pain or his near-miss with death's specter could make him accept what he'd found.

So why did he think Ellie could handle it?

He had to change his direction of thought. Nothing would resolve itself until he and Ellie talked. For one thing, he still hadn't decided what to do about the ranch. His being well able to afford to buy it and make it profitable again didn't overcome the fact that he hadn't really come here to look for investments, despite what he had said to Rockford.

He frowned. He had misled his friend, and he had a suspicion Rockford was putting way too much credence in their discussions about Shane possibly financing a branch of the Van Zandt business in New York. Not that it wouldn't likely be profitable in time, but like the ranch, it would need injections of funds at first. And it was possible, like the ranch, that the business expansion might fail.

But he had been too busy finding excuses to spend time with Ellie—to somehow uncover her true identity, he always assured himself before today—to correct the false impressions between himself and Rockford. Maybe tomorrow he should make it a point to do that.

Shane hadn't maintained the fortune his father left him by sinking more money in failing ventures. Once in a while he did invest in a faltering business, but he chose it carefully. Usually he only financed a loan, with plenty of collateral to repay himself if the business didn't prosper again.

Don't mess with Shane Morgan. You try any shit on Shane Morgan, he'll shit back on you double.

That philosophy, learned from his father, served him well. *Had* served him well, until now. Then he saw how a little slip of a woman gave her all to the people she cared about, even to the detriment of her own future. Saw more guts and determination, more energy and stamina in Ellie's small package than in most men.

Saw her as far more appealing than any other woman he had ever known or been attracted to.

He had no choice. He had thought about that, too, when he woke alone—and damn it, lonely, out on the creek bank. Thought about it all during his lonely ride back to the ranch.

If she got past his disfigurement and still cared for him,

he had to tell Ellie the truth and let her help him either prove or disprove her identity. Either way, it didn't matter to him. He intended to marry her, if she would have his disfigured body.

Damn it, over and above his loneliness when he woke up on the creek bank—a loneliness he had carried within himself ever since Anastasia broke their betrothal—he had realized he loved Ellie Parker. Loved her whether she was Ellie Parker or Cynthia Spencer.

His only reservation—a huge one, but then he had overcome mountainous problems before in his life—was her love for this uncultured state. Surely any woman on earth would choose the easy life he could offer her in New York over living a hard-riding, uncertain life on a ranch in Texas.

A little voice whispered there was another huge obstacle to building a relationship with Ellie Parker. The fact was, he had come into her life under false pretenses. If he had ever had any doubts about Ellie's integrity, the honest, sincere way she discussed their lovemaking on the creek bank with him had put those doubts to bed. She didn't have it in her to lie about anything, even anything as potentially embarrassing as discussing their lovemaking.

He could only imagine how wonderful life with a woman like Ellie Parker would be. No, not any woman, Ellie herself. So even if she could overlook his scars, could she overlook his deceit?

Footsteps sounded in the hallway. Heart in his throat, Shane rose to his feet. Within the next few minutes, his future would be decided, his loneliness possibly over.

Elvina entered the study, stifling a scream when she halted inside the door.

"Who's there?" she asked, making Shane realize he had been sitting there in the dark.

"It's only me, Elvina," he hastened to say. "Sorry, I was lost in thought and didn't realize the wall sconces weren't lit."

Elvina hurried around the room and lit the three sconces,

then settled in the chair behind the desk. "I hope you were thinking about purchasing the ranch," she said with a tight smile. "But please don't let me rush you. However, I talked with the newspaper editor this evening when I saw him at dinner in the hotel. I just wanted to find out how I could go about advertising the ranch, if you did decide not to buy it."

"That was probably a good idea," Shane said, noticing the thinning of Elvina's lips at his comment. "I can tell you that I'm close to making a decision, but I honestly don't know what it will be yet."

"That's fair enough," Elvina said with a sigh, leaning back in the chair. "Were you waiting in here to talk to me?"

"Actually, I had thought to discuss a couple things with Ellie. Have you seen her?"

"Why, yes. She was just coming out of the bathing room when Darlene and I took Rockford into the kitchen to see if Fatima would prepare us something to drink. I guess Fatima must already be in bed, though, and when I noticed the time, I shooed Rockford back to town and sent Ellie and Darlene on to bed."

Had he really been sitting there that long? Shane mused. Lost so deeply in thought he hadn't heard the buggy arrive or three people enter the house?

Yes, that could be. When his thoughts wandered to Ellie Parker, there was little room in his mind for anything else.

He turned toward the door. "I won't bother Ellie tonight, then," he said. "I'll see her in the morning."

Sixteen

As Ellie undressed, Fatima appeared in the corner of the bedroom. "My dear, you look as though you have had a wonderful day."

Ellie ignored her. Pandora languidly stole out from behind Fatima's legs and stood beside the bed, issuing a meow of demand.

"Oh pooh, Pandora. All right," Fatima said. She waved her wand and a rug of gold sparkles swept across the floor and beneath Pandora, lifting her onto the bed. The white Persian lay down and curled its tail around its nose.

"No wonder that cat is so overweight," Ellie grumped. "You never let her get any exercise."

"Pandora is perfectly healthy," Fatima denied. "Now, tell me how it feels to be a woman, Ellie. Tell me how it feels to be in love."

Ellie glared at her, half in astonishment and half in anger. "Were you out there watching us today?"

"No. No, of course not," Fatima assured her, calming Ellie's anger but not her astonishment that Fatima knew what she and Shane had done—knew they had made love.

"Then how do you know what happened?"

"It's written all over your face, Ellie, dear. Might I ask when the wedding will be?"

"It won't be." Ellie threw her dress over the bedpost

and pulled on her night rail. When she glanced at Fatima again, a tight set stretched the fairy woman's lips.

"Why not?" Fatima asked. "That's been my entire purpose here, you know. While I don't have the power to read the future, I am very adept at studying a situation—two situations, really. One a man happens to be in, and one a woman who will suit him exactly is in."

"You guessed wrong this time. Now, if you don't mind, I really would like to get to bed. And since you have obviously failed at your task, I assume you'll be leaving. Good-bye."

Ellie pulled back her comforter, snugging it beside Pandora but not making the cat move, and slid beneath her sheet. Grabbing a pillow, she turned her back on Fatima and settled her cheek. Hopefully, the fairy woman would take her seriously about the hint—no, the order—to leave. She didn't need the complication of worrying about her sanity tonight. Her lost virtue already gnawed at her mind, taking up quite enough space as it was.

She had actually been relieved when Elvina, Darlene, and Rockford arrived back from their dinner at the hotel as she exited the bathing room. She'd been perfectly willing to accede to Elvina's directive to go on to bed due to the late hour. She wasn't ready yet to talk to Shane. Had they continued the vein of their conversation on the creek bank, things might have been different. However, his abandoning her to sleep, as though she were a dalliance he was done with, wasn't easy to forgive.

Someone sniffed as though crying, and for a second, Ellie thought the darned cat had made the noise. Just as quickly, she realized Fatima hadn't left; she still stood over in the corner, beside the window, crying.

Sighing in surrender, she turned back over. "Fatima, you're not going to make me change my mind by crying. I—my word, what are you doing in my bedroom?"

Withers glared at her. Both he and Fatima sat on the

window seat in front of the open window, with Fatima's head buried on Withers's shoulder.

"I am comforting the woman I love," he told her in his prissy English tones. "You are very ungrateful, Ellie. All she has wanted to do since she came into your life is make things easier for you, and you are not being very bloody nice to her at all in return."

"How did you get in here?" Ellie demanded. "I didn't hear you come through the door."

"My love needed me and brought me here with her magic, of course."

Ohmigod. So Withers did know about Fatima's magic. A measure of relief flooded Ellie. Perhaps her sanity was intact after all.

But—that meant the fairy woman actually *could* perform magic!

"Why didn't she go to you instead of bringing you here?" Ellie demanded. "I don't want you in here."

"Perhaps she thought I might talk some sense into you, since I know Master Shane better than anyone else. But for the moment, I am utterly perturbed at you, and I don't know if I have the patience for that."

"I—I—"

"Fatima came here this evening to let you know how pleased she was with your blossoming relationship with Shane," Withers interrupted. "She meant to celebrate with you, but you treated her as though she were an unwelcome intrusion. No, you treated her like a bloody unwelcome dream."

"I—I—"

Fatima lifted her head. The moonlight flooding through the window illuminated her face, revealing tear tracks down her cheeks.

"N—now, Withers," Fatima said brokenly. "Ellie has had a very rough life so far. I guess we can't blame her for being leery of me. No one has ever offered to give her things before. She's always had to work so very hard for anything she got. It comes from her insecurity over being an orphan, you know.''

"My dear, you are so forgiving and so . . . so *giving*." Withers cupped her cheek, then kissed her nose.

Guilt over Fatima's true desire to do something nice for her and her own thoughtless actions filled Ellie.

"I—I—" Throwing back the sheet, she scrambled out of bed and hurried over to Fatima. She knelt in front of her. "I'm so sorry. I didn't realize how I was acting. I had . . . other things on my mind. Please forgive me."

"Why, Ellie dear, that's easy to do. Of course, I forgive you. And I'll help you plan your wedding."

Ellie bit her cheek, but she couldn't allow Fatima to carry on with this misconception. "There isn't going to be a wedding," she said quietly. "You're just going to have to accept that."

"Ohhhhh!" Fatima buried her face on Withers's shoulder again, and the valet glared at Ellie anew.

"Gosh darn it!" Ellie told the two of them, rising to her feet in a rush. "You can't just decide two people should fall in love and get married and have it happen!"

Fatima glanced at her. "I have before."

"You weren't trying to force me and Shane Morgan together before!"

"Are you telling me you aren't in love with Shane Morgan?"

"Of course I am—!" Ellie bit off her words, but it was too late. Too late to keep Fatima from realizing the truth, and too late to keep her own mind—her own heart—from learning it also. Her inherent honesty made her finish the admission.

"Of course I love him. But love and marriage don't necessarily always go together."

"They surely do," Fatima told her firmly. "Withers and I are only waiting until you and Shane are settled before we have our own ceremony. I have looked for a man like Withers for what seems like forever!"

"You and Withers are getting married?" Ellie asked in a shocked voice. "But . . . but . . . how can a fairy woman and a . . . a—"

"Mortal man," Fatima supplied. "It's not a regular occurrence, but it *is* done. There can be problems, but love overcomes them. Just like yours and Shane's love for each other will overcome any problems you have. Or *would* overcome them, if you would give your love even half a chance."

"The half a chance being marriage?"

Fatima nodded sternly.

Ellie wandered over and sat back down on the bed. As though sensing her distress, Pandora rose and ponderously climbed onto her lap. She stroked the cat's soft fur as she spoke.

"Yours and Withers's disparities aren't anywhere near as insurmountable as mine and Shane's," she said in a low voice, "even given the fact that Shane has never indicated that he loves me in return."

Settling herself beside Withers on the window seat as though she were in for a long debate, Fatima asked, "Can you name some of them?"

"Name what?"

"The insurmountable disparities."

"Those are things I should discuss with Shane, if we ever get to that point. But off the top of my head are our different backgrounds. Our different ideas of where we could be happy living. He hates Texas, you know."

"He—" Fatima stared at the door. "He's coming," she whispered. She lifted her wand, and with a flash, she and Withers disappeared.

"Whoops," Ellie heard off in the distance, and Pandora was gone from her lap.

She stared at the empty window seat for long, astounded moments. She would never—*could* never—get used to this magic business! Finally she became aware of the discreet tapping on her door.

"Ellie," Shane whispered loudly. "Ellie, please let me in. Please, Ellie."

She was incapable of ignoring his pleas, as remorseful as he sounded. Or was her longing to see him for the first time since this afternoon the undeniable fact?

Whatever. She rose to her feet and padded soundlessly over to the door.

"Ellie?"

She reached for the doorknob, hesitated, then firmly turned it. But she only opened it a small crack, barely enough to see his face.

"You can't get caught in my room," she said. "I'll come on down to the study."

Lips tightening, Shane curled his fingers around the door and pushed. Although gentle about it, he left her no doubt he was coming in—with or without her permission.

She should have left the door shut and talked through it. Sighing, she stepped back and padded over to the window seat. No way would she sit on that bed with Shane's incontrovertible presence in her room.

But he did. He closed the door quietly, crossed the room and sat down on the mattress. His gaze steadied unwaveringly on her.

"You first, Ellie."

She shook her head. "You're the one who sought me out to talk. What do you want to talk about?"

"What don't we need to talk about is more like it," he said in a musing voice. "It might take us the rest of our lives to discuss all of it."

"If you are insinuating again that you will marry me because you feel guilty about what happened this afternoon, I'll tell you once more to forget it."

"What if that's *not* what I mean?" he asked quietly. "What if the reason I'm talking—trying to talk marriage to you is for a completely different reason?"

She stared at him across the room, hope mixing with self-doubt in her mind. Her hands clenched in her lap, both to still their restless nervousness and to keep her from holding them out to Shane. A long, tense silence settled between them while Ellie struggled to make sense of the turbulent emotions teeming in her thoughts.

It soon became clear Shane would say nothing more; that the next step was hers. Unable to maintain eye contact with him, she turned her head slightly to look out the window.

Her room was in the rear of the house, overlooking the endless vista of rangeland stretching toward the invisible horizon. Silver-blue moonlight scattered across the fence railings and sagebrush, hinting at sparkles where night dew had settled. The pleasantly pungent odor of the sagebrush reached her, the very scent reminding her of Texas.

She had lived every bit of life she could recall here on this ranch. Nearly every person she knew lived in this state. Yet so many times she yearned to see other vistas, other cities, even other countries. She always wanted the ranch to be there for her to return to, however.

Pulling in her bottom lip, she chewed on it in contemplation, then cleared her throat.

"Have you made up your mind about the ranch?" she asked, still gazing out the window.

"No."

He didn't elaborate, and Ellie thought he could have at least asked her what that had to do with the two of them. She thought of Cinder. Her gelding would never be happy anywhere else. Hadn't she read that the only place to exercise a horse in New York City was on the bridle paths in the parks? Heavens, they probably only had ducks there for a cow pony of Cinder's ability to herd.

Should Shane decide to buy the ranch; should she decide to marry him—although he hadn't yet come right out and asked that exact question—what then? He would need someone to run the ranch, but as his wife, she definitely wouldn't be that person. Someone else would ride her ranges, her horses, order her men about.

No, not hers, she reminded herself. Elvina's, and then Shane's.

The mattress creaked and she twisted around to see Shane standing, striding for the door. Her mouth opened to call to him, then clamped shut in pique. Silently, though still wearing his boots, he went out the door and closed it behind him.

What on earth was that all about?

But she knew. He was tired of sitting there like a bump on a log and waiting for her to speak. She had pushed him too far with her silence.

She slid off the window seat and flew across the floor. Hesitating for only a second, she turned the knob and pulled the door free far enough to peek out. Shane was already down at the end of the hallway, opening his bedroom door. He paused for a few seconds halfway through the door, and she got ready to ease her door closed if he turned and looked her way.

But he didn't.

He went on in, and she heard the faint click when the door closed behind him.

Well, she liked that! Shoving her own door shut, she flapped her hands out and strode across the bedroom, halted at the window, turned and glared at her door. What the diddly-darn did he mean by that? He came in here demanding they talk, sat down and refused to say anything, then left without another word before she gathered her own thoughts.

Didn't he realize how important this conversation between them could be?

No. He had said one word after he sat down. *No*.

He hadn't even attempted to carry on his share of whatever conversation he came to her room to foster. It was just like this afternoon. Then he fell asleep. Now, he deserted her!

The heck with him. She stomped across the floor and got

into bed. Flounced to her side and yanked the sheet up over her.

Tomorrow she would talk to Fatima and see if she could take advantage of some of that magic she kept offering her. Persuade the fairy woman to lend her some funds and send her somewhere else. She didn't need much; just enough to keep her going until she found a job. Something like the bookkeeping job the storekeeper had offered her, but somewhere far away from Fort Worth. Maybe out around El Paso.

Uncomfortable, she flounced to her other side and yanked the sheet over her.

She had to have a little bit of a stake. She handled all the ranch funds, but didn't have any money of her own. Not enough to travel that far away and live until she found a job—got a paycheck.

Shoot, this position was uncomfortable, also. She flounced to her back and tried to yank the sheet up. It tangled around her legs, and when she tried to kick her feet to loosen it, it wrapped tighter. She squirmed for several seconds until she finally got loose, nearly falling out of bed by the time she had everything unwound, including the night rail that helped the sheet imprison her legs.

In fact, she was so close to the edge of the mattress, she did start to slide off. Twisting, she managed to land on her feet.

Well, she liked that. And she'd had about enough of this entire situation, furthered by the huge silent man who kept her in such a turmoil!

She stormed over to the wardrobe in the corner and grabbed her robe. Tossing it around her shoulders, she spat a near-curse when her furiously trembling hands tangled it, too, and she couldn't find the armholes.

The heck with it!

She tossed the robe on the floor and, not taking time to find her slippers, headed for the door.

Seventeen

~

Damn it, where was Withers when he needed someone to talk to? Yanking off his shirt, Shane chucked it in a corner. He fell onto the bed and pulled off his boots, almost taking his feet with them. Both boots landed on the shirt, clunking against the wall, muffled on the carpet when they fell.

Nearly tearing the buttons from those damned blue jeans these Westerners wore, which remained stiff and uncomfortable even after he sent them to the Chinese laundry in town, he stood and shimmied them down his legs, then kicked them toward the rest of the clothing.

Let Withers pick them up; he paid him enough to do that!

His nightshirt lay across the pillows, the bed turned down, a neat triangle of snowy sheets showing and the comforter folded trimly. Jerking the top coverings off, he balled the comforter and sent it to join the shirt and boots. Then he tossed the sheet back onto the bed, smiling in grim satisfaction at the untidy mess.

It was too damned hot in Texas for covers! Hell, he could barely stand a sheet over him at night in the New York City summers, let alone during these humid, sweltering breaks in the endless, hot days this dastardly country called nights.

He looked at the nightshirt and deigned donning it, too,

as usual. Wondered briefly if Withers ever bothered to try to figure out why none of his nightshirts ever needed to be replaced.

Hell, who cared.

He sat on the bed again, bent his head and ran his fingers through his hair. Clutched his head and shook it from side to side.

Who the hell cared about nightshirts? Who the hell cared what Withers thought? Those thoughts were only an attempted distraction from the real reason his body heat was up. Damn it, he had perched there looking at Ellie like a schoolboy from the wrong side of the tracks yearning for the belle of the class and knowing there wasn't the remotest possibility of winning her.

She looked like an ethereal dream there in the window, silver moonlight outlining her, the color matching the tumbles of platinum hair cascading down her back and over her shoulders, dancing across the vibrant platinum tresses and curls with her movements. So tiny, yet so full of everything a man could possibly want in a woman. And he wanted her, no doubt about that. He had left the room before his scant control deserted him, as it had that afternoon.

Left with the heat roiling in his veins.

Left before he lost it and grabbed her as he had that afternoon. Let his guard down, and let Ellie at last see the horrible monster he was now; let her realize she, like Anastasia, could never make love with someone like him after seeing the disfigurement without encumbrance.

He cringed inside.

Admit it, Morgan, he told himself. *You thought she might be different—hoped desperately she* was *different.*

But after he got back to the ranch, he gave her three different chances to prove him wrong. She made no bones about not wanting to talk to him in the bathing room. He sloughed that off, because . . . well, because he had no business barging in on her there anyway. If he had, they wouldn't have talked. He would have tried to make love to her again, if he'd been given half a chance.

But she reneged on her promise to come see him in the study, also. Went to her room on the flimsy excuse that "Elvina had told her to do so."

He followed her to her room, took a chance on someone catching them together. And she held him at an across-the-room distance, not wanting him any closer. Not even wanting to discuss things with him.

Pity. She probably felt pity for him now that she knew exactly how marred he was, and didn't quite know how to tell him what she was experiencing. Sure, she was too tenderhearted to actually put it into words, but nevertheless never wanted him near her again, never wanted his hands on her soft skin or his lips on hers.

Despite what he had thought earlier, he found he couldn't bear her pity. He couldn't talk about that. When the faint hope that maybe she could actually bring herself to talk to him now that she knew how hideous he looked faded, he left.

He rose and walked over to the mirror. By standing sideways and craning his neck, he could see most of the damage to his back. He hadn't looked at it since that first surreptitious examination his mother had caught him at well over a year ago.

He recalled her soft gasp, then the look of love and admiration on Mariana's face as she stood in the doorway of his room. She knew he needed to see this. But she wrung her hands in front of her waist, the unconscious gesture confirming her deep worry and dread of his reaction.

I would give anything if it were me instead of you standing there, my son, he remembered her saying.

The loathsome disfigurement hadn't changed much. There weren't the seeping sores and black, charred skin still needing to peel off. But the scars and ridges, pockmarks, and shiny, distasteful-looking areas were just as repulsive.

The door flew open, and Ellie barely caught it before it

banged against the wall. Startled, he watched her in the mirror. There was no time to cover himself, to pretend he had been at the mirror for something other than a grossly riveting examination of his disfigured body. He tensed, ready to throw her little rear end out of here if she made one wrong move—said one wrong word.

"How dare you?" she hissed quietly.

She obviously didn't want to wake anyone and be caught in here any more than he had wanted to announce his presence in her room. To emphasize her words, she slammed her tiny hands on her hips, outlining them beneath the worn-thin night rail and pulling it tight across her well-formed breasts. Shane gulped and his eyes searched the room for his own night covering.

"How dare you?" she repeated, closing the door firmly but quietly, then stalking across the room. Shane backed toward the other side of the bed, but she rounded it with him, keeping between him and reach of the sheet.

Why the hell didn't she say something about his back? She damned sure had seen it, even in the dim light. The moon shone fully through the window, and he had the curtains pulled completely back to take advantage of any scant night breeze in this damned state.

"Are you always like that?" she demanded. "When you want to have a serious conversation, do you either fall asleep or sit there like a bump on a log and wait for someone else to carry the load? Say something! Say something now, or I swear I'm going to scream out my frustration and not care if the entire house hears me!"

"I need to put something on," he answered.

Head swinging wildly, his gaze searched the bed, but he couldn't make out his nightshirt from the tangled, crumpled sheet. He sidled past her and reached for the sheet to shake it out, but Ellie beat him to it.

Swiftly, she grabbed it, slid it loose with a snap, then raced to the window and tossed it out. Shane's mouth dropped, and she turned back to him, a defiant look on her face.

"What happened to your back? I demand you at least tell me that much."

An outraged figure, she reminded Shane of one of the cocky bandy roosters on the estate a friend had outside the city. For a brief second, he almost laughed, but some mental warning saved his hide. He cautiously sat on the bed, his eyes never leaving Ellie in case she went into another flurry of movement. Hopefully, no one would find the sheet before he could retrieve it, but if they did, that would take less explanation than if the comforter and maybe even his shirt and boots joined it.

"I don't like to talk about what happened," he said. Warily, he pulled a pillow across his lap. She dropped her eyes, her curled lip indicating she hadn't missed the movement or the reason for it, but she let him get by with that much.

"You don't like to talk about a lot of things!" she fairly snarled. "Well, I'm tired of *not talking* with you. I have never in my life been this angry. Never in my life even realized I could *get* this angry! I've always had to be Miss Nicey-Nice, satisfied with the leftover crumbs, and then sometimes not even that much."

"You shouldn't have to—"

"Shut up! I'm not done!"

He swallowed another laugh, along with the words telling her he thought she wanted him to talk. Laughing might be more disastrous to him than what had happened on the steamboat. God, she was in a fine fettle. He'd never seen her look so adorable, so . . . desirable.

She paced back and forth in front of the window, flinging her hands out as she spoke and unaware that the moonlight shone through her worn-out night rail with barely any obstruction.

"I understand that things change over time," she berated. "They can't always stay the same—stay the way we want them to. The way we're happy with them. But if things are going to change, I want time to prepare myself for them.''

Shane stared at her in puzzlement. How did they get from the story of his back to this track of reasoning? What was she talking about now?

She stopped in front of the window, blue eyes blazing brighter than starlight and delectable lips pursed in determination. ''So tell me what I want to know. Right now!''

He shook his head and cautiously opened his mouth. Did she really want him to say something now?

''Well?'' she demanded.

Hmmmm. He guessed she did. But he wasn't sure exactly which question she wanted answered. Or even what the question was.

''Ohhhhh!'' She threw her hands in the air. ''There you go again! Mr. Strong and Silent!''

She started around the side of the bed as though leaving, but Shane sprang to his feet and blocked her way. Startled, she gasped and backed up quickly toward the window. He nearly laughed again when he saw the wary look on her face, but he only held out a palm in a pleading gesture. One palm, since he kept the pillow in place with the other hand.

''I'm just trying to figure out if you want to hear what happened to my back or what I've decided about the ranch, Ellie. That's all my hesitation meant.''

''Both, of course,'' she said as if he were as dense as a rock. ''Isn't that what we've been talking about? Or at least, *I've* been talking, while you sit there like Mr. Stone on a Log!''

''Poor analogy,'' Shane said inanely. ''Logs don't usually have stones on them.''

Ellie took a deep breath, which scared Shane more than if she'd lost it and started screaming hysterically at him. Through gritted teeth and a deadly calm voice, which sounded entirely out of place in such a tiny woman, she said, "Start with your back. Now."

"I was burned in a steamboat explosion."

"Where?"

"On my back," he said, confused.

"Gosh darn it! *Where* did it happen?"

"Oh. On the Mississippi River."

"Where?"

"Uh . . . down near St. Louis?"

"If you don't tell me the entire story without my having to pull it out of you like pulling hen's teeth, I'm—"

"Hens don't have teeth, do they?"

"Gosh darn it!" She balled her small hands into even smaller fists and shook them at him. "That's the point, you prim and proper Yankee! Hens *don't* have teeth!"

Shane shook his head, but decided he'd better cooperate here, if he could only figure out exactly what she wanted him to say. He had never talked about the steamboat accident fully with anyone, not since the night he'd tried to prepare Anastasia for the damage to his body. His fiancée's impatience let him know she was more interested in the resulting damage than the way it happened, so there wasn't much discussion about the "how" end of it.

Would it have made any difference with Anastasia? Probably not. Probably not with Ellie, either, but she didn't look like she was going to leave this room until he told her all of it.

Eighteen

"It's one of those things that happens," Shane began quietly, but determinedly. "One you read about, but never think will ever happen to you. We were north of St. Louis, heading for New Orleans, when we breasted another steamship, which was also heading south on the river. The *Lady Rosalyn* was the one we overtook, and our boat was the *Lady Eve*. The captain bragged about how *Eve* was the First Lady of the River, as well as being named after the first lady on earth. Said she'd never been beaten in a race."

"The other boat challenged him?" Ellie asked. "I've read about those races."

Memories strengthened and clamored for escape at the confines of his mind, and Shane shivered despite the heat.

Smells: smoke and charred flesh.

Screams. Oh God, the screams.

He took rigid hold of himself, hoping Ellie hadn't noticed.

"The thing is, the races had been outlawed for years. The steamboats were used at first mostly for cargo, then as settlements opened up along the river, they carried more and more passengers. The *Lady Eve* was strictly a passenger boat, with high-stakes gambling games going on all the time for the male passengers. I don't gamble that much, but there'd been a few problems with our businesses, and I was pretty grouchy and jumpy by the time I got everything straightened out. My mother insisted I take some time off and relax.''

He dropped his head to his chest. Mariana Morgan had blamed herself, lamenting the day she bought him a ticket on the boat and sent him off to his fate. No matter how many times he told her she couldn't have known, wasn't at fault, she worried the blame to death, wore it like a hair shirt.

Ellie took a step toward him, and his head flew up.

"No. Let me finish."

"All right," she said softly, no acrimony left in her voice.

"You're right, the *Lady Rosalyn* challenged the *Lady Eve*. The passengers on the other boat were screaming taunts and making rude gestures at us. I had taken a break from gambling, because I was losing my shirt, and was on deck. I could afford the loss, of course, but the shyster who was winning was a professional. I knew he was cheating, but couldn't catch him at it. I figured I'd go back later and join a different game. Before I could do that, I heard the boilers below deck hissing steam and felt the surge of power when the captain decided to accept the race challenge."

He drew in a breath. "We didn't get very far. I guess the passengers who weren't already on deck, probably at least half the boat, realized something was going on. Afterward, we found out a lot of them were on the stairwells and halls when the first boiler blew."

"My God," Ellie breathed.

"It was hell. The force of the blast flung me into the water, and I helped whoever I could get to shore. I shoved them onto loose timbers or buoys; grabbed one woman who was unconscious and swam to shore with her."

"But . . . but you were hurt."

"Not then," he denied.

"You went back?" she asked in horrified amazement.

"The woman regained consciousness when we got to shore. She started screaming about her daughter. That she was still on the boat. When we looked back, the little girl was at the railing near the prow of the steamboat—where the fire hadn't reached yet. Frantic, the mother went into the water, but she couldn't swim. She tried to find a log or something to float her back out there, but I pulled her to shore again."

He gazed at Ellie. "The little girl was barely three years old. Blond and a pretty little thing. She had her whole life ahead of her. She was standing there with her little arms stretched toward us. She could see her mother, and she was screaming 'Mommie! Mommie!' "

"Oh, Shane."

"I thought I had time to get to her before the fire did. Even if I didn't, I couldn't stand there and let her burn to death right in front of our eyes. The worst part was getting up the side of the boat, but some of the crew had thrown rope ladders over the sides to escape themselves, plus the boat was already foundering, so the climb wasn't that far. I had her in my arms when the second boiler blew. The entire ship went up in steam and flames, but they told me later that I managed to hold onto her when the force of the blast blew me into the water for the second time."

He gave a harsh sound. "The blast itself blew us nearly to shore, close enough for people to wade out and get us. I had her in front of me, so she was protected, but it was days before I regained consciousness. Evidently, the doctor thought it better to keep me out of it until the worst of the pain was over." He sighed, and continued in a musing voice, "If what I still ended up experiencing was less pain, I'm glad I didn't go through the first few days in a conscious state."

Ellie pulled herself up to her full height—not much, but her expression made her seem taller—and settled her palms on her hips again.

"I can't believe you're ashamed of those scars after the

way they happened! You were a hero, Shane Morgan. You saved several people, and you gave a little girl a chance to live her life. How dare you be ashamed of yourself!''

"You aren't the one who saw the woman you thought loved you turn away from you in revulsion," he said in a deadly quiet voice. "Leave you and send your betrothal ring back by messenger less than an hour later.''

Ellie froze. Drawing her lip in, she chewed it for a few seconds, continuing to scrutinize him. What was going on in that pretty head of hers now?

"So—" She bit off her words and shook her head, white curls shimmering in the moonlight and a look he nearly thought might be jealousy on her face. Of course it wasn't.

"Did you love her deeply?"

He quirked an eyebrow. "Love? Honestly, now that I look back on it—no." He tilted his head in concentration. "No, I truly *thought* I loved her. Thought she loved me. Our . . . relationship lasted for over two years.''

"Oh," she murmured.

"Thought so until this afternoon.''

Her eyes flew back to his. "What do you mean?"

"This afternoon I found out what lovemaking really meant. Found the meaning, and lost it, all within the space of a few hours.''

She gazed quietly at him for such a long time, while curls of dread coiled in his stomach. What was going on behind those pretty blue eyes, inside that beautiful head? Was she getting ready to bolt on him again? Admit to him that yes, she had begun to care for him, but now she couldn't overcome her revulsion at his body?

"Why do you think you've lost it?" she asked into the stretching silence.

Hope infiltrated the dread in his belly, but he refused to leave himself open to another bout of humiliation today. Still, "Haven't I?" somehow found its way past his clogged throat.

"I asked you why, Shane. Because I saw your scars, and now you think I'm repulsed by them?"

"Aren't you?"

"Damn it, Shane Morgan! You're making me curse again! I pulled your shirt loose to cover you because I didn't want you to get sunburned, not because I wanted to hide your scars from my eyes. I left because you fell asleep on me and it annoyed me, not because I was repulsed. If you wouldn't go so silent and deep on me, if you'd ask me why I did something rather than read erroneous things into my actions, maybe we'd be able to sort things out!"

He went silent and deep, although he tried to shout out his feelings. Hope crawled past the dread, however, and clogged his throat effectively this time. All he could manage was to hold out a hand—then jerk it back and grab for the pillow that fell on the floor.

Ellie shook her head. "No," she said. "Talking won't do a bit of good. You obviously have to be shown."

She walked over to him, pushed his knees apart and snuggled up to his chest, her breast tips sending a tingling racing to his groin. Circling her arms around his neck, she told him, "I'm glad that other woman was stupid enough to break her betrothal to you, Shane. Otherwise, I couldn't have met you. Or fallen in love with you."

His heart stopped, racing forward almost immediately. He had never imagined hearing Ellie say she loved him would mean so very much, but he needed to tell her the rest of it. Her love meant more than she could ever know, meant his hope might bear fruit this time. He couldn't possibly let her continue with lies still between them.

He couldn't tell her of his love for her in return with a misunderstanding looming largely between them.

"Ellie," he said with a groan. "There's more."

"No, that's enough for tonight."

She kissed him, and he could no more stop himself from kissing her back, from circling his arms around her tenderly yet firmly, than he could have single-handedly held back the blast and flames on the steamboat. She curled her arms tighter, and he swept her with him, lay back on the bed and settled her beside him. He only had time for one final comment.

"Don't make love to me because you pity me, Ellie," he whispered.

"Pity you? Oh, Shane, if there's anything to pity about you, I haven't found it yet. I've been too busy enjoying what I *have* found."

She cuddled every delectable inch of that delectable body closer to him, fitting it exactly where it needed to be against his. The thin night rail was nearly indiscernible between them, except for the way it kept him from enjoying the soft satin of her skin. With one fell swoop, he sent it to join the other clothing in the corner.

Ellie giggled. "I don't guess I'll ever get used to how easily you manhandle me."

Shane froze. "I—"

She kissed him quiet. "I meant that in a good way, Shane Morgan. You took that night rail off me as easily as scattering thistledown on a windy day."

"As easy as that, huh? Well, you're tiny but you pack more womanhood into that beautiful body of yours than a man would ever think possible, Ellie. Don't ever let any of that escape with the thistledown, all right?"

"I promise. Now, are you going to talk all night, or are you going to kiss me?"

Shane smiled evilly at her. "I thought you wanted me to talk. Isn't that what you came in here screaming about? My not talking to you?"

"Look, mister," she said. "I might have been only vaguely aware of what this lovemaking business was all about up until this afternoon, but now I know when it's time to talk, when it's time to act. *You*, on the other hand, must be a very slow learner."

"I've created an insatiable zealot," Shane said with a groan.

Pushing his shoulders back onto the bed with no resistance, she clambered onto his stomach and wriggled into place. Writhing her tiny body in such a manner, she scattered dashes of need through his body. He bit down a rumble of desire that surely would have scared her into retreat had he voiced it. But she evidently knew what she sought—found it when it sprang up to meet her.

The only way he could keep his groans from waking the entire household—betraying their lovemaking and ending it, which was *not* an option at this point—was to give Ellie the sounds. Kiss her, utter them into her mouth, follow the sounds with his tongue and trap them.

Only she learned quickly, did his Ellie.

His Ellie.

She met his tongue with her smaller one, hers so much quicker and fleeter than his, so capable of increasing his desire to that nearly uncontrollable pitch.

His hands skimmed that satin skin, cupped her hips, held her in place to soothe the throbbing part in control of him now.

No, this tiny sprite on his belly controlled him, broke every barrier before it formed, held sway over him more competently with the soft, misty sounds of her own pleasure than if she had demanded her own satisfaction more vocally.

And she left no doubt in his mind he pleasured her; that her movements were meant to show him how much he was giving her. It was as though their minds met along with their bodies. As though the more Ellie gave him, the more she received in return. Never had he felt such power flow between a man and woman.

He parted her legs and nudged at what he wanted, but before he could stop her, she slithered off him like quicksilver. Kneeling over him, she shook her head, breasts heaving with passion and platinum hair cascading over her shoulders to hide them. Still, her nipples peaked far too hard to be lost completely in the tumbled tresses.

"Turn over," she said when he tried to reach for her breasts.

He froze. "No. I won't do that, Ellie."

She lifted an eyebrow in warning. "Either turn over or I'll leave."

Instinctively, he reached to grab her, but she shimmied off the bed, standing beside it in that determined stance once more, palms on hips and legs steady, a mutinous pout on her scrumptious lips.

"I can't, Ellie," he murmured. "Give me some more time."

She backed away a step. Looked around the room, her gaze pausing on the heap of clothing in the corner, with her night rail on top. The other eyebrow questioned him, telling him she only had to retrieve the worn gown and let him linger alone on the wrong side of sated desire.

Slowly, he shifted in the bed, but only to his side. "Only if you promise to not light any of the sconces," he said.

"I promise."

He gritted his teeth, and never removing his gaze from her face, he turned onto his stomach.

She studied his back for a long moment, then flicked a glance at his face. "I saw them this afternoon, you know."

"Yes, but—"

"But what?"

"I didn't know it then."

"I don't understand," she said in puzzlement. "Why is your being aware of me looking at your back different than me looking at in when you don't know what's going on?"

"It just is," he said truculently.

"Well, get over it, buster," she told him, stepping over to the bed and reaching out her hands.

He couldn't keep his eyes open any longer, no matter how hard he ordered them to watch her face. Her caresses weren't caresses now, they were tentative touches of exploration. Her fingers smoothed the puckers he could feel, massaged the scars.

"I want you to let me put some lotion on these later, Shane," she said. "It's something Darlene told me about, that she plans to use when she is with child."

His eyes opened willingly—in astonishment. "You want to put a lotion on me that pregnant women use?"

She laughed. "Darlene says one of her married friends told her about it. It keeps the skin smooth and supple and helps heal any stretch marks that do happen to form. I think it will make the skin softer and not so tight here."

"I see."

Ellie skimmed one hand down his right hip and traced the edge of the scarring just past his hipbone. "At least it didn't get the important part of you."

Shane's laughter burst free and filled the room. Shushing him, Ellie leaped for his mouth to stifle it. He took advantage and captured her waist, dragging her back onto the bed. Opening his mouth, he drew two of her fingers in and lapped his tongue around them.

"Ummmm," Ellie murmured. "The only thing I can think of that feels better is your mouth kissing me."

So he did.

Nineteen

～

Ellie reluctantly slipped out of Shane's room and back to her own before dawn. Yawning, she gathered fresh clothing and took it to the upstairs bathing room, freshened up and dressed, then headed downstairs. Fatima gave her a searching look when she entered the kitchen, and Ellie walked over and hugged the other woman. This morning, she loved the whole world.

"I don't know who you really are, or even *what* you really are," she told Fatima, "but I believe you only want what's best for me."

Smiling, Fatima stroked Ellie's cheek. "Who I am, is your fairy godmother, like I've told you all along. What I am is the same thing—your fairy godmother. And I most definitely want what's best for you, Ellie."

"It appears that you have a productive matchmaking already under way," she said with a grin. "You and Withers make a very unlikely, but nice couple."

Fatima closed her eyes dreamily. "He is such a hunk of human."

"Hunk?"

Ellie's laughter broke through Fatima's thoughts and the fairy woman scowled at her.

"Of course he is. Haven't you noticed how well he's built under all those fussy clothes? And after last night, I'd think you'd know what a well-built man can do to flutter a woman's heart.''

''Were you spying on me again?'' Ellie returned Fatima's scowl with one of her own. ''I—''

Fatima sighed and waved Ellie into silence. ''I've told you and told you that I don't spy on you, Ellie. But wooden floors creak, you know. Down here in the kitchen it's very easy to track a person's footsteps overhead. From Shane's bedroom, to yours, to the bathing room and then down the stairs here to the kitchen.''

''Oh.'' Cheeks flushing in embarrassment, Ellie glanced toward the ceiling. Hopefully Elvina and Darlene hadn't heard the footsteps.

''Don't worry,'' Fatima said as though reading her worry. ''The sounds are much more audible down here than upstairs, especially when a person's walking around in bare feet.''

Ellie heard a new set of footsteps overhead and understood. The heavy creaks of the wooden floor indicated they belonged to Shane. Still, she needed to let Fatima know one thing.

''My relationship with Shane is my own business, Fatima.''

Fatima turned to the stove, but Ellie was almost sure she saw a tiny smirk on the woman's lips before she concealed her face from closer examination.

''Of course your relationship with Shane is private.'' Fatima turned the ham pieces in the skillet, then bent to check the biscuits in the oven. Ellie's stomach growled, and she decided not to take a chance on alienating Fatima until at least after breakfast. The woman truly could cook.

''Ummmmmm, something smells great.'' Shane strode into the kitchen. ''Elvina got a jewel of a cook when she snagged you, Fatima. Good morning, Ellie.''

''Morning,'' Ellie said with a smile, while Fatima giggled in pleasure.

''Have you seen Withers, Fatima?'' Shane asked. ''I

went by his room, but he evidently got up earlier, although I can't figure out what for. His bed was even made.''

The ham suddenly needed serious attention, and Ellie suppressed her giggles as Fatima shrugged her shoulders and seriously tended it.

''You both sit down,'' she said. ''Everything's ready, and I'll fix your plates.''

Shane pulled out a chair for Ellie, one of those unconscious gestures that thrilled her each time he made them. Settling beside her in the chair at the end of the table, he nudged his knee against hers. A thrill raced up her leg and across her belly. He continued his clandestine actions while Fatima served them plates piled high with food and poured steaming coffee. It wasn't until they were half-finished with their meals that Ellie noticed Fatima missing.

Probably she wouldn't have noticed then, but Shane bit into a biscuit and closed his eyes in pleasure, his under-the-table caresses sidetracked for the moment.

''Where did she go?'' Ellie asked.

''Who? Oh, Fatima? I didn't notice. I guess she must have gone out the back door.''

Telling herself that had to be what happened—that the fairy woman couldn't disappear into thin air, no matter what her eyes had told her last night—Ellie frowned at her delicious eggs.

''Shane?'' she asked. ''Have you noticed anything strange about Fatima?''

''Not unless you call being able to cook plain food to make it come out like it was prepared by some French chef strange.''

''There's that. But—well, what about noticing anything going on between Fatima and Withers.''

''Fatima and Withers?'' His tawny brows rose, then danced down to settle over his narrowed eyes. The corner of his mouth twitched in mirth. ''You've noticed it, too, huh? That seems an awfully unlikely match, don't you think? She's probably fifteen years older than him.''

Ellie barely concealed her snort of derision. The Fatima Shane saw looked too old for Withers to be interested in, but the Fatima whom Ellie, and evidently Withers, saw was a different woman. A younger, more beautiful woman, at least in a rather brassy way.

The match between them seemed all the more unlikely to Ellie given that set of differences. Fatima's saloon-girl appearance counteracted Withers's prim and proper Englishness to the point where a person would think the adage about opposites attracting was a blatant lie.

"But . . ." Shane admitted with a sigh. "Like I said, I've seen it going on. I just wasn't quite willing to admit it yet. Although if you've noticed, too, it might be time for me to start keeping an eye open for a new valet."

Ellie clenched her teeth before she asked Shane what he saw Fatima wearing this morning. She wasn't quite ready to get that deep into the facts surrounding her magical fairy godmother with Shane just yet. All she knew was she finally believed magic actually allowed Fatima to foster the illusion of her appearance.

This morning the fairy woman wore a brilliant blue gown, shimmering with sequins and ending two inches above her knees. Her black net stockings even had tiny sprinkles of silver in them, matching the silver heels on her blue high-heeled slippers. Blue-and-black peacock feathers were woven into her bright red hair, which ringed and cascaded around her shoulders in a Southern-belle hairstyle.

But Shane evidently saw the dowdy housekeeper whom Fatima had shown Ellie that one time. Ellie shook her head. It would be different if there were only slight disparities in Fatima's appearance—maybe something explained simply by the woman taking a different stance or schooling her face in various ways. The two identities Fatima showed the world were seriously divergent.

Magic. But magic wasn't supposed to exist, no matter how many times Fatima had tried to prove that a lie to Ellie's eyes.

But it did.

And if Ellie tried to voice her concerns and puzzlement, tried to admit she was starting to believe in Fatima's magic, she might still end up fighting captivity in an asylum. That wasn't an option, given her newfound love, Shane.

Her love pushed his chair back and stood.

"I really wish I could spend the day here at the ranch, Ellie, but I need to take care of a couple of things in town. What if I come back out and pick you up in time for us to have dinner at the hotel this evening?"

"I thought you liked Fatima's cooking." She slipped him a teasing look, knowing perfectly well what his invitation meant.

"Well, I do." He fidgeted with his shirt buttons, a blush tingeing his cheeks—an actual blush. "But—well, I mean— here there are so many people."

"The hotel dining room will be full of people," Ellie reminded him.

Glancing around quickly to assure himself the kitchen remained empty, Shane swooped her out of the chair and whirled her once, then set her down in front of him. He dropped a kiss on her nose and whispered, "Yeah, but it's a long drive back and forth to town. Long and private. With lots of places to stop and rest."

Ellie sighed in anticipation. "Private sounds nice." He bent to kiss her, and she leaned back, placing a finger to his lips. "As does dinner. Don't forget that part of it."

His lips curved in a grin against her finger, and he ran the tip of his tongue across it. Her legs wobbled, and Shane chuckled, pulling her closer with no resistance on her part. No resistance this time when he kissed her fully, either.

They had barely regained their senses when footsteps crossed the rear veranda outside the kitchen. Ellie stepped back just as Withers came in the door.

"Bully good morning out there, Master Shane," he said. "Only time of day to enjoy this country."

Shane gaped at him in astonishment. "You've been out

walking before dawn? You, who thinks a man should ride in a buggy across the street to visit neighbors?''

Withers shrugged. ''Protocol back there dictates you make an *arrival*, Master Shane. You can't do that on foot.''

Shane shook his head. ''I have some matters to take care of in town. I won't need you with me if you'd rather stay around here.''

''Then I believe I shall do that,'' Withers mused, a secretive smile on his normally haughty face. ''There are a few matters I can take care of here myself, such as seeing if any of your clothing needs sent to the laundry.''

Ellie suppressed a secretive smile of her own. She doubted Withers's attention would focus completely on his chores.

Shane came to the same conclusion. ''Try to keep your mind clear enough to send a note with the laundry,'' he said. ''Remind them not to starch my socks, like they did last time. And tell Fatima not to expect Ellie and me for dinner this evening.''

Withers sniffed and walked toward the rear stairwell.

Ellie laughed with Shane and accompanied him out to the barn. They managed a few quiet moments of privacy before each went their own way—Shane toward town and Ellie with her hands out onto the range.

This day dragged for her as no other ever had. Finally Shorty grumbled at her inattentiveness one last time, and Ellie decided to end her day early again. After all, she was the boss. She didn't have to ask anyone's permission to do exactly what she felt.

She rode back to the ranch and, after caring for Cinder, turned the gelding out and raced into the house. The study door was closed, so she assumed Elvina was in there once more, going over her books or something similar. Right then she didn't let it bother her. She only wanted to get through the lower level of the house without notice.

Upstairs she found another new dress on her bed. A little nicer than the gingham one, this one was pale blue with an ivory lace collar. A low-cut collar. Ellie held it up, then turned toward the mirror. Not only was Fatima an excellent cook, she could design dresses that made a woman feel feminine and special. Ellie could tell the dress would fit her perfectly, the collar enticing rather than a blatant display of her not-overly-generous breasts.

She grinned at herself in the mirror. Shane didn't appear to find her attributes lacking.

She supposed she should feel guilty over their lovemaking, but somehow she just couldn't bring herself to do penance for something so beautiful. She had no idea where things between her and Shane would lead, but it was beyond her will to not enjoy what she had for now.

For once in her life she felt like the most important person in someone else's feelings. After living on the edges of relationships all her born days, subsisting on crumbs of affection, working so hard to win even those, she couldn't deny what she had with Shane. Maybe it wasn't permanent, maybe it wouldn't last. Maybe she would end up with her heart shattered into a million pieces.

She had to take that chance. She didn't have the fortitude to deny herself the possibilities if things did work out.

Laying the dress back on the bed, she took her robe and went to the downstairs bathing room, where all the elegant soaps, lotions, and perfumes Fatima had given her were laid out. She spent an inordinate amount of time with her preparations, only hurrying back to her room when she realized how late it was getting. She had barely gotten her dress on and begun to brush her hair before she heard a buggy careen into the ranch yard.

Stepping over to her window, she saw Darlene alone in the buggy. Her sister halted the horse at the front of the house and scrambled out. Had Ellie not heard the buggy, she couldn't have missed hearing Darlene race across the foyer and up the front stairwell. Not only did her feet pound, her sobs filled the house.

Her sister ran into her room and slammed the door. Even

through the walls Ellie could hear her miserable sobs. Laying the brush down on her dressing table, Ellie hurried out of her room, meeting Elvina in the hallway.

"Something is horribly wrong with Darlene," Elvina said, stating the obvious.

"I heard. We better check on her."

Ellie knocked softly on the bedroom door, but Darlene's sobs didn't abate. Elvina reached around her and rapped harder, and when Darlene didn't respond, Elvina pushed the door open.

Darlene lay on her stomach on the bed, tears streaming down her face and sobs by this time nearly choking her. Both women hurried over to her side, and Elvina sat down. Finally noticing them, Darlene surged up and flung herself into Elvina's arms.

"Oh, Mama!" she cried. "It's all over with. I'll be an old maid for sure, because I'll never love anyone like I love Rockford."

Elvina patted Darlene soothingly. "You need to control yourself and tell us what happened, dear. Nothing can be this bad. Everyone has lover's quarrels."

"It's more than that," Darlene insisted. "It's horrible. My entire future is dead."

Moving over to the bed, Ellie sat on the other side of Darlene, adding her comforting strokes to Elvina's. "Dar, you need to tell us what the problem is. Maybe we can help."

Darlene shifted to look at Ellie. "There's absolutely nothing anyone can do. Shane Morgan has made sure of that!"

"Shane?" Ellie said. "What does he have to do with this?"

"He was only toying with Rockford about helping him expand his business in New York," Darlene said around her sobs, making Ellie's heart pound with alarm. "He used Rockford because he was someone he knew in this area. Someone who knew the people around here and who could introduce him. He never had any intentions of following through on his offer of looking into expanding Rockford's business.''

Darlene wailed louder and buried her face on Elvina's shoulder.

''Darlene!'' Ellie grimly took hold of Darlene's shoulders and turned her back to face her. ''Darlene, you have to explain that.''

''Yes,'' Elvina said. ''You know Mr. Morgan was also looking at our ranch with the possibility of buying it. Was that a sham, too?''

''I don't know.'' Darlene wiped the back of her hand beneath her nose, and Elvina sighed and pulled a handkerchief out of her skirt pocket. After Darlene blew her nose, she pushed back and sidled around to sit on the side of the bed. ''I truly don't know. All I know for sure is that Shane admitted to Rockford this morning that he didn't have time to give Rockford the attention he would need for a business expansion. That the other Morgan businesses take up all the time he has at present, and he doesn't want to overextend himself right now.''

''Overextend himself? Well, that doesn't sound like he's interested in the ranch, then,'' Elvina mused. ''This place will take an awful lot of effort to bring it back to the profitability it used to have.''

Focused too deeply on her own misery, Darlene ignored her mother. ''That means Rockford can't afford to get married. The business won't support two families. He said that he and his father would discuss some other ways they might be able to manage to bring in more profits on their own, but that it could take years.'' She wiped her eyes. ''I'll be old and gray by then, much too old to even think of getting married.''

Somehow through her shock and dismay, Ellie comforted her sister. When Darlene got to the point where she could talk again, Ellie asked, ''Did he give any reason other than being too busy, Dar? I mean, you would have thought he

knew that before he came here. Before he mentioned anything to Rockford.''

''I told you, El. It was all a sham. He just wanted an
introduction around the area.''

''But what *was* his purpose here then?'' Ellie insisted.

''I don't know. Rockford said he asked him that, but
Shane said it wasn't any of his business.''

''That doesn't sound like Shane.''

''He didn't say it in those exact words,'' Darlene admitted grumpily. ''But that's what he meant. Rockford said
when he pushed him, Shane admitted he had plans to make
some changes in his personal life, and he just didn't want
to take on another business right now.''

Through the window, Ellie could hear another horse
come into the ranch yard. A moment later, someone
knocked on the front door.

''I'll go,'' Ellie said. ''I haven't seen Fatima around this
afternoon.''

Leaving Elvina and Darlene on the bed, Ellie hurried
down the front stairwell. Darlene had left the door wide
open, and a young boy Ellie didn't recognize stood on the
veranda.

He tipped his hat at her. ''I brought a message from a
Mr. Morgan for a Miss Ellie Parker,'' he said, holding out
an envelope. ''He asked me to deliver it quick as I could.''

''Thank you,'' Ellie said as she took the envelope. The
boy turned to leave, and she asked, ''What if I have a reply?
Can you wait?''

''He said you wouldn't have no reply.'' Tipping his hat
again, the boy raced across the veranda and jumped on his
horse. He was out of the ranch yard by the time Ellie got
the envelope open.

*I deeply regret it, but something has come up, and I
won't be able to take you to dinner this evening. Please
forgive me, and I'll come out tomorrow to explain things.*
The content told her it was from Shane, even if he hadn't
signed it, *My deepest affection, Shane.*

Deep affection, huh? After she told him she loved him last night? And what the heck was going on?

He arrived in their lives, upsetting things to no end. Darlene's looming betrothal might be a thing of the past, as Ellie's virginity was.

Just a few minutes ago, she had placidly accepted what had happened, and what would be forthcoming. At least for the immediate future and as far as whatever hers and Shane's relationship held. Now it appeared Shane was anything but reliable or true to his word. Not only had he broken their date with no explanation—"something has come up" was *not* a valid excuse—he had admitted to misleading Rockford. His actions had sent Darlene's life into turmoil.

Did she know this man at all? Other than physically, which was wonderful but not something to build a life on.

She owed him a chance to explain himself, though. She wouldn't make any judgment until she knew what was going on but she didn't intend to spend a sleepless night waiting for him to show up tomorrow and explain himself.

She glanced down at her dress, then out the door at the buggy Darlene had used. The horse didn't appear tired, just sweaty. She crossed the veranda and took his lead rein, guiding him over to the horse trough on the side of the house. Leaving him to drink and refresh himself, she went back in to tell Darlene and Elvina where she was going.

Twenty

The doorman at the snooty Cattlemen's Hotel could have rivaled Withers with his haughty attitude. Clearly ladies didn't arrive at *his* hotel unescorted. But he snapped his fingers and called a bellboy over to assist Ellie down and stable the buggy horse.

"Might I ask if you are checking in, miss? And if I need to have the boy bring your luggage back with him?"

"You might not," Ellie snarled at him, in no mood for his overbearing posture at the moment. Pulling herself up to her entire height, which still made her tilt her head back to stare the arrogant man down, she lifted her skirts daintily and swept past him. He took a step back, his face wary, probably wondering if he had insulted some major society daughter, Ellie mused.

But her imperious demeanor didn't work at the front desk.

"I'm here to see Mr. Morgan," she told the desk clerk. "Please give me his room number."

The desk clerk looked at her in horror. "I am truly sorry, miss," he said in a voice that belied his regret. "We don't give out our guests' room numbers. And—" He swept his eyes up and down her. "—unescorted women visitors aren't supposed to come in alone."

Ellie's temper snapped. Land sakes, until last night, she

With a visible effort, the woman gathered herself, then smiled exquisitely at Ellie, surprising Ellie but calming her humiliation.

"Shane's gone out to see about renting a buggy, my dear," the woman said. "Would you like to come in and wait for him? I've just received a tea cart in and was going to have a cup while I waited."

"I—" The urge to curtsy filled Ellie, but she managed to control it. "I wouldn't want to be any bother, ma'am."

The woman held out a coaxing hand. "You won't be any bother at all. Please come in."

Ellie moved toward her as though in a fog. Something about this woman tugged at her, filled her with yearning. When Ellie got to the room door, it seemed the most natural thing in the world for this woman to pull her into her arms and give her a warm, strong embrace. Then the woman pushed her back and cupped soft, uncallused hands on her cheeks.

"I heard you say your name, and Shane has told me about you. I'm very glad to meet you, Ellie Parker. I'm Mariana Morgan, Shane's mother. Please call me Mariana rather than Mrs. Morgan, if you will."

Her name, too, niggled something through Ellie she couldn't quite identify. And when the woman stepped back, the loss of contact wrenched her. However, it comforted her again when Mariana Morgan slipped an arm around Ellie's waist and led her toward the tea cart, shutting the door behind them.

"Now," Mariana said, motioning for Ellie to sit on the small settee behind the tea cart and settling beside her, "tell me all about yourself, Ellie Parker."

Ellie stared at her in trepidation. What had Shane told his mother about her? What should she say? She had come to town to lambaste Shane for his deception of Rockford and Darlene, his duplicity, which might ruin Darlene's betrothal. But she couldn't say anything like that to his mother.

"I—" Silence seemed the best, but after a moment, Mariana wouldn't have it.

"Please, Ellie. I have a million questions myself, so if you'd rather, I can ask those." She poured them each a cup of tea into delicate, thin china cups. Without asking Ellie, she added a dollop of cream to one of them and handed it to her.

"How did you know I prefer cream in my tea?" Ellie asked.

"Oh, I'm sorry." She appeared somewhat flustered. "I just assumed since your mo—that is, most women I know take cream in their tea, although I prefer strictly sugar." She selected a lump of sugar with the silver server, dropped it in her tea and avoided Ellie's gaze.

"I do prefer cream," Ellie admitted. "It just surprised me. Your knowing." Picking up her cup, she took a sip, as Mariana settled back against the settee as though prepared for a long conversation.

"So," Mariana said. "Tell me about the ranch where you live. Shane says it would be a very good investment here in Texas."

Elvina would be glad to hear about Shane's continued interest in the ranch, Ellie mused, sipping her tea again to gain time to hold that thought at bay. Instead, she described the Leaning G and its history. She had time for another cup of tea and two of the scones, along with time to tell about the house, before the door to the suite opened.

"I've got a buggy, Mother," Shane said, "but I'd really rather you'd wait until tomorrow to—" He caught sight of Ellie, and a huge grin broke out on his face. "Ellie! Well, that settles that then."

Her insides went cold when she saw his false delight. Evidently he intended to maintain his lies even in front of his mother. She glanced from Shane to Mariana in time to catch what she interpreted as a warning look on Mariana's face, another strange action on this woman's part that Ellie couldn't interpret. Shane probably didn't see it, however, since he kept his eyes on her as he walked across the room. Pulling up a side chair, he sat down near enough to her for her to feel his presence.

"Have you and Mother had a nice chat? If you'd told me you wanted to come into town anyway, I would have come back out and gotten you, you know."

"Your messenger didn't wait for a reply," Ellie informed him curtly, although he didn't appear to notice her tone. "And I only decided after he left anyway."

"Well, we have reservations for dinner here in the hotel, so don't fill up on scones. I imagine Fatima can make some just as delicious, if you want more after you get back to the ranch."

"I won't be staying for dinner," Ellie said, and Mariana gasped beside her.

"Oh, but please do, Ellie," Mariana said. "I've only just met you, and I truly do want to get to know you better. In fact, why don't you let us send another messenger out to the ranch and tell them you're staying here overnight. This suite has two bedrooms, and you can stay with me."

Ellie stared back and forth between Mariana and Shane, her puzzlement at their actions turning into irritation. Ever since she had met Mariana in the hallway, it seemed that the woman was trying to envelop her totally. Not that it wasn't somewhat pleasant at first for someone to want your company that badly, but it grew annoying the longer it went on. Ellie was used to making her own decisions.

"I couldn't do that," she said. "There are chores and things at the ranch I need to do in the evening. I can't just leave them without giving orders for one of the men to take care of them."

"Wouldn't Shorty be able to handle that?" Shane put in.

Ellie shot him an angry look. "No." She couldn't have her conversation with him, either, in Mariana's presence, so she might as well head back to the ranch and wait for another time.

"But Ellie—"

Mariana broke off when Ellie swung back to face her, and it wasn't until Ellie saw the look of apprehension on the other woman's face that she realized her own expression still mirrored her anger at Shane. She worked a smile onto her lips.

"I'm sorry, Mariana, I really am. But I do have responsibilities at the ranch, and Shorty won't realize I'm gone unless he goes out and sees my share of the chores undone. He was still on the range with the rest of the men when I left."

"But we could send a messenger, my dear," Mariana said cautiously.

"No." Ellie carefully placed the china cup back on the tea cart and stood. "I do need to go."

"Maybe we could come out with you and visit," Mariana said, an almost desperate plea in her voice, which puzzled Ellie further and didn't calm her vexation one bit.

Ellie shook her head. "Elvina, my stepmother, would have my hide if I brought unannounced visitors out. Especially someone of your . . . well, your social standing. I will tell her of your arrival, however, and I'm sure she'll want to entertain you. Maybe for dinner tomorrow evening."

"Will you at least come in for lunch tomorrow and let me know?"

"I—" She glanced at Shane, studying the worried look on his face. "I don't think I can get away. But I'll have someone come in and deliver Elvina's dinner invitation."

Mariana sighed. "I guess that will have to do."

"I'll walk you out," Shane said, following Ellie toward the door.

She whirled on him. "No! No, you won't. I don't want you to accompany me."

He stared at her with a frown, which narrowed into an uneasy perplexity. Ellie didn't give a diddly-darn—a *damn*—right then. What she had to say to him couldn't be said in a public place—either in his mother's presence or on the streets of Fort Worth.

"Ellie," he said in a low voice he didn't mean to reach his mother's ears, "let's step over into my room and talk."

"No," she repeated for what seemed like the dozenth time. Though he waited for a further explanation, she couldn't come up with one right now. He deserved every bit of the worry and frustration showing on his handsome face, and she still carried enough anger at him to be satisfied with his befuddlement at her actions.

She hadn't realized it would be so hard to actually face him, though. To see him and know that his delight in her presence was feigned, his words to her covering up lies and deceit. It had taken every bit of effort she could dredge from deep inside her not to let her newly recognized temper fly at him—tell him she knew about his duplicity with Rockford. Tell him how it had broken Darlene's heart.

"No," she said one last time, then nodded over at Mariana and went out the door, closing it firmly behind her.

"What on earth have you done to that child?" Mariana asked Shane.

He turned and held out his hands in an innocent gesture. "I don't know, Mother. She wasn't like this this morning. In fact—" Well, he couldn't tell his mother about that. "—she was very agreeable this morning."

"This is more than just your breaking your engagement with her for the evening," Mariana mused. "What else have you done today that could have upset her life?"

"Upset her life? Mother, you're here to possibly tell Ellie that she's not who she's thought she was for her entire life, and that she's an heiress with a fortune waiting for her that's probably as large as our own, given the investments I've made with it over the years. And you think anything *I* could do could upset her life more than that?"

Mariana was unperturbed. "Evidently it has. That is *not* the girl you described to me earlier today."

"She's not a girl," Shane said instinctively, feeling his

cheeks heat at Mariana's sharp scrutiny. "I mean, well, she's the exact age she should be if she's Cynthia Spencer."

"Make no mistake about that, Shane. That young woman *is* Cynthia Spencer. I'd stake my life on it. I brought some pictures of Rose and me together, and I've got more pictures back home, even some baby pictures of Cynthia before she was taken. Ellie has William Spencer's mouth, but everything else on her is Rose at that age."

"I'd still like to have some sort of actual proof."

"There isn't any. Rose's sister destroyed everything after Rose and William died. Or were killed, if what I believe is true."

"Were killed? What do you mean, Mother?"

Marian motioned for Shane to sit and settled herself once again on the settee. She poured two cups of tea and handed one to Shane before she leaned back.

"I believe that Rose and William's deaths weren't an accident, no matter what the coroner ruled, Shane. I think someone drugged that horse and made it bolt and wreck the carriage. Or perhaps hid in the brush and shot something at the horse. You were too young to be aware of it, but that animal was skittish. William took pride in the fact that he could handle the gray, and I'll admit, it made a beautiful sight pulling their carriage. But anyone close to the family knew what that horse was like."

"But why kill them, Mother?"

"Greed, of course. Rose's sister, Lily, was an evil woman. She was as wicked as Rose was generous. They were actually twins, but no one would ever mistake one for the other. Lily's evilness gave her a stark, deadly beauty, whereas Rose was soft and gentle."

"I still don't understand what benefit their deaths would have for Lily."

Tears glinted in Mariana's eyes, and Shane leaned forward to comfort her, but she shook her head.

"Let me finish," she said.

She took a steadying sip of tea. "It was as though Fate somehow had this in mind. An evil Fate, that wouldn't be denied. Soon after Rose and William married, both sets of parents died. To be honest, I believe their deaths were natural, as they were all elderly and in poor health. William was an only child and inherited everything. Rose and Lily's parents had their lineage, but they'd fallen on hard times, and there was nothing left of the family fortune. Rose didn't need it, but Lily became dependent on William's generosity."

"So Lily got rid of Cynthia and killed her sister and brother-in-law," Shane concluded to save his mother the agony of repeating the tale. "Lily inherited everything."

"Not for long." Mariana shook her head. "She died of yellow fever within a month of Rose and William's deaths. We both shared the same attorney, and I went to him, demanding that he search the estate papers and find out anything he could to help me search for Cynthia, since I truly believed Lily was behind the child's disappearance. He told me there was nothing there; that Lily had evidently destroyed a lot of papers. You see, he'd had his own suspicions, but she must have known about them and took pains to protect herself. That made me sure Lily had either killed Cynthia or sent her away where no one could find her."

"I can't believe she was so evil."

"Believe it, Shane. And it's taken me years to unravel all this evil and deceit. I'm not going back to New York without telling Ellie who she really is and making sure she receives her proper due as my best friend's daughter."

Twenty-one

~~~~

Shane halted Blackjack at the end of the wide arc he rode to approach the Leaning G from behind the barn and listened to the night noises. A month ago, he wouldn't have known a coyote from a cow, but tonight he could identify different sounds, thanks to Shorty's patience. The rasping yet pleasant noise was katydids calling to their mates. Far off in the distance, a pair of coyotes howled, and closer in, a fox yipped.

The smells were different, too. Sagebrush and clear night air, at variance with the odors of New York, which the women counteracted with perfume on their bodies and scented handkerchiefs. Dust lingered in the air, stirred up from Blackjack's hooves, but here it fit the atmosphere rather than annoyed.

When had he changed his mind and decided maybe a few things about Texas weren't that unpleasant? Maybe when he realized this state sheltered the woman he hadn't even known he was searching for, and not because his mother insisted on it.

The woman he had found—Ellie—could be the heiress his mother thought, or she could indeed be Ellie Parker, adopted daughter of George Parker and some completely different person from the orphan train. No matter what his mother said, Shane wasn't positive yet of Ellie's identity.

Either way, it wouldn't bother him, however.

The Ellie he wanted was the other half of him, his soul mate. Heiress or poor orphan girl—he didn't care one whit either way.

And he wasn't about to wait until morning to see why she had held him at such arm's length today in the hotel, when she had been the other half of his heart and body last night. Even this morning. Last night she had insisted he talk to her instead of being Mr. Stone on a Log. He was here to do that.

He told himself her actions today were because of his mother's presence. Perhaps Ellie had sensed the disquietude Mariana had tried to hide until she could find the right time to talk to Ellie openly. He was at last certain Ellie wasn't repulsed by the scars on his back, not after the way she had acted last night.

Dismounting, he tied Blackjack to a bush and removed something from his saddlebags, placing it in his shirt pocket. He supposed he could ride up to the front of the house and announce himself, even this late at night. But if Ellie refused to see him, he wouldn't dare barge on in.

No, he would keep to his decision made on the ride out of town.

Cautiously he crept toward the barn, keeping a watch for any prowling ranch hands. He knew all of them, and he was sure that, if necessary, he could talk any of them, including Shorty, into being a participant in his secretive visit to Ellie. Still, it would be better to keep this private, since Ellie would murder him if she found out he had let someone else know he planned to visit her in her room at night.

Something exploded in the brush beside him, and Shane instinctively flung himself to the ground. As soon as he saw the jackrabbit's wild, veering flight into some brush a few yards away, he chuckled and rose. Brushing the dust from his clothing, he shook his head. Shorty hadn't mentioned jackrabbits being dangerous.

One of the horses in the corral nickered and lifted its

head in alarm, but Shane recalled the soothing, clicking noises Shorty made when he chose a mount for the day each morning. He clicked his tongue in imitation of the sound, and the horse bobbed its head and trotted over to the fence. Shane moved over and patted it for a second, then headed for the shadows on the side of the barn.

No one was on the rear veranda; they shouldn't have been anyway, at this late hour. A light shone somewhere deep inside the house, reminding him to be as quiet as he could. He dashed across the yard, just in case someone was wandering about there. At the back of the house, he halted far enough out to see over the rear veranda roof to the bedroom windows above, all of them dark.

Shane studied the trellises on the end of the veranda. No way would they hold his weight. He supposed he could try to sneak into the house and up the stairwell, but those old wooden floors squeaked loud enough to announce any intruder. And after the way Ellie acted in the hotel, he had his doubts as to whether or not she would agree to come down and talk to him if he woke her by scattering gravel against her bedroom window. The bottom portion of the window was open anyway, and he would probably end up flinging gravel into the room and hitting something.

He supposed he could change his mind once again and just go to the front door and walk in. Whoever was in the study would wake Ellie for him. Or he could go on up to the room that had been assigned to him, detouring to Ellie's room on the way. Unless Ellie had informed the household that he would be staying in town with his mother. That would mean more explanation than he wanted to take time to give this evening. There were more important things to straighten out.

"What are you doing down there?"

Ellie's voice! Shane stared up at the window. She was obviously on her knees on the window seat, head thrust through the lower part of the window.

"I need to see you," he hissed back.

"What?"

"I need to see you!"

"Hush! Someone will hear you."

"They will if you don't come down here and talk to me," he threatened. "I'll wake up the entire house if you don't explain why you acted like you did this afternoon at the hotel."

"Forget it. Go back to town. I don't have anything to say to you."

"We'll see about that!"

Shane leaped for the veranda roof, managing to get a firm grasp on the edge of it with both hands.

"What are you doing?" Ellie whispered harshly.

Ignoring her, he swung one leg upward, his heel thudding a connection on the slate shingles. Heaving, he threw his body onto the veranda roof with one thrust. It made a much louder crash than his heel.

"Get out of here," Ellie hissed. "I told you I didn't want to talk to you."

Lifting his head, he shot her a glance, then pushed himself to his hands and knees. "We're going to talk, Ellie."

"We are *not*."

She slammed the window closed and turned the latch to lock it before Shane could lunge over and push it open once more. He stared at her through the window, almost expecting her to stick her tongue out at him, given the so-there look she had on her face.

He held her glare for a long moment as he studied the situation, then sighed in resignation and sat down on the roof. Keeping a sidelong gaze for Ellie's reaction, he removed his boot. He tossed it in the air once and caught it, noticing her face change to a wary alertness. Then he turned to the window and held the boot heel outward.

"You better move back," he said loudly enough for her to hear through the window. "I don't want you to get cut by flying glass."

"You wouldn't dare," she said deliberately, lips moving

so he could clearly understand her words even though he couldn't hear them.

He pulled his arm back. Ellie stared defiantly at him, moving her face right up to the windowpane. She was right; he didn't dare try to break the window now. The flying glass would imbed in her lovely face.

Jamming the boot back onto his foot, he pushed his hands through his hair. "What on earth are you mad about? Damn it, Ellie, I can't think of anything I've done to set you off like this!"

"Go away!" She turned from the window and disappeared from his sight.

Rising to his feet, Shane considered the situation further. Suddenly it dawned on him that the windows on either side of Ellie's were both open to catch the night air. Darlene's room was on the right of Ellie's, while the one on the left was Elvina's. It was probably Elvina in the study at this hour, so her room would be empty. He could enter that way without discovery.

If Elvina wasn't on her way upstairs already, in which case she would probably catch him either in the room or in the hallway. It was a chance he would have to take.

He started toward Elvina's window, but the window on Ellie's room flew up with a rush.

"What are you doing?" she asked.

He turned to her, but didn't move in that direction. "There are open windows on either side of yours."

Even this far away, he could hear her grit her teeth. She glared at him in such a deadly manner, he was surprised the force didn't knock him off the roof. Then she whirled around and disappeared, leaving her window open.

Cautiously, Shane moved closer to the window. He had sense enough to check inside to see where she was before he went through. The mood she was in, he wouldn't be shocked to find her waiting beside the window seat with something in her hands to break over his head.

She stood on the other side of the bed, the room too dark

for him to see the expression on her face now. Keeping his gaze on her, he swung a leg through the window. It was a tight fit to get the rest of him inside without losing sight of Ellie, but he managed with only one hurtful scrape on his right shoulder. Gaining his feet, he stayed where he was in case prudence dictated a speedy escape.

His mother was absolutely correct. The Ellie he saw today was a far different woman than the Ellie to whom he had made sweet love the previous night.

He glanced at the rumpled bed, realizing he had had a faint hope of being in it later on tonight with Ellie, after they straightened out whatever foolish idea she had in her mind. A closer look at Ellie as she moved a few steps closer to him made him realize needing the safety of the window wasn't out of the realm of possibility, and ending up in bed was. Her platinum hair swirled around her with her angry movements, her blue eyes shooting something other than reflected starlight his way.

"You are a liar, Shane Morgan," she spat. "I wonder how many other things you've lied to me about?"

Thoughts rushed through Shane's mind, and he realized she had made the one comment he had no defense for. It also had the power to sink him even deeper into her bad graces, since he wasn't exactly sure which lie she referred to—leaving him with no alternative defense, in case he defended the wrong untruth.

Could she have possibly listened outside the room earlier today and heard what he and his mother discussed? Or was she referring to something else?

Honesty—at least as much as he was able to give her without totally shattering his image in her eyes—seemed the best policy. Evasive honesty.

"I tried to talk to you last night. I told you there were things I needed to tell you."

"You rat!" she said. "So now you're saying that I gave myself to you without reservation, more interested in making love to you than getting to know you better!"

"No! Ellie, of course not. You're twisting my words. Listen—"

"Now I'm twisting your words, a liar myself, huh? And I'm not a listener. I don't want to listen to you, do I?"

"Damn it, I didn't mean that—"

"What were you going to tell me about? The fact that you were only leading Rockford on about his business? Or the fact that you didn't give a darn that what you'd done would ruin my sister's hopes for the future?"

At least now he knew what she was angry about. The measure of relief didn't help much, though. He still had to make it right.

"If that's all that's bothering you, I'll take care of it."

"All? You call what you've done just some little problem you can wave your hand and *take care of*? You aren't concerned about what your stupid, heedless actions have caused? How giving false hope, then admitting you misled someone, has caused so much pain and misery? Get out of here. I never want to see you again."

"I'm not going," he said sternly. "Not until you tell me what you mean. I'll help Rockford, if that's all it takes. What else is bothering you?"

"Oh," she said musingly. "So there *is* more than one lie between us. You want me to enlighten you as to whether this is the only one I've found out about."

"No. I mean, yes, but— Damn it, Ellie, there's a logical explanation for everything I've done since I got here."

"Even making love to me?"

He studied her closely, unable to lie about the most wonderful thing that had happened to him in his life. He knew his next words were the most important he would ever utter.

"Never," he whispered. "Making love to you wasn't logical. It was completely illogical and unexpected. And the sweetest, most wonderful thing to ever come into my life."

It didn't work; he could tell by her tight face.

"It was a lie, too, Shane. Given the fact there was a

mountain of deceit between us, all our lovemaking was a sham. I wish I'd never met you.''

Shane's shoulders crumpled, and he shook his head. ''I don't know what else to say to you. But will you please at least talk to my mother again before you shut us out of your life?''

''Us? What does your mother have to do with this?''

''Ellie?'' A firm knock sounded on the door, and Elvina called again, ''Ellie? Are you talking to someone in there?''

Ellie stiffened, whirling to face the door, then casting Shane an apprehensive look. She remained silent for a few seconds, until Elvina repeated her request and shook the doorknob. Lucky for them both, Ellie had stuck a chair beneath the doorknob. Probably to keep him out, but it worked for Elvina.

''Ummmm—'' Ellie said as though waking from sleep. ''Is that you, Elvina?''

''Yes,'' Elvina replied. ''I heard you talking in there.''

''I was having a dream, Elvina. It's all right. I'm fine. You can go on to bed.''

''All right.''

Her footsteps indicated she left, and Ellie glared at Shane once more.

''Please get out of here. It will only cause me a lot more grief if you're caught in my bedroom.''

Her grief wouldn't even begin to touch his own once she talked to his mother tomorrow, Shane realized, having concluded that she still didn't know about his initial reason for coming to Texas. And it wouldn't be grief she felt. Given the inflexibility of her ire this evening over his deception of Rockford and her unwillingness to even discuss whether he could make it up to her sister's fiancé, Ellie would have built an impenetrable wall of anger at him by tomorrow evening. Tonight it was his deception with Rockford she was angry about. Tomorrow it would be the confirmation of his deception of her—a deception she would be even less willing to overlook.

Giving her one last, longing look, as though to fix her in his mind, although he knew he wouldn't desert his mother and leave for New York just yet, he turned back to the window. He didn't bother to watch her this time as he crawled through. If she wanted to conk him with something, it couldn't hurt him as much as this heartache.

Twenty-two

~~

"Ellie, you're acting extremely childish!"

Recognizing the fairy woman's voice, Ellie searched the room, but she didn't see Fatima anywhere.

"Where are you?" she demanded. "You told me you didn't spy on me! But better yet, don't show yourself. Get out of here and leave me alone!"

"You're going to spend the rest of your life alone if you don't try to work things out with Shane." Fatima remained invisible, but her voice rang clearly in the room.

"Someone's going to hear you and come to investigate," Ellie said. "Elvina's already stopped by here once. If she finds me talking to thin air, she'll haul me off to the insane asylum!"

"Pooh," Fatima said. "Haven't you figured out by now that I can block anyone from hearing me, as well as seeing the real me?"

"I wish *I* could block you out," Ellie gritted. "Go away. Leave me alone."

"You're being very childish," Fatima repeated.

"Then let me!" Ellie demanded, slamming her hands on her hips, and unable to keep the tears at bay. "Go away and let me be childish! Leave me alone. I'm sick and tired of people thinking they know how I should feel or how I should act when they deceive me! You're deceiving me as much as everyone else.''

''How do you explain that remark?''

''You claim to be magic, but you didn't tell me about the lies Shane was spreading while he was here. You could have let me know he wasn't what he appeared and that he was only using Rockford instead of being honest about not having any plans for Rockford's business expansion.''

''Even if I knew these things, it's not my place to interfere that way in your decisions, Ellie.'' Fatima's voice was quieter and hesitant now. ''I can only lend assistance. Your decisions have to be your own.''

''My decisions have been based on deception,'' Ellie whispered. ''I fell in love for the first time in my life, and it had to be with a liar. I deserve better love than that.''

''Maybe Shane does, too,'' Fatima cautioned.

''I know what he deserves, and it's not my love!'' Racing across the room, she scrambled into bed and pulled the pillow over her head. Even through that, she thought she heard Fatima sigh, but a second later, she sensed the room was empty.

Still she kept the pillow over her head. It wouldn't do for Elvina or Darlene to hear her wracking sobs. Darlene might come to see what was wrong, but she doubted Elvina would, as she had with her blood daughter. And one more confirmation of her stepmother's indifference for her was more than Ellie could take on top of everything else today.

Fatima appeared back in her bedroom where Withers waited for her, stretched out on the bed with Pandora curled beside him. He laid down the book he had been reading and held out his arms.

''I gather it didn't go well, my dear.''

''No, it didn't.'' She crawled onto the bed and snuggled close to him. She had never imagined for a moment that having a mortal man hold her could feel this blissful. If it weren't for her concern for Ellie, she would have gloried in his caresses.

"I hope you're not giving up, darling," Withers said. "Master Shane might not know it, but Miss Ellie—or Miss Cynthia, whoever she is—is the best thing that could happen to him."

Fatima pushed herself up and looked at Withers in confoundment. "What do you mean, Miss Cynthia? What do you know about this situation?"

"Why, of course, Master Shane's here to try to find out if Miss Ellie could be the missing New York heiress, the one who's the daughter of his mother's best friend, Rose Spencer. Madame Spencer is departed, as is her husband and the rest of that branch of the family. Master Shane told me all about everything on our trip down here."

"And you didn't tell me you were aware of all this?" Fatima asked angrily. "You knew very well I was trying to make a match between Ellie and Shane, and you didn't think I needed someone to discuss things with when things started to go wrong?"

Withers winced and shrugged, a wary look settling on his haughty face. "It didn't dawn on me that you didn't know what I knew."

Fatima moved off the bed. "I'm a fairy godmother, not a gypsy fortune-teller," she said in a near-yell, sending Pandora scrambling off the other side of the bed. "Why don't you and Ellie realize that? Don't you mortals have any idea what magic's all about?"

"My dear—" Withers began.

"Dear, schmear!" she shouted. "You mortal men are so dense at times. No wonder Ellie is having such problems with Shane. He's a man."

A hurt look replaced the wariness on Withers's face, and he got off the bed and took a step toward her. Fatima weaved out of his reach and pointed a finger at the door.

"Go on back to your own room," she demanded. "I don't want you here tonight."

"We should talk—"

"No! I'm not in the mood to talk. Go!"

He went. After a supercilious sniff that told Fatima his hurt had changed to irritation, he left the room. She flounced back over to the bed and flung herself belly down.

Now what was she going to do? The dictates of her set boundaries didn't allow her to tell Ellie about her possible heirship or the other "misleading information" Shane had given out. Shane needed to be the one to advise Ellie of everything instead of Fatima, since if Fatima did, it brooked on the verge of interference in the relationship.

Darn it. Why hadn't Withers told her what he knew so she'd have someone to work this out with?

Because he thought you knew it already, with your magic powers, her mind repeated.

"Mortals!" she spat.

The bed sank, and she looked up to see Pandora ponderously moving toward her from the other edge of the mattress. The cat sat down and fixed Fatima with a stern cat look.

"Meowr," she said, the sound strangely similar to the word *mortals* and the tone chastising Fatima's disgust with that race of beings. Then Pandora paced to the edge of the bed once more and leaped to the floor. Tail curved over her back and nose high in the air—darn it, Pandora looked as if she were trying to imitate Withers's supercilious posture—she pranced out of the room after Withers.

Fatima curled into a miserable, lonesome ball, finally falling asleep hours later.

As tired as though she hadn't slept a wink, although she had sobbed herself to sleep finally sometime between midnight and dawn, Ellie made her way into the kitchen the next morning. She barely glanced at Fatima, only long enough to see that she wore a stark black gown this morning. It gave Ellie a start for a second to realize her own vision of the fairy woman was in the guise of the dowdy housekeeper she displayed to the rest of the world, but Ellie didn't feel like puzzling it out at the moment. Instead, when Fatima ignored her in turn, Ellie went over to the stove and poured herself a cup of coffee.

Back at the table, she sat down and took a sip of the coffee—and nearly spat it back out. It tasted as if Fatima had boiled a cup of kerosene in it. Shoving the cup aside, she waited to see if Fatima would offer to serve her.

Fatima did, but a moment after the plate was placed in front of her, Ellie wished she hadn't. The biscuits were as hard as rocks, and she couldn't even cut them to spread the butter. The eggs were greasy, with a crust of burnt edges, and the bacon crumbled to pieces when she tried to pick up a strip.

Giving a sigh of disgust, she rose and left the kitchen. Maybe Cookie would have something extra left over.

Ellie was just finishing a plate of Cookie's fried mush and ham when Withers hesitantly entered the bunkhouse.

"Do you think perhaps I might get something to eat out here this morning, Miss Ellie?" the valet asked.

Ellie waved him to the chair beside her. "Fatima's mad at you, too, huh?"

"Devastatingly," he said.

"What's her problem with you? Have you been childish, too?"

"I'm not sure." He grabbed a plate from the end of the table and reached for the ham. "Does obtuseness fall under the same definition as childishness?"

"Probably. At least as far as your punishment is concerned."

Ellie finished her meal and stood, then remembered what her plans were for that evening. "Would you mind taking an invitation in to Mrs. Morgan for dinner this evening?" she asked Withers. "Tell Elvina about it, and I'm sure she'll prepare one for you."

"Madame Morgan?" Withers swallowed audibly. "Madame Morgan as in Master Shane's mother?"

"He didn't tell you that she'd arrived in town?"

"No. No, he didn't." Withers shoved his plate away as though he'd lost his appetite and rose to his feet. "I'll let Madame Parker know. I gather you invited Madame Morgan to dinner this evening? And Master Shane?"

"Yes," Ellie confirmed.

"Oh, lordy," Withers muttered. "I wonder if you should ask Cookie to do the meal?"

"Surely Fatima wouldn't embarrass us like that. Would she?"

Withers shrugged. "I'll do what I can."

He left the bunkhouse, and Ellie followed after him. Withers strolled toward the house, very slowly and hesitantly to Ellie's mind.

The heck with it. Fatima was Elvina's problem. Let the two of them work it out. She had enough other things on her mind.

One of whom rode out to join her and her men barely an hour after they hit the range. She wasn't truly surprised at his arrival, although the ravaged look on his face, mirroring her own troubled night, niggled a serious hole through her anger. As he rode toward them, she debated whether to ask her men to turn him away. But all three of them looked at one another and turned their horses in some unspoken agreement, riding off and leaving her to meet Shane alone.

She straightened her shoulders and held Cinder's reins firmly as the gelding danced sideways at Blackjack's approach. Shane halted the stallion within touching distance of her, but to what she found was her dismay, he kept his hands away.

"I'm not leaving today until we talk," he said without greeting. "I left my mother a note, so don't think after you hear what I have to say that she's the one who sent me out here. This is between you and me alone, Ellie. If you have even one iota left of the love you claimed to have for me, you'll hear me out."

"And if I don't, you'll call me childish just like Miss Fairy Woman Fatima, I suppose," Ellie said childishly.

Shane frowned. "What's Fatima got to do with this? And why did you call her that?"

Ellie might as well tell him, since he appeared to be on an honesty mission this morning. Part of her musings, however, were still that—musing suspicions. Maybe Shane would confirm or deny some of them.

"You did admit that you've noticed that Fatima and Withers are a couple."

"I've noticed," Shane agreed.

"Then since Withers knows about Fatima having magical capabilities, I assume you also know. And that's something else you've been hiding from me. All of you have let me think I'm going bonkers and might be carted off to an asylum any minute."

Shane's frown deepened into a scowl, and he shook his head at Ellie. "I don't know anything about Fatima being magic, Ellie. But I wouldn't presume to make a judgment on your feelings and declarations about such a thing. I've come to know you fairly well, although not completely. What I do know about you tells me you have a valid reason for saying what you've just said, as crazy as it sounds."

"Then you believe in magic?" Ellie asked in astonishment.

"Not necessarily, but I do know there are things that can't be explained logically in this world. I found that out during and after the steamboat explosion. People lived and died at seemingly arbitrary mandates, even me. My mother believes that I had things left to do here—and that maybe one of those things was to find you."

Shane stared away from her for a moment. "When I was fighting for my life the first few days after the explosion, my mother swears my father came to her in New York. That he left, telling her he would stay with me until she got there. I remember something in the room with me, but

I can't decide now if I really felt it, or if it's what my mother later told me was there.''

Recalling the evidence of his fight for life on his back, Ellie had to hold Cinder's reins tightly and remind herself about the problems between her and Shane. Otherwise, she would have been off Cinder in a heartbeat, sharing Black-jack's broad back with Shane and holding him to help him fight the misery of his remembered pain. But when he looked back at her, there was wonder, not pain on his face.

"So if there is magic in the world, all it can do is make it a better place, not a worse one.''

"What Fatima does isn't spiritual magic. It's not some-thing like Fate or angels or a Being who can perform mir-acles. It's things like new dresses and doing her housework by magic. She probably even uses it for her cooking.''

"Does she have a reason for using it?''

Ellie avoided his gaze this time. Yes, the fairy woman had what she considered a very valid reason—to help her matchmaking attempts. So far, however, it hadn't worked with that. Thank goodness Fatima drew the line at tamper-ing with human will.

Startled at the thought, Ellie sat up straighter in her sad-dle and studied Shane. His direct eyes held shadows of worry, an indication of just how much Ellie's anger was bothering him. Fatima hadn't interfered and explained any-thing to either one of them. But, of course, Fatima had no idea what to do about Ellie's deep anger at Shane's de-ceiving her.

Other than to tell Ellie she should quit acting childish and confront Shane. Listen to his explanation.

She turned Cinder away from Shane's stallion. "It's not far to the creek. It'll be a cooler place to talk there.''

As soon as the words left her mouth, she wished she could take them back. Wished she could blame Fatima for putting them in her mouth and that she had thought of an-other place to go. But she couldn't. The yearning to be at the creek again with Shane, to be where she had first made love to him, was undeniable.

And she couldn't ignore the fact that her hopes were high that they could make a new beginning at the place where the full impact of their love had hit her.

Twenty-three

~~~~~~

Shane dismounted at the creek and reached to help Ellie down. She ignored his polite gesture. Longed for it, but ignored it anyway. *Childish* rang in her mind, but she ignored that, too.

The foreboding that had been building incessantly during the ten-minute ride to the creek burgeoned through her, almost as though some magical warning told her that she wouldn't like what she was about to hear; that her future hung in the balance of some spiritual justice scale, which was ready to tip one way or the other in the next few minutes.

Shane's face didn't even hint at any clues. As blank and uncommunicative as during the ride, only the uneasiness and misery in his tawny eyes hadn't changed. For some reason, that permeated her with guilt.

She shoved guilt aside, also. She had lived with guilt all her life. Guilt because she must have done something to make her parents not want her and send her on an orphan train rather than keep her and love her. Guilt because she hadn't been able to make the Parkers love her like their own either. Newer guilt that she had succumbed to Shane's proffered love without building a firm foundation for it first. She had wanted for once in her life to have a love all her own so badly, she might have mistaken passion for love.

Was that what Shane meant to tell her? Was he about to give her an affirmation of her accusations last night, when she had thrown the allegations of their love being a sham at him?

Shane loosened Blackjack's girth strap while Ellie did the same with Cinder, and they turned the horses loose to graze while they talked. Ellie made for the downed log, but Shane wandered back and forth on the creek bank, head bent in concentration. The longer he kept her waiting, the more agitated Ellie grew, until at last she either had to explode or descend into an icy calm. She chose the false calm, resolutely waiting for him to open his mouth, as she had done many times previously in their relationship.

Still, when he finally faced her, Ellie wondered if she was ready for this. Knew she wasn't but had no choice.

"I'm not going to pussyfoot around," Shane said. "I did mislead Rockford, but I'll take care of that immediately this afternoon. I'll have him get in contact with one of my managers in New York who has the experience the Van Zandts need to expand, and make funds available to him."

Ellie nodded her head carefully, certain from his attitude that he had more than this to say. "Darlene will be ecstatic."

But how come *she* wasn't overflowing with happiness herself? Ellie wondered. Because something on Shane's face told her that what was coming was going to be worse than his deceit with Rockford?

He dropped his head again as though gathering strength, then stuck his fingers in his back pockets and faced her directly.

"I came here at my mother's request initially. She began her search over seventeen years ago, and continued the search until recently, after hiring the Pinkerton Agency two years ago."

As his words sank in, Ellie's heart pounded so thunderously she had to strain to hear his voice. A little over seventeen years ago was when she had been put on the orphan train, at least according to George Parker. Shane's further explanation heightened her confusion and failed to alleviate her anxiety one bit.

"Mother seemed to think the last Pinkerton report she got meant she had finally been successful in tracing a child who was kidnapped in New York when she was a little over two years old," Shane informed her. "The child of my mother's best friend, Rose Spencer. Everyone associated with the child's disappearance died shortly after it happened, but Mother refused to give up. She sent me down here to check out the Pinkerton report, and after seeing you yesterday, she's certain. She feels you're Cynthia Spencer, the missing heiress to the Spencer fortune in New York."

Stunned, Ellie couldn't move. Many nights she had fantasized that her parents had indeed wanted her, but had lost her through no fault of their own. Dreamed that some day—

Oh, lordy, she recalled the childhood dream now. She had imagined that her fairy godmother would show up in her life and make everything right, taking her back to her true parents, who would sob with gratitude at her return, holding her, hugging her and loving her to pieces.

Had her yearnings actually brought Fatima into her life?

Had Fatima put the wheels into motion to make Ellie's dream a reality—righting the wrong that had been done to a young child?

She clenched her hands in her lap and looked at Shane. "You said everyone is dead. My parents?"

Shane started toward her, but she held up her hands in protest.

He halted. "I'm very sorry, Ellie. Yes, they're both dead. A buggy accident. And your aunt, who Mother believes was responsible for your kidnapping, died a month after them."

Slowly Ellie rose to her feet. She should feel something, some sort of grief. But she hadn't even known them, and her turmoil over Shane's revelations was barely held in check. If she let the barriers down, she might collapse.

"What name did you mention? Cynthia?"

"Cynthia Spencer. Your parents were Rose and William Spencer."

Suddenly she stared at Shane in misery. "But you came here to prove I *wasn't* this Cynthia Spencer, didn't you? Otherwise, you would have told me openly why you were here."

He spread his hands. "You have to understand, Ellie. I didn't know you at the time, but I love my mother. However, in all honesty, I didn't come here to prove or disprove anything. I came here to find out the truth, one way or another."

"So some charlatan wouldn't deceive your mother. As you deceived me."

"After Mother saw you—"

"You've been with me for over a week, Shane. You've made love to me. You've told me you loved me. Yet it was only yesterday that you believed I truly might be Cynthia Spencer? Just who did you think you were falling in love with? Or didn't you care? Was your declaration of love also a lie?"

"No! Ellie—"

"I really need to be alone, Shane. Please leave."

"No, damn it! I—"

"Then I'll leave. Please don't follow me. I'll throw your own words back at you. If you have any feelings at all left for me, give me some time alone right now, Shane."

She walked up the creek bank, aware with every particle of her being of Shane's eyes on her. She could sense his obedience of her request to leave her alone.

Damn it, she almost wished he would ignore her demand and race after her, capturing her in his strong arms and wiping away her fear and distrust. But she called Cinder to her without interference on his part, tightened the girth and swung into the saddle.

"Ellie?"

His voice was soft, and she realized she had been hoping desperately that he would at least say something. And she couldn't ignore him any more than she could have performed one of Fatima's magic feats. She couldn't answer, either, through her clogged throat. Instead, she sat on Cinder, waiting.

"I want you to know, Ellie, that there was one thing I never lied to you about. Whether your name is Ellie or Cynthia, I love you. Maybe I've deceived you about my reason for being here, but I think if you're fair with me, you'll realize I had to do things the way I did. At least, I thought I had to at the time."

He took a deep breath, pulling his hands from his back pockets and removing his hat. "I started to tell you at one point all about this, but if you'll remember, we got sidetracked. I'm not making excuses. I'm just being totally honest with you now."

Tears misted her eyes, but she resolutely blinked them back. "I can't think straight. What you've told me is a tremendous burden on my mind right now. I need to be alone to sort everything out."

"I see." He started to say something further, bit it back, then lifted his head as though deciding to continue. "Maybe you're the one who's having trouble being honest, Ellie. Both to me and to yourself. The way I look at it, if you cared for me, you'd fight for what we have. Or have the potential to have, anyway. Instead you're allowing the misunderstandings to take control of our lives. Instead of attempting to work things out, you're letting something beautiful die."

She pondered his words, admitting the truth of them yet unable to handle doing what he wanted at the moment.

"You don't understand. You aren't the one who's had your entire life turned topsy-turvy within the last few minutes."

"The life I thought I had was shattered not that long ago," Shane reminded her.

She shook her head. "You had to handle that your way,

and I have to handle this mine. I can't explain it any better than that. I've always had to go it alone.''

''Maybe in the past, but you have a choice now. You can let me into your life to share it, or you can let the past freeze me out. I'm willing to work things out, but I won't wait forever.''

She stared at him for a long moment. Then she neck-reined Cinder around and urged the gelding into a gallop. But no matter how fast Cinder ran, Ellie couldn't outrun her thoughts. It was impossible to outrun the knowledge that what Shane said made perfect sense, but that something inside her refused to break loose and allow him inside.

She instinctively headed for the house, but when she had it in sight, she pulled Cinder up. Ahead of her lay another lie—the lie that made up the life she lived all these years.

Had Elvina known all along, and withheld the truth from her?

She gazed around her. The sky was still blue; the sun still shone. Everywhere, lives swirled along their own paths, diverging and connecting without rhyme or reason. Or so it seemed.

Almost eighteen years ago, her life had veered off course. What had Shane said? That her aunt had instigated the kidnapping? What sort of family did she have for something like that to happen? Only a truly evil person would wreak this sort of misguided vengeance on a small child.

Realizing she had a million other questions needing answers before she could sort everything out in her mind, Ellie nudged Cinder onward. Her answers lay with Mariana Morgan, and she would see her this evening.

And while both Shane and his mother appeared to be satisfied as to Ellie's true identity, she wasn't sure at all in her own mind. It was too big a step to take to believe that she might have gone from being a very poor little orphan girl to a rich New York City heiress in the space of one conversation with the man who held her heart.

Because Shane still held it. She couldn't reason herself

out of that emotion, although she didn't see how she could forgive his deceit. Look at what the deceit of others had already done to her life, if she truly was Cynthia Spencer. It had stolen her very identity from her.

She rode Cinder into the barn and spent a long half hour currying the gelding before she turned him into the corral. Still she came to no firm conclusions in her troubled thoughts; had no startling revelations. Too many things remained cloudy. Too many questions held a "what if" slant attached to them.

Avoiding Fatima successfully, she went to her room. She opened the closet door, disgusted when she felt a surge of disappointment at not seeing another new gown that she might wear to dinner this evening. How quickly she had come to depend on Fatima's magic!

She took her second-best gown with her to the bathing room, using the one upstairs instead of chancing Fatima being in the kitchen. At least she had smelled something cooking down there, so Withers or Elvina must have convinced Fatima to prepare dinner for the Morgans this evening. Hopefully the food would be edible.

After bathing, Ellie spent the rest of the afternoon in her room, attempting to read but finally giving up and staring out the window. Hearing a noise, she gave a start and opened her eyes. Darn, she had fallen asleep, head pillowed on her shoulder as she leaned back in the window seat. Now she had a crick in her neck and felt the need to wash her face.

At least the nap had given her a respite from her thoughts. But the noise had been a buggy arriving—no, two of them. Both the Morgans and Rockford Van Zandt had arrived.

Ellie stood and went over to her water pitcher and basin, kept full for the times when Elvina hogged the bathing room. After washing her face and brushing her hair, she headed downstairs.

As she descended the stairwell, Ellie found Elvina and

Darlene in the foyer, greeting their visitors. Mariana Morgan crossed the floor and held her hands out to Ellie in greeting.

"Ellie, I'm so glad to see you." Sotto voce after they gripped hands, she said, "Shane told me about your discussion this afternoon, and we'll talk between ourselves later. If you want. Until then, I'll continue to call you Ellie until you tell me different. "

"Please," Ellie replied. "And I do want to talk later. I have dozens of questions, and I'm still not sure about all this."

"I understand."

From the corner of her eye, Ellie saw Elvina watching them closely. Her stepmother's wariness surprised Ellie. She would have thought Elvina would fall all over herself to make points with someone of Mariana Morgan's social standing. Instead, Elvina appeared reluctant to have her as a guest.

Her eyes didn't linger on her stepmother, however. Unerringly, they veered to the tall man standing just inside the door. He had hung his hat on the wooden rack provided in the entrance foyer, and his broad shoulders nearly blocked the doorway. He held her gaze, making no bones about the fact that his interest lay in Ellie, not any of the other people in the group. He started toward her, but Elvina stepped into his path—deliberately, it appeared.

"We haven't had many guests recently," she said, "but I do want to welcome you to our ranch, Mariana. I asked Withers if he would serve us some libations before dinner in the parlor. It's right this way."

She took Mariana's arm and led her across the hallway to the parlor. As she passed Ellie, Elvina hooked her other arm in hers, leading her along with them. Short of digging in her heels and embarrassing both Elvina and herself, Ellie had no choice but to go along.

Withers waited in the parlor, and when Ellie managed a questioning look at him, he shrugged his shoulders. Evidently he had no idea of Fatima's mood, and Ellie could only hope the coming meal would go smoothly.

"I've always wanted to see New York," Elvina said, motioning Mariana to the settee and Ellie to sit beside her.

"Well, maybe you'll get your chance, Mrs. Parker," Rockford said.

"Oh?"

"Yes." He took Darlene's hand and held it to his mouth, kissing it briefly. "I haven't had a chance yet to tell Darlene, but Shane and I have come to an agreement about the business expansion. It looks like I might be able to support a family soon. And that I might be doing that in New York."

Ellie gave Shane a grateful look as Darlene disregarded propriety and flung herself into Rockford's arms. Excited chatter flew around the room, but Shane only nodded, his gaze never leaving Ellie's. In fact, Ellie had felt his eyes on her continuously since his arrival. But there would be no chance for privacy this evening.

She fervently hoped not, anyway. She felt as ill-prepared to deal with her feelings for Shane tonight as she had when she rode away from the creek earlier.

Amid the discussion of the city Darlene would call home, Ellie noticed Withers slipping out. A moment later, he came back in and announced dinner. Rockford escorted Darlene, of course, and Elvina captured both Mariana and Ellie once more, leaving Shane to tag along behind. Ellie didn't understand her stepmother's actions, since Elvina hadn't paid this much attention to her in years, but she accepted the chance to avoid Shane for a while longer.

In the dining room, Ellie halted in shock until Elvina pulled her forward. The table hadn't been set this gorgeously since George Parker died and Elvina gave up formal entertaining.

"What a lovely table," Mariana Morgan said, confirming Ellie's thoughts.

She was right. Though the extensions weren't added in

the middle, in order to keep the small party more intimate, nothing else had been spared. A snowy white cloth covered the table, with short candles burning in two candelabras, so as not to impede conversation across the table. They sat on either side of a low centerpiece of white and pink roses, a match for the china at each place setting. The floral scent lingered pleasantly in the air, and water and wine goblets were already filled. Silverware gleamed in reflected candle-light.

Ellie breathed a sigh of relief, hoping this indicated Fatima's acceptance of her duty to serve a nice meal to their guests.

They settled at the table, with Elvina asking Shane if he would take the seat at the far end from her. Since she placed Ellie in the chair on her left and settled Mariana on her right, Elvina's seating pattern effectively separated Shane from Ellie once again.

Conversation continued to swirl as Fatima silently carried in containers and set them in front of Elvina to serve.

"This is very lovely," Ellie told her after Fatima set down the bowl of whipped potatoes. Fatima didn't answer, but only nodded and disappeared back into the kitchen. A stab of unease hit Ellie.

Though everything appeared delicious and she dutifully took a serving of each portion as it passed, Ellie had no appetite. No one except Shane seemed to notice that she merely toyed with her food. Finally she caught his frown, then his eyes drifted down to her full plate. With a sigh, she stabbed a piece of roast beef on her fork and forced it into her mouth.

She nearly spat it out a lot quicker than she had picked it up. It was loaded with salt! Under the guise of wiping her mouth, she enclosed the meat in her napkin and lowered it to her lap.

Staring around the table, she noticed everyone else relishing their meals. Except Shane.

"You do have a wonderful cook," Mariana told Elvina

just then. "I'll have to ask her for her recipe for this marvelous cheese sauce on the asparagus."

"Fatima is incredible," Elvina agreed. "Wait until you taste her rum sauce on the bread pudding for dessert. Why, I have to watch myself with her, or I'd gain weight just looking at the food."

Elvina laughed in accompaniment to Mariana's chuckle, then glanced at Ellie's plate, lifting her brow in question. Ellie cut off a piece of asparagus and dipped it in the cheese sauce. A moment later, it joined the beef in her napkin. Grabbing her water glass, she gulped and tried to rinse the sour taste out of her mouth. If she kept this up, her entire meal would end up in her napkin. Why didn't the nasty food appear to bother anyone else?

She looked down the table at Shane's plate and saw it now empty. When she caught his gaze, he flicked his head ever so slightly at the plant sitting on the floor behind him. Evidently his food was resting beneath one of the broad leaves now.

Fatima! Fatima's magic had spoiled only hers and Shane's food. Not giving anyone a chance to stop her, Ellie shoved her chair back and stood.

"I'll be right back," she said. "I need to see Fatima briefly."

Hurrying into the kitchen, she found Withers there alone. He gave her a guilty stare, and she noticed one of the plates from the bunkhouse sitting on the counter. Another plate was in the sink, scraped fairly clean but with a few remnants of the meal clinging to it.

"You went out and got a plate from Cookie," she accused Withers.

"Did she ruin all the food for dinner?" he asked worriedly.

"Evidently just mine and Shane's. Where is she?"

"A headache, she said. She went to her room after asking me to serve the dessert. And—" He gave the dessert dishes on the tray a contemplating look. "She said the two on the end were yours and Master Shane's."

Ellie stomped over to the tray and removed the two undoubtedly offensive bowls of bread pudding. "Where did she put the rest of the pudding?"

Withers went over to the pie cupboard and opened the doors. Inside Ellie saw a covered bowl and a small pitcher beside it. She doubted Fatima would have spoiled the leftover pudding, since someone might ask for a second helping. She took two fresh bowls down and placed them on the counter for Withers to fill.

"I'll bring it right in, Miss Ellie," he said.

Nodding her head in satisfaction, Ellie returned to the dining room. When Withers came in a few seconds later with the dessert tray and a pot of coffee, she managed to give Shane a surreptitious nod, indicating the pudding was safe to eat. He smiled his gratitude and dug into the bowl Withers placed in front of him.

Twenty-four

~

Shane openly approached Elvina when she rose to indicate they would retire to the parlor again for an after-dinner drink or more coffee, whichever anyone preferred.

"I'll escort Ellie," he said when Elvina started to take Ellie's arm. He suited action to words and nudged his hand in to capture Ellie's elbow first. Elvina's face indicated surprise, which faded into something Ellie almost thought was apprehension before she shuttered her eyes. Moving over to Mariana, Elvina walked out of the dining room with her.

"How did she do that?" Shane asked.

Instinctively, Ellie knew he referred to the meal, but his hand on her arm was so warm, so comforting. So . . . Shane. She had yearned for this closeness all day, even when she kept the barrier of distance between them, both physically and with her sharp words.

"The meal," he explained when she didn't answer his inquiry. "How could she make our food taste so bad when we took our servings from the same containers as everyone else at the table?"

"I told you this morning. She claims to have magical powers."

"I see." His tone indicated he didn't, but this was one subject Ellie didn't intend to pursue yet.

Ellie started to walk away from the table, but Shane

caught her other arm and held her in place. Looking around, she saw they were alone in the dining room, since Rockford and Darlene had followed the other women.

"Ellie, I'm not going to leave things like they were this morning," Shane told her firmly. "I'll give you time to think about things, since so much was dropped on you all at once. But if you won't fight for our love, I intend to."

"That's the problem, Shane," she said sadly. "I don't know if there really is love to fight for."

He stifled a shocked gasp, and Ellie pulled her arms free. "It's all been built on a relationship between two people who don't really exist. Who aren't who they're supposed to be—aren't really the two people who fell in love. You're not a nice businessman from New York, who came here and whom I fell in love with. You're someone who had a hidden agenda for your trip."

She pushed a loose tress of hair threatening her vision back in place, noticing a lock of Shane's hair in disarray at the same time. But she refused to give in to the urge to smooth the tawny curl back from his forehead.

"And I'm not Ellie Parker," she continued. "Or I might not be. I'm not Cynthia Spencer, either, because her life was taken from her nearly eighteen years ago. How can I even think about letting someone else share a life with me until I know what that life entails? Until I know who I am myself?"

"If you cared as much for me as I do for you, Ellie, you'd let me help you through this confusion."

"That's unfair, Shane! You can't tell me how I should handle this, because you can't have the slightest idea what this is doing to me. If you feel I'm selfish because I don't have room in my emotions right now to take your feelings into consideration, I'm sorry about that. But it's the way things are. Besides, don't forget that your own actions helped create my predicament."

"You're the unfair one, Ellie. I *have* gone through something similar. After the explosion, I wasn't the same man I was prior to it. And I can tell you truthfully that I wished many times for someone to share that confusion with me and help me sort it all out. I had Mother, but the woman I loved walked out on me, leaving me to handle everything alone.''

It was Ellie's turn to be shocked. He was right; she was being unfair. But unfair or not, she had to sort through things and decide who she was before she could trust her own feelings once again. She didn't even know if her feelings were her own, for that matter, or whether they belonged to a woman inside her, whom she had yet to meet and understand.

Shane took her hands. ''Just give me a chance, Ellie. Don't cut me out of your life completely right now. Have dinner with me tomorrow night, and let's talk. Let's talk honestly. By then you'll have had some time to initially sort through some of this in your mind. And if you can tell me truthfully that you don't want to see me again after tomorrow night, I'll believe you. I'll accept your decision and leave you alone.''

''Ellie,'' Darlene said from the doorway. ''Mother has something she wants to talk to you about.''

Ellie tugged at her hands, but Shane refused to relinquish his grasp.

''Tomorrow?'' he asked.

''All right,'' she agreed, a glow of relief filling her at his persistence and recognizing that this was truly what she had wanted all along. She wanted him to explain things, make her see that there was a reason for the way he had gone about his investigation.

She wanted a future that lingered out there somewhere beyond reach right now, in the netherworld of misunderstandings.

''Ellie?'' Darlene repeated.

''We're coming.''

Darlene's skirts whispered as her sister left, but instead of following immediately, Ellie stood unmoving. Shane's head was bending, and he meant to kiss her. She wanted that kiss with everything in her, and she intended to have it.

His lips met hers softly, firmly, lingeringly and with a yearning that matched the deep need inside her. All too soon he raised his head and left a sense of loss on her lips instead of the warmth and succor she craved—the flicker of desire even this slight caress stimulated.

He stared at her for a long moment, his gold-dust eyes filled with deep, shadowed feelings. For one brief instant, she considered asking him to sneak out of the house with her and find some privacy to sift through their difficulties now instead of tomorrow night. But Shane dropped her hands and wrapped an arm around her waist, steering her out of the dining room and toward the parlor, where either some answers or more questions waited for her.

All eyes were on the two of them when they entered the room, and Ellie couldn't help but wonder what Mariana had told Elvina and Darlene. Elvina took a sip from a glass of sherry in her hand, then motioned for Ellie and Shane to sit on the settee she had occupied earlier.

''I have something to discuss,'' Elvina said. Then she reached for another glass of sherry, handing it to Ellie. Beside it was a smaller glass holding an amber liquid, which she handed to Shane.

Although Ellie seldom drank, she accepted the sherry. She had heard spirits actually helped a person handle strain, as long as one didn't drink too much. She sipped from the glass, and after a few seconds, did actually feel a loosening in her shoulders.

Instead of seating herself, Elvina continued to stand in front of the empty fireplace.

''Mariana has told us why she and Shane came to Fort Worth,'' she said. ''And I want you to know, Ellie, that I really haven't been hiding anything from you. I truly didn't remember this until after I saw Mariana this evening. George had intended to tell you what he knew and give

you what I'm about to give you on your eighteenth birthday. But he died three years before that, and with my own
troubling adjustment to widowhood and not knowing how
to help you handle the ranch problems, I just completely
forgot about it.''

"What are you talking about, Elvina?'' Ellie asked impatiently. Shane reached for her hand, and she allowed herself that comfort, although she noticed Mariana looking at
their clasped hands with a tiny smile on her face.

Elvina set her sherry glass down and walked over to one
of the pictures on the parlor wall. Removing it, she placed
it on the floor and spun the dial on a wall safe Ellie wasn't
even aware was in the house. When it opened, Elvina
reached inside and pulled out a small, black-velvet jewelry
bag.

Rather than going over to Ellie, Elvina approached Mariana, who sat in one of the side chairs. Opening the drawstring on the bag, she took out a gold locket.

"I think you might recognize this,'' Elvina said.

Nodding her head in agreement and seeming unsurprised,
Mariana reverently reached for the locket. She pushed the
spring lock, and the locket face opened. After looking at
what was inside it for a long moment, a tear slipped down
her face. Mariana rose and handed Ellie the locket.

Ellie pulled her hand from Shane's grasp and held the
locket on one palm, touching it with a finger on her other
hand. Two women's faces peered back at her, one of them
a younger Mariana Morgan. She didn't recognize the other
one, but it looked familiar in spite of that. A beautiful
woman gazed back at her, a smile on her lips and her platinum hair swirling around her much the same way Ellie's
did when she let it hang before she braided it.

"Is this my mother?'' she asked quietly.

"Yes,'' Mariana said. She knelt in front of Ellie and
clasped her own hands around Ellie's. "We had this made
soon after you were born. There was another one, with

George and Rose in it, but I found it among their things after Lily died.''

"Lily?'' Ellie asked.

"Your aunt, child. An evil woman. I'll tell you all you want to know about her later, but right now this locket is the last bit of proof of your identity, although I firmly believed who you were the moment I saw you in the hotel.'' She looked over at Elvina. "Where did you find this?''

"Ellie had it in one of her shoes,'' Elvina said. "George knew it was expensive, and he immediately had suspicions about Ellie's true background. But there was no way to follow anything up. We discussed it, and decided to give Ellie a home and see if anyone came searching for her. As you know, they never did. But George still knew the locket would mean something to Ellie some day, so we saved it. Still, he intended to search for her true parents if she ever asked him to.''

Mariana nodded. "It was too large for Cynthia to wear, but she absolutely loved this locket. So Rose allowed her to carry it around in her shoe or pocket or wherever she wanted to carry it. She never once lost it.''

Standing, Mariana pulled Ellie up with her. "You're Cynthia Spencer, my dear. My godchild and the daughter of the dearest friend I ever had. You're also the only heir to a very substantial fortune waiting for you back in New York. I hope you'll come home with me for a while, at least until we can get all of the paperwork straightened out.''

Even though she thought she had prepared herself for this possibility, Ellie could hardly speak. In an attempt to forestall dealing with her confusion, she studied the people around her for their reactions. Elvina wore a strangely sad look on her face. Rockford merely looked stunned, the way Ellie felt, but excitement danced across Darlene's face.

"I'd like to see where my mother lived,'' Ellie admitted.

Darlene uttered a cry and raced across the parlor, flinging her arms around Ellie. "Oh, Ellie, how wonderful! I'm so happy for you! And you'll be able to visit with me when I move to New York.''

Ellie returned Darlene's embrace, knowing without doubt her sister was truly, unselfishly elated for her. Darlene pulled back, and Ellie reached to wipe a tear of happiness from her sister's cheek.

"Or should I call you Cynthia now?" Darlene asked.

"I'll always be your sister, Ellie," Ellie said. Then she looked once more at Elvina.

Her stepmother crossed the room, and Darlene stepped back. Ellie sensed Shane close beside her, but her world at the moment centered on Elvina's reaction.

"I am truly happy for you, too," Elvina said, taking her hands. "I know you think I don't love you like Darlene, and maybe you're right. But I've always wanted what was best for you, Ellie. I've felt very inadequate since George died. You were always his special little girl, and Darlene was mine. When you needed me, I had no experience in the things you'd learned from George. I tried to educate myself, but you were always so busy, I didn't want to add that burden to you.''

"I did my best with the ranch, Elvina.''

"I realize that. And I guess the least I could have done was tell you how much I appreciated that, instead of trying to figure out what I could do to help and ending up making the wrong decisions.''

Elvina squeezed Ellie's hands. "I finally decided that both of you girls needed to get off this ranch and find lives you couldn't get here. Darlene found Rockford, but you kept yourself buried in work. And the longer it went on, the more I felt the ranch was a losing proposition. That's why I decided to sell it—so you could live a life becoming to a woman instead of trying to do a man's job.''

"Will you sell the ranch to me now, Elvina?''

She nodded. "If that's what you want, but only because I know how much you love it. But think it over carefully, Ellie. And we'll talk about it later.''

"I've wanted to talk so many things over with you, El-vina."

"I know that now. Before, I felt I was supposed to be the adult and take care of you. Instead, you had to take on responsibilities you shouldn't ever have had to carry on your young shoulders."

Ellie tentatively pulled her hands free and reached for Elvina. Her stepmother sobbed and pulled Ellie into her arms. She held Ellie for long moments, stroking her hair and murmuring comfort and admissions of wanting to hold her but not knowing how to approach after all the lost years. At last, Elvina released her, very reluctantly, then cupped her cheek.

"I hope we can truly become a mother and daughter, Ellie. I do love you, even though I haven't been the best of mothers to you."

"It was partly my fault," Ellie admitted. "I've pretty much held everyone at bay."

She heard Shane's sound of agreement beside her, and she turned to smile at him.

"Well, Shane and I are going to get back into town and leave your family alone to talk," Mariana said. "Coming, Shane?"

Ellie received one last, longing look from Shane. "To-morrow, then?" he asked.

"Yes. We'll have dinner tomorrow. I haven't forgotten."

He set his glass down and took Mariana's arm when she approached. Rockford murmured a leavetaking to Darlene and joined them as they left the parlor. Before Ellie could miss Shane too much, Darlene grabbed her and pushed her back onto the settee, settling beside her.

"Now, Ellie," her sister demanded. "Tell me how it feels to be rich. And tell me what's going on between you and Shane Morgan. And tell me how soon we can both go to New York. And tell me what on earth you want with this ranch when we could—"

"Darlene," Elvina said in chastisement. "Let Ellie catch her breath."

Ellie laughed along with Darlene when her sister clapped her hands and broke into giggles in the face of Elvina's rebuke. Then Ellie held out a hand toward her mother.

"Come join us, Mother. Let's have a long girl talk."

Elvina smiled tolerantly and settled on the other side of Ellie.

They talked deep into the night, healing old wounds and making new plans. Long after midnight, they went upstairs, and as Ellie prepared for bed, she realized she was watching for Fatima to appear. But the fairy woman never showed up, and Ellie fell asleep an instant after her head hit the pillow. She slept better than she had for weeks, but when she woke the next morning, her thoughts immediately flew to Shane.

What would the result of their evening be? Darlene had been ecstatic last night over the possibility of her and Ellie both living in New York, if Ellie ended up marrying Shane.

But Shane hadn't asked her that final question. And if he asked tonight, Ellie had no idea what her answer would be.

Twenty-five

That morning, Ellie discovered further changes in her life.
Even this early, Elvina and Darlene were already in the
kitchen, and Fatima stood at the stove, a huge smile on her
face. Well, at least they would get a decent meal this morning, Ellie mused tolerantly when Fatima waved and winked
at her.

Darlene and Elvina still wore their robes and yawned
sleepily when Ellie joined them at the table.

"Why are you both up this time of day?" she asked as
Fatima came over with a steaming cup of coffee for her.
The steam tickled her nose delightfully, and she didn't have
to wait for it to cool to sip before knowing it would taste
delicious.

"I wanted to catch you and also talk to Shorty this morning," Elvina said. "I think it's time we gave him full responsibility for running the ranch and hired another hand,
so you don't have to spend all your time out on the range."

"And," Darlene put in, "I heard your comment about
having dinner with Shane this evening. You and I are going
to spend the day making over one of my dresses so you'll
have something beautiful to wear, so you're not going to
have time to boss the men around today. I suppose we
could take a chance on there being something appropriate
in one of the dress shops in town, but I think it will be

more fun doing it ourselves. We'll see the dressmaker in Fort Worth later.''

"You two are spending money I don't have yet," she cautioned them, but grinned at their enthusiasm.

"I have some money put back that will get us by for a while," Elvina said. Ellie glanced at her in amazement, and Elvina actually laughed at her. "George always allowed me what he called 'pin money,' but he always insisted on paying any bill I ran up. So I've got that money in the bank in an account of my own."

"I don't even know how much this supposed fortune is," Ellie cautioned. "It might not be enough to pay you back and also buy the ranch."

"Then we'll get by somehow," Elvina said firmly. "I don't want you to worry about it. And—" She frowned at Ellie. "—I don't want you handling everything by yourself from now on. I want you to remember that you're part of this family. A very important, much-loved part of it."

Fatima began to hum behind Ellie, and she looked around to see the fairy woman dancing a little jig as she turned the fluffy flapjacks on the griddle.

This morning Fatima wore green. Bright green silk. Oh, and some red here and there. She almost looked as if she were dressed for Christmas, although Ellie sensed part of the gaudiness was some sort of celebration.

Her dress bodice dipped low, and the skirt flared out with red and green net underskirts, but ended well above her knees as always. Green silk stockings with a black seam up the back encased her legs, and sparkling green high-heeled slippers with square decorations made of what looked like diamonds sparkled with each tiny prance of her feet. She wore her hair pinned up in beautiful swirls, held in place with emerald-tipped hairpins.

Ellie ate breakfast with her stepmother and sister, then Darlene went to her room to dig in her closet while Ellie and Elvina went to talk to Shorty. Another surprise waited for Ellie. Shorty didn't seem at all upset over being handed the reins of the ranch or finding that Ellie intended to move to a more feminine style of management. In fact, the discussion demonstrated to Ellie that Elvina and he were old, if wary, acquaintances.

Afterward, she and Darlene had so much fun together, Ellie almost felt reluctant for the day to end. They made over a beautiful blue watered-silk dress, shortening it and tucking it in to fit Ellie's smaller figure. She let Darlene talk her into helping her dress and fixing her hair, which they did in Darlene's more adequately stocked bedroom.

Feeling somewhat scandalous, Ellie even allowed her sister to brush a faint dusting of rouge on her cheeks and tip her lashes with kohl. She drew the line at lip rouge, though, promising her sister she would bite her lips prior to meeting Shane, to bring some color into them.

"Now, let's go get Mother's verdict on how you look," Darlene said at last. "Oh. Wait a minute." She dug in her jewelry box and pulled out some gold earrings. "I assume you'll want to wear your locket, and these will go with them."

While Ellie put the earrings on, Darlene smirked at her in the mirror. Then she took one of her crystal perfume bottles from the dresser and spritzed Ellie between the breasts.

"That smells wonderful," Ellie said.

"It was a gift from Rockford, remember? On my birthday last month?"

"I remember."

Although Darlene's feet were larger than Ellie's, they found a pair of shoes in Elvina's closet that went well with the dress. Unaccustomed to the higher heels, Ellie tottered for a second when she stood, but quickly adapted. She even made it down the stairs and to where Elvina waited in the parlor without difficulty.

"You look wonderful, Ellie," Elvina said. "You've always been a pretty girl, but now you make a gorgeous woman. Shane's going to be falling all over himself."

Ellie frowned.

"Oh, don't," Elvina said with a laugh, wiping away the crease on Ellie's forehead. "You'll give yourself early wrinkles.

It was something Ellie wished her own mother could say, and she squeezed Elvina's hand in appreciation. But her stepmother's words were still a cause for worry.

"What's wrong?" Elvina asked astutely.

Ellie walked over to the settee, and Elvina joined her. When Darlene pulled a chair up and sat across from her, Ellie realized both women truly cared about what troubled her.

"It's Shane," she admitted. "I'm having trouble with the fact that he came here under false pretenses."

Elvina nodded. "Even well-intentioned lies dig at a person's trust," she said wisely.

"That's it exactly. And I do love him. The problem is, I'm not sure if I love the Shane who came here at first, or the man he is now."

"No," Elvina said. "The problem is, Shane is both these men. And you're not sure you can forgive him for his deception."

"What should I do?" Ellie begged.

"Follow your heart," Elvina told her. "But while you're following it, make sure you know where it's leading you."

Ellie reached out and took the hand Elvina held toward her. "I wish we could have been closer years ago."

"You've grown into a wonderful woman despite my neglect, Ellie."

"It wasn't really neglect. It was the two of us being unable to overcome our insecurities with each other."

Elvina smiled at her, then glanced through the parlor window as they heard a buggy drive into the ranch yard. They jumped to their feet, and Elvina and Darlene both began primping and adjusting various things on Ellie: her hairpins, her bodice, her skirt. Finally Ellie laughed and pushed their hands away.

"Shane's going to think I can't dress myself if he comes in here and finds the two of you all over me like this."

They giggled like conspirators, but when Shane's broad shoulders filled the parlor door, her stepmother and sister stepped back so he could view Ellie unobstructed.

A stunned expression on his face, Shane crossed the floor, his eyes never leaving Ellie.

"You've always been beautiful," he said. "But tonight you take my breath away."

Giggling, Elvina and Darlene sneaked out of the parlor, with Shane seeming not to notice. He offered his arm, and Ellie took it. Her own eyes filled with him, his evening dress and stark white shirt perfectly tailored to suit him, so very masculine. His scent of sandalwood and evening air drifted to her nose as she walked out of the house with him. He handed her into the buggy as though she were a precious jewel, climbed in after her and set the horse in motion.

Good thing the horse knew the way back to town, Ellie mused after a while. Shane, quiet as was his normal bent, kept his eyes mostly on her. Until they came in sight of town, however. Then he steered the horse over beneath a huge cottonwood tree.

Ellie finally spoke, her voice husky. "I thought we were going to dinner."

"We are. But first—"

He cupped his fingers under her chin and gently tilted her face up. He kissed her gently, and he kissed her harder. She lost track of time while the evening deepened around them, and he kissed her nose, her cheeks, her ears. Kissed her neck in that special spot she hadn't even known was sensitive until Shane found it. The spot probably wasn't even sensitive unless it was Shane kissing it.

She didn't come to her senses until his tongue traced her breast mounds, peeking above the low dress bodice. Even then, her cautionary words raced right out of her mind when he slipped a hand inside her bodice and swept her right breast free to his wet caresses.

He was the one who finally called a halt, because he could have swept her out of the buggy and under the tree with no resistance on her part. Breathing harsh and heavy in the evening air and abandoning her breast to cool while the nipple puckered even tighter with longing, he released her. Laying his head back against the buggy seat, his eyes closed and his chest rising and falling, he moaned a sound that made her want to fling herself back into his arms.

"My God," he said after a moment, eyes glittering with passion when he turned his head to face her. "I nearly ravaged you right here on the buggy seat."

She smiled cockily. "Ravage means with force, doesn't it? I wasn't giving you any reason to believe I wasn't fully cooperating, was I?"

His eyes swept down her face and over her bodice, and centered on the breast she hadn't been aware still perked from her dress. The indiscretion heated her cheeks in embarrassment, something his caresses hadn't been able to effect. But when she reached for her breast, Shane grabbed her hands.

Gently, he laid her hands in her lap and took the breast himself. Gently, he bent and kissed it, then tucked it back into place, covering it with the silk material of her bodice. He looked at the mound with regret, traced a finger along the top of it, then laid his head against the seat back again.

"We'll go in a minute," he said with another groan.

That was fine with Ellie. Right now she felt on the very edge of exploding with the passion Shane stirred in her, and the motion of the buggy might just send her over that mountain. She laid her head back, also, but her breathing brushed her breast tips against the silk, and she finally sat up straight. Hadn't Darlene said something about putting a lady's fan in her reticule?

She found the reticule on the floorboard and opened it.

Yes, there was a fan. Pulling it out, she spread it and waved it back and forth in front of her face.

"Got another one of those?" Shane asked.

Ellie laughed delightedly and fanned his face a few times. Shaking his head at her, Shane picked up the reins.

"I don't suppose you would consider staying in town with me tonight," Shane said as they drove into town a few minutes later.

"I would *not*," Ellie replied in mock haughtiness. "Why, whatever would people think?"

He laughed, drove on and halted the buggy in front of the hotel a few minutes later. The hotel doorman hurried out and tied the horse to a hitching rail, but when he reached to help Ellie from the buggy, Shane waved him off. He climbed down and turned back, lifting her easily when she trustingly placed her hands on his shoulders.

Shane dug a coin from his pocket and gave it to the doorman, then led Ellie up the hotel steps. Inside, a prim and proper waiter met then, greeting Shane and leading the way through the restaurant, toward the back. The waiter opened a door to a private dining room, which contained a table already set with sparkling china and lighted candles. A single, gorgeous red rose lay across one of the plates.

"It's beautiful," she said.

Shane waved the waiter off, closing the door on him and seating her himself, at the place setting where the rose lay. Silver platters and covered dishes over low flames sat on the sideboard, along with a wine bottle in ice and sparkling glasses. Shane ignored all that for the moment.

"There's a way you could spend the night with me, Ellie," he said as though picking up the previous conversation.

He knelt on one knee beside her, and Ellie's hand flew to her throat. Without taking his eyes off her, Shane picked up her other hand in his left and removed a small velvet box from his suit jacket pocket with his right.

"I love you, Ellie," he said. "I need you in my life.

Without you, there's an unbearable, empty hole. With you, I feel complete.''

He turned her hand over and kissed her palm, then flicked the velvet box open with his thumb. Holding out the beautiful diamond-and-sapphire ring to her, he said, ''Marry me, Ellie. Be my wife.''

Her breath, which she hadn't even realized she was holding, rushed out, destroying the dam against her turbulent thoughts at the same time. The ring shone in the candlelight, beckoned her with everything she had thought she wanted so many nights after a hardworking, emotionally draining day on the ranch. A life of ease and freedom to work when she wished, play when it suited her. Most of all, a life with a man by her side who loved her above all others, who would walk with her into the sunset years of her life, never leaving her lonely again.

So why did the ring glow mockingly rather than enticingly?

Because she wasn't ready to make that final commitment until she sorted through all the things that had happened in the last week. Because she wanted to be sure which woman accepted Shane's proposal—Ellie Parker or Cynthia Spencer. Or the third woman perhaps waiting inside her for acknowledgment.

With an enormous effort from the bottom of her soul, she made the only decision possible for herself at the moment.

Ever so slowly, so very, very slowly, Ellie shook her head, watching Shane's face crumble as she did so.

''I . . . didn't expect this,'' she managed to say, at the same time knowing it wasn't a complete surprise. ''We . . . we were going to talk.''

Closing the ring box and flinging it onto the table, Shane rose to his feet. He jammed his hands into his trouser pockets and walked over in front of the window curtains, closed to give the room privacy.

Swinging around, he said, ''Then talk.''

Twenty-six

~

Rising to her feet, Ellie clutched the locket around her neck as though seeking courage. She might need it. The man in the room with her was twice her weight, probably ten times her strength.

Then one of the candles on the sideboard flared, lighting up Shane's face. The ravaged, pained look in his eyes filled Ellie with remorse at what she had done. She needn't fear this man physically, she reminded herself. What she needed to remember was how easily she could hurt him.

Which she had obviously done quite effectively.

She took a step toward him. "Shane, I thought I explained to you yesterday that I needed some time. I do love you—"

"No," he interrupted. "Not really," he qualified at her puzzled look. "Love includes trust and complete acceptance."

She bit her lip, unable to dispute that.

"I don't blame you," he continued in a musing voice. "In fact, I understand completely. Had I known the woman I would find when I came here—were I able to go back and change things, I would. But it's not possible. I've done what I've done, and if forgiveness is beyond you, it's for the best. I want completeness with you or nothing."

He returned to the table and held the back of her chair,

standing as far away from her as he possibly could. "We can at least eat before I take you back to the ranch."

She shook her head. "I've lost my appetite. I thought you wanted to talk."

"There's nothing more to say, Ellie. You say you need time, and if that *is* all it takes, you know how to contact me if you decide a life with me is what you want. *If* I happen to end up a part of your final decision."

"Oh, Shane—"

He continued as though she hadn't tried to interrupt. "But I don't think time's going to heal the deception I so stupidly played out. If you're ready, I'll take you home now."

She bit her lip, trying to decide how to make him talk to her. He avoided her gaze and silently waited for her answer, as he had so many previous times. After a moment, his silence flicked her anger into rearing its ugly peak, and she straightened her shoulders. With a frosty toss of her head, she walked out of the room, Shane following.

The waiter in the hallway looked askance at both of them, but quickly masked his face. Hurrying ahead, he glanced back once to confirm they were indeed leaving the hotel. He snapped his fingers at the doorman, who covered up his own surprise and hastily retrieved the buggy he had moved on down the street.

They rode back to the ranch in silence, with Ellie utterly furious at Shane's refusal to reopen their conversation. Damn him, it was a good thing she wasn't going to marry him. She would never survive the rest of her life having to suffer these silences that were such a huge part of him.

She might not survive without him at all, either.

He kept the horse at a trot, and they reached the ranch fairly quickly. Climbing out of the buggy on her side as soon as it stopped, she walked onto the porch without waiting for Shane. He caught her at the door, stared at her for a lingering moment as he handed her the rose from her plate, then turned and went back to the buggy.

Silent again.

She held the rose to her nose as he left, only realizing she was crying when the tears clouded her eyes so densely she couldn't see the buggy. Backhanding them away, she watched until the buggy disappeared in the distance, and even the dust settled.

Shane never looked back. And she didn't even realize that was what she was waiting for until he was gone from sight.

After turning the buggy over to the doorman again, Shane shoved his fists into his pockets and strode down the street. He would never be able to sleep yet—maybe not at all tonight. And if his mother heard him back in his room, she would be over there in a flash, demanding to know how his evening with Ellie had gone.

I asked her to marry me and she turned me down flat, Mother.

Shane could see the dismayed look on his mother's face in his mind, a look not even close to matching the bitter pain in his heart.

"How many times are you going to open your heart and let some woman cut pieces out of it, Morgan?" he murmured as he walked down two steps leading to an alley bisecting the tall building. A sound in the darkness drew his attention, and he halted, peering toward it. A rangy hound raised its head from a pile of garbage, but the streetlight showed a collar on the animal's neck and a well-fed body. Someone's pet who preferred rummaging in rubbish to his own dish of food, he guessed.

The animal snarled at him, obviously preferring his meal of rubbish well enough to defend it.

"Shit," Shane grumbled as he strode on across the alley. "Even animals hate me tonight."

Spying a crowd ahead of him, an unforeseen experience this time of evening, he decided to investigate. It would give him something to do instead of fighting to ignore his aching heart and loneliness as he strolled alone through the night.

As Shane approached the train depot, he saw that most of the activity was centered further back on the baggage and flat cars, where men unloaded crates and some sort of machinery. As he drew closer, he saw animal cages and, at one car, men leading horses down a ramp.

Another circus. He shook his head. Full circle here in this town.

Someone tugged on his leg. Shane looked down into the excited eyes of a boy around ten.

"Ain't it wonderful, mister?" the boy said. "Someday I'm gonna join the circus!"

"What's your name, son?" Shane asked.

"Lucky, sir," he said.

"I bet you've enjoyed yourself recently, then, Lucky," Shane told him tolerantly. "Two circuses the past couple of weeks."

"Yeah, but this 'un's the big circus. T'other one, it was just sort of a tease for this 'un, my grampa said. This 'un's got trapeze artists and a bunch a elef . . . elef . . . them animals with them long, snaky noses."

"Elephants."

"Yeah. T'other circus, it only had a couple of them. This 'un's got . . ." He lowered his voice in awe. "This 'un's got six of 'em."

Another boxcar door opened, and Lucky's eyes rounded. Shane followed his gaze and saw an elephant stroll ponderously down the wooden ramp, followed by another one with the first one's tail in its trunk. Then another. The boy forgot all about Shane and raced through the crowd to get a better look.

Without Lucky's lively, excited presence, the sad hole in Shane's mind expanded. Glancing at the idle engine again, he made up his mind. He turned into the depot where, given the arrival of this late train, the stationmaster would still be working.

"Can I help you, sir?" the man behind the ticket counter asked when Shane approached. He wore a badge with the name Cletus on it, and Shane nodded at him.

"Hope so, Cletus. When does your next train leave?"

"Not till day after tomorrow."

Shane frowned. "What about this train here?"

"This one here ain't scheduled to go on tonight. It'll just move to a side track and wait for its next load. If it don't get one in the next two days, the circus will load back on and go to its next stop."

Shane studied the schedule behind the ticket counter. Now that he had made up his mind, he didn't feel like waiting.

"You wanting to leave tonight, sir?" Cletus asked.

"If I could. I'm trying to get back to New York City. I—something has come up that needs my immediate attention back there."

Cletus picked up a piece of paper from the counter in front of him. "You can get there from over in Dallas early tomorrow morning," he said, handing Shane a train schedule. "But that train leaves at six, and the engineer on it don't wait for no one."

"How long a ride over to Dallas is it?"

Cletus glanced at the clock, which indicated ten-thirty. "You could be there around one A.M., you have a fast horse. Even a slower one oughta take you there in plenty of time for the train."

"What about lodging over there?"

"There's a nice hotel a couple blocks from the train station. It's never full this time of year."

"I imagine everyone who can afford it leaves town and goes somewhere north in this heat," Shane mused.

"Yes sir."

Shane shoved the schedule in his pocket. "Thanks, Cletus."

Cletus bobbed his head, and Shane left the depot building.

On his way back to the hotel, he paused at one point, realizing the heat really hadn't bothered him that much the last few days. In fact, he had found himself strangely drawn to the wild, dusty, unending land around him.

His own ancestors had been among the original settlers in the New World, yet they had never spread beyond New York. Still, some of their adventurous genes may have been lying in wait in Shane, raising their adventurous heads when they found themselves in Texas.

Funny, he could even say the name of the state now in his mind with liking rather than revulsion.

He wondered how much of this new feeling was the result of actually coming to enjoy the land and how much of it was a direct result of the wonderful woman he had found here, who would be forever beyond his reach because of his own self-centered erroneous decision on how to investigate the matter his mother had begged him to handle.

Shrugging, he crossed the alley, spying the dog still at its odorous meal as he hurried to the hotel. Pulling a large bill from his pocket, he handed it to the doorman along with his room key, and gave him instructions. Then he went on to the stables, returning on Blackjack a while later to pick up the bag the doorman handed him and give the man a note to put in the message box for his mother's room.

Settling himself deep in the saddle for the long ride, he nudged Blackjack into a smooth canter toward Dallas.

Twenty-seven

The instant she woke the next morning, Ellie knew she had made a huge mistake. Eyes swollen from sobbing nearly all night, she turned her head and saw the crushed and mangled rose on the pillow beside her. With a gasp of dismay, she reached out and smoothed the petals.

"Ellie, are you all right?"

Through puffy eyes, Ellie made out Fatima sitting in the window seat.

"No," Ellie admitted. "I've made a huge mistake. I turned down Shane's proposal."

Fatima's jaw clenched, and Ellie prepared for another round of nearly inedible meals. She scooted up in bed and leaned against the headboard. Picking up the rose, she sniffed it, the scent revitalizing the tears in her eyes, although she couldn't understand where they found the necessary moisture in her body. She had cried all night, both consciously and unconsciously, waking with a wet face even after the few hours of restless sleep she'd managed.

"I knew you'd be extremely angry with me," she choked to Fatima. "After all, you've been very clear that you wanted a match between Shane and me."

Fatima sighed in—was that maybe understanding? Ellie wiped at her eyes, trying to see the fairy woman's expression.

"Perhaps you weren't ready to accept it," Fatima said grudgingly. "I want a lasting match and your happiness, Ellie. Not just an end to my assignment, but the right end."

Standing, Fatima picked up the black wand from the window seat and waved it at Ellie. Amid a sparkle of gold dust, the rose returned to its former beauty.

"And," Fatima said with a cautioning finger, "don't get me wrong. I am severely perturbed, because you've been an extremely difficult assignment. However, I'm willing to make allowances for your error in judgment, since I found Withers after I met you."

"Then you and he have worked out your own differences?"

"Excellently." Fatima smirked in satisfaction. "Shane's going to have to find a new valet, since Withers and I will wed as soon as I tie up this assignment."

Ellie scooted over to the edge of the bed. "If Shane will still have me, that might be very soon. I'm going to see him. This time if he refuses to talk to me, I'll do the talking."

Suiting action to words, Ellie dressed and ate breakfast, glad to find the meal enjoyable instead of a plate of burned offerings. She was ravenously hungry after missing dinner the previous evening. But the moment she heard movement overhead, indicating that either her sister or stepmother was awake, Ellie hurried out of the house and to the barn.

Knowing she would prefer riding Cinder, she had dressed in her riding clothing, although Fatima had disagreed and thought she should let her conjure up another new dress. Saddling the gelding, she mounted, only to find Fatima waiting in the shadows inside the barn door as she started to ride out.

"I'll want to know what happened, Ellie," the fairy woman said. "And I want you to know that I *do* wish you happiness."

"Thank you," Ellie said honestly. "I wish you and Withers the same, Fatima."

Ellie rode out the door, her thoughts following her. *After last night, I'm going to need more than just best wishes. I might really need Fatima's magic. So it's a good thing she's not angry at me.*

What she found in town made her wonder if even magic could help her. At the front desk, a different clerk informed Ellie that Mr. Morgan had checked out.

Ellie stood stunned as though her entire world were crumbling around her—which she felt might actually be happening. Through the fog of her remorse, she heard the clerk continue to talk, saying Mrs. Morgan was still in residence, at the moment having breakfast in the dining room. Although reluctant to face Mariana, Ellie slowly walked away from the desk.

In the dining room, she found Mariana Morgan with a forlorn look on her face matching the feeling in Ellie's heart. She crossed the room, and Mariana rose as soon as she saw her.

"My dear," Mariana said, rounding the table and giving Ellie a hug. "Please join me. I would very much like to know what happened last night."

Ellie sat, and Mariana waved the waiter over. The well-trained man already carried an extra coffee cup, and he poured Ellie a cup from the silver server, pushing the silver tray holding cream and sugar closer before he discreetly left.

Ellie toyed with the cup handle. Given the acid feeling in her stomach, coffee didn't appeal right now.

"Would you rather have some tea or juice?" Mariana asked.

Ellie pushed the cup away, shaking her head in denial. She didn't want anything. Not food, anyway. In fact, the food she had eaten at the ranch lay heavy amid the sick feeling in her stomach.

"I turned down Shane's proposal last night," she said without preamble.

Mariana gasped in dismay, and Ellie avoided looking at

her, knowing she would see deep disappointment in the older woman's eyes. But that wasn't even close to the devastating knowledge in Ellie's own mind that she had turned down the only man she could ever love. She had made possibly an irreversible mistake, since she doubted Shane would ever want her again after this.

What man could want a wishy-washy woman who didn't know her own mind? What man could forgive her after she turned down such a heartfelt offer of love, especially a man with a recently healed broken heart from another woman?

"He didn't say what had happened in the note he left for me," Mariana said, drawing Ellie's attention back to her as surely as though she had dangled Shane's presence in front of her.

Mariana had to know where Shane was. But when Mariana continued, Ellie's spirits dove right through the floor.

"He only said he was going back to New York," Mariana said. "I checked with the doorman to see when he left, but the one who's there now isn't the one who was on duty last night. I was on my way to the depot to ask the stationmaster which train Shane took. I have a train schedule, but it appears to indicate it will be another two days before I can leave myself."

Ellie nodded sadly. "Might I go with you?" she asked, fully expecting Mariana to tell her that she had no business making another assault on Shane's emotions.

But Mariana said, "Of course, dear," and Ellie's hopes rose. Perhaps she could catch up to Shane before his resolution set too firmly and destroyed any chance she had to convince him she had changed her mind.

Mariana rose, and the waiter hurried over, staring at the still full table. "I hope nothing was wrong with the meal or coffee," he said.

"No, everything was fine," Mariana assured him. Holding out a hand and refusing to make any further explanation, she took Ellie's arm and led her out of the hotel.

As soon as they got out on the street, Mariana removed

a fan from her reticule, waving it in front of her face and reminding Ellie how much Shane had hated the Texas heat. It didn't really bother Ellie, accustomed to it since she worked out in it daily. But Darlene and Elvina both moved slowly through the summer afternoons, as did a lot of the other women Ellie knew.

Thinking of the heat reminded her of how Shane's skin glistened with sweat after they made love, slick under her palms. Knowing she was the cause of his passion had once stirred her femininity and a desire to give her own passion to him in return. Now she didn't know how she would ever make it through the rest of her life without ever being with him again.

Despite the fact that Mariana was not able to read her mind, Ellie glanced guiltily at Mariana, knowing her thoughts weren't something she should be fostering in the company of Shane's mother. Her cheeks flushed, and when Mariana saw that, the other woman offered Ellie her fan. Ellie shook her head.

The train depot came into view. When they reached it, they went inside and questioned the stationmaster. Mariana questioned him, anyway. Ellie stood there falling deeper and deeper into the gloomies, as she had called them when she was a small child. Shane had been determined to leave last night. He evidently went to not a little trouble to find a way to get away from her. If what the stationmaster indicated was true, Shane had ridden Blackjack all the way over to Dallas in order to catch a train.

Outside the depot once again, Mariana led the way to one of the waiting benches on the side of the building. She sat and motioned for Ellie to join her.

"Well, I guess that's that," she said. "The stationmaster said that was the last train headed for New York until the day after tomorrow, either here or over in Dallas. I'll wire Shane and tell him I'll be on that train, so he can have someone pick me up at the station."

She scooted around to face Ellie. "In the meantime, I

hope you don't change your mind about accompanying me, Ellie. And that you'll let me spend some more time with you here. I do want to get to know you better, and even if things don't work out between you and Shane, I want us to be friends.''

''I already like you a lot, Mariana,'' Ellie said, taking the hand the other woman offered.

In the middle of the mutual squeeze, she and Mariana heard a commotion somewhere away from the depot building. Gazing in that direction, Ellie focused on a huge striped tent rising into the air, and smaller outlying tents interspersed among animal cages.

''Another circus,'' Ellie said. ''I've had so much on my mind, I wasn't even aware another one was scheduled, although we do have several over the course of a summer.''

''I saw the posters around town,'' Mariana admitted, ''and I'd been hoping to be able to attend. I do like a good circus.''

Ellie glanced at her in surprise before she recalled Shane saying his mother enjoyed circuses.

Mariana chuckled. ''What? You think a New York society woman wouldn't be interested in a circus? I'll have you know, both my side of the family and Shane's father's family have highly adventurous genes in our makeup.''

Ellie stood. ''Would you like to go over and watch them set up, then?'' she asked. At least it would give her something to occupy her mind other than her horrid sadness.

''I would indeed.''

Mariana rose, and they walked down the depot steps, heading toward the activity of the circus preparations. They covered perhaps half the distance before a small figure appeared around the side of one of the smaller tents, racing in their direction, legs windmilling and feet kicking up puffs of dust in the hot air. When he got nearer, Ellie recognized one of the town children, a small boy around ten years old named Lucky.

Curious as to the trouble, she held out her hand to stop

Lucky when he got close. Lucky plowed to a halt, his small chest heaving as he panted.

"Ain't neither one of you ladies a midwife by no chance, are you?" he asked when he caught his breath.

"No," Ellie said. "But I've helped at animal births on the ranch."

Lucky grabbed her arm in a dirty hand and tugged. "Then you'd be what they need," he said urgently. "They sent me to find Doc, but I didn't figger he'd come to help a horse birthin'. And she's a'gonna die for sure if someone don't help her."

Mariana gasped, but Ellie ignored her and followed Lucky, joining the boy's run when he found his second wind and raced toward one of the small tents. He didn't stop at the tent, though; he pounded around behind it, where a mare lay on her side. Head stretched out, her flanks heaved in agony as she tried to birth her colt.

An overweight man stepped in front of Ellie. "Ma'am, this ain't no place for you. I might have to shoot this mare, and I don't think you want to see that."

Ellie shoved him aside, not taking time to respond to his orders. Kneeling at the mare's head, she stroked her muzzle and breathed into her nostrils until the mare opened her eyes and gazed at her.

"You're going to be all right," she promised the horse. "I'm here to help, and we'll get through this. Then you'll have a beautiful little baby to love you."

The mare nickered faintly, and after one last pat, Ellie moved to the back of her. "Someone get me a bucket of water and some strong soap."

Evidently they already had this ready, because one of the other men there handed it to Ellie. Glad she had worn a short-sleeved blouse, she washed her hands and arms, then covered her right arm again with soap suds. Sending the men into gasps of amazement, she reached inside the mare, feeling to see what was wrong with the colt.

She found the little head turned back onto the colt's

shoulder instead of straight out, as it should have been to lead the way down the birth canal. With a firm effort, she managed to tug the head into the proper place just as another contraction wracked the mare.

Ellie managed to jerk her arm free before the contraction crushed it, and she watched closely, giving a cry of joy when she saw the colt's muzzle appear. The mare heaved again, and a small brown-and-white colt slid out onto the straw beneath its mother.

Something was wrong, though. After a few seconds, the mare struggled to her feet and turned, nuzzling her baby and urging it to rise and suckle. The colt tried to comply, but Ellie saw that one of its rear legs was deformed. Still, after a few attempts, the colt made it up, its stance wobbly but effectively allowing it to walk. It nudged its head beneath the mare and grabbed a teat, tail switching as it enjoyed its first nourishing meal.

"Hell," the fat man said. "I'll let it eat, I guess. Won't matter whether I kill it with a full belly or an empty one."

Ellie whirled on him, spying Mariana beside him for the first time.

"What do you mean?" she asked the fat man with narrowed eyes.

"Deformed colt ain't no good to me," he said with a shrug. "Can't be trained for the ring. It'll just cost me money to feed it, and I ain't got no money to feed no animal that don't pay me back by performin'."

Ellie caught Mariana's eyes, and almost as though they communicated without words, Ellie knew what the heartbreak on Mariana's face meant. Shane had faced some of the same snide, bigoted remarks when he became deformed. Her horror at the way she had treated Shane last night deepened until she could barely breathe.

Someone handed the fat man a rifle.

Ellie rushed forward and jerked it away from him. "I'll give you five hundred dollars for that mare and colt," she said.

"What?" He pulled his hands back from trying to retrieve the rifle, a contemplating frown settling into his piggy eyes. "Well, now, missy, that there mare *is* one of my performin' horses. She's worth quite a bit to me, even if her colt ain't."

Mariana stepped forward. "Didn't your circus perform in New York City once?"

The man puffed out his fat chest even further. "It sure did, ma'am. And we're goin' back in the fall."

"You won't if I decide you won't," Mariana warned him. "My name is Mariana Morgan, and I'm on the board of the organization that decides just what type of entertainment we allow in our city. And also what we *don't* want there. Ellie has offered you two hundred and fifty dollars for this mare and colt. I'd suggest you take her offer."

The fat man glared at her. "She said five hundred!"

"Two hundred," Mariana said.

The fat man gulped. When Mariana began to speak again, he interrupted her.

"Sold," he said. "But you'll have to figger how to get her and the colt out of here yourself. I can't spare nobody to help you haul her off."

"I'll arrange for that," Ellie said. "And go by the bank before you leave town. My banker will have the money ready for you."

"Here." Mariana dug in her reticule and pulled out a roll of bills. She peeled off a few and handed them to the man. "Ellie can pay me back. I don't want her to have to deal with you again."

Her sarcasm didn't bother the fat man. Shrugging, he grabbed the bills and shoved them into his pocket, then hurried away.

"So what are we going to do with this little mite and its mother now?" Mariana asked.

"Maybe I can help."

When Ellie looked up, Fatima stood across from them, with Withers beside her. They must have just appeared, because they hadn't been there a moment ago. Aware of Fatima's attire, Ellie glanced at Mariana to see her reaction.

Mouth open in awe, Mariana asked, "Are you Fatima's daughter? The woman who cooks out at the ranch?"

Fatima laughed gaily. "Actually I'm Fatima."

Ellie dropped her gaze. Obviously from Mariana's expression, she saw Fatima as she really was: her red hair piled willy-nilly and held in place with multitudes of jeweled hairpins flashing every color under the sun; her gold dress bodice cut scandalously low; her red, yellow, green, purple, and black skirt swirling above knee length; and black stockings with a red diamond pattern encasing her legs and feet. Red-and-black high-heeled slippers completed the ensemble.

Then Ellie realized she had been judging the fairy woman, also, just as other people had judged the colt and Shane. Lifting her head, she walked over to Fatima and hugged her.

"I'm so happy to see you," she said, and a huge smile worth every bit of humility Ellie tried to put into her words spread across Fatima's face. "I need you."

Fatima cupped Ellie's cheek. "I'm your fairy godmother, Ellie. I'm here to grant your wishes."

"Thank you." Ellie nodded at the mare and colt. "Could you whisk them out to the ranch, into one of the stalls?"

Fatima lifted her wand and pointed it at the mare and colt. When the gold dust subsided, they were gone.

"Done," Fatima told Ellie. "And I'll make sure Shorty gets the urge to check in the barn. What else?" But before Ellie could speak, Fatima continued, "I hope your next wish has to do with finding Shane and accepting his proposal."

Ellie glanced at Mariana, but the other woman had actually sunk to the ground and was staring at Fatima as though about to faint. Ellie hurried over to her side and helped her back to her feet.

"She's real," Ellie assured Mariana. "Please don't think

you're crazy. I did at first, but believe me, Fatima is real.''

A glass of ice water appeared hovering in the air between them, and Ellie handed it to Mariana. The older woman stared at it in awe for an instant, then drank it gratefully. Handing the glass back to Ellie, she stared at Fatima again.

''I saw it, so it *has* to be true,'' she mused. ''And I've lived long enough that I should be able to accept this. It was just a huge shock initially.''

She gracefully rose and walked over to Fatima, holding out a hand. ''I'm very pleased to meet you. Again,'' she said with a smile.

Ellie breathed a sigh of relief, then looked at Fatima. ''Shane's gone back to New York, and we can't get a train out of here for two more days.''

Cocking her head, Fatima tapped an index finger on her cheek in contemplation. ''I can get you there, but I'll want to do it my way.''

''Any way at all,'' Ellie pleaded. ''Just get me to Shane.''

''He's probably still on the train,'' Mariana murmured. ''It's a full three-day trip to New York City from here, and the train only left Dallas this morning.''

Fatima shrugged. ''I can take care of that.'' She waved her wand, then said, ''There. He's back home now.''

Mariana gasped. ''But he must be frightened to death! To be on the train one second, then back at our home the next.''

''Then I suggest we hurry there and explain things to him,'' Fatima said.

Both apprehensive and eager for whatever Fatima had in mind, Ellie nevertheless grabbed Mariana's arm to steady them while the fairy woman performed her magic. Fatima waved her wand again, and a nearby empty animal cage turned into a huge, round, orange carriage. Splendid beyond measure, it sat there in the sunlight, white trim nearly blinding them and for some reason reminding Ellie of a pumpkin.

Next, Fatima waved her wand at another cage, where a male and female lion paced. The door opened, and the lions stared at it for a moment, then leaped free. Immediately Fatima changed them into a pair of beautiful white horses, already harnessed with black and silver leather, with feathery white plumes dancing on their heads. They trotted over in front of the carriage, and Fatima hitched them with one brief wand wave.

Hearing a noise, Ellie swallowed her astonishment and glanced to the side to see two monkeys chattering to each other, staring back and forth from the carriage to the group of people. Fatima must have waved her wand, because the monkeys changed into two young boys dressed in footman's gear. They hurried over to the carriage and took their places, standing on footrests on each side of the driver's seat.

"Withers and I will drive," Fatima informed them, a pleased smile at her work on her face. Waving her wand, she opened the carriage door, and a set of steps appeared.

Mariana swayed for a second, and Ellie gripped her hand tighter. They started for the carriage.

"Oh, wait," Fatima insisted.

Ellie stopped, and Fatima waved her wand. A second later, Ellie wore a beautiful white silk gown, the bodice covered in seed pearls matching the diamond-and-pearl necklace around her neck. Lifting the heavy skirt, Ellie saw crystal high-heeled slippers on her feet.

Fatima waved the wand a final time, and Ellie's hair swirled up onto her head, wispy tendrils feathering around her face. Noticing something on her ears, she raised a hand and fingered dangly earrings with square-cut stones in them, which surely were diamonds.

She smiled gratefully at Fatima. "I feel beautiful," she admitted.

"You are, my dear," Fatima said. "But then you've always been beautiful where it counts. Inside."

"I've made some very huge mistakes, though."

"You're only human, my dear. The biggest mistake would be to let your errors ride and not correct them."

"Let's go then." Pulling her skirts higher so she could climb the carriage steps, Ellie hurried forward. "I want to go correct my mistakes." She paused at the carriage door and stared back at Fatima. "If I can."

"Shane's human, too," Fatima said with a shrug, "so I can't predict how he'll react. However, I have a good feeling about this."

"Oh, I hope you're right."

Ellie climbed into the carriage, and Mariana joined her, relaxing in the deep cushioned seats. Shane's mother finally looked like she was accepting the startling happenings. Patting Ellie's hand, Mariana said, "I hope she's right, too."

Withers closed the carriage door, and the carriage swayed as he climbed into the driver's seat. A moment later, all Ellie could see was gold fairy dust swirling around them, although she felt the sensation of flying through the air. She and Mariana held hands, but neither of them asked Fatima to stop. After what seemed an all-too-brief moment later, the fairy dust around them died, and the carriage door opened.

Withers pulled down the steps, and Ellie took a deep breath. She courteously waited for the older woman to descend first, but Mariana shook her head and motioned for Ellie to proceed. Withers gave Ellie a comforting wink, and Ellie smoothed her damp palms down her silk dress and stood. Bending her head, she went through the carriage door, pausing on the top step.

Twenty-eight

The carriage and horses stood in what appeared to be a huge ballroom, and music swelled from an orchestra in the corner of the room. Instead of couples dancing, however, there was only one other occupant of the room in addition to the orchestra members and the group that had arrived in the carriage: Shane.

He stood conscious but paralyzed, mouth open and amazement filling his face. When Ellie appeared, he lifted his hands and viciously rubbed his eyes. The second he dropped his hands, Ellie winked at him. Maybe his shock would allow her to say what she needed to before he recovered his senses and told her he didn't want to see her.

But for once in their relationship, Shane spoke before she could.

"I am totally crazy and hallucinating," he mused. "I'm leaving to check myself into the asylum."

"Don't be silly, Shane," Mariana said from behind Ellie.

If possible, Shane's shock deepened. Mariana pushed gently on Ellie and, steadied by Withers's hand, Ellie went down the carriage steps. As Ellie waited uncertainly beside the carriage, Withers assisted Mariana's descent.

Rather than approach them, however, Shane staggered backward, feeling for a chair he evidently remembered sat against one of the walls. He fell more than settled into it, gazing from his mother to his valet to Fatima, his eyes inevitably coming back to Ellie as though seeking refuge in the madness. When Withers held a hand up to Fatima and she rose and floated serenely off the carriage and through the air to join him, Shane's face blanched.

Ellie hurried over to him. "I tried to tell you she was magic," she said, biting her cheek to hold back her laughter. "Is there somewhere we can go to talk?"

She held out her hands to him, and Shane grabbed them as though they were a lifeline. He gulped, closed his eyes briefly, then opened them and looked at Fatima.

"If you're the one responsible for this, I thank you from the bottom of my heart," he said, then turned his tawny gaze back on Ellie. "I'm assuming you're here of your own free will."

"More than that," she admitted. "I'm here as a result of my deep certainty that I made a huge mistake in asking you to wait for me. I love you, Shane Morgan. I want to spend every minute of the rest of my life as your wife, if you'll still have me."

"Still have you? Ellie, there's nothing I want more than to marry you and find you beside me every morning from now on. I want to have children with you and to sit by your side watching our grandchildren and great-grandchildren play in the yard. And I don't care whether that yard is in Texas or here in New York."

Ellie threw her arms around his neck. "Why can't we have it both ways?"

"We'll work it out."

He wrapped his arms around her and kissed her. The music swelled and filled Ellie's senses. When he finally lifted his head, Ellie heard the orchestra playing a beautiful waltz. Smoothly, Shane glided her onto the dance floor.

"I don't know how to dance," Ellie murmured.

He kissed her again, then said, "Just hold onto me."

"Forever," she agreed.

Turn the page for a preview of
Jill Marie Landis's newest novel

BLUE MOON

Coming in July from Jove Books

Prologue

SOUTHERN ILLINOIS
LATE APRIL, 1819

She would be nineteen tomorrow. If she lived. In the center of a faint deer trail on a ribbon of dry land running through a dense swamp, a young woman crouched like a cornered animal. The weak, gray light from a dull, overcast sky barely penetrated the bald-cypress forest as she wrapped her arms around herself and shivered, trying to catch her breath. She wore nothing to protect her from the elements but a tattered rough, homespun dress and an ill-fitting pair of leather shoes that had worn blisters on her heels.

The primeval path was nearly obliterated by lichen and fern that grew over deep drifts of dried twigs and leaves. Here and there the ground was littered with the larger rotting fallen limbs of trees. The fecund scent of decay clung to the air, pressed down on her, stoked her fear, and gave it life.

Breathe. Breathe.

The young woman's breath came fast and hard. She squinted through her tangled black hair, shoved it back, her fingers streaked with mud. Her hands shook. Terror born of being lost was heightened by the knowledge that night was going to fall before she found her way out of the swamp.

Not only did the encroaching darkness frighten her, but so did the murky silent water along both sides of the trail. She realized she would soon be surrounded by both night and water. Behind her, from somewhere deep amid the cypress trees wrapped in rust colored bark, came the sound of a splash as some unseen creature dropped into the watery ooze.

She rose, spun around, and scanned the surface of the swamp. Frogs and fish, venomous copperheads and turtles, big as frying pans, thrived beneath the lacy emerald carpet of duckweed that floated upon the water. As she knelt there wondering whether she should continue on in the same direction or turn back, she watched a small knot of fur float toward her over the surface of the water.

A soaking wet muskrat lost its grace as soon as it made land and lumbered up the bank in her direction. Amused, yet wary, she scrambled back a few inches. The creature froze and stared with dark beady eyes before it turned tail, hit the water, and disappeared.

Getting to her feet, the girl kept her eyes trained on the narrow footpath, gingerly stepping through piles of damp, decayed leaves. Again she paused, lifted her head, listened for the sound of a human voice and the pounding footsteps which meant someone was in pursuit of her along the trail.

When all she heard was the distant knock of a woodpecker, she let out a sigh of relief. Determined to keep moving, she trudged on, ever vigilant, hoping that the edge of the swamp lay just ahead.

Suddenly, the sharp, shrill scream of a bobcat set her heart pounding. A strangled cry escaped from her lips. With a fist pressed against her mouth, she squeezed her eyes closed and froze, afraid to move, afraid to even breathe. The cat screamed again and the cry echoed across the haunting silence of the swamp until it seemed to stir the very air around her.

She glanced up at dishwater-gray patches of weak afternoon light nearly obliterated by the cypress trees that grew so close together in some places that not even a small child could pass between them. The thought that a wildcat might be looming somewhere above her in the tangled limbs, crouched and ready to pounce, sent her running down the narrow, winding trail.

She had not gone a hundred steps when the toe of her shoe caught beneath an exposed tree root. Thrown forward, she began to fall and cried out.

As the forest floor rushed up to meet her, she put out her hands to break the fall. A shock of pain shot through her wrist an instant before her head hit a log.

And then her world went black.

One

Noah LeCroix walked to the edge of the wide wooden porch surrounding the one-room cabin he had built high in the sheltering arms of an ancient bald cypress tree and looked out over the swamp. Twilight gathered, thickening the shadows that shrouded the trees. The moon had already risen, a bright silver crescent riding atop a faded blue sphere. He loved the magic of the night, loved watching the moon and stars appear in the sky almost as much as he loved the swamp. The wetlands pulsed with life all night long. The darkness coupled with the still, watery landscape settled a protective blanket of solitude around him. In the dense, liquid world beneath him and the forest around his home, all manner of life coexisted in a delicate balance. He likened the swamp's dance of life and death of the way good and evil existed together in the world of men beyond its boundaries.

This shadowy place was his universe, his sanctuary. He savored its peace, was used to it after having grown up in almost complete isolation with his mother, a reclusive Cherokee woman who had left her people behind when she chose to settle in far-off Kentucky with his father, a French-Canadian fur trapper named Gerard LeCroix.

Living alone served Noah's purpose now more than ever. He had no desire to dwell among "civilized men," especially now that so many white settlers were moving in droves across the Ohio into the new state of Illinois.

Noah turned away from the smooth log railing that bordered the wide, covered porch cantilevered out over the swamp. He was about to step into the cabin where a single oil lamp cast its circle of light when he heard a bobcat scream. He would not have given the sound a second thought if not for the fact that a few seconds later the sound was followed by a high-pitched shriek, one that sounded human enough to stop him in his tracks. He paused on the threshold and listened intently. A chill ran down his spine.

It had been so long since he had heard the sound of another human voice that he could not really be certain, but he thought he had just heard a woman's cry.

Noah shook off the ridiculous, unsettling notion and walked into the cabin built over the water. The walls were covered with the tanned hides of mink, bobcat, otter, beaver, fox, white-tailed deer and bear. His few other possessions—a bone-handled hunting knife with a distinctive wolf's head carved on it, various traps, some odd pieces of clothing, a few pots and a skillet, four wooden trenchers and mugs, and a rifle—were all neatly stored inside. They were all he owned and needed in the world, save the dugout canoe secured outside near the base of the tree.

Sparse but comfortable, even the sight of the familiar surroundings could not help him shake the feeling that something unsettling was about to happen, that all was not right in his world.

Pulling a crock off a high shelf, Noah poured a splash of whiskey in a cup and drank it down, his concentration intent on the deepening gloaming and the sounds of the swamp. An unnatural stillness lingered in the air after the puzzling scream, almost as if, like him, the wild inhabitants of Heron Pond were collectively waiting for something to happen. Unable to deny his curiosity any longer, Noah sighed in resignation and walked back to the door.

He lingered there for a moment, staring out at the growing shadows. Something was wrong. *Someone* was out there. He reached for the primed and loaded Hawken rifle that stood just inside the door and stepped out into the gathering dusk.

He climbed down the crude ladder of wooden strips nailed to the trunk of one of the four prehistoric cypress that supported his home, stepped into the dugout *pirogue* tied to a cypress knee that poked out of the water. Noah paddled the shallow wooden craft toward a spot where the land met the deep dark water with its camouflage net of duckweed, a natural boundary all but invisible to anyone unfamiliar with the swamp.

He reached a rise of land which supported a trail, carefully stepped out of the *pirogue* and secured it to a low-hanging tree branch. Walking through thickening shadows, Noah breathed in his surroundings, aware of every subtle nuance of change, every depression on the path that might really be a footprint on the trail, every tree and stand of switchcane.

The sound he thought he'd heard had come from the southeast. Noah headed in that direction, head down, staring at the trail although it was almost too dark to pick up any sign. A few hundred yards from where he left the *pirogue,* he paused, raised his head, sniffed the air, and listened to the silence.

Instinctively, he swung his gaze in the direction of a thicket of slender cane stalks and found himself staring across ten yards of low undergrowth into the eyes of a female bobcat on the prowl. Slowly he raised his rifle to his shoulder and waited to see what the big cat would do. The animal stared back at him, its eyes intense in the gathering gloaming. Finally, she blinked and with muscles bunching beneath her fine, shiny coat, the cat turned and padded away.

Noah lowered the rifle and shook his head. He decided the sound he heard earlier must have been the bobcat's cry and nothing more. But just as he stepped back in the di-

rection of the *pirogue*, he caught a glimpse of ivory on the
trail ahead that stood out against the dark tableau. His
leather moccasins did not make even a whisper of sound
on the soft earth. He closed the distance and quickly realized what he was seeing was a body lying across the path.

His heart was pounding as hard as Chickasaw drums
when he knelt beside the young woman stretched out upon
the ground. Laying his rifle aside he stared at the unconscious female, then looked up and glanced around in every
direction. The nearest white settlement was beyond the
swamp to the northeast. There was no sign of a companion
or fellow traveler nearby, something he found more than
curious.

Noah took a deep breath, let go a ragged sigh and looked
at the girl again. She lay on her side, as peacefully as if
she were napping. She was so very still that the only evidence that she was alive was the slow, steady rise and fall
of her breasts. Although there was no visible sign of injury,
she lay on the forest floor with her head beside a fallen log.
One of her arms was outstretched, the other tucked beneath
her. What he could see of her face was filthy. So were her
hands; they were beautifully shaped, her fingers long and
tapered. Her dress, nothing but a rag with sleeves, was
hiked up to her thighs. Her shapely legs showed stark ivory
against the decayed leaves and brush beneath her.

He tentatively reached out to touch her, noticed his hand
shook, and balled it into a fist. He clenched it tight, then
opened his hand and gently touched the tangled, black hair
that hid the side of her face. She did not stir when he moved
the silken skein, nor when he brushed it back and looped
it over her ear.

Her face was streaked with mud. Her lashes were long
and dark, her full lips tinged pink. The sight of her beauty
took his breath away. Noah leaned forward and gently
reached beneath her. Rolling her onto her back, he straightened her arms and noted her injuries. Her wrist appeared
to be swollen. She had an angry lump on her forehead near
her hairline. She moaned as he lightly probed her injured

wrist; he realized he was holding his breath. Noah expected her eyelids to flutter open, but they did not.

He scanned the forest once again. With night fast closing in, he saw no alternative except to take her home with him. If he was going to get her back to the tree house before dark, he would have to hurry. He cradled her gently in his arms, reached for his rifle, and then straightened. Even then the girl did not awaken, although she did whimper and turn her face against his buckskin jacket, burrowing against him. It felt strange carrying a woman in his arms, but he had no time to dwell on that as he quickly carried her back to the *pirogue*, set her inside, and untied the craft. He climbed in behind her, holding her upright, then gently drew her back until she leaned against his chest.

As the paddle cut silently through water black as pitch, he tried to concentrate on guiding the dugout canoe home, but was distracted by the way the girl felt pressed against him, the way she warmed him. As his body responded to a need he had long tried to deny, he felt ashamed at his lack of control. What kind of a man was he, to become aroused by a helpless, unconscious female?

Overhead, the sky was tinted deep violet, an early canvas for the night's first stars. During the last few yards of the journey, the swamp grew so dark that he had only the yellow glow of lamplight shining from his home high above the water to guide him.

Run. Keep running.

The dream was so real that Olivia Bond could feel the leaf-littered ground beneath her feet and the faded chill of winter that lingered on the damp April air. She suffered, haunted by memories of the past year, some still so vivid they turned her dreams into nightmares. Even now, as she lay tossing in her sleep, she could feel the faint sway of the flatboat as it moved down river long ago. In her sleep the fear welled up inside her.

Her dreaming mind began to taunt her with palpable memories of new sights and scents and dangers.

Run. Run. Run, Olivia. You're almost home.

Her legs thrashed, startling her awake. She sat straight up, felt a searing pain in her right wrist and a pounding in her head that forced her to quickly lie back down. She kept her eyes closed until the stars stopped dancing behind them, then she slowly opened them and looked around.

The red glow of embers burning in a fireplace illuminated the ceiling above her. She lay staring up at even log beams that ran across a wide planked ceiling, trying to ignore the pounding in her head, fighting to stay calm and let her memory come rushing back. Slowly she realized she was no longer lost on the forest trail. She had not become a bobcat's dinner, but was indoors, in a cabin, on a bed.

She spread her fingers and pressed her hands palms down against a rough, woven sheet drawn over her. The mattress was filled with something soft that gave off a tangy scent. A pillow cradled her head.

Slowly Olivia turned her aching head, afraid of who or what she might find beside her, but when she discovered she was in bed alone, she thanked God for small favors.

Refusing to panic, she thought back to her last lucid memory: a wildcat's scream. She recalled tearing through the cypress swamp, trying to make out the trail in the dim light before she tripped. She lifted her hand to her forehead and felt swelling. After testing it gingerly, she was thankful that she had not gashed her head open and bled to death.

She tried to lift her head again but intense pain forced her to lie still. Olivia closed her eyes and sighed. A moment later, an unsettling feeling came over her. She knew by the way her skin tingled, the way her nerve ends danced, that someone was nearby. Someone was watching her. An instinctive, intuitive sensation warned her that the *someone* was a man.

At first she peered through her lashes, but all she could make out was a tall, shadowy figure standing in the open doorway across the room. Her heart began to pound so hard she was certain the sound would give her consciousness away.

The man walked into the room and she bit her lips together to hold back a cry. She watched him move about purposefully. Instead of coming directly to the bed, he walked over to a small square table. She heard him strike a piece of flint, smelled lamp oil as it flared to life.

His back was to her as he stood at the table; Olivia opened her eyes wider and watched. He was tall, taller than most men, strongly built, dressed in buckskin pants topped by a buff shirt with billowing sleeves. Despite the coolness of the evening, he wore no coat, no jacket. Indian moccasins, not shoes, covered his feet. His hair was deep black, cut straight and worn long enough to hang just over his collar. She watched his bronzed, well-tapered hands turn up the lamp wick and set the glass chimney in place.

Olivia sensed he was about to turn and look at her. She wanted to close her eyes and pretend to be unconscious, thinking that might be safer than letting him catch her staring at him, but as he slowly turned toward the bed, she knew she had to see him. She had to know what she was up against.

Her gaze swept his body, taking in his great height, the length of his arms, the width and breadth of his shoulders before she dared even look at his face.

When she did, she gasped.

Noah stood frozen beside the table, shame and anger welling up from deep inside. He was unable to move, unable to breathe as the telling sound of the girl's shock upon seeing his face died on the air. He watched her flinch and scoot back into the corner, press close to the wall. He knew her head pained her, but obviously not enough to keep her from showing her revulsion or from trying to scramble as far away as she could.

He had the urge to walk out, to turn around and leave. Instead, he stared back and let her look all she wanted. It had been three years since he had lost an eye to a flatboat accident on the Mississippi. Three years since another woman had laughed in his face. Three years since he moved to southern Illinois to put the past behind him.

When her breathing slowed and she calmed, he held his hands up to show her that they were empty, hoping to put her a little more at ease.

"I'm sorry," he said as gently as he could. "I don't mean you any harm."

She stared up at him as if she did not understand a blessed word.

Louder this time, he spoke slowly. "Do-you-speak-English?"

The girl clutched the sheet against the filthy bodice of her dress and nodded. She licked her lips, cleared her throat. Her mouth opened and closed like a fish out of water, but no sound came out.

"Yes," she finally croaked. "Yes, I do." And then, "Who are you?"

"My name is Noah. Noah LeCroix. This is my home. Who are you?"

The lamplight gilded her skin. She looked to be all eyes, soft green eyes, long black hair, and fear. She favored her injured wrist, held it cradled against her midriff. From the way she carefully moved her head, he knew she was fighting one hell of a headache, too.

Ignoring his question, she asked one of her own. "How did I get here?" Her tone was wary. Her gaze kept flitting over to the door and then back to him.

"I heard a scream. Went out and found you in the swamp. Brought you here—"

"The wildcat?"

"Wasn't very hungry." Noah tried to put her at ease, then he shrugged, stared down at his moccasins. Could she tell how nervous he was? Could she see his awkwardness, know how strange it was for him to be alone with a woman? He had no idea what to say or do. When he looked over at her again, she was staring at the ruined side of his face.

"How long have I been asleep?" Her voice was so low that he had to strain to hear her. She looked like she expected him to leap on her and attack her any moment, as if he might be coveting her scalp.

"Around two hours. You must have hit your head really hard."

She reached up, felt the bump on her head. "I guess I did."

He decided not to get any closer, not with her acting like she was going to jump out of her skin. He backed up, pulled a stool out from under the table, and sat down.

"You going to tell me your name?" he asked.

The girl hesitated, glanced toward the door, then looked back at him. "Where am I?"

"Heron Pond."

Her attention shifted to the door once again; recollection dawned. She whispered, "The swamp." Her eyes widened as if she expected a bobcat or a cottonmouth to come slithering in.

"You're fairly safe here. I built this cabin over the water."

"*Fairly?*" She looked as if she was going to try to stand up again. "Did you say—"

"Built on cypress trunks. About fifteen feet above the water."

"How do I get down?"

"There are wooden planks nailed to a trunk."

"Am I anywhere near Illinois?"

"You're in it."

She appeared a bit relieved. Obviously she wasn't going to tell him her name until she was good and ready, so he did not bother to ask again. Instead he tried, "Are you hungry? I figure anybody with as little meat on her bones as you ought to be hungry."

What happened next surprised the hell out of him. It was a little thing, one that another man might not have even noticed, but he had lived alone so long he was used to concentrating on the very smallest of details, the way an iridescent dragonfly looked with its wings backlit by the sun, the sound of cypress needles whispering on the wind.

Someone else might have missed the smile that hovered at the corners of her lips when he had said she had little meat on her bones, but he did not. How could he, when that slight, almost-smile damn had him holding his breath?

"I got some jerked venison and some potatoes around here someplace." He started to smile back until he felt the pull of the scar at the left corner of his mouth and stopped. He stood up, turned his back on the girl, and headed for the long wide plank tacked to the far wall where he stored his larder.

He kept his back to her while he found what he was looking for, dug some strips of dried meat from a hide bag, unwrapped a checkered rag with four potatoes inside, and set one on the plank where he did all his stand-up work. Then he took a trencher and a wooden mug off a smaller shelf high on the wall, and turned it over to knock any unwanted creatures out. He was headed for the door, intent on filling the cook pot with water from a small barrel he kept out on the porch when the sound of her voice stopped him cold.

"Perhaps an eye patch," she whispered.

"What?"

"I'm sorry. I was thinking out loud."

She looked so terrified he wanted to put her at ease.

"It's all right. What were you thinking?"

Instead of looking at him when she spoke, she looked down at her hands. "I was just thinking . . ."

Noah had to strain to hear her.

"With some kind of an eye patch, you wouldn't look half bad."

His feet rooted themselves to the threshold. He stared at her for a heartbeat before he closed his good eye and shook his head. He had no idea what in the hell he looked like anymore. He had had no reason to care.

He turned his back on her and stepped out onto the porch, welcoming the darkness.

TIME PASSAGES

__**CRYSTAL MEMORIES** *Ginny Aiken* 0-515-12159-2

__**A DANCE THROUGH TIME** *Lynn Kurland*

0-515-11927-X

__**ECHOES OF TOMORROW** *Jenny Lykins* 0-515-12079-0

__**LOST YESTERDAY** *Jenny Lykins* 0-515-12013-8

__**MY LADY IN TIME** *Angie Ray* 0-515-12227-0

__**NICK OF TIME** *Casey Claybourne* 0-515-12189-4

__**REMEMBER LOVE** *Susan Plunkett* 0-515-11980-6

__**SILVER TOMORROWS** *Susan Plunkett* 0-515-12047-2

__**THIS TIME TOGETHER** *Susan Leslie Liepitz*

0-515-11981-4

__**WAITING FOR YESTERDAY** *Jenny Lykins*

0-515-12129-0

__**HEAVEN'S TIME** *Susan Plunkett* 0-515-12287-4

__**THE LAST HIGHLANDER** *Claire Cross* 0-515-12337-4

__**A TIME FOR US** *Christine Holden* 0-515-12375-7

Prices slightly higher in Canada All books $5.99
